Change

Lives Apart: A World War Two Chronicle

Part Two

Carole McEntee-Taylor

Copyright © Carole McEntee-Taylor, 2015.

The right of Carole McEntee-Taylor as the Author of the Work has been asserted by her in accordance with the Copyright, Designs and Patents Act, 1988.

First Published in 2015
by GWL Publishing
an imprint of Great War Literature Publishing LLP

Produced in United Kingdom

Apart from any use permitted under UK copyright law, this publication may only be reproduced, stored or transmitted, in any form, or by any means, with prior permission in writing of the publishers or, in the case of reprographic production, in accordance with the terms of licences issued by the Copyright Licensing Agency.

All characters in this publication, with the exception of any obvious historical characters, are fictitious and any resemblance to real persons, either living or dead, is purely coincidental.

ISBN 978-1-910603-14-7 Paperback Edition

GWL Publishing
Forum House
Stirling Road
Chichester PO19 7DN
www.gwlpublishing.co.uk

Carole loves writing and loves history, so it's no surprise that she writes historical books! She enjoys writing both military history and historical fiction and the idea is to give the author royalties of any military history titles to military charities, whilst proceeds from the fiction go to Carole, to help fund the research into both – at least that's the theory! She currently has six military history books published with Pen & Sword, with more in the pipeline.

Carole lives on the north east Essex coast with her husband, David and, when not writing, she works full-time at the Military Corrective Training Centre (MCTC) in Colchester.

Also by Carole McEntee-Taylor

Fiction:
Separation: Lives Apart - A World War Two Chronicle Book One

Non-Fiction:
Herbert Columbine VC

A Battle too Far: The True Story of Rifleman Henry Taylor

From Colonial Warrior to Western Front Flyer: The Five Wars of Sydney Herbert Bywater Harris

The Battle of Bellewaarde, June 1915

Surviving the Nazi Onslaught: The Defence of Calais to the Death March for Freedom

Military Detention Colchester from 1947. Voices from the Glasshouse

Dedication

To my father in law, Ted Taylor, without whom I would never have started writing

Acknowledgements

I would like to thank the following:

My husband David for his continual help and support and for putting up with burnt or undercooked dinners, little or no conversation and me continually forgetting things while my mind was stuck in the 1940s!

My colleagues in the MCTC for encouraging me and Jane da Silva for reading draft copies of the books.

Finally, my publisher, Wendy Lawrance for her considerable perseverance and continuing support and belief in me.

Cast of Characters

English/in England

Joe Price:	Soldier, Rifle Brigade
Pauline Price:	Joe's mother
Fred Price:	Joe's younger brother
Frank 'Rob' Roberts:	Joe's friend
Pete Smith:	Joe's friend
Mitchell Lewis:	Joe's friend
Bert Stapleford:	Joe's friend
Cyril Green:	Joe's friend
Peggy Cooper:	Joe's girlfriend, student nurse at Lambeth Hospital, London
Helen Macklin:	Peggy's friend, student nurse at Lambeth Hospital, London.
Annie Macklin:	Helen's sister
Chris:	Student doctor
Ethel:	Peggy's friend
Colin:	Ethel's boyfriend
Sally:	Peggy's friend
Peter:	Sally's boyfriend
Pamela Lloyd-Smyth:	Peggy's friend
Captain Richard Denis:	Pamela's boss
Giselle:	Pamela's colleague
Anthony:	Pamela's brother
Jane Harrison:	Peggy's friend

Alf Harrison:	Jane's son
Olive Cooper:	Peggy's cousin, switchboard operator at Lewisham Council
Kurt Ritter:	Olive's boyfriend
Tom:	Local villain
Kath:	Switchboard operator, Lewisham Council
Bernard Dickson:	Local villain
Lilly:	Marcel's girlfriend

French/in France

Jacques Servier:	Farmer
Marie Servier:	Jacques' wife
Louis Servier:	Older son of Jacques and Marie
Marcel Servier:	Younger son of Jacques and Marie
Brigitte Fabron:	Louis' girlfriend
Rolf Keller:	German officer
Henri:	Louis' friend
Gerald:	Louis' friend
Pierre:	Marcel's friend
Paul:	Marcel's friend
Antoine:	Marcel's friend
Charles:	Marcel's friend
Jean-Paul:	Teacher and refugee
Claudette:	Jean-Paul's wife
Jeanne:	Daughter of Jean-Paul and Claudette
Angel:	Orphan
Suzanne Siemens:	Jean-Paul's friend
Adele Fourier:	Angel's friend's mother
Gabriel Valence:	Deputy Commissioner, Police
Eve Poitiers:	Receptionist, Police Station

Prologue

London

December 1940

Olive re-read Kurt's letter and tried hard to recapture the warmth she had felt previously, but there was nothing. She felt completely numb inside and, after sitting for several moments, unable to think of anything to write in reply, she opened the new bottle of whisky and poured herself a large drink.

My darling Kurt,
It seems so long since you held me in your arms.

She stopped and took another gulp of the inviting amber liquid. It was over a year since she'd seen Kurt and now, because of that bastard, she couldn't remember how she'd felt about him anymore. Everything was ruined and she had no idea how it was ever going to be alright again.

I wish you were here with me.

Sadly, she was no longer sure her words were true, but if she didn't have Kurt, she had nothing, so she had to hang on to the idea of him and hope that, when he was finally able to come back to England at the end of the war, her feelings for him would have returned. When she thought of everything she'd lost, she could feel the tears pricking her eyes and she blinked angrily. If only he hadn't left her, none of this would have happened.

The bottle of black market whisky was almost half empty and she frowned. Normally a couple of glasses in the evening helped her forget, but tonight she couldn't shake off the memories. Another glass might help. After all, there was plenty more where this bottle came from. She laughed, but there was no mirth in the drunken cackle that filled the flat, only despair, loneliness and regret.

Part One

July - August 1940

Chapter One

Toulouse, Southern France

The silence in the apartment was shattered for the third night in a row, when Angel's piercing scream rent the air. Jeanne leapt out of bed and Claudette rushed into the girls' room, closely followed by Jean-Paul. Angel was sobbing, her long blonde hair tangled in sweat and tears as she thrashed about on the bed. Jeanne sat down and scooped up the little girl in her arms

"Angel, sweetheart, don't cry. You're just having a bad dream. Wake up, darling." It took her several minutes to break through the child's nightmare, by which time, her shoulder was drenched in Angel's tears.

Angel opened her eyes and stared fearfully at Claudette and Jean-Paul, standing by the bed. She tightened her grip on Jeanne and then gradually began to relax.

"Do you want to tell us what you were dreaming?" Jeanne asked.

Angel shook her head frantically, her eyes still wide with terror.

"The nightmares might stop if you talked about them." Claudette smiled at Angel, who was still hanging on to Jeanne.

Angel shook her head again and closed her eyes.

"Alright, you don't have to if you don't want to," Jeanne said gently. "Would you like some hot milk?"

Angel shook her head but still didn't speak. Jeanne suddenly felt uneasy. The previous two nights, when she had woken screaming, she had answered them when they'd spoken to her.

Jeanne tried to think of something to ask which Angel couldn't answer by shaking or nodding her head.

"Where's your doll?" Jeanne was unable to see her amongst the messy bed clothes. Angel's doll was her most prized possession and she always slept with it.

Angel shook her head but, again, didn't answer.

Thoroughly alarmed, Jean-Paul knelt beside the bed and spoke to her. "Angel, please say something to us, even if it's rude," he added trying to make her smile. But she didn't answer; she just looked at him with her deep, soulful blue eyes. "Why don't you want to speak? Are you frightened?"

Angel shook her head again.

"I think we should settle her down. I'm sure she'll be fine in the morning." Jean-Paul spoke with a confidence he didn't feel. He had heard of cases like this, where delayed shock brought on some kind of temporary speech loss. They would just have to make sure she felt safe and secure and, hopefully, her speech would return. If not… He watched while Jeanne put her back to bed.

Then he saw Angel's doll, naked and lying face down at the bottom of the bed. Jean-Paul quietly pointed out the figure to Jeanne and Claudette before turning his attention back to Angel, who was staring sightlessly at the ceiling above her bed. He spoke softly. "Good night, sweetheart. Do you want us to stay in here with you until you fall asleep?" Angel nodded, closed her eyes and, within minutes, was in a deep sleep. They waited a little longer and then quietly left the room.

"What's she done with the doll?" Jeanne asked.

"I don't know for certain, but I would think that's how she saw her mother after she'd been raped by the Germans and they'd killed her father. She's reliving the whole thing."

"What on earth can we do?" Claudette's face was serious.

"I think we just have to wait and see how she is in the morning. If she's not better, then we'll have to take her to a doctor."

"Isn't that dangerous?" Jeanne looked worried. "How can we explain what has happened to Angel without giving ourselves away?"

"I don't know, but we must do what is best for Angel, don't you think?"

Jeanne and Claudette nodded in agreement. Eventually, after several minutes of silence, wondering what the next day would bring, they said goodnight and went to their separate rooms. Sleep eluded Jean-Paul and, after a couple of hours, he got up and went and sat in the living room. He yawned widely; the constant strain of having to be careful and watch over their shoulders for the past few months was beginning to tell. This latest episode with Angel was the final straw and he could feel himself beginning to wilt.

Only a few days earlier, she had overheard him and Jeanne discussing the dangers of being Jewish. They had quickly changed the subject, but he was terrified Angel would remember at some inopportune moment, perhaps when she started school, where anti-Semitic comments were likely to be common. He shook his head. *One thing at a time.* He would deal with that eventuality if and when it happened. The more serious problem was Angel's sudden lack of speech. He could only pray Angel would be sufficiently better in the morning, and a doctor wouldn't be necessary, but if not, he needed to concoct a story close enough to the truth to help Angel, yet without giving them away.

****

Lambeth Hospital, London

"Chris, how did your leave go?" Peggy was pleased to see him back, although he seemed distracted.

"Hello, Peggy. Not great. Bit of a long story. I'm pleased not to be traipsing backwards and forwards to Gravesend, though." He fiddled with his stethoscope and glanced up at the clock on the wall. "Perhaps we could have lunch together?" He saw her hesitation. "I could really do with someone to talk to."

In Peggy's experience, men never asked for help, so she immediately forgot her reservations and nodded. "Of course. I'll meet you in the canteen at one thirty?"

He face lit up and he smiled. "Thanks, Peggy. I'll see you there."

****

Bethune, Northern France

Brigitte was quite enjoying having two men running around after her and it certainly made a change from them using her like they had in the past. Perhaps things were looking up. A few more months and she would be able to afford to move. She still hadn't decided where to go, but the idea of living somewhere warm appealed to her. Maybe, by the time she was ready, Louis would have changed his mind about leaving his mother and the farm. She hoped so. She really wanted him to come with her and then they could start again, somewhere fresh.

She put on her make-up, checked her appearance and headed downstairs.

"Glad to see you and Louis have patched up your differences." Her father, Fabian, was cleaning the tables and did not see the look of astonishment on her face. "He's a good reliable lad. You could do a lot worse."

"Yes. I'm seeing him later." Brigitte was amazed he was being nice to her and she wondered if there was a catch.

"Then we won't be seeing the Boche officer round here again?" This time he was looking straight at her. Brigitte blushed.

"I can't tell the Germans what to do, Papa. If you don't like them coming here, perhaps you should tell them."

Fabian stared at his daughter, contempt flooding his face. "I really have no idea what I have done to deserve a daughter like you. You're behaving like a whore and the German is only using you. He'll dump you soon enough, when it suits him."

Brigitte ignored him. She wasn't going to let his continual sniping spoil her good mood. Rolf would be round to collect her later and she couldn't wait.

****

Simonsdorf, Poland

Facing Joe and the other POWs were the usual lines of German guards, rifles at the ready, their expressions grim and unwelcoming. Large Alsatian dogs were barking incessantly and straining at their leashes, trying to get at the prisoners lined up in front of them. The Germans began the laborious task of counting.

"Wouldn't take half as long if they'd learnt to add up when they were at school," Pete muttered.

"Well, all armies do things in triplicate, so perhaps that includes counting." The answer came from one of the soldiers in the row behind. He sounded American. The nearest guard was quite a long way down the platform, so Joe took a chance and turned round quickly to get a better look.

The voice came from a young freckle-faced man with reddish hair and a cheeky smile standing directly behind him. He was in a British uniform and wore the shoulder title of the Kings Royal Rifle Corps.

"Are you a Yank?" Joe kept his voice low.

"How'd you guess? Did the accent give it away?" the soldier responded good-humouredly. "Mitchell Lewis, originally from Brighton, Michigan, now a proud member of the KRRCs."

"Joe Price, Rifle Brigade and this is Pete Smith, East Yorks. Were you at Calais?"

"Yeah, fun wasn't it?" Mitchell was grinning and Joe smiled back.

"So what made you join up?" Joe was curious.

"My mum's English. She met my dad when he was wounded serving with US Forces in France. She was a nurse and they fell in love while he was recuperating in hospital during the Great War. When she married him, she came over to the States to live, so us kids were all born Americans. There's five of us in total, three boys and two girls. My older brother joined the Eagle Squadron about two weeks before I joined up. He's based in Biggin Hill, or at least he was, last I heard. My younger brother's still in high school, so perhaps by the time he's old enough, the rest of America will have woken up and we'll all be fighting beside you guys."

He was about to say more when the guards shouted and they were marched along the platform towards the gate at the end and out of the station.

Joe looked around him trying to get his bearings, but there wasn't much to see, other than the name of the railway station which appeared to be *Simonsdorf*.

"God, this is boring." Mitchell's voice carried forward quite clearly. "I reckon they just move us around and make us march up and down so we don't have time to plan escapes."

"If only!" The man next to Mitchell joined in. "They're using us for slave labour. They don't have to pay us, or even feed us properly and they can use us to do the jobs the men in their armed forces used to do. So, while they're jack booting it around Europe, we're keeping things going."

"Can they do that?" Joe was scandalised he could be doing something to help the Germans invade England.

"Who's gonna stop them?" Mitchell's voice dripped cynicism. "At the moment they've got everything all their own way and there ain't no-one to tell them not to do something."

There was silence while Joe and Pete digested his words. Unfortunately, it all sounded uncomfortably near the truth.

"Cheerful bugger, isn't he?" Mitchell's companion was grinning. "I'm Bert, by the way, Bert Stapleford, also of the KRRCs, captured on that wonderful week's trip to Calais."

"I'm starting to feel outnumbered." Pete sounded miffed. "I'm going to have to look for some more East Yorks to give me some support."

"That's alright, you can be an honorary rifleman; we won't tell anyone," Joe chipped in. He was enjoying the banter and felt more cheerful than he had since he had first found out he was to be moved.

****

Aldershot, England

Marcel sighed. Other than the relentless training, there didn't seem to be an awful lot happening. He had been into Aldershot on previous occasions with the others, but had soon grown bored. All they wanted was to find girls and then talk about their conquests. Marcel really wasn't interested. Not only was he in love with Jeanne, he had also seen the films about the diseases you could catch, which had put him off completely. He couldn't understand why this didn't stop his friends too, but he was too shy to ask, so he just let them think his reluctance was because of Jeanne.

The only excitement had been a trip to London to be vetted for the Free French Forces by two British policemen. They had stayed under canvas in the large arena in Olympia Hall, a building that, before the war, had been used for trade fairs and show jumping competitions.

Although he had been nervous at first, Marcel soon realised he had nothing to worry about. He answered all their questions and was told to come back the next day. To his disappointment, they were not allowed to wander around London so he spent the night drinking and playing cards with his friends. The following day, he was cleared and sent to Aldershot, where he had been ever since.

He stared out of the tent, wondering when they were going to start fighting. He hadn't fled to England to sit around in an army camp. He wanted to throw the Germans out of his country because, until they left, he couldn't go home to his parents and brother or look for Jeanne and his adopted family who'd helped him escape the Nazis.

****

La Couture, Northern France

Now he had a purpose, Louis felt much better. He felt slightly guilty when he thought back to how he'd lied to his friends about Brigitte. But his girlfriend was none of their business and he wasn't stupid enough to tell her anything anyway. He put thoughts of Brigitte out of his mind and concentrated on thinking up ways to disrupt the Germans. He couldn't wait for the evening to come, when he and his friends could make their plans. He stood up and went into the fields to harvest some of the vegetables and to make sure they were all properly watered. While he was doing this, an idea came to him.

On their visit to the farm, the Germans had made an inventory. They were obviously going to help themselves to a percentage of his crops. He needed to find somewhere to hide any surplus so the Germans didn't get their hands on them. The question was, where?

After racking his brains, he wondered whether the answer was to build some kind of secret space in the farmhouse. He would have a look before he went out. Maybe somewhere near the loft, or perhaps he could block off part of the cellar. Lost in his thoughts, something caught his eye. He straightened up and stared in the direction where he had seen the sudden movement, but there was nothing there. Shrugging, he bent down and carried on, returning back to his thoughts of where to hide food, when… there it was again. This time he did not react in any way, but pretended he hadn't seen anything. There was definitely someone out there.

****

London

Pam watched the guests circulating, drinks in one hand, programmes in the other. She'd only volunteered to help because she had nothing to do, but she was even more bored now and she wondered whether she could slip away without being noticed. London had not proved to be any more exciting than Dover and she still hadn't found a proper job.

Her family's London house in the Bayswater Road had a wonderful view over Hyde Park and she'd spent the first few days in the city watching the activity in the park. However, the initial feeling of excitement and being part of something, soon palled. Most of her London friends were busying themselves with various wartime activities and some had joined up. Even her old friend, Peggy, was busy nursing and they'd only been able to meet up once since she'd moved to London.

Fed up with her continual moaning, her father had eventually put her in touch with a 'friend of a friend' at the Home Office who offered her some secretarial work, but, like the numerous fundraising events she attended on a regular basis, this wasn't enough. Frustrated beyond belief, she felt the war was passing her by without giving her an opportunity to 'do her bit'.

"Wonderful paintings. Know the artist do you? I'd love to meet him." She glanced up. Although the man had asked a question, she had the strangest feeling he wasn't interested in the answer, so she was surprised when he continued to stand in front of her, one eyebrow raised.

"I'm sorry, I don't actually. I'm only helping out a friend. But I believe that's him over there." Pam pointed to a rather flamboyant man in black trousers and a very bright shirt standing next to one of the paintings, a nervous expression on his heavily perspiring face. He looked totally out of place in a room crammed with men in expensive-looking suits and women in designer dresses and very exclusive hats. The room reeked of money and Pam sighed. She didn't mind being rich, she just wanted desperately to do something to help the war effort, other than type up meaningless reports no one wanted to read, serve endless cups of tea or host boring charity events to raise money.

"You look bored stiff!" The statement caught her by surprise and she started guiltily. She was about to deny his accusation, but looking into his intelligent brown eyes, she changed her mind and smiled instead.

"Guilty as charged, I'm afraid. Still, the event's in a good cause." She was unable to think of anything positive to say.

"Grahame Thompson." The man extended a hand which she took automatically, unconsciously noticing the firm handshake.

"Pam, Pamela Lloyd-Smythe. The gallery is owned by one of my mother's friends."

"But it's not really your style?" Grahame was smiling at her.

"No. To be perfectly honest, I'm bored rigid. I'd prefer to go and do something a bit more useful." She stopped and returned his smile. "But I'm sure that's not what you want to hear. Would you like me to introduce you to some other people... people who are interested in art?"

"No, I'm quite happy talking to you."

She stared at him in surprise. She was sure he wasn't chatting her up, not in the usual sense, anyway, but she did have the feeling there was more to this conversation than there appeared.

"So, what would you prefer to be doing?"

"I don't know. Something where I can use my brain and feel I am actually making a difference, I suppose. Why? Are you here to offer me a job?" Pam was half joking and was rewarded to see a fleeting look of surprise cross his face, which was gone almost as soon as it had appeared.

"Maybe," he conceded after a few seconds of silence. "I have an office not far from here. Come and see me tomorrow afternoon at three o'clock and we'll talk." He gave her a small card, which she read. When she looked up again, he had gone. She scanned the room, but there was no sign of him. Intrigued, she stared back down. The only words written on the card were Room 36, Northumberland Hotel, London. There was no phone number and no further information. Suddenly feeling a lot less fed up, she slipped the card into her pocket. Now, all she had to do was to keep herself amused until tomorrow afternoon.

****

Catford, London

Olive hurried home. She had a half day off and was hoping there would be a letter from Kurt via their correspondence address in Glasgow. She was still reeling from the excitement of becoming supervisor and had just finished her first week in charge. She had worked so hard and then, when she had all but given up hope, the job had simply fallen into her lap. Unfortunately, with the good luck, came the realisation that Tom, the blackmailer, would want more money once he knew she was earning a higher salary, but maybe there was some way she could use the job to get rid of him. The key might lie in his relationship with Kath. They definitely knew each other and maybe she could use her position to influence Kath and find out something about him? Even while the thought passed through her mind, she knew this was unlikely. Kath hated her. Feeling her good mood dissipating, she turned her attention to Kurt. She had written straight away to tell him her good news, knowing he would be very proud of her and she was looking forward to reading his response.

Ignoring the warm sunny afternoon, Olive let herself into the communal entrance to her flat, her heart beating with expectation. But her face fell when she saw there was no post for her at all.

"Looking for something?"

She spun round, her heart thumping loudly against her chest.

"What are you doing here?"

"Tut tut, you sound very angry, Olive. That's no way to speak to a friend, not one who's come to congratulate you, anyway." Tom brushed an imaginary speck of dust off his sleeve and treated her to a full view of his yellowing teeth.

Olive resisted the temptation to lean back against the wall and, instead, faced him squarely.

"What do you want?"

"Let's go upstairs, shall we? I'm sure you don't want your neighbours listening in…"

Olive was about to argue when she realised there was no point. Clamping her mouth shut so she didn't give him the satisfaction of asking if there had been a letter on her doormat, she turned to walk up the stairs.

"Oh, there wasn't any post by the way. Were you expecting anything important?"

Grateful he had not found a letter from Kurt, her heartbeat almost returned to normal. Ignoring him, she opened the door and waited for him to enter, bracing herself for whatever he had come to demand.

Chapter Two

Lambeth Hospital, London

"So, how was your family?"

"Not great." Chris rubbed his face. He looked tired. "My little brother has run away and joined the merchant navy. He's only fourteen, but he's tall and quite well built, so they didn't question him." He sipped some more of his tea.

"But, if he's under age, can't you get him brought back home?"

"We don't know where he is at the moment. We can't do anything until he arrives back in a British port. And, even then, we have to find him. We don't know what ship he's on, so it's a bit like looking for a needle in a haystack."

Peggy was silent. She had no idea what to say, other than silly platitudes about being sure he would be alright, so she said nothing. She wanted to reach out and hold his hand, but that would be much too forward. When he continued, she was glad she hadn't said anything

"But that's not the worst. My younger sister is pregnant and her boyfriend was in France, or at least she thinks he was. She hasn't heard from him in weeks, so she doesn't know whether he's been captured, killed, is hiding out in France somewhere or just doesn't want to know about her now. In her last letter to him, she told him she was pregnant, so…" He tailed off. "My Da's alright about it, strangely enough, but Ma… well, that's another story."

Chris' Welsh accent, which was often barely noticeable, grew stronger as he recited his problems.

"I'm sure your mother will come round, won't she?"

Chris gave a wry smile. "It's the shame, you see. Ma's a good Chapel girl, her family are very strong in the church. She feels she can't hold her head high and face people, so she's cut herself off from her church, which means the rest of the family are having to put up with her."

He saw the look on Brenda's face.

"Sorry, my mother is not what you'd call the warm and loving type. She was brought up in a strict Presbyterian household. You know, lots of bible bashing, duty and holier than thou… Love didn't really come into things. My Da's totally different. It's him I really go home to see. I can never understand why they got married: total opposites." He sighed. "Anyway that's all my misery; not much really, when you compare it with what we've seen on a day to day basis lately."

"Are you very close to your sister?"

"We all are. There's six of us; four boys and two girls. As well as the two younger ones, I have two older brothers and one older sister, Catherine. She's married with two children. My oldest brother, James, he works the farm with my Da and the next one down, Llewellyn, is in the Army." He drained his tea. "Thank you for letting me talk. I know there's not much I can do, although I'd like to help Connie if I could."

"Connie's your younger sister?"

"Sorry, yes. I didn't say, did I?"

"There might be nothing to worry about. Her boyfriend might not have got her letter." Peggy gave a rueful smile. "I know I'm probably the last one to say 'stop worrying' considering the terrible state I was in."

Chris smiled back. "You're right, though. I'm going to take your very good advice and…" He glanced at the clock on the wall. "Christ! I'd better get back!"

Peggy stared at the clock in disbelief. "Goodness, I had no idea it was so late. Matron will have my guts for garters if she spots me."

They said a hasty goodbye and Peggy headed back to the ward. Chris was such a nice man, she wished she could do more to help him.

****

La Couture, Northern France

Louis wasn't armed, other than with his hoe, but presumably whoever this was, didn't want to attack him or they would already have done so. If they didn't want to be seen, they weren't likely to be the Boche, but maybe someone trying to hide from them. Feeling his blood racing, he decided to take a chance. Without standing up, he looked in the direction where he had last seen movement and shouted, "There's only me here. It's safe to come out." Nothing happened. Perhaps the person didn't understand him.

He tried to remember some of the English he'd learnt at school and his father had taught him when he was younger.

"Safe. Me here only." He stumbled over the unfamiliar words.

Nothing happened and he was about to call out again when he saw a man climbing slowly out of the ditch in the far field. He was wearing the uniform of a British pilot. Not wanting to scare him, Louis stood up slowly, glanced around quickly to make sure they were still alone and hurried across the field to greet him. He drew closer and could see the man was injured. There was blood dripping down his right arm and, judging from the expression on his face, he was in pain.

Louis didn't hesitate. Helping to support the wounded airman, he led him towards the farmhouse. They approached the building and Louis stopped, motioning the airman to hide behind the hedge while he went ahead to make sure there was no one about. Opening the farmhouse door, he called quickly to Marie, "Mama, quick, give me a hand."

Marie started awake and looked at him in surprise. She hadn't seen him look so happy since he returned and she wondered at the reason for the miraculous change.

She rose slowly out of the chair where she'd been dozing, to see what he wanted. She'd been feeling very tired lately and had started falling asleep in the afternoon. She had no idea why; it was most unlike her. Her eyes opened wide. Louis had reappeared in the doorway supporting a man in uniform. Her first thought was the man was British; the second, while blood dripped on her clean kitchen floor, was he was wounded and the third, quickly following the others, was that if the Germans came back now, they would all be shot.

****

Catford, London

"What do you want?" Olive licked her lips nervously. Tom had been inside the flat for nearly ten minutes and still hadn't told her. Instead, he was watching her, an expression of amusement on his face. He swirled the sherry round in his glass before swallowing. He grimaced.

"I can't believe you've only got sherry here." He shook his head.

"I don't drink very often." For some obscure reason Olive felt the need to defend herself.

Tom grinned and placed the glass on the cheap, worn sideboard, ignoring the coaster. Olive winced and, without thinking, took a step closer to him, picked up the glass and placed the tumbler on the coaster. He grabbed her arm and leered, his face inches from hers.

"Oh dear, Olive. That was very careless." He was laughing at her and she pulled away angrily.

"Just tell me what you want and go." She tried to keep the desperation from her voice, but she could tell from his expression she had failed.

"I hear from a little bird you've been promoted."

Olive knew she should look surprised, or he would guess she knew about his involvement with Kath, but she was too tired.

"News travels fast." She made no attempt to hide the sarcasm in her voice.

"That's how I keep on top of things." Tom took a step closer and Olive moved backwards, but the wall was behind her and there was nowhere to go.

He placed his hand on the wall, effectively trapping her. Olive swallowed and tried to stare back at him, but her heart was beating so hard she couldn't hold his gaze and her eyes dropped.

"You're not frightened of me, are you?" His mouth was close to her face and she could smell the alcohol on his breath.

"Of course not!" Her voice faltered and he began stroking her hair. Olive squirmed and tried to wriggle away. His fingers stopped stroking and, grabbing a small amount of her hair he tightened his grip, pulling her closer. Olive kicked out, catching him on his knee. Tom cursed but loosened his grip, allowing her to duck away from him. Reaching out for something to defend herself with, her hands alighted on his empty glass and she acted instinctively. Smashing the tumbler on the sideboard, she thrust the broken glass towards him.

"If you touch me again, I'll kill you." To her surprise, her voice was steady and didn't betray the fear coursing through her.

****

Outside Bethune, Northern France

"You haven't forgotten my instructions have you?" Leutnant Rolf Keller stared at her, his voice full of rage, his eyes boring into her skull. He had driven her to his commandeered house in virtual silence, but Brigitte was used to this, so his sudden anger caught her by surprise.

Brigitte shook her head nervously and she felt sick. She had no idea what he was talking about. He couldn't possibly have seen her with Louis; they'd been very careful. Unless he was watching her… She shivered and her heart began pounding. She was standing opposite him, just out of reach, her eyes lowered. His swagger stick hit the table between them, making her jump.

"How can you say 'no' when you do not know to what instructions I am referring?"

Brigitte opened her mouth to say something then closed it again. Whatever she said would be wrong. She searched her brain for an answer to satisfy him.

"I haven't disobeyed any of your instructions." She kept her head down, not daring to make eye contact.

"You're quite sure?"

She heard his chair creak and knew he was coming towards her. Her stomach squirmed and she could feel herself growing wet.

"Yes."

"Yes, sir!"

"Yes, sir," she repeated.

She could hear him pacing behind her and her legs began to tremble, but whether through fear or excitement, she couldn't tell.

"I don't believe you. You're a whore and whores lie." The stick cracked again, this time on the floor and she winced.

"Come here."

She turned around. He was seated behind her. She walked towards him and he grabbed her, pulling her over his knee. Before she could react, he'd lifted up her dress and pulled down her silk knickers. His hands caressed her buttocks and then he slapped her.

"I'm going to punish you." His voice was cold, devoid of emotion. Brigitte waited. Nothing happened for a few seconds and she could feel his hand fumbling for something down by the side of the chair.

"I was going to spank you, but I've done that before and it doesn't seem to make any difference to your behaviour."

Brigitte didn't answer; instead she tried to move. He slapped her hard again and then shoved something under her nose. She had only just recognised the item was a slipper, when he transferred the footwear to his other hand and began pounding her bottom.

****

La Couture, Northern France

"Quick, shut the door. No one saw you, did they?"

"No, there's no one about, Mama. He's wounded. Will we need a doctor?" Louis looked like an excited puppy and Marie resisted the impulse to slap him. How could he be so stupid? He should at least have waited until dark. Of course she would help, but sometimes her son had no sense at all.

"I don't know. Let me cover the settee then you can help him there and I'll take a look." She rushed to the linen basket to get some old sheets and, laying the cotton over the worn settee, she smiled at the injured man. His face was ashen and she could see he was in considerable pain and had lost a lot of blood.

"Quick, lay him down, before he faints. While I'm examining him, wash the floor and make sure you clear up any traces of blood outside."

Louis rushed to obey while Marie gently helped the pilot remove his jacket. The effort was too much for him and he passed out, leaving Marie to tear off what was left of his shirt sleeve so she could reach the wound.

After a few moments, she nodded at Louis. "The wound's not too deep or infected. He's lost a lot of blood, which is why he's fainted, but I should be able to bandage the injury sufficiently well for it to heal." She fetched her first aid box, then returned to the pilot who was now conscious again.

"Merci." He spoke with a dreadful English accent which made Marie smile.

She patted his good arm. "Not a problem," she replied in French, knowing he probably didn't understand but hoping the words and her tone would be reassuring, nonetheless. "I'm going to bandage you up and then we'll get you up the stairs to bed." She continued to clean the wound, causing the pilot to wince and moan with pain and then she covered the injury in some of her herbal balm which smelt dreadful but would aid the healing process. Having covered the wound with a fresh bandage, she called to Louis, "Go upstairs and make up Marcel's bed and then come down and give me a hand to get him up there."

Louis sped upstairs to his brother's room, which was still as he'd left it on the morning of his abrupt departure. Within minutes, he was back and they helped the pilot upstairs and into the freshly laundered bed.

"Patrick Andrews," the pilot mumbled much to Marie and Louis' confusion. Seeing they didn't understand the pilot pointed to himself. "Patrick Andrews," he repeated.

"Oh!" Marie nodded. "I'm Marie and this is Louis."

Patrick nodded and, after thanking them again, he closed his eyes and was instantly asleep. Marie stared at him for a moment and then she and Louis went back downstairs.

"I'm sorry, Mama, but what could I do?"

"I just wish you had been a little more careful. You mustn't tell anyone he is here, Louis. I mean it, not anyone, not your friends, not anyone. Do you understand?"

Louis nodded "I know. I have to act normally, but how will we get him away if we can't speak to anyone about him?"

Marie sighed. "I don't know. We'll worry about moving him when he's better. At the moment, we probably couldn't anyway."

Louis nodded in agreement but he had no intention of not telling his friends. After all, this was exactly what they had been waiting for; a way to hit back at the Boche and the pilot had literally fallen straight into their waiting arms. Marie watched him anxiously. She knew only too well when Louis was lying to her.

"Louis!" She caught hold of his shirt. "It's really important you don't tell anyone. You do realise how dangerous this is, don't you?"

"Of course I do, Mama." Louis wouldn't meet her eyes and her heart sank even lower. There was silence. "I had arranged to meet Henri and Gerald tonight. If I don't turn up, they'll be suspicious. We have been talking about doing some sabotage."

Marie thought quickly. They were good boys; she had known his friends for years and, if anything, they were better than Louis at keeping secrets. At least he wasn't still seeing the dreadful Brigitte. Although her instincts told her they would be safer if no one knew, she realised they would need help to get the pilot back to Britain. Louis was bound to tell them anyway, he wouldn't be able to help himself, so maybe she should suggest he talk to them. At least then she might have some control over what happened.

"Alright, tell your friends but make sure you are not overheard. In fact, I think you should get them to come back here before you say anything. We can then put our heads together and work out what to do next." She suddenly realised she had taken control and she glanced at Louis, who still seemed perfectly happy. "Is that alright with you?"

"Yes, Mama. It's probably better you all decide what to do next. I'm better at acting than thinking!" He smiled at her and, for the first time since he had come home, she caught a glimpse of the real Louis, the Louis who had gone away all those months ago. "I'll go and finish in the field and then get over to Henri's."

Marie agreed. "We need to make sure we act normally and we must assume we can't trust anyone. Our lives may depend on what we do next."

Louis caught the seriousness in her voice and the urgency and danger of the situation finally communicated itself to him. He nodded soberly.

Marie went to prepare some food, her brain racing while she tried to work out how on earth they were going to get a British pilot out of occupied France and back to England.

****

Aldershot, England

Curiosity and loneliness finally got the better of Marcel and he reluctantly allowed himself to be taken out to the local pub.

Pierre had already chosen some company for him for the evening and, after ensuring Marcel had drunk a couple of glasses of beer, he introduced him to one of the local girls. Pierre had seen her before and he noticed she never had more than one glass of cider and always went home with her friend at the end of the evening. She would make a good companion for Marcel, much better than some of the more experienced girls who would eat him for breakfast.

"Come with me, Marcel. There is someone I would like you to meet. Her name is Lilly." He ignored Marcel's feeble protests and, knowing he would follow, walked over to where Lilly was sitting with her friend.

With a mixture of reluctance and excitement, Marcel followed and said a shy "hello" to the attractive red-haired girl smiling up at him. She was pretty in a different way to Jeanne and Marcel warmed to her upturned nose and faintly freckled face. She moved up and indicated he could sit next to her and then introduced him to her friend. "This is Anita," she said, speaking slowly, not sure how much English he could understand. Marcel nodded and said hello to Anita after remembering to thank Lilly for the seat.

Before long, the language barrier had been forgotten, together with their initial shyness and, with the help of gestures and repetition, the conversation almost flowed. Marcel was amazed to find the pub was closing and he felt shy again when he offered to walk Lilly home.

"That would be lovely, thank you. Can we drop Anita off first." It took Marcel a couple of attempts to understand this, but then he nodded. For a moment, Jeanne came into his mind but she wasn't there with him and, if he was realistic, he didn't even know if he would ever see her again. The thought made him sad but then he shrugged. Lilly was very pretty and she was there with him now. She wasn't just an image he was carrying around in his head. He wasn't sure whether what he was doing was fair or right, but he couldn't help himself. He was lonely and he wanted to feel the warmth of a girl's arms around him, he wanted to kiss her pretty lips and feel her body next to his. He was a long way from home, he had no idea whether he would ever see his family – either of his families – again and if he went off to fight, he could be dead in a matter of weeks, so surely this wasn't wrong?

****

La Couture, Northern France

"I don't believe you!" Gerald slammed down his coffee and stared at Louis in astonishment. "You've really got an RAF pilot upstairs?"

"Shhh." Louis glanced around warily, even though they were in the relative safety of the farmhouse. "Yes. He was hiding in the back field. He's injured, so we put him in Marcel's room."

Henri was also suitably impressed. All they had done was to express a vague wish to do something to resist the occupation and, within a few weeks, this happened. It was altogether too much to take in.

"You realise now why I couldn't tell you anything until we were here," Louis said. "We need to find a way of getting him out of the occupied zone and into the south. Either we have to figure out a way of doing this ourselves, or we have to find contacts who already have things in place."

"How long do we have?" Gerald asked.

"At the moment, he's injured, so it would be best to let him heal more before he moves," Marie answered. "But he obviously can't stay here indefinitely and, if we can't find a way of getting him out ourselves, then whoever we approach must be trustworthy. We don't need to make a decision tonight, but if we all think and then meet back here again in two days' time, we can discuss what we've come up with. How does that sound?" The others nodded in agreement. "In the meantime, none of you must do anything stupid to draw yourselves to the attention of the Germans. You will all have to be model citizens!" Marie finished with a twinkle in her eye. They laughed, relieved to have something less serious to think about, finished their coffee and then took it in turns to leave.

After they had gone, Marie turned to Louis. "We should help Patrick outside to the barn when he wakes up in the morning. Other people know he is here now and, however much we trust them, we don't know how long they would keep quiet if the Germans were threatening to shoot their families."

Louis frowned. "I think we should wait until he's better before moving him." Having rescued the pilot, Louis felt responsible for his welfare. He would hate him to die from his injuries having gone to all the trouble of helping him. He changed the subject before Marie could argue. "I've also been thinking. Maybe we could use the old cow shed that backs onto Giraud's land. They never use the land themselves and the shed looks almost derelict. It's a long way from either farmhouse and, conceivably, he could have found the shelter himself, so that removes his connection from us. Providing he doesn't say anything, of course. I'll go and have a look tomorrow, during daylight. If it's usable, I'll tidy it up and we'll get him up there." He hesitated. "I'm sorry, Mama. I really didn't think before I brought him straight back here, but I will in the future." He kissed her on her cheek and was gone before she could ask him what he meant by his last remark. Surely he didn't mean he was going to do this again?

Chapter Three

Aldershot, England

Marcel suddenly realised that, while he had been wrestling with his conscience, they had reached Anita's house. He had no idea how they had got there, so he would never be able to find his way back, but for once he wasn't worried. Anita said goodnight, winked at Lilly and went in, leaving them on their own. They walked on and, tentatively, he put his arm round her. He was delighted when she moved closer to him and they continued in silence for a couple of streets. Having got this far, Marcel had no idea what to do next. He knew he wanted to kiss her, but he wasn't entirely sure how to go about it. Should he stop and kiss her or wait until they reached her house? He was so busy thinking about this, he wasn't immediately aware they had stopped.

"This is where I live." Lilly gazed up at him. The moon was shining down on her face and she looked so appealing, Marcel completely forgot his shyness and gently brought his lips down on hers. After a slight hesitation, she began to kiss him back. Instantly Marcel was lost in a world of pleasure he wished would go on forever and the war, his conscience, homesickness and loneliness, all vanished, leaving him feeling happy and struggling with a large erection.

She finally pulled away and, smiling up at him, said quietly, "I'd better go in now. Thank you, Marcel, for a wonderful evening. I've really enjoyed myself."

Marcel was surprised by just how dejected he felt. Reluctantly he let her go, his disappointment obvious. "Can I see you again?"

Lilly's face lit up and she nodded with enthusiasm.

Marcel pulled her back towards him and began to kiss her again, this time with more passion. Laughing, she pulled away, said, "Goodnight," and disappeared in through the front door before he could ask her the way back to camp.

Marcel looked up and down the road but it was deserted. He began walking back up the street and then he had an idea. As a boy, he had always watched the stars and used them to find his way back to the farm on the rare occasions he had slipped out at night to watch the foxes or badgers, so he should be able to do the same here. The camp was north of the town, so he stared up until he had his bearings and then headed towards where he thought the camp was. To his relief, he was soon back at the pub and, from there, he had no problem finding the camp. Unfortunately he took much longer to find his tent because they all looked the same in the moonlight. Several mistakes later and, after profuse apologies to those he had woken, he eventually found the right one.

Everyone was asleep, except Pierre, who was reading. When he crawled quietly in through the entrance, Pierre glanced up and, seeing his expression, grinned. "I don't need to ask whether you had a good evening then?"

"Yes, I did. A wonderful evening. Thank you, Pierre." Marcel fell onto his camp bed. "Do you think it's possible to be in love with two women at the same time?"

Pierre laughed. "I think you have to decide for yourself. You're very young and we are in the middle of a war which could go on for a very long time. When they deploy us, we could go anywhere and we could be away for years. You shouldn't tie yourself down to the first or even the second girl you meet. Enjoy yourself and don't make any promises. It's not fair on them either to fall in love with you and then you get yourself killed. Live for today and let tomorrow take care of itself. Oh, and if you want to do more than kiss and cuddle, be careful!" He ignored Marcel's blushes. "You asked me my opinion and I've told you. Now go to sleep. Tomorrow is another day and the sooner you go to sleep, the sooner you can see her again!"

******

Bethune, Northern France

"Don't think you're going swanning off with that Kraut for the day. There's work needs doing."

Brigitte closed her eyes and ignored her father's shouts. Her buttocks were still stinging from the previous day and she felt her stomach squirm when she thought back to their encounter. Obviously Rolf must have seen Louis but she couldn't understand why he hadn't stormed up to her bedroom and thrown him out. Why hadn't he mentioned seeing them together before? The last time they'd been out, Rolf had given her some earrings, taken her to a nice restaurant, then back to the cottage where he had made love to her and then taken her home. Perhaps he was playing some strange game where he imagined things, so he could have an excuse to punish her. She knew she should be worried about his attitude to her but, for some reason she couldn't fathom, she didn't feel like she was in any real danger.

"Brigitte, are you getting up, or am I going to have to come up there and make you?" Her father's angry voice made her jump. She would have liked to ignore him, but there was no point in antagonising him any more than necessary.

"I'll be down in a minute!" she shouted and turned over on her side, her thoughts returning to Rolf.

She couldn't say she liked him; they hardly had any conversation, but for some bizarre reason she did look forward to seeing him. Maybe she liked the sex? She shook her head. No, it couldn't be that. Then she frowned. Actually she did find the sex exciting and strangely satisfying. Brigitte frowned and stared up at the ceiling, trying but failing miserably, to understand why she should enjoy being physically chastised. After a few moments, she gave up and wondered what Louis was doing instead.

She hoped he was going to come over and see her soon. She missed him more than she wanted to admit to herself. If only his mother wasn't so difficult. Brigitte had no idea why Marie should hate her so much, but she was worried Marie would turn Louis against her. A horrible thought struck her. If Rolf did know about Louis, perhaps he was in danger. Maybe she should warn him? But what could she say? She had promised Louis she wouldn't lie to him anymore and here she was having a relationship with a German behind his back. Louis would hardly take kindly to sharing her with the enemy. No, her best bet would be to keep quiet. She was sure Rolf didn't know about Louis, so there was nothing to worry about.

"Brigitte!" Her father's roar sounded much too close for comfort and she leapt out of bed, grabbed some clothes and began to get dressed.

****

La Couture, Northern France

At first light, Louis made his way up to the far edge of their land and, after checking no one was in sight, walked the short distance to the disused cow shed. As he had correctly surmised, the building was completely derelict but the walls were quite sturdy, although the roof had definitely seen better days. Louis looked around him thoughtfully. Although he had been joking when he'd said next time he would be more careful, maybe the idea wasn't so stupid after all. Yes, he would have to find some way to get allied airmen out of the occupied zone, but while they were here, maybe he should devise some way of hiding the men properly. Stepping into the barn, he scuffed his foot along the ground. Perhaps the answer would be to dig a large underground room, create some kind of trapdoor covered with soil, so it was completely invisible and undetectable. He wasn't an engineer, so he would probably need to take advice. Henri was a builder, so he should know all about tunnelling and how to build safe structures underground. He would ask him.

For his mother's sake, he would tell her nothing. He would say the cow shed was unsuitable but he had found something else and it would be safer not to tell her where. He and Henri would be the only ones who would know where the hiding place was and any airmen would be blindfolded before being hidden and again when being taken out. The more he thought, the more he was sure his idea could work. But, before he made any more plans, he would have to consult with Henri and he would not be back until the evening.

Not the most patient of people, Louis found it quite difficult to get through the rest of the day. But he knew his idea needed careful planning and execution, or they would all be shot. To keep himself occupied, he began to think about how to move the pilots on. Providing them with a safe place to rest was one thing, but they couldn't stay on the farm indefinitely. Somehow, they had to be taken across the lines into Vichy and from there across the border into Spain, but that wouldn't be his problem; his was to get them across the demarcation line and he had no idea how.

If they crossed through check points, they would need papers good enough to satisfy the guards. If they didn't go through the check points, they would have to find other routes that didn't involve passing through manned posts. He had no means of getting papers, so this seemed to be the most likely way. But how could he find the safest places to cross? It was very difficult to move about now, especially without the correct documentation and there were constant rumours of people being shot out of hand for trying to cross in either direction.

Again, he decided he would need to talk to the others, then there would be more than one brain trying to think things through. He turned his attention to his friends. He trusted Henri the most, which was a good thing, because the whole plan hinged on Henri. If he couldn't build the underground room, the whole scheme would fall apart.

****

Lambeth Hospital, London

"Look!" Helen pointed upwards. "I wonder if that's Jimmy." Peggy's gaze followed Helen's finger and she watched the all too familiar sight of British and German planes duelling in the cloudless skies above London.

"Yes!" Helen was delighted when a puff of smoke appeared on the tail of the German plane and the aircraft began to plummet downwards. They could hear loud cheers from the other side of the wall of the hospital grounds, where people were making the most of the hot weather.

"Don't you feel bad about cheering over someone's death?"

"Not really, Peggy. If the German plane was alright then the English pilot would be dead and I know which I prefer. Anyway, they started the war, we didn't."

Peggy couldn't really disagree and, whenever she felt sorry for the Germans, she only had to think about Joe stuck in a POW camp somewhere and any vestiges of pity soon vanished. Peggy sighed heavily. Surely, it shouldn't be that simple to put aside her Christian beliefs and justify killing the enemy? Helen looked at her in concern.

"Are you alright?"

"Yes, sorry. I was just trying to work out why I find it so easy to say killing Germans is fine, when I've always been brought up to believe taking a life is wrong."

"But if we don't take their lives, they will take ours and those of other people, so of course its justified," Helen replied with total confidence, and Peggy envied her the ability to see things in black and white. She wished she was as certain of her own convictions instead of continually questioning things.

"Come on, back to work. Just ask yourself who you would rather was dead – a German or British pilot?"

Peggy nodded, although she wasn't entirely convinced and the two girls went back to work. They had been expecting things to become quieter once the Dunkirk evacuation finished, but the hospital was still quite busy.

"Is Annie coming round tomorrow?" Peggy asked as they went back in. "She hasn't been to see you and your mum for ages and you know you're always welcome to borrow our living room."

"No, she's feeling a bit sick and the heat isn't helping. They've not had too much sleep either over the past couple of weeks thanks to Hitler's planes flying over all the time. In her last letter, she said that because John's parents are worried about the possibility of being bombed, they are all having to sleep in the shelter every night, which is really getting on her nerves."

"But they haven't bombed any towns yet, have they? They're concentrating on the airfields and the RAF."

"I know, but having lost John, they're not taking any chances with his son."

"What if Annie has a girl?"

"Oh, I don't think they'll mind whether the baby's a girl or a boy, but Annie is starting to worry about how possessive they are. She says she's beginning to feel like she's a prisoner, even if she's in a very gilded cage."

"I thought she seemed a bit quiet the last time she came up, but I presumed she was just tired." Peggy looked worried. "If they're like that now, what will they be like when she has the baby?"

"Exactly! Between you and me, I think she's more worried than she's letting on. I'm beginning to wonder whether she hasn't just jumped out of the frying pan with our dad and into the fire."

"What on earth will she do if they don't get any better?"

"Who knows? Maybe once the baby is born, they'll relax a bit. They might just be nervous because they're frightened something'll happen before she gives birth."

"Let's hope so. She really doesn't need this, does she?"

"No. She's had more than enough."

Peggy hesitated for a moment. "It *is* just because she's tired that she's not coming up, isn't it? I mean they're not making things difficult for her or anything?"

"Oh, Lord. To be honest, I don't know. I just took what she said at face value. I never gave any thought that there might be something else behind it." Helen looked worried now and Peggy wished she hadn't said anything.

"I think…" But whatever Helen thought was forgotten as a loud droning noise drowned out her words. Looking at each other in astonishment, their conversation temporarily forgotten, they rushed down the corridor, in through the nearest ward door and over to the window.

The sound grew louder and louder and, in the distance, they could see a German plane spiralling out of control towards the river, smoke and flames streaming from its tail. Following behind, was the familiar sight of a Spitfire and, while the German plane disappeared beneath the waters of the Thames, the Spitfire did a victory roll. The plane flew off to engage in another dogfight and Peggy and Helen smiled at the sight of young men and women, some with children chattering excitedly, standing on walls and roofs and in the street below, cheering madly.

"They don't have a problem knowing who to cheer for." Helen's pointed words went home and Peggy smiled, her earlier doubts forgotten.

****

Lewisham Council Offices, London

Olive was having difficulty concentrating. Her thoughts returned to Tom and she shuddered. He was possibly the most unpleasant man she'd ever met. She'd been relieved when he'd backed off after she'd threatened him, but he still wanted more money and she had no option but to pay him. Or did she? The idea that had popped into her mind after he left was ridiculous but, if he touched her again, she might have no option. She stared sightlessly at the girls on the switchboard and her heart missed a beat. Killing him in the heat of the moment was mad and would only lead to her being arrested, even if she could prove she had acted in self-defence. Questions would be asked about why he was there in the first place… and then there was Kath. What would she do if Olive killed Tom? Would she go to the police and tell them Tom was blackmailing Olive because she had killed Mary, or would that be too incriminating? Even if Kath didn't go to the police, there was nothing to stop her blackmailing Olive instead.

In any case, there was also no guarantee Olive would succeed in fighting off any assault. Tom was bigger than her and much stronger. Mary had been drunk, with her back turned to Olive when she'd struck the fatal blow. Tom was unlikely to give her the same opportunity. The thought of his hands pawing her, touching her in places where only Kurt had, made her feel physically sick. Unfortunately, she had a feeling it was only a matter of time. She shuddered again and turned her attention back to how she could protect herself. There was only one way. She would have to kill him and, to be successful, she would have to make a plan, rather than just react to circumstances.

The sound of laughter broke into her thoughts and she looked around to see two of the girls chattering while there was a red light on the switchboard.

"You two girls, pick up the line immediately."

The ladies in question jumped. They had been sure Olive was not paying any attention.

"Yes, Miss Cooper." Their reply was simultaneous and Olive experienced a brief surge of pleasure at her new-found power. If she could deal with silly giggling girls, she was sure she could put a stop to Tom and Kath's games. At the thought of Kath, Olive's face fell. Even if she got rid of Tom, there was still Kath to deal with. Olive twisted round in her seat and glanced at the girl in question. She was busy answering a call, her back to Olive. As Olive stared hard, her resolved stiffened. Well if Kath got in her way, she would just get rid of her too.

****

Simonsdorf, Poland

The day after their arrival was spent doing the menial tasks they would normally have called camp fatigues or 'jankers'. Whilst some were sent to clean the toilets, the bathhouse and the hut, others had to dig patches and beds to grow vegetables in. Those who weren't digging, occupied themselves by picking the stones out of the beds and pulling up any remaining visible weeds.

Although not hard work, it was quite boring and, after a while, Joe found himself hoping this wasn't what they were going to be doing every day. While this was much easier than the work they had done before, time passed very slowly. After what seemed like ages picking up pebbles and stones, Joe was depressed to find only an hour had gone by.

"Is this all they do here?" he asked one of the other men who was helping him.

"Nah, you'll be allocated to working parties tomorrow. The last lot they brought in were so exhausted, the NCO managed to get the Jerries to agree that the day after any new people arrive, they spend on camp getting their strength back. Don't worry, you'll be wishing you were back here tomorrow, take my word for it."

"It's not so bad," another of the men piped up. "All depends what they get you doing. Most of us seem to end up repairing the damage to the railways and building new lines so our glorious captors can move their armies around easier and conquer some other poor sods."

"So how long have you been here?" Joe asked.

"About a month, but we've been on the sick, so we've been doing this for a couple of days," the first man replied.

"Well I've been on the sick," the second soldier said with heavy emphasis on the 'I'. "Jenkins here is always on the sick. He's so sick, I'm not sure how he ever managed to get in the army at all. In fact, he so sick, I'm surprised he's still breathing."

Used to the friendly banter of his friends, Joe looked up, expecting to see the second soldier smiling, but he wasn't and Joe shivered at the look of hatred on his face. He decided to say nothing and instead concentrated on looking for stones. The next hour passed inexorably slowly and Joe spent the time wishing he was somewhere else. The atmosphere between the two men was quite poisonous and Joe really didn't want to get involved.

****

London

By ten to three, Pam was standing outside the requisitioned Northumberland Hotel which was situated just behind the War Office. At first glance, the hotel appeared to be full of young women, arms loaded with papers, bustling from one floor to another and her heart sank. Perhaps he just wanted a secretary. She almost changed her mind and went back home but, deciding she had nothing to lose, Pam familiarised herself with the room numbers, made her way to room number thirty-six and knocked briskly. After hearing his voice inviting her to go in, she entered. The room was empty, other than a square table, two fold-away chairs and a blackout curtain; even the light hanging from the ceiling was just a naked bulb.

Grahame smiled and indicated the chair nearest her. "Punctual. Good. Please take a seat and, if you don't mind, we'll just have a chat about various things."

Her initial curiosity returning, Pam sat down and waited for him to say something else.

"Your maternal grandmother was French, I believe?" The question took her by surprise. "She lived in Arras?"

"Yes, she did. Why?"

He ignored her question. "And you speak French?"

"Oui," Pam answered automatically, before her brain had even registered he had asked his question in French.

"And how long since you last went to France?" The questions continued in French, each more probing than the last. Eventually, the interview seemed to come to a conclusion and she waited, an expectant look on her face.

There was a silence which she finally felt compelled to break. "Mr Thompson… Grahame… I've answered all your questions to the best of my ability but I'm still none the wiser. Why are you asking me all these things? Are you offering me a job, or not?"

"All in good time. Yes, there could be a job for you, but first I have to make sure you are the right person." He raised his hand to stop her interrupting. "Can you come back here again tomorrow at six o'clock?"

"And after that, will I know what this is all about?"

Grahame smiled and led her to the door but made no attempt to answer. "Oh, and we would prefer you do not mention anything about this to anyone else. Careless talk and all that."

Thoroughly exasperated, Pam stopped in the hallway and turned, but he had already gone back inside leaving her face to face with the closed door.

Chapter Four

Honor Oak Park, London

Peggy hurried home. She was looking forward to catching up with Ethel, who had a thirty six hour pass from her RAF base. She hadn't seen her for a few weeks, so it would be good to spend some time with her before Colin came round. She missed Ethel. Sally was busy with Peter, her fiancé, and Peggy often spent the evenings on her own now, so very different from when the three of them had first moved into the house.

The house was hot and stuffy when she arrived home and she immediately opened the downstairs windows. A gentle breeze rustled the curtains and the heat slowly dissipated. Upstairs was even warmer and, when she opened her bedroom window, the sounds of the children playing in the street reached her, bringing a smile to her face. Fleetingly, she wondered how long she would have to wait before she had children of her own. Of course, Joe would have to come home first and, if she was realistic, now was definitely not the time to be having children, however much she might want them. Thinking of children reminded her of Annie and her conversation with Helen. She did hope the behaviour of Annie's in-laws was just a reaction to John's death, otherwise Annie was going to find life very difficult once she'd had the baby.

The sound of the front door closing brought her out of her reverie, followed by Ethel's cheerful voice shouting up the stairs: "Peggy? Are you home?" Not waiting for an answer, she continued, "Do you want some fish and chips?"

"I'd love some. Do you want some money?"

"No, it's alright. Pay me when I get back. See you in a minute." The door slammed loudly behind her. Peggy changed out of her uniform into a cool sleeveless summer dress and went back downstairs to lay the table.

Ethel was not gone long and the two girls sat down and tucked in, catching up on each other's news between mouthfuls. While Peggy licked the last of the salt off her fingers, Ethel said hesitantly, "I've been thinking, Peggy…"

"Sounds ominous?"

"We have no idea when this beastly war is going to end, so I wondered whether you wanted me to move out. I don't want to, of course, but I'm a bit worried about paying my way out of my wages. I'm already stumping up for my quarters, so maybe you should look for someone else."

Peggy didn't answer for a minute. "Even if we do take in another person, the way things are, there's no guarantee they won't be moved around too. Maybe we could look for someone else who's in the services or based somewhere else who just wants to come here on leave and you could then share the room and the rent. What do you think? Then you'd still have your room here. You'd have to coordinate your leave, but it could work."

Ethel breathed a sigh of relief. "That sounds like a really good idea. I was worried you might be hurt or upset and I don't really want to move out; I just couldn't see a way of paying for both Uxbridge and here."

"We need to talk to Sally first, to make sure she agrees and then we can start to look round for someone. Do you know anyone?"

Ethel shook her head. "No, but I can ask." A thought struck her. "What about Helen?"

"No, that's not a particularly good idea. First of all, Helen would need a full time flat, but more importantly, her dad would know about this address, which would make it difficult for Annie and her mum to meet here."

"Oh, of course. Oh well, I'm sure we'll think of someone." She smiled. "What about Pam?"

"Good idea. I'll ask her." Peggy was about to say more when there was a knock on the door.

Ethel leapt up from the table and rushed into the hall to answer the door.

"Hello, Peggy." Colin's cheerful face appeared in the doorway.

Peggy smiled back. "I'm sure you two have got plenty to talk about, so I'll clear out."

"No, don't go, Peggy. We don't want to push you out of your own home," Colin protested.

"I don't mind, really. It's such a nice evening, I thought I'd go for a walk in the park and give you both some time on your own."

"Thanks, Peggy." Ethel's eyes sparkled. "We'll talk about the room later, when you come back?"

"What's this about a room?"

"I'll leave you to explain." Peggy stepped out into the warm evening sunshine. There were several children playing hopscotch in the street and she turned the corner and came across some more girls skipping. For a little while, she envied them their childhood innocence and ignorance of the real danger they were all in. Her thoughts returned to Joe. While she walked, she thought about all the things she wanted to say to him and decided, even if she couldn't send him a letter, there was nothing to stop her writing one and then, when she did have an address, she could post it. If the letter was out of date, then she could just pen another one. Telling him all about her everyday life would be like talking to him and would make her feel closer to him.

****

London

Pam's brother, Anthony, had managed to get a twenty-four hour pass and had just arrived from his fighter station when she got home, so she had little time to think any more about the strange interview.

"Tony!" Pam was shocked by his appearance. He looked tired and grey and several years older than when she had last seen him, which had only been just under a month ago. She knew the RAF were busy, but she couldn't believe how awful he looked and, for the first time, she realised the warnings about an imminent invasion had probably underplayed the seriousness of the situation.

"I know. I look dreadful but it's nothing a few hours' sleep won't cure, honestly, Sis. Things are a bit hot at the moment, so none of us are getting much kip." He smiled and, although she could see glimpses of the old Tony, the strain was only too apparent. He put his arm round her and she could smell the stale alcohol on his breath. She stared at him with even more concern but, seemingly unaware of this, he continued, "So what have you been up to? You look very smart and mysterious and you were deep in thought when you came through the door."

Pam shook herself mentally. "Nothing. I'm thoroughly bored, to be honest. Crazy, isn't it? You're rushed off your feet and I don't have enough to do. Maybe I should've joined the WAAFs after all."

"You would have spent most of your time on a charge!" He gave her another hug. "Honestly, Sis, you'd never have coped with the discipline."

Pam shrugged, suddenly feeling despondent and rather useless. She wondered whether these strange interviews would really end in a job or whether she was destined to spend the rest of the war doing mindless, mundane things when her soul cried out to be doing something useful.

"Is everything alright, Sis? I was only joking, you know. You'll find something, I know you will."

"Yes, of course I will." She linked her arm through his and began dragging him towards the drawing room. "Come on, let's have a drink to celebrate the fact you're here." The words were out of her mouth before she had really thought them through. But there was no time to retract them before Tony nodded with alacrity.

"Sounds good to me."

He left his overnight bag in the hall and they entered the large drawing room. The windows were open and, outside, they could hear the traffic in the distance. Pam poured some whisky while Tony flung himself down in the comfort of the large armchair by the open fire which, although laid, was not lit. The weather was still warm and sultry and Pam felt hot in her smart dress and cardigan.

"I'm going to go and change out of these clothes." She drained her drink in two large gulps but there was no answer. She looked across at Tony and wasn't surprised to see he was fast asleep, his mouth slightly open and his drink barely touched. She crossed over to him and carefully removed the glass from his hand and, after placing it on the coffee table, she quietly left the room.

****

Simonsdorf, Poland

They had finished and were headed back to the huts when the second soldier came up to Joe.

"Jenkins is not to be trusted, mate. Be very careful what you tell him or what you say within his earshot. We think he's passing information to the Germans in exchange for a cushy life and some little luxuries. There's sod all wrong with him health wise we can see, but the Jerries seems quite content to let him shirk off the work parties, whereas they make the rest of us go, however sick we are."

Joe was appalled. However bad things were, he couldn't envisage any situation where he would help the Germans at the expense of his fellow soldiers.

"Are you sure?" he started to say, then seeing the look on his companion's face, he stopped.

"Don't worry. It took us a while to even begin to think like that. I'm Frank, Frank Stevenson, by the way and I came here about three weeks ago. I picked up some kind of stomach thing, so I've been on camp for a couple of days but I should be back to work tomorrow. Can't wait!"

Joe looked at him, wondering if he was being sarcastic but he seemed quite genuine. Seeing Joe's bemused expression, he suddenly smiled.

"Sorry, I should explain. If you're sick, you get put on half rations and, as you've probably seen, there's not too much to do here, so the time really drags. At least out on the working parties, there's opportunities to scrounge stuff and meet the civvies. The locals are alright, well most of them anyway. Right, here we are." They were approaching the entrance to the feeding hut. "See you tomorrow, probably." He smiled and started to walk off, when suddenly he turned back. "Don't forget what I said." He looked straight at Joe. The expression of menace Joe had seen earlier returned, lingered for a moment and then disappeared and he smiled again, turned round and went towards some other friends who had just returned from a working party.

"You alright, mate? You look like you've seen a ghost." Pete's voice was a welcome relief and Joe quickly recounted what had been said. Pete frowned. "Probably best to keep out of it. Just be careful what you say and to whom." Joe nodded and they joined the queue to get their food. As Frank had predicted, their rations were much smaller than the previous day and Joe looked at his in disappointment.

They found themselves a space at the end of one of the tables near Mitchell and Bert who were looking fed up.

"Food should be better again tomorrow, if they put us on working parties." Joe attempted to cheer them up.

"Great, I can't wait." Mitchell finished his paltry ration and, resting his head on his hands he began watching their fellow prisoners. After a few minutes, he said quietly, "Wonder what the beef is with that guy?" Joe and the others looked to where he was surreptitiously pointing.

"What do you mean?" Pete asked, ignoring Joe who was frantically trying to get his attention.

"All the other guys are avoiding him like the plague. Maybe he's upset them…" Mitchell started to say and then saw Joe's expression. "Okay, Price, what gives? You know something; I can tell by the look on your face."

Joe hesitated and then repeated what he had been told. Mitchell nodded slowly. "Well, let's hope they're right and they're not victimising the poor guy for nothing." The others digested this in silence.

"I still think we should keep out of it and, if we do have to get involved, we should make up our own minds," Pete said.

"I've got no quarrel with that," Mitchell agreed and adroitly changed the subject. "So, do we get to choose working parties or do they pick us out?"

Joe shrugged. "They choose us. I can't see them suddenly giving us a choice about something, can you?"

****

London

Pam came back downstairs, looking resplendent in a rippling brown silk dress that fitted the curves of her body like a second skin. She heard voices coming from the drawing room. She could identify the tones of her mother, father and Tony but there was another, deeper baritone she didn't recognise. As she entered the room, the conversation stopped and Pam's mother rushed over to greet her. "Pam, you look lovely, darling. Isn't it wonderful to have Anthony home again? Even if it's only for twenty four hours." Without waiting for an answer, she took her daughter by the arm and led her towards the only stranger in the room: a tall, dark haired man in army uniform with deep blue eyes and a gentle smile.

"Pam, I want you to meet Captain Richard Denis. He's the son of Lord and Lady Denis; you remember them, I'm sure. Anyway, Richard is en route somewhere or other and was at a loose end, so I thought I'd invite him to dine with us."

Pam smiled at the captain, who bowed his head and said graciously, "It was very kind of your mother to invite me, but I'm even more grateful now I've seen the company I am to dine with."

Pam laughed. "Flattery will get you nowhere, Captain, but I don't mind if you keep trying."

He laughed with her and, leading her gently towards the window, he pointed towards the park which backed onto the house. The barrage balloons were swaying gently in the cool evening breeze and the sun was slowly sinking towards the horizon.

"It's a beautiful evening, isn't it?" They watched the children playing happily on the green and further away, in the distance, they could just make out the men of the Pioneer Corps digging up large chunks of turf and turning over the soil, ready to plant vegetables for the winter. She was about to respond when the sound of an aircraft in the distance caught her attention. She only realised afterwards that it was not the aircraft that had startled her, but Tony's reaction to it. He had jumped up and was frantically searching for something on the carpet. Then he suddenly flung himself flat on the floor, his hands clamped over his head.

"It's alright, Tony. You're off duty." She rushed over to him, speaking loudly and firmly while everyone else froze, not knowing what to do. "Tony, it's alright."

His eyes lost the glassy unfocused look and he stared at her, first in confusion and then embarrassment. "Sorry. Thought I was on the base. Automatic reaction, you know." He tailed off and then abruptly changed the subject. "Right, time for another drink, don't you think, Sis?" He headed over to the drink's cabinet without waiting for an answer and Pam could see his hands were shaking violently when he reached for the whisky decanter.

"Thanks, Tony." Pam was grateful when Richard also chipped in. "I'd love another whisky, old chap."

Her parents gradually recovered and everything slowly returned to normal. The aeroplane disappeared into the distance and Anthony resumed his conversation as though nothing had happened. Pam and Richard took their drinks and went back to the window

"Thank you. I didn't realise just how bad he was."

"Unfortunately, the RAF can't spare them to take any proper time off. They don't have enough pilots and the situation is too critical." Seeing her concerned face, he carried on, but this time with a smile: "One of the things this war has taught me is you should only worry about things over which you have some control. Everything else you deal with by ignoring or getting drunk – whichever is the most appropriate at the time."

Pam smiled back and raised her glass. "I think that's a very good sentiment. In fact I'll drink to that!"

They laughed and the rest of the evening passed off quietly, Richard leaving just before midnight after promising to keep in touch. She climbed into bed, reflected on the last couple of days and wondered what the next few would bring. She was rather taken with Richard and, for the first time since she had met Grahame Thompson, she had something else to think about. As she drifted off to sleep, her last thoughts were of Richard and, even though she was almost asleep, she was vaguely conscious of a warm glow spreading through her body.

****

Bethune, Northern France

Brigitte climbed out of the car and crept upstairs. She was very confused. She'd spent the evening with Rolf and two of his friends, playing cards. Rolf had been the perfect gentleman, filling her glass, holding her chair when she stood up and patiently explaining the rules of poker to her, even though this had slowed the game considerably.

To her surprise, his friends were also polite and courteous, treating her like Rolf's girlfriend; something she wasn't used to. Her previous experiences with men had not prepared her for this and she found herself gradually warming to Rolf. He spent much of the evening making her laugh and she had been looking forward to having sex with him when his friends left. They had finally gone and Brigitte had moved closer to him. To her astonishment, he'd taken her hand and led her out to his car instead. Thinking he wanted sex in the car for a change, Brigitte was even more astounded when he climbed in and drove her home.

Brigitte hesitated before getting out, but he just smiled and said goodnight. This had thrown Brigitte completely. All men expected sex, didn't they? Maybe he didn't like her anymore? She undressed and stared at herself in the mirror to see if she had suddenly lost her sex appeal. She couldn't see anything different, so she climbed into bed and lay there worrying until the early hours.

****

Toulouse, Southern France

Jean-Paul went into the kitchen and made himself some ersatz coffee, wincing at the taste. He didn't really mind chicory, but for once he would have loved a cup of real coffee. He was having trouble sleeping even though, for the first time in days, Angel had not woken. A noise made him jump and, looking round, he saw Jeanne standing in the doorway, her body silhouetted in the light from the moon.

"I couldn't sleep."

"No, I couldn't either, but you should try, you've got work to go to."

"So have you and I'm younger than you."

Jean-Paul smiled. "Do you want some coffee?"

"Please." She nodded. "Papa, I know we have more than enough to worry about with Angel, but…" She stopped.

"What's the matter?" Jean-Paul was concerned at the expression on his daughter's face.

"Mama is very thin. Haven't you noticed?" Jeanne began haltingly and then carried on in a rush. "She's always tired too and I'm sure she is in pain quite a lot, although when I ask her, she says there's nothing wrong." She searched for some kind of denial on her father's face but found none.

Jean-Paul suddenly looked older than his years. "I thought I was imagining things. Then I thought…" He stopped. "I don't know what I thought really, probably if I didn't notice anything, then there was nothing to worry about."

"What do you think is wrong?"

"I don't know, but I think we should ask her, don't you?" Jean-Paul suddenly seemed more like his old self. "I'll talk to her in the morning and try to persuade her to see a doctor."

Jeanne felt slightly reassured. "I'll distract Angel while you talk to her. The last thing she needs right now is…" She broke off. "… Is something else that isn't 'normal' happening around her." Jeanne had been about to say something so unspeakable, she was horrified with herself for even thinking it, but the words were there in the back of her mind and now she had allowed them to surface, however momentarily, she couldn't shake off the feeling of foreboding. "So, what do we do about Angel?" She made a conscious effort to change the subject and think about something else.

"I don't know, to be perfectly honest." Jean-Paul replied distractedly. Now Jeanne had mentioned how tired and thin Claudette looked, he could no longer pretend everything was fine. He had not been entirely convinced by Claudette's blithe assurance she was just tired after the doctor had examined her before they left what was now occupied France. But there had been more pressing things to worry about, so he had allowed his concerns about her health to be subsumed under the need to get his family all safely away from the advancing Germans and, he reluctantly acknowledged, he didn't want to think anything could possibly be wrong with her that a few weeks of rest and recuperation couldn't cure. He tried to put his fears out of his mind and concentrate on what they could do about Angel.

"I think the best thing is to give her time. Now she feels safe, maybe all the trauma is coming out. If she continues to feel secure, hopefully she will gradually go back to being the bright cheerful little girl we've got to know."

"I agree." Claudette's voice, coming from the door, startled them. "I think we may also start to get behavioural problems with her while she tries to come to terms with what has happened. But we'll cope. As long as we continue to show her how much she is loved and reassure her she is safe, she should gradually recover. We are just going to have to give her time."

"Come and sit down, my love." Jean-Paul took her arm and led her gently towards one of the comfortable armchairs. Although he'd intended to wait until the morning, feeling how bony her arm was galvanised him into action. "Claudette, I am really concerned about the amount of weight you've lost and Jeanne and I both think there is something you are not telling us?"

There was silence while they watched her face. Eventually she spoke. "I'm sorry, there's no easy way to tell you. I have been trying to find the words and the right time but…" Her voice trailed off and she looked away, unable to bear the worry on their faces and knowing she was only going to add to their concerns.

"The time to tell us what?" Jean-Paul prompted, trying to ignore the ominous thudding of his heart as he stared into her eyes.

Claudette took a deep breath and said clearly, "I have cancer. It's probably only a matter of time now… I'm sorry, my loves, but you are going to have to manage without me." She tried hard to smile but it was no good. The expression on their faces was enough to release all the tears she had been suppressing. Jean-Paul put his arms round her and held her tight, his head buried in her shoulder. Jeanne had not moved, the shock leaving her completely stunned. Then she too rushed forward and flung herself into her mother's arms.

****

London

Pam was woken suddenly by a loud shout and then what sounded like garbled talking. She reached for the clock by the side of the bed and saw it was three o'clock in the morning. She had left the blackout down and the moon was shining directly through the window, lighting the room. The voice was coming from further down the corridor and she hurried towards the door. The night was warm, she didn't need her dressing gown or slippers and her bare feet moved silently along the carpeted corridor. The noise was coming from Tony's room and she hesitated, wondering whether she should knock or just go in. After a couple of seconds of indecision, she opened the door and found Tony fighting with an invisible enemy, his sheets wrapped tightly round him while he struggled and shouted indecipherable words at his unseen opponent.

"Tony." Pam spoke gently but there was no response. "Tony, you're alright. You're dreaming."

She came closer and put her hand on his shoulder, repeating the calming words several times until eventually his struggling began to subside and the rapid talking ceased. She stayed there for nearly half an hour until he seemed to be in a more peaceful sleep and finally she left and made her way back to her own room where she lay awake, her thoughts full of fears for her brother.

Chapter Five

Toulouse, Southern France

"Is there nothing they can do? Perhaps you should seek a second opinion. The doctor could be wrong, couldn't he, Papa?" Jeanne appealed to Jean-Paul. He was about to agree, when he turned to Claudette and looked at her properly for the first time in a long while. He stared at her face. The shadows under her eyes and the prominence of her cheek bones through the translucence of her skin told him there was no hope. He couldn't understand why he hadn't noticed. How could he have been so blind?

Claudette took his hand. "You have nothing to reproach yourself for. Without you, we would all be trapped in occupied France and Angel would not have a new family. Not to mention there is a good chance Marcel reached England and delivered the note so that poor prisoner's mother knows he is safe. You are a wonderful man and you have been a perfect husband and father."

Jean-Paul turned away, not wanting her to see the grief he knew would be etched on his face. It was her use of the past tense that really brought home the truth of her situation.

"I don't know what to say," he said eventually, when he had his emotions back under control. "Are you in pain? Is there anything I can do to help you?"

"I'm alright most of the time. The doctor has given me some pain killers, but there is a shortage, so I am trying to only take them when necessary." She smiled at him. "You have no idea what a relief it is to have told you; I feel like a giant weight has been lifted from my mind. Now, some coffee would be nice, even if it is only ersatz."

"I'll make some." Jeanne was still unable to take in what was happening and needed to be on her own, just for a few moments. Not for the first time, she wished Marcel was there with her. She missed him so much and not even being able to write to him, it was like he was dead to her too. The tears welled up in her eyes again and she brushed them away angrily. The last thing her parents needed now was for her to fall apart. She would have to be strong for them both and for Angel who was about to lose someone else she loved. How on earth was she going to tell the little girl? She sighed heavily; at the moment there was no need to tell her, so she would face that problem when she had to.

They sat in silence, drinking the coffee and trying not to think of the future.

"You should both get some sleep; you have work to go to." Claudette yawned. "I'm sorry. I think I'm going to have to go back to bed too, or I will never get up in the morning."

Jean-Paul took her arm and gently walked back into the bedroom with her. Jeanne didn't move. Although she was tired, she knew she wouldn't sleep. She had too much on her mind. A while later, Jean-Paul returned to the sitting room and Jeanne was suddenly struck by how much he had aged over the past few hours. She looked at him standing by the window, staring into the deserted street below and she suddenly felt very afraid. The news her mother was dying was devastating enough, but her father had always been invincible and to think of him getting old was immensely frightening. She went over to him and put her arms round him, suddenly realising she was no longer the child whose parents would always protect her. Their roles had reversed and she would have to take over the responsibility for looking after them. They stayed there until the sun rose and bathed the street in its warm dawn glow.

"We need to get ready for work." Jean-Paul shook himself reluctantly out of his reverie. Jeanne nodded, although she couldn't imagine how she would get through the day.

****

Catford, London

Olive watched the hands on the alarm clock move slowly towards dawn. Yet again she couldn't sleep. She stared at the wall, sipped her hot milk and wished she could come up with a satisfactory plan to get rid of Tom. She had just under a week before he arrived on her doorstep again, so she needed to think of something. Of course, he might just turn up, collect his money and go, but she doubted it. She had felt the unspoken menace from the first time she had met him, but she had fooled herself into thinking he only wanted to intimidate her. Men had never wanted her sexually; that's why Kurt's interest had been such a surprise. The thought that Tom could want her in any physical way was laughable. She had no idea why he was behaving in that way towards her; she'd not led him on at all, yet he seemed to find her attractive. The feeling wasn't reciprocated; she found him repulsive and, not for the first time, she cursed the war for taking Kurt away and leaving her defenceless.

Thinking of Kurt failed to provide the normal warm, cosy glow and she hugged her knees to her chest and sighed. She wished he'd hurry up and write. Once again, she considered telling him about her problems but what help could he give her? Putting her predicament in writing would be madness and the last thing she wanted to do was to alienate the only person who loved her. No, this was one problem she would have to deal with on her own.

****

Outside Bethune, Northern France

Giving up on sleep, Brigitte got up early and wandered down to the café. The place was silent, her father not yet up. She would go and see Louis. He would be awake and she was sure he would be pleased to see her. If Rolf didn't want her, Louis would.

She let herself out quietly, fetched her bike and began pedalling towards La Couture. The sun was warm and already high in the cloudless blue sky, and she quickly began to feel better.

Rolf watched from across the street. He finished his cigarette, threw the butt on the ground and climbed into his car. He was pretty sure he knew where she was going, but he would follow her anyway. The thought crossed his mind that, perhaps he should do something about the farm boy, but then he smiled. Louis could wait. Punishing Brigitte was much more fun and she was so predictable. Louis was no threat. He'd had him checked out and Louis was just a boy. He would soon lose interest in Brigitte when he had to worry about quotas and keeping his German masters happy. Rolf had known exactly how Brigitte would react when he brought her home straight after his friends had gone. He congratulated himself on not losing his touch.

Unaware Rolf had seen her, Brigitte continued on her way, her thoughts now full of Louis and how she could see him without his mother catching her.

****

Toulouse, Southern France

Walking through the quiet streets helped clear her head and, by the time Jeanne reached the police station, she felt slightly better, although her face was still tear streaked.

"What's wrong?" Eve asked within minutes of her walking through the door.

Jeanne hesitated for a moment, knowing that to say the words out loud would make everything real.

"Come on, Jeanne. I know we haven't known each other long but I have grown very fond of you and I hope you feel the same. You can trust me, you know." Jeanne nodded. The tears began to fall and she said the dreaded words aloud. Eve gasped in horror and instinctively put her arms round Jeanne in sympathy. "Oh, Jeanne," she said. "I am so sorry." She held her in her arms for a few moments. "How is your father?" she asked.

"Not good. In some ways, that's making everything worse. He has always been able to deal with everything and now he suddenly seems so old."

"From everything you've told me about your father, he will cope. It's just a shock at the moment. Once he comes to terms with the news, you will find he becomes more like his old self."

Jeanne wasn't so sure. They had been through so much recently. She would have to hope Eve was right.

"And how is my beautiful receptionist this morning?" Gabriel Valence's voice cut through the air as he strode purposefully towards the reception desk. Instantly taking in the situation, he continued, "Jeanne, what on earth is wrong? Can I help at all?" The sincerity in his voice caught her by surprise. He had been flirting with her light heartedly ever since her first morning at work, but she had not allowed herself to be fooled into thinking he was interested in her. Gabriel flirted with every woman under thirty and she had also heeded Eve's warning. The last thing she needed to do was to draw attention to herself by upsetting his fiancée.

But this morning, her guard was down and she allowed him to steer her to a side room where he sat her down. He waved at Eve to bring some coffee, closed the door and handed her a pristine white handkerchief. "Here. Now tell me what the problem is."

Jeanne found it easier to speak the words aloud the second time and, much to her disgust, she found a part of her mind was telling her how awful she must look with tears flowing down her cheeks. Angrily, she pushed the thought away; she couldn't care less what he thought of her. At the moment, she felt like her life was falling apart and she didn't know what she could do to take away the pain.

"Jeanne, I'm so sorry. This must be dreadful for you. Perhaps you should take some time off work?"

"Thank you, but I think I'm better here at the moment. I don't really want Mama to see me so upset. It will just make everything worse for her and we don't want to tell Angel until we have to." She stopped abruptly, aware she was just about to launch into an explanation of the problems they were having with Angel. That wouldn't be wise until they'd come up with a sanitised version of the truth they could all use. She could feel Gabriel's eyes on her as she frantically tried to think of something to say. Luckily, they were interrupted by the arrival of Eve with two cups of steaming coffee.

"Who's Angel?" Gabriel asked, as they sipped their drinks.

Even though she was back on reasonably safe ground, Jeanne avoided his eye. "My sister. She's only five."

Gabriel replaced his cup on the table. "Of course you must stay at work, if you think it's for the best, but remember, I am only upstairs if you need someone to talk to or you just want some time on your own."

"Thank you, you've been really kind." Jeanne wiped away the tears and tried unsuccessfully to blow her nose quietly. She stared down at the screwed up handkerchief in her hands and said wryly, the beginnings of a tentative smile on her face, "I'll wash your hankie and let you have it back."

"Whenever you're ready. I'm sure I have another." He stood up and opened the door. "Don't forget… any time."

****

La Couture, Northern France

"Brigitte! You're up early?" Louis was delighted to see her. Marie was still asleep, so there was no danger of her seeing Brigitte. He grabbed hold of her arm and pulled her into the barn.

They were only just inside when she began kissing him, her tongue snaking through his mouth, her hands rubbing his penis through his trousers. Louis forgot all about closing the door. He kissed her back, his hands already exploring her breasts while she began pulling off his shirt. He laughed. "You're in a hurry…"

Brigitte didn't answer. She wanted to feel loved and Louis' passion was just what she needed to make her feel attractive again. With fumbling fingers, she began undoing his trousers and Louis lifted up her skirt, tearing her knickers as he fought to pull them off. His passion completely aroused, he shoved her back against the open barn door, slid his hands under her bottom and lifted her until he could thrust inside her. His movements became faster and he grunted as she began to move against him. He could hear her panting, her muscles closed tightly around him, pulling him in deeper and then everything else was forgotten and he climaxed. Brigitte held him close, her arms linked around his neck, enjoying her success. She hadn't lost her power after all…

Rolf lowered his binoculars and leant back against the car. The sight was quite arousing and he had an erection. He climbed into the car and quickly brought himself off, his mind recalling every detail of their coupling. He wiped himself with his handkerchief and sighed. Maybe he should do something about the boy, after all. He didn't want her running back to him every time she was dissatisfied; that wouldn't suit his plans in the least. He needed to make her totally reliant on him. Then she would do whatever he wanted.

****

Simonsdorf, Poland

After a breakfast of ersatz coffee and suspiciously mouldy-looking bread, Joe was marched back down to the station where he was put to work digging in some sand pits on the railway line. The work was hard and Jenkins' words about wishing he was back in camp doing menial tasks returned to haunt him as the sun rose higher and higher in the sky. His muscles began to ache, his eyes stung and the sweat dripped continuously from his forehead. He soon learnt that trying to brush the perspiration away was not a good idea. His hands were covered in sand which immediately made its way into his eyes. The morning seemed endless and he was relieved when they were told to stop for a short break and given some water.

****

La Couture, Northern France

Louis gulped down his lunch and headed over to Henri's parents' house. Seeing Brigitte had been a pleasant surprise. It was a shame he hadn't been able to spend more time with her, but she seemed satisfied with a quick romp in the hay and he'd promised to try and get over to see her soon. To be perfectly honest, he'd actually been in a hurry to get rid of her once they'd made love. He hadn't wanted Marie to see her and he was worried she would find out about their house guest. He also couldn't wait to share his idea with Henri, who was in one of the outhouses when he arrived.

"I thought we could make this into a kind of meeting place, rather than use the house. Then Mum and Dad don't need to be involved. I think the less our families know the better, now."

Louis nodded. "My sentiments exactly." He checked outside to make sure there was no one about. "I've got an idea, but I need you to tell me whether it's feasible."

Henri was intrigued. "Go on."

"The way I see things, we have two immediate problems. We can't just go and ask anyone how to get someone across the lines, we need to be really careful and take our time. But time is not something we have too much of, because Patrick – that's the pilot's name, by the way – is still in our house, as Mama doesn't think he should be sleeping in the barn while he's still recovering and the longer he is there, the greater the danger of discovery." Louis glossed over the fact it had been his idea Patrick should stay in the house. "To find a safe route out or someone who is able to help us, we have to be able to hide him safely.

He can't stay in the house much longer; it's too dangerous. The Boche could come round at any time. So, if we can find somewhere else to hide him, that will give us the time we need. Agreed?'

Henri nodded. He was quietly impressed by this new, sensible Louis.

"I went to look at the deserted cow shed bordering our land and Giraud's but it's no good as it is now. However, I was wondering if we could build an underground room in there. The entrance would be through a trapdoor which would be covered with soil. Anyone we hide there would have to be blindfolded, so they don't know where they are. I know it's not ideal long term, but safety has to come first. What I want to know is whether it's feasible."

Henri thought for a few moments. "In principle, the idea's not a problem, and wouldn't be too difficult to do but the location is very important. If you put the hide in too isolated a spot, you could draw attention to it if anyone sees movement there and it would be very difficult for those hiding to get any fresh air or to take food to them on a regular basis."

Louis looked crestfallen. "I hadn't thought of that – you're right of course."

"I'm not saying the idea won't work, Louis, just the location's wrong. We need to put the hide somewhere no one will think anything of, if you're going there regularly and also where those you are hiding can come out without being seen."

Louis realised Henri had accepted the idea Patrick would not be the first and he smiled. "Alright then, what about my barn. I know my original idea was to locate the room somewhere away from the house, but if the hiding place is anywhere on our land, the Boche will still blame us, so we may as well locate it in the barn. I can go there without raising suspicion, there's cover during the day and they can use the upper level for a look out and hide away in good time if anyone comes. What do you think?"

"Yes, I think that will work. Let's go and have a look now."

Delighted with their plans and looking forward to putting them into action, they headed towards Louis' farm, discussing their ideas in low voices while they made their way through the fields.

****

Simonsdorf, Poland

The rest was over all too quickly and they were soon back working under the merciless glare of the noon sun. The afternoon was even worse and Joe was more than relieved when the whistle finally blew and they returned to camp. Pete's face and back were burned bright red by the sun and Joe wondered if he looked the same. The sunburn grew worse and, by the evening, Joe and Pete felt like their bodies were on fire.

"I'm going to keep my shirt on tomorrow." Joe was fed up trying to get comfortable.

"Me too." Pete was suffering even more than Joe and it didn't help having the others make fun of the colour of their faces. "If anyone else says anything, I'm going to hit them." Pete grimaced. "At least, I will if I can get off this bunk."

But Joe wasn't listening. He'd spotted some new arrivals and realised from the divisional signs on their arms they were from the brigade his father's unit was attached to. He waited until they were dispersed amongst the huts and then went in search of the staff sergeant he had seen earlier.

"Excuse me, Staff. My names's Price, Joe Price. My father, David Price, is a corporal in the Army Service Corps. I know this is a long shot, but I just wondered if you knew him or if you had any idea what's happened to him or the rest of his unit…" He tailed off, not knowing what else to say.

"Hello, Joe." The staff sergeant looked him over and smiled. "As it happens, I do remember your dad. I think he was amongst the lucky sods who got taken off from Dunkirk. Of course, I can't guarantee he got back home safely, but the last time I saw him, he was amongst those queuing to board one of the last destroyers. After that, only the small fishing boats and trawlers were able to get in. I should imagine he's back home now, having a pint and enjoying himself; unlike us," he finished ruefully.

"Thanks, sir." Joe was relieved to know his father had got home safely. At least one of them was back in England, well for the moment anyway. Of course he didn't know whether he was wounded, but at least he was free.

****

Toulouse, Southern France

The police station remained busier than usual throughout the day, which left Jeanne with little time to think and she was surprised by just how quickly five o'clock came round.

The disrupted night, together with the worry and distress over Claudette, plus the busy day, left her feeling very tired and, for once, she wasn't looking forward to the walk home. She said goodnight to Eve and set off. At least the weather was nice, she thought; she was gradually adjusting to the continuous warmth of the southern climate, although it was strange to know each day was likely to be warm and sunny instead of the forever changing weather patterns she was used to.

"Can I give you a lift?" Jeanne looked around in astonishment to see Gabriel smiling at her from the driving seat of a shiny green Bugatti T46 'Petite Royale' sports saloon.

Jeanne wanted to say yes, but she wasn't sure whether she should let him know where she lived. Then she realised how ridiculous she was being. He was a senior policeman and she worked at the police station. It would hardly be difficult for him to find out her address, if he hadn't already done so. A quick look at her employment registration would suffice. "Won't it take you out of your way?"

"It's not far," he responded, confirming her thoughts.

"Then, thank you. I am really tired and I wasn't looking forward to walking." Knowing it would look suspicious to refuse, she gave in gracefully, walked around to the passenger seat and climbed in. The interior of the car had an expensive wood trim with tan coloured leather seats and she found herself admiring its luxurious comfort.

"So, have you lived here long?"

"Not long, no. We fled the invasion and were lucky enough to find somewhere quite quickly." Jeanne wondered how much she should tell him. Instinct told her to change the subject and ask him questions instead. "What about you? Have you always lived in Toulouse?"

"Yes. I was born here, grew up here and, when I left school, I joined the police force. Very boring really." He smiled at her and Jeanne found herself smiling back. "So, have you been to any of our wonderful restaurants since you arrived?" Gabriel sensed she was not ready to talk about anything too personal.

Jeanne shook her head.

"No? Then you must allow me to take you to one, perhaps tomorrow night?"

Jeanne couldn't hide her astonishment. "I thought you had a girlfriend," she blurted out and then began to blush furiously when she realised she had implied he was asking her out on a date, rather than just as a friend.

Gabriel laughed. "I see the gossip mill works well. Yes I do have a girlfriend but she doesn't own me and, in any case, you are a colleague who is in need of cheering up."

Jeanne tried frantically to backtrack. "I'm sorry. I just meant I didn't want to cause you any problems." She realised she was digging herself in deeper with every word. She was now implying she would be a threat to his girlfriend. She wished fervently she hadn't accepted the lift and the floor would open up and swallow her. She looked out of the window feeling miserable and suddenly realised they were pulling up outside the apartment.

"Thank you for the lift," she mumbled. She couldn't get out of the car quickly enough.

Gabriel seemed totally unaware of her discomfort. "We can discuss our dinner tomorrow at work, so don't go making alternative arrangements, will you?" He waved, let the clutch out and drove effortlessly down the street leaving her standing there looking bemused.

****

London

The evening was cloudy and an ever present threat of rain hung in the air. Pam arrived slightly earlier this time and positioned herself quietly on the corner of the street, watching. As before, the only people who seemed to come and go were women but then, to her surprise, Richard appeared at the other end of the street and strode purposefully towards her. She was so startled, she almost called out to him, but something held her back. He wasn't wearing his uniform. In fact he was dressed in a very nondescript way, his hat at an angle, shading his face so she almost doubted it was him. But no, she was right and, as he drew closer, she began to wonder what she would say to him; what excuse she could invent for her presence.

Before he reached her, though, he stopped at the hotel and ran up the steps, disappearing inside. Thoroughly intrigued, Pam looked at her watch. Ten to six. She entered the building, telling herself there could be lots of reasons for his being there. There were, after all, several other offices he could be visiting. But why the suit and where was his uniform?

She went straight to room thirty six and knocked on the door. Grahame answered curtly, "Come in."

Pam turned the knob, pushed open the door and almost stumbled, so surprised was she to see Richard sitting on the other side of the table next to Grahame. She recovered quickly. "I wondered if you were coming here when I saw you enter the building just now."

She was gratified to see the surprise on his face and then he smiled. "I'm sorry for all the subterfuge, but it is necessary, I can assure you." He raised his hand to stop her interrupting and continued, "I'll explain a lot more in a moment but, briefly, Grahame works for me and I sent him to meet you the other day in the gallery. His report after your first interview was very favourable, so I thought I would take a closer look for myself last night." He ignored the growing hostility in her face. "Quite frankly, Pam, we are looking for people with particular talents, whose loyalty is not in question. One of the talents we need desperately is to find people who speak French fluently enough to pass as French citizens if necessary."

The anger left her face, replaced by a look of bemusement. "But France is occupied by the Germans and Vichy France is almost as bad."

"Yes, that's right," Richard replied.

There was silence. "Are you looking for spies?"

Richard nodded, his face deadly serious. "In a sense, yes, but there are other roles too."

"But I wouldn't know where to start." Pam tried to think things through logically, whilst trying to ignore the voice in her head crying out with glee, and to stop herself from jumping up and down with excitement.

"We would give you training if you volunteered for this kind of work. However, make no mistake, the work of an agent is very dangerous and exacting. The odds of you surviving are about evens. The life of a spy is not glamorous, because no one can ever know what you are doing and, although some of it is exciting, much of the work is dull and routine, which is often the most dangerous time of all, because you must never let down your guard and you can never trust anyone."

Pam sat still and said nothing, her eyes scrutinising their faces. They waited for her to speak first. Eventually she looked at Richard. "Do I have to make a decision here and now or can I go home and then let you know? I would prefer to give the idea some thought."

Richard smiled; unbeknown to her, she had passed the final test of the interview phase. Although they were looking for bold and decisive people who were capable of making instant decisions, they also needed candidates who would think things through before acting, who could react to changing circumstances and who weighed up actions and consequences before making decisions.

"Yes, we want you to go home and think things through." He stopped and looked straight into her eyes, his face serious again. "You cannot discuss this with anyone at all. In fact, before you leave this room you will have to sign the Official Secrets Act. When you have made your decision, ring this number and just say your name and either 'yes' or 'no'. Obviously your answer will determine what happens after that." He handed her a piece of paper with a telephone number printed on it. She looked at the note and then handed it back to him. Seeing the expression on his face, she smiled.

"It's alright. I haven't already made a decision or anything. I've just got a really good memory for numbers, so I won't need the piece of paper."

She stood up, feeling more relaxed than she had in days. "Is there a time limit?" she asked.

Richard stood up and held out his hand. "We need to know by five o'clock in two days' time. If you decide not to accept, there is no stigma or shame attached. We would much rather people were honest with us and we know this is not an easy decision to make, mainly because you can never tell your family or friends what you are doing. They may guess, but you can never confirm their suspicions." He shook her hand. "Goodbye, Pam and thank you for coming in. I'll look forward to hearing from you."

Pam left the office calmly. Her biggest decision was how long to wait before ringing to accept. She had hesitated only because she knew instinctively they expected her to, but in reality she'd made her mind up before she had even left the office.

Chapter Six

Honor Oak Park, London

"Thanks again for the lift." Peggy smiled at Chris as she climbed out of his car. "You have no idea what a luxury it is to be driven home."

"See, I do have my uses!" He laughed. "So, when are you going to come out with me for a drink again? I promise not to leap on you, or bore you with all my family problems."

Peggy grinned. "Maybe this weekend?" She still wasn't entirely sure about the wisdom of going out with him, but he was nice and they were only friends.

"Sounds wonderful. I'll pick you up at seven and we'll go to the pub."

Peggy started to answer when she spotted Colin standing on the door step. Chris saw him at the same time. "Looks like you've got a visitor."

Peggy frowned. "That's Colin, Ethel's boyfriend. I wonder why he's here. I hope everything's alright." She had a sudden premonition Colin had brought bad news. His shoulders were slumped and his usually happy face looked pale and drawn.

"Do you want me to stay?"

"No, you'd better not." Peggy was suddenly embarrassed by his presence.

Chris hesitated, but he could tell she wanted him to go. "Goodnight then," he said.

"Bye." Peggy was already heading towards Colin. Chris watched while she opened the door and they disappeared inside, then he drove off.

****

London

Pam travelled home, her mind made up. She could wait before phoning and accepting, but what was the point? She wasn't sure who she spoke to on the phone, because she didn't recognise the voice, but she was told to pack a small bag and to await further instructions. In the meantime, she was to tell her parents she had joined the First Aid Nursing Yeomanry and was waiting for her deployment papers to come through.

After making the call, from the public telephone box in the nearby park, she went home, began packing her bag and prepared to lie to her parents. She managed to catch her mother on the way back from an important charity event and her father on the way home from a busy day at work. Her mother nodded vaguely in the way Pam had got used to when her mother had her mind fixed elsewhere, but her father stopped and looked at her curiously.

"I thought you hated nursing." He appeared somewhat mystified.

"Well, I need to do something and they do other things too," she answered, which seemed to satisfy him.

He kissed her on the cheek and made a mental note to check which branch of the FANY his daughter had joined. Everything seemed a little too sudden for his liking and, he knew Pamela would hate doing first aid, she would need something more challenging and that was what was bothering him. He had heard rumours the FANYs were involved in secret work and, given his daughter's fluency in French, he would not be surprised to find out this was all a front for something else. He hoped he was wrong. It was bad enough having his son on the front line with the RAF. He really didn't want his daughter, the apple of his eye, in danger too. Not that he would rock the boat. After all, there was a war on and Hitler didn't seem to distinguish between civilians and the military, which meant they couldn't either, but that didn't mean he would approve.

Unaware her father was quite so perceptive, Pam congratulated herself on not arousing her parents' suspicions and, having finished packing her bag, she settled down with her mother to listen to the wireless and wait for her orders. Unfortunately, she couldn't quite hide her excitement and eventually she had to stop herself jumping up every time the phone rang, because her parents were beginning to get suspicious.

"What on earth's the matter with you?" Her mother was exasperated at being nearly knocked out of the way in Pam's haste to reach the phone first.

"Sorry." Knowing they would never believe she was excited at the prospect of what appeared to be a routine job, Pam was suddenly inspired. "I thought it might be Richard. He said he would ring." She managed to make her face look suitably embarrassed, which seemed to work because her mother sighed.

"Honestly, Pam, you'll never find a man if you throw yourself at him. Men like to chase after a woman; makes them feel they are in charge. You need to act with a little more decorum."

Pam nodded, suitable chastened. "I know, Mummy, but you have to agree he is really 'lish."

"'Lish? What does that mean?"

Relieved her diversionary tactic had worked, Pam smiled. "Delicious of course!"

"What's delicious?" Her father asked, coming into the room.

"Captain Denis," her mother replied. "You know; he came to dinner the other night? I was just telling Pam she shouldn't throw herself at him because it will probably put him off." She frowned and rubbed her temples. "I really do have a splitting headache. I think I'll go up to bed. Good night, darling." She kissed him on the cheek and headed up the stairs.

Pam smiled. "I'll just have to learn to be patient, won't I?" She followed her mother upstairs. Fooling her mother was one thing but her father was another and she was sure he was watching her more closely than usual. Once in her bedroom, she lay on the bed and wondered what Richard was doing at that moment. Although she had used him as a convenient excuse, she was actually rather taken with him. Still, she had no intention of throwing herself at him: at the moment she was more interested in her new job.

****

Honor Oak Park, London

The colour drained from her face and Peggy shook her head. Reaching backwards, she grasped the arm of the chair behind her and sat down heavily.

"She can't be. There must be some mistake."

There was silence while Peggy struggled to accept the dreadful news. How could Ethel be dead? Her kind, gentle friend who had just wanted to do something useful to help the war effort. Gradually, haltingly, his voice hoarse from emotion, Colin explained what had happened.

"She was transferred to Detling Airfield near Maidstone for a few weeks. She rang me after she arrived and said she had a weekend pass so we arranged to meet on Saturday. She sounded really pleased, you know, looking forward to her new duties, although she wouldn't tell me what they were, of course. I'm so grateful the conversation was happy, Peggy. At least I can always remember her laughing. It would have been awful if we'd had a row and that was the last time I'd spoken to her." He swallowed. "She was queuing in the mess when the Stukas arrived."

Peggy found herself picturing everything in her mind: Ethel queuing, laughing and joking with her friends and then the bombs falling, smashing through the roof and bringing the building down on top of them. She could only hope Ethel had died instantly and didn't know what was happening; anything else was unthinkable.

As if he could read her mind, Colin continued, "She died instantly, she didn't suffer at all. One of her friends was with her. She came out with barely a scratch." He paused, while the feelings of guilt he had felt for momentarily wishing the friend had been killed and not Ethel, resurfaced. Hurriedly he pushed them away and carried on, "They were almost at the front of the queue when the bomb fell. There was a tremendous noise and everything went black. When she came round, the raid was over and she could hear rescuers searching through the wreckage trying to find people. She called out to Ethel but there was no reply and, because she was trapped under some wreckage, she wasn't able to move. When they finally reached her, they also found Ethel. There wasn't a mark on her, so it must have been the blast that killed her."

Colin was unable to go on and Peggy reached out to hold his hand, relieved Ethel wouldn't have suffered.

Eventually she broke the silence. "How's Martin? He must be devastated?" She couldn't even try to imagine the way Ethel's widowed father must be feeling.

Colin shook his head. "She was the reason he carried on after Ethel's mum died. All he wanted was to see her happily married with a couple of children of her own and he would have been happy. He can't accept she's dead and he's still alive." Colin stopped, unable to continue while the flood of emotion coursed through him. "Oh, Peggy, what am I going to do without her? I loved her so much. I was going to ask her to marry me on her next leave." He got up and walked over to the window. "Why didn't I ask her last time?"

Peggy didn't answer. Ethel had been a kind, gentle person and such a good friend, she couldn't imagine not ever seeing her again. She looked at Colin standing by the window, his shoulders bowed and shaking. She got up and put her arms round him and they cried together.

****

Toulouse, Southern France

"Is everything alright, Jeanne?" Claudette looked at her daughter with some concern. She was looking very flushed and had seemed preoccupied while they were preparing dinner. She knew Jeanne had received a shock, but somehow Claudette didn't think that was the problem. If she hadn't known better, she would have thought perhaps Jeanne had met someone. But she knew how her daughter felt about Marcel, although when and if they would ever see each other again was debatable, given the circumstances.

"I'm fine, Mama, honestly. Just a little tired."

Claudette wasn't convinced, but she felt Jeanne had enough things to cope with at the moment and didn't want to push her. She only hoped that, if she had found someone, he would be good to her. She would need someone she could lean on during the next few weeks which she knew would be very difficult. She hadn't said any more to either Jean-Paul or Jeanne but she could feel herself weakening already. The pain was much worse and she also felt nauseous. Somewhere deep down, she realised she had kept going before because they didn't know and she needed to hide her illness from them. Now she had told them her secret, it was as though she had given her body permission to give up and she knew she didn't have much time left.

"You look tired, Mama. Let me do this. You go and sit down." Jeanne had watched the waves of pain crossing Claudette's face and all thoughts of Gabriel were forgotten. Her fears for her mother superseded everything else. "Do you want me to take some time off work to look after Angel?" she asked, checking first that Angel was not in earshot.

Claudette shook her head. "No, not at the moment. You may have to later on, but not yet." She winced while another wave of pain hit her body. "I'd like to try and keep things normal for a little longer. I'm still hoping she'll start to speak again."

Jeanne nodded. She had been hoping when she walked in that Angel would run up to her, chattering away, but although Angel had run to her, she had just hugged Jeanne in silence. Despite Jeanne's attempts to prompt her to speak, Angel had remained resolutely silent and eventually Jeanne had given up trying. Instead, she had given the little girl a big hug and tried not to let her see any concern on her face.

"Jeanne, there's something I need you to do for me?"

"Anything, Mama. You only have to ask."

Claudette indicated they should sit down at the kitchen table, then she took her daughter's hands and spoke in a low voice. "When I die, Jeanne, you can't do anything to draw attention to yourselves, like laying my body on the floor and lighting candles. You have to leave my body on the bed and call a priest. I will have to be buried in a coffin, not straight into the earth and the casket will have to remain open until the funeral. You must be on your guard and not forget the danger you are in. After the burial you cannot have a meal of condolence or sit shiva, because of Angel."

Jeanne gasped. They had never been strong orthodox but not to follow their life long traditions would be an insult to her mother. Claudette smiled and patted her hand. "God will not mind if you bury me as a Catholic, I'm sure. We didn't run away from the Germans for you to give yourselves away for something that really doesn't matter to me." She could sense Jeanne was about to argue and interrupted her, "You and your father will need to read about Catholic burying rituals and learn some prayers, so when the time comes, you do not do anything suspicious."

"Have you spoken to Papa about this?"

"Yes, but I need you to be strong for him and make sure you are both prepared." She saw the expression on her daughter's face and sighed. "When the war is over and you are safe, your father can recite kaddish for me, as I have no son to do it. I'm sure God will forgive us for being a little late. Please promise me, Jeanne?"

Jeanne nodded. Her mother was right. She would do some research in the morning.

******

La Couture, Northern France

Lost in his plans, Louis worked past dinnertime and only realised how late it was when Marie arrived, a concerned expression on her face.

"I was getting worried about you when you didn't come in." She was relieved to find him working hard in the fields.

"Sorry, Mama. I was concentrating so hard, I forgot the time."

Glancing round to make sure there was no one about, she continued in a quieter voice, "Did you have a look at the cow shed?"

Louis nodded. "It's no good but I've found somewhere else. It needs some work first. I don't want to tell you where, though, because the less you know the better."

Marie was about to argue but then she realised what he said made perfect sense. "I'll go back and leave you to your plans." She yawned and began heading back to the farmhouse, wondering why she felt so tired. It was most unlike her to keep dozing off; perhaps her body was just reacting to all the strain. She had been through a horrendous time and it was only natural her body should rebel and want some time to repair itself.

Louis finished the rest of the digging and, when the sun began to sink gently westwards, he headed back to the farmhouse for his evening meal. Although he was tired, he found it hard to suppress his excitement and he couldn't wait to finish his dinner so he could rush off to see the others. Marie was upstairs taking some food to Patrick when he arrived back and Louis was pleased to see he was sitting up in bed and looking much better.

"How are you?"

"Much better." Patrick responded in English, nodding while he spoke. Marie had been trying to teach him some French and he had managed to understand a few words. Unfortunately, understanding was easier than speaking and, although he and Marie had spent a lot of the day laughing at his atrocious attempts, he didn't really feel his speaking skills had improved much. Still, one thing at a time. He really was feeling better, thanks in part to the enjoyable day he had spent with Marie. However, he was concerned he was endangering them by his presence and his limited French was not good enough to ask when he could be helped on his way.

"Good." Louis turned back to Marie. "Is my dinner ready yet? I'm starving."

****

Outside Bethune, Northern France

"You've been with farm boy again. You were seen with him." Rolf's tone was almost as icy cold as his eyes, which were boring into her.

Brigitte was horrified. How could he know? Was he watching her? Had he seen her with Louis? She frowned. They had made love in the barn and the door was closed. Or was it? She couldn't remember. "We were only talking," she lied.

"Did I tell you to speak?"

She shook her head, careful to keep her eyes on the floor.

"You do remember, don't you? I told you if you were seen with any other men, I would punish you."

Brigitte nodded and a warm glow spread through her body. She squirmed uncomfortably while she waited for the orders she knew would come next. She could feel herself growing wet, remembering the last time when he'd put her across his knee and used a slipper to beat her. Too late, she realised he was speaking.

"I said strip!" he yelled. Brigitte hurried to remove her clothes, her fingers trembling so much, she struggled to undo the buttons on her skirt. He stood watching until she was naked.

"Go upstairs. I've prepared a special punishment tonight." Brigitte began walking up the stairs, Rolf close behind her. She had never been in the bedroom before but the cottage was small and there were only two doors. One was open and was a bathroom, the other led to the bedroom. She stepped through the doorway and peered through her lashes. Everything seemed normal and she felt a flush of disappointment.

"Lay down on the bed, face down." She obeyed and then he was pulling her legs apart and tying her feet to either side of the bed. Before she could react, he took her arms and did the same, leaving her spread-eagled on the bed and unable to move. Lying face down, she was also unable to see what he was doing.

There was a rustling sound and then she heard him approach the bed. Her own excitement was mounting and he grabbed her chin, turning her head towards him and forcing his erect penis into her open mouth. She began sucking hard, trying not to gag, then yelped when he slapped her across her naked buttocks. Just when she thought she couldn't take any more, he stopped and loosened the ties on her feet. Brigitte thought he'd finished. She was wrong. Instead he climbed on the bed and, straddling her, he slipped his hand under her hips and raised her slightly from the mattress before plunging his erection inside her. His fingers began exploring her anus, forcing their way inside until her moans mingled with his. Then, just when she was about to climax, he pulled out and exchanged his fingers for his erection. Brigitte gasped and, while he rode her faster, he began slapping her hard, rhythmically in time with his thrusting penis.

****

Toulouse, Southern France

It was not until Angel had gone to bed that Jeanne remembered Gabriel's invitation. She waited until her mother had also retired, and then told Jean-Paul.

"What do you think I should do?"

"Do you want to go?"

"I don't know, really. He's very nice but he's not Marcel and I'm worried about him asking too many questions. I don't think he's asking for any reason other than he wants to get to know me. But he's a policeman and I'm not sure how much I should say, and yet if I keep avoiding his questions, he may get suspicious. I really don't know what to do for the best."

"Perhaps you should just thank him, but explain with your mother so ill, you don't feel it's appropriate to be out enjoying yourself. You are needed at home to do the housework, and cooking to help your mother. What do you think?"

Jeanne jumped up and hugged him; relief flooding through her. "That's brilliant. He can't possibly object and it's not likely to make him suspicious either."

"Good. You look tired. I would suggest getting some sleep. I have a feeling we may need all our strength over the next few weeks."

"She's getting worse very quickly, isn't she?" Jeanne asked, her relief instantly forgotten when she remembered the look of pain on Claudette's face earlier in the evening.

"Yes. I think she was only holding on until she told us. Now I feel the end will be sooner rather than later." He stopped and looked at her, tears streaming down his face. "I don't know how I am going to manage without her, Jeanne. She's always been there; we've never been apart. How on earth am I going to carry on?"

Jeanne put her arms round him; there was nothing she could say. There would be time to talk about the funeral arrangements later. They stayed like that, each lost in their own thoughts, while darkness fell and the shadows lengthened around them.

Chapter Seven

Aldershot, England

"Are you sure?" Marcel could hardly believe he was about to make love to Lilly. He was struggling to restrain himself, but he wanted to make sure she was happy for him to carry on.

"Yes. You do love me, don't you?" Her voice was little more than a whisper and Marcel nodded in the darkness.

"Of course I do." Her body was warm and, without waiting any longer, he slid his hands into her knickers and his fingers began rubbing her short pubic hair. His breathing was laboured and he pushed her legs open and slipped two fingers inside her. Lilly groaned but made no attempt to resist him. Instead, her legs opened wider and he inserted another finger, reaching deeper inside her. She felt warm and wet and, with his other hand, he began to ease her panties down her legs. Lilly closed her legs to help him, trapping his hand and he almost climaxed. Unable to contain himself any longer, Marcel climbed on top of her and tried to push his erect penis inside. But she was tight and there was an obstruction stopping him entering. The impetus to climax was so strong he began shoving harder until he felt something give. At the same moment, she gave a small cry, but Marcel was no longer aware of anything other than her muscles tightening around him. To his horror he climaxed almost immediately.

"I'm sorry." He was embarrassed but Lilly didn't seem to have noticed. She cuddled up to him and he put his arm around her. She ran her fingers over his chest, tracing delicate patterns in the short fair hair covering his upper body. For a moment, he wished Jeanne was lying next to him, then he put her firmly out of his mind. He could see the outline of Lilly's breasts in the moonlight, their pointed nipples still hard and he reached for them, squeezing and pulling until she groaned and tentatively lowered her hand to his penis. To his surprise, he was hard again and he rolled over until he was on top of her again. This time he lasted longer and he could hear her panting as they both grew used to the unfamiliar rhythm.

"Was it alright?" Having never slept with a woman before, Marcel was anxious she had enjoyed the experience.

"Mmm, yes." She kissed him and then hurriedly pulled her skirt down as the sound of voices echoed across the moonlit park. He pulled her close, but the noise was only another courting couple and they were too busy to notice Marcel and Lilly.

They lay quietly for a few moments, then Marcel stirred. "I have to go back to the camp and you must go home." He gazed down at her tenderly.

"Can't you stay a bit longer?" Lilly snuggled up closer but Marcel shook his head. He would have liked nothing better than to lie there with her until morning but he would be in trouble if he didn't get back and he didn't think Lilly's parents would be too pleased if they knew she'd stayed out all night.

****

Toulouse, Southern France

Jeanne fought to prevent her eyes closing. Claudette had suddenly taken a turn for the worse and she and Jean-Paul were keeping a silent vigil by her bed. The speed with which she had deteriorated had taken them both by surprise but both knew the end was not far away.

"Jean-Paul…" Claudette's voice was little more than a whisper.

"I'm here my love." Jean-Paul's grip on her hand tightened as if, by holding her, he could keep her there.

"You must remarry. You are a wonderful man and much too loving to live the rest of your life on your own." She ignored the pain on his face. "You have my blessing my love, in fact I insist you find someone else to look after you and Angel. Please promise me you will do this."

Jean-Paul shook his head in horror and began to protest but Claudette interrupted him. "Jeanne you must follow your heart and do what makes you happy." She tried to smile but the pain was too great and she grimaced instead. Jean-Paul reached for the remaining medicine and held the small cup to her lips. She swallowed, lay her head back down on the pillow and closed her eyes.

Claudette made one more attempt to smile and then her breathing became laboured, gradually slowing until she took one long, rasping breath. The room fell silent; the only sound, Jean-Paul and Jeanne sobbing.

****

Guildford, England

Pam finally received her orders, telling her to catch a train to Woking where she would be met at the station. The train was on time and the journey was short and uneventful. A car was waiting for her at the station and drove her swiftly through the leafy lanes, pulling up at a large country house buried deep in its own grounds.

Pam was one of the first few female recruits for the SOE so, when she arrived, most of the other inhabitants of the house were men. On arrival, she was greeted by a stern sergeant major who informed her that, whilst she was living in the house, she was to use the code name she had been given. He impressed on her that under no circumstances was she to divulge her real name or any other personal information. She was also to speak French at all times. If she violated these orders, she would find herself on the first train back to London. There would be no appeals, no second chances.

Pam was given the codename Violette and everything in her bag was then vetted to ensure there was no personal correspondence of any kind to identify her real name. Her ration cards and driving licence were removed and put in the safe in the commanding officer's room which was locked at all times. There were only two keys for the office, one was held by the Commanding Officer, Colonel X, as he was known, and the other by the sergeant major, named McGovern, a dour Scotsman with a receding hairline, a very wiry physique and eyes in the back of his head, or so the recruits thought after a couple of days under his exhaustive training.

Pam was given a key to room sixteen and, taking what was left of her bag's contents, she went upstairs to the room she had been allocated. She had already been told she was sharing with another woman, Giselle, and she was looking forward to meeting her new roommate.

****

Lewisham Council Offices, London

Olive's eyes strayed to her handbag again. She couldn't wait to get home and read Kurt's letter. Because of concerns about Tom getting into her flat, she had begun walking the long way to work so she could pass the postman. Although she'd checked her strongbox and couldn't see any signs of tampering, she wasn't certain, so she'd emptied the box and put all Kurt's letters into her handbag, which she never let out of her sight.

The sound of aeroplanes broke into her thoughts and she stood up and stared out of the window to the skies above, where a fight to the death was taking place. She clutched her hand to her heart and instinctively began praying for the British pilot: for once Kurt was forgotten. The girls had left the switchboard and were all standing with her, gazing upwards, the ringing phones temporarily ignored.

"Yes! Got 'im!" For once, Kath's shriek did not annoy Olive, who joined in the cheering while the German plane spiralled out of control and disappeared out of sight. There was a brief silence and Olive took the opportunity to reassert her authority.

"Back to work, girls." Her eyes met Kath's briefly and Olive held her gaze until the younger girl looked away. With a few brief mutterings, the others had already returned to their desks and, within moments, were answering the lines which were busier than ever.

Olive sat back down, her eyes automatically checking her bag was still there.

"Everything alright, miss?" The voice was insolent and Olive jumped. She hadn't noticed Kath's approach.

"Why shouldn't it be?" Olive snapped.

"No reason. You just looked a little concerned." Kath smiled and carried on before Olive could answer. "I'm sure we've nothing to worry about. The RAF'll soon sort out them Nazis."

Olive nodded. "I expect you're right. Now please get back to work." Olive tried to keep the antagonism out of her voice. She knew Kath was not referring to the Luftwaffe. Kath smiled again and returned to her desk. She wondered what the old girl had in her handbag. Something she was worried about, that's for sure. She'd mention the bag to Tom when she saw him later. Kath frowned. Tom was behaving very strangely. Although she received her share of the blackmail money, regular as clockwork, he was beginning to look decidedly shifty whenever she mentioned Olive. She'd have to keep a closer eye on him. He was up to something.

****

Simonsdorf, Poland

The day had started the same as any other. They were marched back down to the railway station and given their tasks. Everything progressed normally until just before lunch, when there was an enormous bang, followed by clouds of dust and the sounds of shouting and swearing in both English and German. Startled by the noise, Joe and Pete rushed over to the site of the commotion to find five trucks had derailed. The scene that met their eyes was one of complete chaos. The trucks had splintered and fallen apart, shedding their loads of sand all over the rails. The German guards were shouting and gesturing frantically at the mess, while the British POWs were standing around scratching their heads and looking very confused. Some of the bolts holding the rails in place had not been put in properly and, when the trucks rolled over the weak spot, the rails had moved, derailing the trucks and spilling sand everywhere.

Joe looked at Pete and they both had trouble hiding their smiles. Obviously this was sabotage, but it was very important the Germans couldn't prove it. With a bit of luck, they might believe the derailment was just inexperience on the part of the workforce.

"Do you want us to help?" Joe asked one of the guards, purposely getting in the way of someone trying to salvage some of the sand from one of the derailed trucks.

The guard gestured angrily, so Joe shrugged and looked questioningly at him.

"Sorry, I don't understand? Did you want me to help?" The guard was becoming increasingly agitated. "Oh! You want me to move!" His face brightened as understanding dawned.

While the guard was trying to make Joe move out of the way, other prisoners had come over and were also getting in the way whilst appearing to be trying to help. The guard eventually managed to make them understand they were to get shovels and start clearing the sand. In their haste to obey, they walked into one another and managed to knock more sand out of the trucks. Joe and Pete struggled even harder not to laugh. Finally returning with shovels, they began to move the sand to the area indicated by the guards. However, the guards were frantically giving orders and they were not watching the men, so while some prisoners moved the sand, others shovelled the same sand back again onto the original piles.

****

Toulouse, Southern France

Gabriel stood by his window watching Jeanne walking across the square. She'd declined his invitation to dinner and he understood why. Normally that would have been enough for him to drop the matter, but in Jeanne's case it hadn't put him off. He was becoming increasingly interested in her and he wasn't sure why. She was very pretty, but although he was attracted to her, that wasn't the only reason for his curiosity. He felt sure she had a secret, although what someone so young and seemingly innocent could be hiding, was beyond him. If he had some time later, perhaps he would have a dig around and see what he could find out.

He frowned. Even from his office on the third floor he could see how unhappy she looked, her shoulders slumped, her head down. Perhaps her mother was worse? His heart went out to her and his suspicions faded to the back of his mind. He grabbed his jacket and headed towards the stairs. He had a few moments to spare and would just pop down to see if there was anything he could do to help.

****

Guildford, England

Giselle was stretched out on one of the two beds in the sparse room. There was an old-fashioned chest of drawers in between the two beds which were sited along either side of the room. The single window was opposite the two beds and had flowery curtains, seeming completely at odds with the rest of the plain room.

"I see they've had the decorators in." Pam gave the room a first cursory glance. "Hello, I'm Violette." She stumbled slightly over the unfamiliar name and hoped her roommate wouldn't notice. "Giselle, I presume?"

Giselle glanced up from the book she was reading and smiled at Pam, who was immediately taken back by the stunning beauty of her companion. She had long blonde hair, tied up in a loose pony tail, and deep blue eyes set in perfect proportion to her aquiline nose and firm jaw line.

"Hello, Violette. I am so pleased you've arrived. I was really fed up being the only woman." Pam had spent enough time in France to recognise the gentle drawl of her companion's southern French accent and she wondered whereabouts she came from, although she resisted the temptation to ask.

"How many of us are there?" She wondered whether she was breaking the rules by asking.

"There's about a dozen men and us two. Normally I would say the odds were to my liking, but it does get tiresome not having another woman to talk to." Giselle laughed, revealing a set of perfect white teeth. "I've taken the top two drawers. You'll get the rest of your uniform either tonight or early tomorrow morning. My favourites are the knickers. They are unbelievable." She opened the drawer while she spoke and pulled out what appeared to be a pair of large shapeless bloomers made of some kind of heavy material in a rather unpleasant shade of green.

Pam burst out laughing. "Good grief! Who on earth designed those? Obviously they're to stop us getting too involved with our fellow recruits. I reckon if we show them these, we'll have no trouble fending them off."

Giselle joined in and they were laughing so much, neither heard the first tentative knock on the door. When there was no response to the knocking, the door opened and a head appeared round the corner.

"Sorry, I did knock. My name's Irène and I have the room next door." Irène was small and very thin with jet black straight hair, dark eyes set quite close together under heavy brows, a small nose and thin pursed lips.

Pam gave Giselle back the knickers. "Hello. I'm Violette and this is Giselle. Have you just arrived?"

"Yes. What about you?"

Pam nodded and Giselle added. "I arrived last night." She looked at her watch. "Come on, let's go downstairs and you can meet some of the others."

She climbed off the bed and they followed her downstairs into a large, airy room with antique furniture and heavy carpets which muffled the sound of their shoes. At the far end were some French doors leading out onto a paved area with some chairs and tables. There were already a few people sitting out there and their voices and laughter travelled easily across the room.

Giselle led the way and, once outside on the terrace, she introduced them. "Hello everyone, this is Violette and Irène. They've just arrived. Would you like a drink?" Giselle helped herself to some whisky and poured out some for Pam and Irène. Having distributed drinks, Giselle proceeded to start the introductions. "Raul, Jean, Ralph, Bénarde, Ricardo, Serge, Claude, Samuel, Christophe and Felix." She indicated each person with her finger and finished with a bow, making everyone laugh. "I gather the others haven't come down yet?"

Pam was impressed; she was quite good with names but not that good and Irène looked totally intimidated. One of the men stood up and offered Pam his seat while another offered his to Irène.

"Thank you…?" Pam accepted and sat down.

"Ricardo." He smiled at her and she smiled back. It was a while since she had heard French spoken by so many people, but after a little while she found she could understand without any problem and eventually realised she had also reverted to thinking in French again; something she hadn't done for several years.

****

Simonsdorf, Poland

The prisoners continued to shovel the sand from one pile to another and back again for some considerable time, Joe and Pete joining in with enthusiasm and struggling to keep the smiles off their face. Lunch time came and went, the piles of sand remained stubbornly the same size and finally the Germans realised what was happening. Furious that the mess was no nearer being cleared up, one of the younger guards lost his temper and fired some shots in the air.

The POWs immediately stopped what they were doing and began arguing amongst themselves about the most efficient way to move the sand. The argument gradually grew heated with men pushing, shoving and threatening each other and Joe had trouble not laughing out loud. Eventually the Germans managed to calm the situation down and, after another round of shouting and angry gestures, the sand was moved to the correct place. However, the whole thing had taken most of the afternoon and, in disgust, the guards gave up and marched the men back to the camp.

****

Lambeth, London

The pub was lively and Peggy was pleased she'd decided to come. After Ethel's death, she'd tried to cancel but Chris had been surprisingly persistent, insisting no one knew what was going to happen next, so they should enjoy themselves while they could. Eventually Peggy had given in and now she was glad. He had driven her to a pub in Lambeth, close to his flat and Peggy could see he was a regular visitor by the number of people who greeted him.

An elderly man was playing the piano and all around her people were singing. Although she was still devastated by Ethel's death, she felt her spirits rising and soon she was singing along with everyone else.

Chris watched her, an expression of amusement on his face. He was pleased to see her looking happier and he was glad she had agreed to come out with him. He really liked Peggy and he found her very attractive. He knew she had a fiancé and she only wanted them to be friends but he was hoping, somewhere along the line, she might change her mind. He wasn't sure he was being very honourable, especially when Joe wasn't there to defend his interests. But Peggy was an adult and if she really did love Joe, she'd brush him off and he would have to admit he'd been wasting his time.

Peggy was laughing at something and her eyes were shining. Chris crossed his legs and tried to think of something else. He had promised not to pounce on her and he intended to keep his word. He would be her friend until she changed her mind. And if she didn't? Well, he would cross that bridge when he came to it.

****

Aldershot, England

Despite Pierre's warnings about keeping an emotional distance, Marcel was now madly in love. It was obvious to his friends that he'd finally done 'it' and Paul teased him mercilessly, but Marcel had learned to give as good as he got, much to Pierre's amusement.

"What's so funny?" Marcel said after another quick fire exchange with Paul in which Marcel had emerged the winner.

"I was just thinking how much you've changed from the shy innocent chap who joined us only a few weeks ago. The Marcel who caught the train to the recruiting office with us would never have been able to deal with Paul."

"He's right, Marcel. You've really grown up," Paul agreed. "Of course I'm not sure that's necessarily a good thing…" He trailed off, a big smile on his face.

Marcel grinned.

"So, although this conversation is fascinating, are any of you coming into town tonight?" Charles asked. "Perhaps you could manage to not see the lovely Lilly and come out with your friends one night for a change?'

"Yeah, Marcel, we're missing you," Paul quipped.

Marcel grinned widely. "Sorry, lads. Duty calls and anyway, you're only jealous. That's why you want me to come out with you poor sad people who don't have a warm pair of loving arms to hold you through the dark night."

His remark was greeted with howls of laughter and more ribald comments.

****

Guildford, England

Dinner was a lively affair while they got to know each other. The food was good and there was plenty of wine to wash it down. Pam was seated between Ricardo and Claude who, although vying with each other to keep her amused, were careful not to divulge any personal information. The talk was mainly about the war and General De Gaulle and the formation of the Free French Forces. Opinion was divided about how successful he would be. Some feared he would antagonise Frenchmen with his extreme right wing views. However, when the conversation moved on to first Vichy France and then the sinking of the French Fleet by the British, opinion was no longer so divided. There was total agreement that the Vichy Government should be considered traitors to France and that Britain had had no choice but to sink the French fleet, lest the ships fall into the hands of the Germans.

Pam listened with interest to the conversation and the political opinions of those around her, but contributed little, instincts telling her any outspoken or extreme political views could lead to an abrupt termination of their training. She amused herself by trying to pick out the genuine French people, as opposed to those, like herself, who had French relations or were just fluent in the language. On the whole, she had little difficulty in identifying the natives. They were, in the main, quite outspoken with strong opinions about what should be happening in their country, but there were a few she wasn't sure of. She noticed early on Ricardo was adept at avoiding direct questions and, by the end of the evening, she still had no idea what his politics were. Claude seemed to favour a middle path and spent a lot of time defusing arguments between the more volatile members of the group.

The evening wore on and they adjourned to the terrace to make the most of the warm evening, the alcohol flowed even more freely and some of her companions became quite drunk. Serge and Jean got into a fierce argument about De Gaulle and communism which almost came to blows, its intensity fuelled by the amount of alcohol both had imbibed. A fight was only avoided when Jean lunged drunkenly at Serge, fell over a chair and sprawled head first into one of the flower beds. Claude and Ricardo carefully extracted him and, after saying a cordial goodnight, escorted him out of the room whilst Christophe and Felix managed to persuade Serge it was time to call it a night and also left.

The temperature continued to drop and the others decided to leave the terrace and return inside. Whilst some carried on drinking, Pam and her two female companions went up to bed.

Pam had been careful to only drink one to every three the others drank and she noticed both Giselle and Irène did the same. In between, she drank water and, in the morning, she was pleased she had been so judicious.

Chapter Eight

Outside Bethune, Northern France

"You can't leave me here!" Brigitte shrieked at Rolf as he opened the car door and pulled her out.

"The walk will do you good. You're getting fat."

"I'm not!" Brigitte wailed, more upset by his insult than the fact he was going to leave her several kilometres outside Bethune.

He ignored her and walked back to his side of the car, climbed in and drove off. Brigitte stared after him in disbelief, then sat down by the side of the road and waited for him to come back.

She waited for some time but he did not reappear and, eventually, she realised he wasn't coming. Reluctantly, she stood up, brushed the gravel from the back of her skirt and began the long walk back to town. She was furious and spent several minutes plotting her revenge, until her feet began to ache and she had to stop. She bent down, took off her high heeled shoes, leant against the hedge and decided to wait for someone to come along, reasoning it couldn't be too hard to get a lift, even if she had to offer something in return.

She didn't have to wait long, though.

"Brigitte!"

She spun around, delighted to see Louis alighting from his bicycle.

"What on earth are you doing here?" she asked in astonishment.

"I could ask you the same thing," Louis replied. His smile had been replaced by a frown and Brigitte flushed. She couldn't think of any reason for being stranded and then she smiled.

"I was missing you and the day was so lovely, I thought I would walk out to see you. But I didn't realise how far it was and then I got blisters on my feet, so I decided to turn around and go back home."

Louis' face lit up. "Brigitte you are really wonderful. I was on my way to see you, too. What an amazing coincidence!" He gave her a big hug and squeezed her buttocks, which still smarted from Rolf's punishments. She winced and he pulled back. "I'm sorry, are your feet really hurting? Let me have a look."

Brigitte held up her right foot. She couldn't quite believe Louis was so gullible, but she was relieved he didn't seem to want to ask her any more questions.

He glanced around. The road was quiet and there was no one about. He grinned and, reaching towards her, he began to kiss her.

Brigitte tried to push him off.

"Don't, someone might see!"

"So? Who cares?" Louis was already reaching under her skirt and pulling down her knickers. "Turn around!"

Brigitte was terrified Rolf would come back and she tried to stop him. "Louis, we can't! Not in the road!"

"Course we can, if we're quick. Don't worry I'll keep an eye out in case anyone comes." He was already forcing himself inside her, shoving her forward into the hedge. Brigitte held her hands out to stop the twigs scratching her face and prayed he would be quick. He was. The thought of being caught spurred him on and reminded him briefly of the time he'd made love to the girl when he was on the run from the Germans. He couldn't remember her name now, or even what she looked like, but he could still see her tight rounded buttocks when she scrambled out of the bush. The thought was enough and he climaxed. Brigitte breathed a sigh of relief, pulled up her knickers and quickly looked up and down the road, but they were still alone. Louis recovered and slapped her playfully on her bottom, grinning when she winced.

"Come on, hop on my bike and I'll drop you home."

****

Guildford, England

Breakfast was a quiet affair and Pam made sure she ate plenty of the good food on offer. She could only count eight men and she looked around to see who was missing. Neither Serge nor Jean were there and she wondered whether their drunken behaviour had resulted in them being sent packing. Two other men were also missing and she silently speculated as to why. She finished her eggs and thought back over the previous evening. There had been no members of staff around so, if their fellow recruits had been dismissed because of their behaviour, this opened up some interesting possibilities. Either one or more of their fellow recruits were not who they seemed, or someone had reported them, or alternatively there were some listening devices deposited around the building.

She glanced around and Ricardo caught her eye. "Seems several of our companions have failed the first test," he muttered before returning to the early morning paper. Pam said nothing but was relieved to have her suspicions confirmed. She glanced at the headlines of his paper which reported the escalation of air raids on the south coast and briefly sent up a silent prayer for Tony, who she knew would be in the thick of the fighting. Turning her attention back to her own circumstances, she resolved to be even more on her guard. She had no intention of being sent home because of a silly mistake.

While she drained the last of her coffee, the thought occurred to her: if there were 'spies' there, one must be a woman. How else could they keep an eye on them too? She knew the spy wasn't her, so that left either Giselle or Irène. About to ponder this further, she was interrupted by the sergeant major shouting at them to get their kit and get changed so they could begin their training. Pam glanced at the clock. It was six o'clock. She couldn't remember the last time she'd got up this early and here she was, dressed, breakfasted and about to start training. She, Irène and a few of the other men who had arrived late, followed the sergeant major to a small store cupboard where they were given their kit and told they had ten minutes to change and be back outside the front door lined up with everybody else.

The training began with series of physical exercises and then a cross country run. Having not run since she'd been at school, it wasn't long before Pam thought she was probably dying. Her chest felt like it would burst, she couldn't breathe and she was light headed and dizzy but the sergeant major had no sympathy and, other than allowing her to slow to a jog until she got her breath back, he harried her mercilessly.

Finally seeing the house looming on the horizon, Pam steeled herself for one last push and threw herself bodily across the imaginary finishing line. Lying on the floor, her chest heaving with the exertion, she assumed she was finished, so to be told they could have a ten minute break before weapons training with pistols and sub machine guns, was a nasty shock. By lunchtime, she was even more grateful she had not had much to drink the night before, because every bone and muscle in her body was aching and they were still only half way through the day. By now, she hated the sergeant major with a passion she would not have thought possible. In fact, she thought she hated him even more than the Germans, so she was surprised when he came up to her after lunch and quietly congratulated her on the effort she had made.

****

Bethune, Northern France

Fabian watched his daughter climb off Louis' bike and head for the back door of the café. He finished drying the glass in his hands, placed it on the bar and stepped into the hall just in time to catch her creeping in. Her face was flushed with the sun and she jumped when he stepped out of the shadows.

"You need to make up your mind who you're going out with, or you're going to get hurt." She had left with the Boche and returned with Louis. He had no idea what was going on. But he did know his daughter was heading for a fall unless he could talk some sense into her.

"Does the Boche know about Louis?"

Brigitte hesitated then shook her head.

"What do you think he'll do if he finds out?"

Brigitte blushed even more and Fabian stared at her. "For God's sake, girl, what is the matter with you? He could have Louis killed or carted off to a labour camp in Germany. Is that what you want?"

A look of horror crossed Brigitte's face. "He doesn't know," she lied. Perhaps her father was right. At the moment, Rolf seemed content to punish her, but what if he got bored? Perhaps she should warn Louis? But what could she say? She wasn't supposed to be seeing anyone but him. No, she reassured herself, she was certain Rolf wouldn't bother taking some petty kind of revenge. Louis was quite safe. There was no need to ruin everything.

****

Aldershot, England

"At ease, men." The colonel indicated they should sit down again. "This is a totally informal, off the record, chat. Over the past few weeks we've been carrying out lots of different exercises. Although much of the reason for this is to make sure you are properly trained to deal with all eventualities, there was also another purpose." He paused. They were watching him intently. "We are going to set up a training academy to train young men, like you, to be officers. Your trainers consider you are all possible officer material, so I wondered what you thought?"

There was complete silence for a moment, then they all began talking at once, their excitement and enthusiasm giving the colonel his answer.

Smiling, he raised his hand to stop their chatter. "I gather then, you would all be interested?"

The answer was unanimous and the colonel smiled. "Once I have more information, I will let you know the details, but for now I will put all your names forward. There will, of course, be some written and practical tests. I would suggest reading De Gaulle's theories of modern warfare at least, and give some thought to why France, whose army was bigger than the Germans's, capitulated so quickly. Officers need to have a grasp of history as well as tactics. Thank you, gentlemen. Carry on." He left.

"What's the matter, Marcel?" Pierre suddenly realised Marcel was not joining in the excited conversation and was looking rather crestfallen.

"I was never good at school; I'm not sure whether I can pass written tests."

"We'll help," Paul said confidently. "We've got plenty of time. We'll start tonight; if we all work together, we can make sure we all get through. Agreed?"

The others nodded and Marcel started to feel better. Perhaps with their help, he would be able to qualify after all.

"Of course, your love life might have to suffer," Paul added mischievously and everyone laughed, including Marcel.

Pierre opened his mouth but whatever he was about to say was drowned out by the air raid siren which shrieked through the camp.

Grabbing their equipment, they ran for the defensive trenches and threw themselves in just as the bombs started to fall. This was the third raid that month and they were beginning to get used to it. Pointing their guns skyward, they began to fire at the German planes. The heavy ack ack guns boomed out repeatedly, the deafening sound punctuated by the small arms fire coming from the various trenches around the perimeter of the camp. To the defenders, the attack seemed to go on for hours but, in reality, only lasted minutes before the bombers turned and headed for home.

The 'all clear' sounded and they emerged to view the damage.

"They're getting more frequent." Pierre's eyes were smarting from the smoke. "Come on, let's put the fire out before it spreads." They quickly had the blaze under control and, surveying the damage, realised they had probably escaped quite lightly.

They made their way back to their tents, Marcel feeling proud of himself for acting like a soldier and not panicking when the bombing started.

Paul's voice broke into his thoughts. "So Marcel, where do you want to start?"

Marcel stared at him blankly for a moment and then realisation dawned and he grinned. "I think I probably need help with everything, so I'm not sure. What do you suggest?"

"Let's go and see if we can borrow a copy of De Gaulle's book to start with," Antoine said, surprising them. Normally, he would let the others take the lead and then follow effortlessly behind.

"Where can we get one from?" Marcel asked.

"There's bound to be a copy on the camp somewhere." Pierre grinned. "You'll have to tell Lilly tomorrow that you've got some work to do over the next few nights, so you won't be able to see her."

Marcel's face fell then he shrugged. Becoming an officer was more important than seeing Lilly. He was sure she would understand.

****

Lambeth Hospital, London

They sat down wearily in the rest room, relieved to have a break. Peggy switched on the wireless and then wished she hadn't. The gloating, sneering tones of Lord Haw Haw greeted her: *"…For those of you wondering where the Luftwaffe is tonight or those thinking your depleted RAF are winning in the skies, let me reassure you. London will be attacked soon, the planes were slightly delayed owing to strong south westerly winds, so if…"*

She cut him off mid-sentence and glanced at Helen who was deep in thought. "Penny for them?"

Helen glanced up from reading the latest letter from Annie, which Peggy had given her.

"I was just thinking how things have changed so much in such a short time."

Peggy nodded "I know. This time last year…" She tailed off. There was no point dwelling on the past. It wouldn't change anything.

Helen was quiet for a moment. "Jimmy says the airfields are really taking a pounding. They are on constant standby now. If they get a few hours off, they leave the airfield, otherwise they can get called back in, even if they've just come off duty. He says he thinks we're only hanging on by a thread. If things don't change soon, we could go under."

Both girls lapsed into silence while they considered the seriousness of Helen's words.

"Surely things can't be that bad?" Peggy asked after a few moments.

Helen shrugged and then her voice became brusque. "Well, there's no point worrying about something we can't control. Changing the subject for a minute, Annie isn't coming up again at the weekend. I'm getting really worried about her. This letter doesn't sound like her at all."

"What do you mean?"

"Oh I don't know, she seems distant, I suppose. Perhaps it's just being pregnant…"

Peggy didn't want to worry Helen but she didn't think Annie's remoteness was anything to do with being pregnant, but to do with John's parents' possessiveness. But before she could answer, the rattle of machine gun fire shattered the calm. They rushed to the nearest window and found themselves with a grandstand view of the aerial battle being fought above their heads. The night sky was lit up with tracer and anti-aircraft fire and searchlight beams fighting to keep the intruders visible and an easier target for defending fire. Helen watched for a couple of minutes and then turned away.

Peggy's thoughts turned to Ethel's funeral. She was dreading going and she knew things must be a hundred times worse for Colin and Martin. She hoped they would find some comfort from the formal goodbye and, in time, they would all be able to think of Ethel with fun and laughter and remember the good times.

Chapter Nine

Simonsdorf, Poland

The morning was bright and sunny and Joe was looking forward to the evening and the practice for the concert party.

"So, Joe, what can you do?" The question came from Wilf, who was in charge of putting together the entertainment.

"Well, I'm a carpenter, so maybe I could help with scenery or something, or I can have a go at acting?" Joe was looking forward to anything that broke the dull monotony of the days and eased his longing for Peggy and the comforts of home.

"Sounds good. We can always do with some back stage scenery and extra actors. We're going to do a variety show and one of the lads has written a play called…" But what the play was called Joe never found out because Wilf stopped abruptly, his attention caught by the arrival of a German staff car speeding noisily into the yard and screeching to a halt.

Other than the driver, who remained seated, there were two occupants in the back of the car. They were both wearing the dreaded SS uniform and, when they climbed out of the car, Joe felt the first stirrings of unease.

"Aye aye, trouble." Wilf's face had gone pale under his tan and, looking round, Joe could see varying degrees of fear on the faces of the other prisoners.

"What's the matter?" he asked, but Wilf waved at him to be quiet.

"Whatever you do, try to be invisible; don't draw attention to yourself." He needn't have worried, because the last thing Joe planned to do was to draw the attention of the two menacing characters in their black trench coats. He swallowed nervously and, like the others, fell swiftly into line when shouted at.

The new arrivals stood watching and then shouted something which the guards swiftly translated into halting English and then Polish.

"There has been sabotage here. Those responsible must step forward now or we will shoot two prisoners. You have one minute."

A collective gasp went through the assembled men, followed by silence while they all stared ahead, praying they would not be chosen. The seconds ticked by. Joe could feel his heart racing and pounding so hard against his chest, he was sure the Germans could hear.

"Time is up," the guard said and, pointing at two men further down the row of Polish prisoners, he raised his rifle and fired twice.

****

Honor Oak Park, London

The house seemed unnaturally quite when Peggy got up. She was later than normal because she had a day off. Sally had already left for work, and would meet her at the church and, of course, Ethel was no longer there. The realisation finally sank in that she would never see her kind, gentle friend again and it was all she could do to make herself get dressed for the funeral. For once, she wasn't hungry. If anything, the thought of food made her feel sick. Ignoring her exhaustion, she forced herself to leave the house and walked towards the church, trying to think about other things, about what a beautiful day it was and how lucky she was to be alive, but nothing seemed to remove the dark heavy feeling of depression hanging around her like a thundercloud. She was beginning to forget what life had been like before Joe went away, before Ethel had been killed.

****

Toulouse, Southern France

Gabriel walked away from the docks and into the nearest bar. He had been investigating yet more complaints from the Germans that their fruit and vegetables were rotten on arrival in Germany. He had shown his face, made all the right noises and done nothing whatsoever to search for the culprits, who were probably dropping decaying pieces of fruit into the cargo boxes to ensure the produce went off on the journey. Personally, he admired them. At least they were doing something constructive to fight against the Germans, unlike him who had unwittingly become their glorified lackey. Although they were not officially occupied, the Vichy French police seemed to be dancing to the same tune as their colleagues in the occupied zone and he was becoming increasingly despondent. He knew there were several active resistance groups already, with more springing up all the time and he was tempted to join them. But the fact he knew about them meant their security wasn't very good and that worried him. So far, all he'd done was to think about it, but he had a feeling the time was coming when he would have to act on his conscience and do something to help his country.

He downed his cognac and returned his attention to how he could fudge the report so the contamination of German produce didn't look like sabotage.

****

La Couture, Northern France

Louis cycled back home from Henri's after another meeting to discuss their plans, a broad grin on his face. Everything was coming together. He was getting his own back on the Germans and Brigitte was his again. Perhaps they should get married after all. The idea was appealing until he thought about Marie. She was bound to be difficult but she would just have to accept his choice and support him.

He was concentrating so hard on how he could persuade Marie that Brigitte was good for him, he failed to hear the rapidly approaching car. The next moment, a vehicle rushed past, almost putting him in the ditch. He swerved, fighting to control the bike and somehow managed to stay upright. He was about to shake his fist at the car disappearing round the bend in the narrow country road, when he realised the car was being driven by a German. The driver seemed vaguely familiar, although he'd only caught a glimpse of him.

Louis wondered where he'd seen the officer before and then shrugged. Who cared? He wasn't going to let the Boche ruin his day.

****

Simonsdorf, Poland

Joe looked straight ahead, unable to believe they had just shot two men at random.

"Back to work!" In total shock, the men went back to where they had been working.

It was several minutes before anyone spoke.

"What I want to know is, who told them." Wilf's voice was harsh and uncompromising

Joe, Pete and Mitchell exchanged glances.

"You think someone told them?" Joe asked

"They had no idea two days ago. Now, all of a sudden, they are totally sure someone deliberately derailed the trucks. What does that say to you?"

"Well maybe they aren't sure; perhaps they just want to make certain it doesn't happen again. Even if it was an accident, by accusing us of sabotage, it will make us all much more careful in the future," Pete suggested.

"You're too trusting by half," Wilf muttered. "You mark my words, we've got a traitor amongst us." He looked around to make sure they weren't overheard and then continued, "The trucks were derailed by

British soldiers, not Polish. There were no Polish anywhere near the trucks when they went off the rails. So why shoot the Poles?"

Joe looked confused. "I don't understand?"

Wilf sighed impatiently. "Think about it! No Brit soldier is going to agree to the Germans shooting his own, however despicable he is, even if he does want extra rations. By promising him they will only shoot Poles or French, he's more likely to cooperate, isn't he?"

Joe still looked unconvinced but then realised Wilf's theory did seem to make some awful kind of logical sense. But he still couldn't bring himself to accept one of his fellow prisoners would cooperate to that extent with the Germans.

Seeing he wasn't entirely convinced, Wilf shrugged. "You'll see. Look, Price, this isn't a holiday camp; this is about surviving the best way you can. Just take my advice and don't trust anyone, lad, or you won't get through. I know it's hard, but we have no idea how long the war is going to last, or if we're ever going to get home again. This is our lives for the foreseeable future so we just have to accept the realities of where we are. Forget about the outside. Your life is here, now. You need to harden up. Sorry if that sounds harsh, but it's how things are."

Pete and Joe exchanged glances. Whilst they could understand the logic behind what Wilf was saying, it went against everything they knew. They carried on working in silence; the heat and humidity were rising and the sweat began to pour off them. Glancing up briefly, trying to catch his breath, Joe was relieved to see some ominous black clouds approaching.

"Looks like a storm brewing," he said in relief and, before long, his prayers were answered. Jagged forks of lightning crackled off the surrounding hills, followed by dazzling bursts of sheet lightning brightening the ever darkening skies. Within seconds, the clatter of thunder could be heard and then the heavens opened, soaking them completely in a matter of minutes.

Reluctantly, the guards called a halt and the men fell into line, ready to march back to camp. Their mood was sullen and there was little conversation. Not only were they shocked to the core by the casual shootings but rumours were already circulating that there was a traitor among them. Wilf was not the only one who suspected the traitor was British, which made things even worse, because the more established prisoners viewed the newcomers with suspicion. Despite the heat, Joe shivered. He could've cut the atmosphere with a knife. Like the other newcomers, he felt personally under suspicion, even though he knew he had done nothing wrong.

"I don't like this." Pete kept his voice low. "The last thing we should be doing is getting together a lynch mob. It's probably just what the Krauts want."

"Best to keep out of it." Mitchell also lowered his voice. "There's not a lot we can do and the way the mood is at the moment, if we try to interfere, they may think we're guilty too."

"I think he's right," Bert agreed. "Best to just say nothing and keep low."

"But what if they get the wrong man? Or worse still, what if there isn't a stooge at all, just bad luck or, like Pete said earlier, some plot of the Krauts to make us fight amongst ourselves?" Joe sounded worried.

Mitchell shrugged, although he looked uncomfortable and Pete nodded. "Sorry Joe, I think he's right. We don't know enough of what's been going on here to interfere."

Joe was about to argue when the conversation was interrupted by one of the guards drawing level. He stayed there for the rest of the march, so there was no further opportunity to discuss the possible traitor and, once back in camp, Joe finally decided they were probably right and there really wasn't anything he could do.

****

Honor Oak Park, London

The service had been lovely, the pastor paying such a glowing tribute to Ethel that Peggy's tears had flowed unchecked, but she felt the service was too short to really celebrate her friend's life. She'd been shocked by Martin's appearance; he looked so much older than when she'd last seen him and the light had gone out of his eyes, but Colin seemed much better. He had dressed smartly and had taken charge of everything. She'd felt touched he was being so efficient, suppressing his own sadness and allowing Martin to take a back seat and time to express his grief. The wake had been subdued, war time rationing adding to the gloom of the occasion and Peggy was silently relieved when the whole gathering was over and she was able to return home.

****

Toulouse, Southern France

Jeanne stared sightlessly across the reception hall, her mind still on Claudette's funeral. The end had come so quickly, it seemed no sooner had she told them she was dying, than she was gone. Angel remained stubbornly silent, even the death of Claudette not bringing her out of her shell. If anything, she retreated deeper into herself and neither Jeanne nor Jean-Paul could reach her. Trying to deal with their own grief and resolve Angel's problems was too much, so they came to an unspoken mutual decision to wait and hope time would heal her without outside intervention.

Jean-Paul was inconsolable with grief and, for the first time ever, Jeanne felt unable to lean on him. Instead, she took control and made all the day-to-day decisions. The strain of having to be strong for Jean-Paul and Angel and being unable to release her own emotions began to take its toll. Without realising it, she began to rely more on Gabriel, who always seemed to be there when she needed him. She was too confused to really analyse her feelings for him and was only too glad to have someone to lean on. Marcel faded into the deep recesses of her mind and she struggled to recall his voice or remember what he looked like. She knew the feelings she had for Marcel were real, but he wasn't there when she needed him. She didn't even know if he was still alive or if she would ever see him again.

"I'll pick you up at seven and we'll have a nice quiet dinner." Gabriel's voice broke into her thoughts and she glanced up to find him looking down at her, his eyes full of concern. She nodded, suddenly unable to speak for the tears threatening to overwhelm her.

"Are you sure you don't want some time off?" Eve was also concerned but Jeanne shook her head. How could she explain that, this time, the tears were not for her mother but for Marcel. She had finally accepted that, as far as she was concerned, he too was dead and it was time she moved on. The thought shocked her at first but then a small but insistent feeling of relief flooded her body and she knew she was doing the right thing. If they both survived and Marcel came back after the war, then they could start again but for now she had to put him out of her head. Gabriel was here, he was real and she needed someone to help her through the depths of her despair, otherwise she couldn't support her father and Angel.

****

Lewisham, London

Kath sipped her gin and tonic and winced. She was convinced the barmaid was watering down the gin to make the rations go further. She turned her attention to Tom.

"I think the old cow is hiding something in that handbag of hers."

"Oh? What makes you think that?" Tom's ears had pricked up. He'd been disappointed to discover the box under the mattress was empty. Perhaps Olive had got wise to him and decided to move whatever she was hiding to her handbag. "Perhaps you should try and get a look?"

Kath stared at him. "Why?"

Tom improvised quickly. "Well if she's got another secret, we might be able to squeeze some more money out of her."

Kath shrugged. "I don't see how. You said she was already paying all she could afford."

"Well, until we know what's in there, we can't decide anything, can we?" Tom downed the rest of his pint and raised his hand to the girl behind the bar. "Another pint and a gin and tonic, love."

"Not for me thanks, Tom. I've got to go. I have a date."

Tom was delighted she'd changed the subject. "Good for you, girl. Anyone I know?"

"Nah, met him at a dance on Saturday. We're going to the pictures. Night, Tom, see you tomorrow." And she was gone.

Tom breathed a sigh of relief. Kath was right about Olive's finances but that wasn't the reason for his interest. If she had a secret boyfriend, there must be a reason she was keeping him quiet, which could mean he'd make another good target for blackmail. There was another reason for his secrecy. He was finding it hard enough to accept his bizarre sexual reaction to Olive, and he wasn't about to broadcast his strange behaviour to anyone else.

****

Aldershot, England

Arriving at the pub, Marcel was delighted to find Lilly waiting for him. After greeting her with a passionate kiss, he disentangled himself and started the speech he'd practised with Pierre. "I can't stay tonight, Lilly." He was rewarded by the sight of her face dropping with disappointment. "I'm sorry, my love, but I have the chance to go to officer training school and the others have offered to help me pass the entrance exam. I can't do this without their help. I missed so much at school and it's something I really want to do. I can't miss this opportunity."

Lilly pulled out of his arms and pouted. "You've found someone else, I know you have."

"No!" Marcel was astonished and looked for signs she was joking.

"Yes, you have. You've got what you wanted, so now you don't need me anymore."

Marcel suddenly realised she wasn't messing about; she was serious. "This is crazy. I've told you. We're only talking about a few days… while I catch up and give myself the best chance." He was starting to feel angry that she didn't believe him. "There's no other reason. I promise."

"My dad warned me about you Frogs. He said you're only after one thing and I was stupid to listen to you. Well, he's right, isn't he?" Lilly's normally quiet voice had risen several octaves and people were watching them.

"This is stupid, Lilly. You should calm down and stop talking rubbish." Marcel's rehearsed speech was long forgotten and he was struggling to find the right words, now alternating between French and English.

"So, who is she?" Lilly was shrieking at him.

Marcel had had enough. "I've just told you, there is no-one else. You know how important it is to me to be able to go home and chase the Boche out of my country. How can you be so shallow and selfish?" He had given up speaking in English because he couldn't think of the words, so the last sentence was delivered in French.

Lilly looked at him uncomprehendingly and Marcel shrugged, suddenly realising he had no wish to continue this conversation and he really didn't care whether she believed him or not. His good mood had evaporated and he began to silently berate himself for having betrayed Jeanne for this vacuous girl.

"I have to go now." Suddenly unable to get away quickly enough, he left the pub hurriedly and headed back to the safety of the camp, her insults following him until he was out of earshot.

Seeing the expression on his face, Paul couldn't resist: "Went well then, did it?"

Marcel scowled. "No. The stupid girl accused me of seeing someone else. I can't believe she's so shallow. I should never have gone out with her."

The others smiled and Pierre said comfortingly, "Just put this down to experience, Marcel. Now you know why we told you not to get involved. We're here to fight for our country; everything else takes second place."

"I won't be making that mistake again." Marcel had a sullen expression on his face.

"Come on, start reading this. It's more than enough to keep your mind off her." Paul handed him a book entitled *Vers l'Armée de Métier* by Charles De Gaulle.

Marcel took the book and began to read. To start with, he found it difficult to put Lilly out of his mind and concentrate. He wondered whether he had been too harsh but, when he replayed the conversation over and over in his head, he realised he was glad the relationship was over. They had little in common and, if he was honest with himself, her only attraction had been her very accommodating body and, much as he hated to admit Paul and Pierre were right, he knew they were. He could find sex anywhere; for a relationship to mean more, there had to be something else.

"Probably best if you concentrate on the book and forget about her." Antoine had been watching him. "Plenty more fish in the sea and, anyway, we want to read it after you!"

Marcel felt better. He had his friends and that was more important than anything, certainly some girl he would never see again.

****

Catford, London

At last she was on her own with Kurt. Olive made a conscious effort to push aside her problems and savour every moment of his letter.

My darling Olive,

Congratulations on your promotion. I am so proud of you, my darling. I do so wish I could kiss you and show you just how much.

It seems so long since you were in my arms and I could feel your wonderful body pressed up against mine. Do you still remember how it only took the slightest caress from you set me on fire. Oh, darling, I miss you so much. I would like to continue recalling our love but the memories make me too sad, so instead I will try and think of more mundane things to talk about.

I am becoming increasingly concerned about your safety, especially when I hear about the fighting in the skies above London. I hope you are not in any danger from the damaged aeroplanes falling onto the capital. I hope you do not have any friends who are in the RAF. I fear they are being hit very hard. No doubt your anti-aircraft guns are firing constantly. You must be so worried, not knowing what is going to happen next.

I expect you are very busy in the council. I found your description of the councillor arguing with your arms manufacturers over all the rules and regulations very amusing, and I can understand why you are scared after the hurried retreat of your army from France. Try not to be too afraid. When our troops arrive, you'll only have to tell them about me and I am sure they will treat you less harshly. They will only make examples of your leaders who have led you into this madness. The ordinary people are of no concern to us. We know you have had no choice but to fight against us, your closest cousins. I can't understand why your leaders decided to support the French of all people… and look what they did to you? Surrendered as soon as they could, leaving your army trapped. Still, once we are there, you won't have to worry and at least then I can come and see you openly and we won't have to remain apart any longer.

Olive stopped reading and thought about what Kurt was saying. He made a lot of sense. The French had let them down and left them to fight on their own. If the Germans invaded, at least she could be with Kurt and they wouldn't have to worry anymore. Her heart soared at the thought of seeing him again and then sank when she thought of Tom and Kath and all her problems. If Kurt was here, they wouldn't dare blackmail her. The thought was comforting but didn't resolve anything and she turned back to the letter.

Well, my darling, I suppose I had better end now, but before I go, close your eyes and remember my hands exploring your body, your nipples erect with passion when I insert my fingers inside you. Remember how you writhed and moaned, your legs splayed open while I thrust my penis inside you faster and faster, your arms hugging me closer pulling me deeper into your sacred place. Can you feel me, my darling?

Olive put the letter down, her legs were trembling and there was an ache in her stomach that wouldn't go away. Tentatively she reached down and ran her hand across her pubic hair. She'd never touched herself before and she felt guilty at first but, within seconds, this was replaced by something else. She started to rub faster and faster. In her head, she could see Kurt, his face inches from her, she could feel his hands on her buttocks pulling her closer so he could pound harder. The orgasm took her by surprise and she lay panting, her head swimming and a contented smile playing on her lips. The rest of the letter could wait until later.

Chapter Ten

Toulouse, Southern France

"Thank you so much for driving me home again." Jeanne gave Gabriel a shy smile.

He smiled back. "It's my pleasure, Jeanne." He was about to say more when Jean-Paul came out.

"You really are very kind." He had no idea how he'd managed to survive since Claudette's death but he knew Gabriel and Eve had played a large part by supporting Jeanne, who in turn had somehow kept the family together. Angel was still quiet but she would be starting school soon and he hoped she would then make some friends.

"Like I said to Jeanne, whatever I can do to help, I will." He could see the pain etched in Jean-Paul's face and, although he would have liked to stay, he said goodnight and drove away.

"He's very nice." Jean-Paul was watching Jeanne's face and he saw her eyes light up. He smiled. "Your mother would not want you to shut yourself away, Jeanne. Her last words to you were to follow your heart."

"But what about Marcel? I said I would wait for him."

He could hear the despair in her voice. "Marcel is not here and you may never see him again. Gabriel is obviously very fond of you. I think he will ask you out once he feels you are ready. You should go, if you want to, of course."

"And Marcel?" Jeanne was still hesitant.

"Stop feeling guilty and get on with your life. Your mother would say the same and she'd be right."

Jeanne didn't answer. She hadn't told her father Gabriel had a fiancée, because she was hoping Gabriel would break off his engagement and ask her out. If she told Jean-Paul, he would be horrified and forbid her to go out with him. In any case, Gabriel had not done anything to encourage her, other than behave like the perfect gentleman. For all she knew, he had no romantic feelings for her at all.

****

Lambeth Hospital, London

Helen was becoming seriously concerned about Annie's non-appearance and the increasingly stilted letters, which far from easing her mind, just added to her worries.

"Do you think I'm worrying about nothing?" Helen sighed. "Sorry. I don't mean to keep asking you. I don't know what to do and I don't want to make Mum any more worried than she already is."

"It's alright really, Helen. I don't mind. I like Annie and I think it's very strange the way she's behaving." An idea came into Peggy's head. "Why don't we take a day off and go to see her. If we speak to Colin, perhaps he could drive us, if he's got enough petrol coupons. If not, we could swap some of our food ones for petrol or, if the worst comes to the worst, we could just go by train. What do you think?"

Helen's face lit up and she stopped what she was doing and gave Peggy a big hug "You're a genius. When do you think we could go?"

Peggy laughed. "We've got to talk to Colin and find out whether he can drive us and if he's got time off, then we'll ask matron if we can have a day off. It'll take a few days to organise; you'll have to be patient!"

"Yes I know, but now we have a plan, I just want to get on with it!"

"I think we should aim for some time towards the end of next week; before the end of the month anyway. I'll talk to Colin tonight and let you know tomorrow."

****

La Couture, Northern France

"Evening Louis, Madam Servier." Henri popped his head around the kitchen door. "Any chance of a chat, Louis?"

Louis jumped up. "Yes, of course. I won't be long, Mama." He was about to leave when something in her expression caught his attention. He stared more closely at her; she was very pale. "Are you alright?" he asked.

"Yes, I felt a little strange, that's all. I'm probably just tired."

Louis frowned. "Can I get you anything? Some coffee perhaps, or a glass of water?"

"No, thank you. I think I'll go to bed." Marie stood up, took one step forward and then the world began to tilt. From a long way away, she heard Louis' voice and then everything went black.

Louis stared in horror at his mother's prone body on the floor where she had collapsed and called Henri. After trying unsuccessfully to bring her round, Louis decided they should get help.

"I'll go, you stay here." Henri rushed out into the night to fetch the doctor.

After Henri had left, Louis continued to try and revive his mother and, after a few moments, her eyes fluttered open. "What happened?" She looked at Louis in surprise.

"I don't know. I think you fainted but Henri has gone for the doctor."

"I don't need a doctor."

"Well, he's on his way now and, anyway, we need to make sure there is nothing seriously wrong, don't we?" he pleaded and, seeing the obvious concern on his face, she gave in with good grace. If she was honest, she was worried about her heath too and it wouldn't hurt to be reassured.

Louis gave her some water and she slowly sipped the cool liquid, gradually feeling better.

After a little while, they heard the sound of a car pulling up and Louis rushed to the window. "I'm sure that's the doctor, but I'd better make certain." It was, and Louis opened the door in relief.

Marie looked embarrassed. "I'm sorry to call you out. I feel better now."

"You collapsed and, quite rightly, Henri came to get me. Now, let me do my job and I'll be the judge of whether you're wasting my time." The doctor spoke kindly, a twinkle in his eye. He turned to Louis and Henri. "If you'd like to leave us alone while I examine your mother?"

Louis nodded and they both went into the small hallway and sat waiting silently at the bottom of the stairs. In a remarkably short time, the door opened and the doctor appeared with a smile on his face. "You can come in now, Louis. Don't worry… your mother is absolutely fine, but she does have some news for you." He tipped his hat and spoke firmly to Marie. "Now take my advice for once. Get plenty of rest. Goodnight, my dear."

Henri and Louis stared at Marie who appeared stunned.

"I'll leave you to talk," Henri said. "I'll be back early in the morning, Louis. Alright?" Louis nodded absently, his eyes focused on his mother.

Marie took a deep breath, and tried to find the words. Although she knew the doctor was right, the news was still a shock and she wasn't entirely sure how to tell her son.

"The day before the Germans came, your father and I…" Her voice trailed off and she tried again: "We had a picnic in the back field and had some wine and…" She stopped again. "It was a beautiful day and it was like when we were young… Louis I'm not ill; I'm pregnant."

****

Catford, London

"What do you want? You aren't due until Saturday!" Olive's protests were ignored as Tom pushed past her. He was carrying a large box which looked heavy and, once inside, he placed the container carefully on the floor.

"Shut the door, then, and I'll pour us a drink."

"I don't want a drink, I want you to leave." He wasn't paying any attention, so Olive changed the subject. "What's in the box?"

Tom grinned and tapped his finger on the side of his nose. "Just a few things I'm selling. I needed a safe place to store them and I thought of you."

Olive blanched and her voice rose an octave in panic. "You can't leave black market goods here!"

"Why not?" Tom looked surprised. "You and me, we're friends now, aren't we? And who better than a friend to help me out of a bit of a pickle."

"What do you mean?" Olive ignored the reference to their friendship. He never took any notice of her rebuttals, so she had given up. If he wanted to delude himself, that was his problem.

Tom shrugged. "Nothing to worry your head about. I just need a safe place to hide a few things."

"No, you can't leave whatever that is here." Olive tried to sound firm but she was becoming increasingly desperate.

Tom was already by the cupboard, helping himself to two glasses. He turned round, pulled a small bottle of whisky from his pocket and poured them both a generous measure.

"I don't want a drink. I want you to leave."

"You're not being very friendly, Olive." Tom was no longer smiling and she shivered. "On the other hand, you're quite attractive when you're angry. Drink!"

Olive picked up the glass, her hand trembling. Tom placed his free hand over hers. "You're the one making this difficult, Olive. I just want to be friendly."

She snatched her hand away and he laughed. He downed the whisky in his glass, replacing it on the sideboard, and stared at her. Her fear was making him excited. His eyes strayed to her breasts and he stepped closer. Olive moved backwards, only to find she was pinned against the sideboard. She glanced around for something to defend herself with but there was nothing. She could feel his sour breath on her cheeks and he began stroking her hair. Olive struggled but he tightened his grip on her hair, his free hand unbuttoning his fly.

"No, please..." Her protests only seemed to excite him and he forced her to her knees. She tried to stop him but he was too strong and she found her face level with his crotch, his enormous erection rammed against her cheek. One hand was on her head forcing her forward while the other tugged her hair hard until she opened her mouth. He shoved his penis deep into her mouth, touching the back of her throat and she gagged, her eyes watering. He began to thrust faster and faster until finally he exploded, filling her mouth with hot liquid. She waited for him to pull out but he didn't. Instead, he rammed her head forward again forcing her to swallow.

Satisfied, he pulled out, picked up his glass and the bottle, and moved towards the table where he sat down and poured himself another drink.

"Well that was fun, wasn't it?" He smiled. "Plenty more where that came from." He looked down at his flaccid penis and began stroking himself. To Olive's horror, she could see him growing hard again. "Come and have another drink and we can get to know each other better."

****

Bethune, Northern France

The café was busy and Brigitte was rushed off her feet. Most of the clientele were German and they were very noisy. The French customers sat in one corner of the café and glared at them and she spent the evening alternating between the two. The French were mainly old and friends of her father's, so she reserved her best smiles for the Germans who were young and generous with their tips.

"No, Hans, I'm spoken for." She pushed his hands away for the third time, only for him to grab her round the waist and shove her down on his lap. Brigitte laughed along with them but she had one eye on the door. It was unlikely either Rolf or Louis would come in, but she couldn't risk any problems with either.

"Just a quick kiss, Brigitte." Hans pulled her head towards him and his tongue was in her mouth before she could stop him. Brigitte tried ineffectually to push him away but he tasted nice and, after a couple of seconds, she began kissing him back. The café was noisy and she had her eyes closed, so it came as a shock when she felt strong arms pulling her away from Hans and dumping her unceremoniously on the floor. The room went deathly quiet and Brigitte stared up in horror. Rolf was standing in front of her, his eyes blazing, his face pale with fury. Self-preservation kicked in and Brigitte opened her mouth.

"I told him I was spoken for, but he wouldn't listen."

Hans blanched and he opened his mouth to dispute Brigitte's version but Rolf didn't give him a chance. Ignoring Brigitte, his eyes on the soldier, Rolf spoke in a measured tone. "Back to your barracks, now, all of you. You don't know what you'll catch hanging around here." His voice was deceptively quiet but the men all stood up and left, leaving Brigitte still sitting on the floor. He bent down, his face inches from hers.

"I'll pick you up in the morning when I've thought of a suitable punishment." His eyes lingered on her for several seconds then he stood up and was gone.

Brigitte got shakily to her feet, trying to ignore the rising fear. Or was it excitement? She no longer knew. She could hear the French customers laughing but she didn't care.

****

La Couture, Northern France

Louis stared at his mother in disbelief. "I don't know what to say."

"I know; I'm shocked too but I couldn't be happier. I will always be able to look at this child and remember the wonderful afternoon we had together, knowing we were still so much in love after all those years together. We were lucky in so many ways. Many people do not have those memories to look back on, so I will count my blessings and look forward to the birth of our child." Her face fell. "I only wish I knew what had happened to Marcel. He would love to know he is no longer the baby of the family."

Louis smiled. "I'm pleased for you, Mama and providing you are alright I will look forward to having a brother or sister." His expression changed and he carried on more seriously, "But this makes it even more important that we are careful. Henri and I had a plan but now… I'm not sure we should go ahead."

"What plan?" Marie looked at her oldest son's serious face and her heart swelled with pride. He finally appeared to have grown up. "Maybe you should let me decide?"

Louis quickly outlined his plan and Henri's modifications. Marie considered them carefully.

"I agree, if they are found anywhere on our land, no matter how far away from the house, the Boche will not believe we didn't know. And Henri is right, if we hide them somewhere where there is no reason to go to regularly, it would look suspicious. Maybe we should think about the problem in a different way?"

Louis looked puzzled.

"The difficulty is to find somewhere perfectly normal to visit regularly. That's why you thought of the barn. But the barn is really much too close to the house. It's too dangerous."

Louis nodded.

"So, could we not find a reason to build something on the very edge of the land, something you would need to visit every day and then hide the airmen there?"

Louis considered her idea, looking for flaws. "What though?"

"I don't know. But there must be something"

They sat in silence for a while and, just when Louis was about to give up, Marie began to smile. "I think I have an idea."

Louis looked at her and waited.

"The Boche said we have to give them a percentage of our produce, yes?"

Louis' face darkened but he said nothing and just nodded.

"So, why don't we build a special barn or outhouse on the edge of our land to store their produce. If we build something near the back road, we can argue it is there for their convenience to collect their produce, especially in the winter when the road into the farm can get blocked. They will never think to search somewhere they go regularly, which is there purely for them. Even if they get suspicious of us, which pray God they don't, they will search the house and barn before they even consider looking there. What do you think?"

Louis grinned. "Yes. I think it could work. Of course, whoever hides there would have to be very careful, but I think you are right. That would be the last place they would think of looking. The only problem is our neighbours may think we are too friendly with the Boche."

Marie shrugged. "Then, unfortunately, we will have to let them think that way. Our lives may depend on the Germans thinking we are collaborators." She yawned. "And now, I have to go to bed. I have had more than enough excitement tonight."

She stood up and Louis kissed her on the cheek and then gave her a big hug.

"Good night, Mama. Sleep well." He watched her go up the stairs to bed, his brain racing while he considered her idea. He couldn't see any flaws but he would see what Henri thought in the morning. He knew he should go to bed but, despite being physically tired, his mind was still busy. The next problem was to find an escape route out of occupied France.

Chapter Eleven

Honor Oak Park, London

"Annie! What a surprise." Peggy suddenly noticed the suitcase in her hand and Annie's red rimmed eyes. "What on earth's happened?"

Annie's eyes filled with tears. "Oh Peggy, I've left them. I can't stand living there anymore, they just don't give me a minute's peace." She began sobbing uncontrollably. "I'm really sorry, but can I stay here for a few days while I find somewhere else to live? I can't go home and I didn't know where else to turn."

"Of course you can." Peggy took the suitcase from her shaking hands. Annie followed her into the hall and Peggy shut the door. "You can have Ethel's room." Annie was still crying and Peggy stared at her, shocked by how fragile she appeared. Although there was quite a sizeable lump where the baby was, the rest of her seemed very thin and her face was etched with lines of worry, making her look considerably older than her twenty-four years.

"Come on, sit down. You look exhausted and that can't be good for the baby. You're safe now." She put her arms around Annie, feeling the bones of her shoulders through her thin blouse. "I'll make a cup of tea while you rest." Peggy helped Annie put her legs up on the comfortable settee and, as she closed her eyes, Peggy went into the kitchen and put the kettle on.

While the water boiled, Peggy considered the options. Obviously Annie was in no fit state to be living on her own, certainly not at the moment and there was an empty room upstairs where she would be among friends and where Helen and her mum could visit regularly. She was sure Sally would agree, although she felt obliged to ask her first, rather than just assume she would be happy with the arrangement. In any case, Sally was hardly ever at home now; she spent most of her time with Peter and their wedding wasn't far off. Then she would be moving out altogether.

The kettle boiled and Peggy quickly made the tea and took two cups into the sitting room

Annie gave a watery smile and took the cup Peggy was offering her. Sipping gently, she closed her eyes in appreciation. "Thank you so much, Peggy. I didn't know what I was going to do or where I was going to go." She stopped and her eyes filled with tears again. "I still don't. If I can just stay until I find somewhere?"

"I need to make sure Sally agrees, but as far as I'm concerned you can stay here as long as you want." Annie started to say something but Peggy waved a hand and carried on, "We were going to start looking for someone else to have the room anyway, so you'd be doing us a favour."

Annie dissolved into tears again and Peggy looked at her in alarm, until she realised she was crying with relief not despair.

"Come on, drink up and we'll take your things upstairs. I've got some spare sheets and blankets you can have. I'll go and look them out while you finish up, unless you'd rather talk?"

"No, I think I'd rather sleep now and talk later." The relief was visible on Annie's face.

"Well, you go up to bed and I'll pop out and ring Helen." Peggy quickly explained the plans they had been making to visit her and Annie looked at her in surprise.

"I had no idea everyone cared so much." She dissolved into tears again. "I'm sorry, I don't seem to be able to help crying, I don't know why. I haven't cried this much since John died."

Peggy hugged her. "Don't worry. You'll feel much better after you've had some sleep."

Annie was soon settled into Ethel's room and, within minutes of lying down on the comfortable bed, she was asleep.

****

Bethune, Northern France

Brigitte existed in a state of nervous anticipation all morning, but there was no sign of Rolf.

"For God's sake, stop mooning around, girl. Why don't you go and see Louis?" Fabian was becoming increasingly concerned over Brigitte's behaviour. Louis seemed like a nice enough lad and at least he was French. Perhaps if he encouraged her more in his direction she would forget all about the Boche officer. He was a cold bastard and his Brigitte needed someone to love her, not order her about. He'd heard the German shout at her a couple of times and it made his blood boil but there was nothing he could do, other than clench his fists and hope he treated her better when they were on their own. He was under no illusion about his daughter, but she didn't deserve to be badly treated.

"He's probably working," Brigitte responded. She looked downcast and Fabian tried again.

"That's never stopped you before. Go on, go up and see him."

Brigitte stared at him for several seconds. Her father was right: she could go and see Louis. Rolf obviously wasn't interested in her. But then, she reasoned, what if Rolf called round and she was out? He'd be even more angry. "No," she said. "I'll go and see him another day."

****

La Couture, Northern France

Henri couldn't see any real problems with Marie's idea but suggested they think about the plan for a few days, in case anything else came to them. Louis agreed reluctantly. He knew Henri was right. He would just have to curb his impatience.

Seeing his disappointment, Henri smiled. "I think I might have an idea about an escape route into the unoccupied zone." Louis' face lit up. "I'll know one way or another in a few days. How's the patient, anyway?"

"Much better. He's ready to move if he needs to, although another couple of days won't hurt and it'll give him more time to get his strength back."

Henri glanced round the expanse of the farm and an idea came to him.

"Perhaps you should get a dog or some geese, to give you some warning of anyone approaching."

Louis nodded. "That's a good idea. Do you know anyone who's got any geese for sale? Or a dog? I haven't got lots of money, but perhaps I can do a deal?"

"Don't worry. Girauld's collie bitch has just whelped. He was moaning the other day about what he was going to do with all the puppies, what with rationing and everything. He didn't think anyone would want a dog, however good its breeding. Leave it to me; he owes me a favour."

"Thanks, let me know how much I owe you."

Henri shook his head. "This is as much my fight as yours. The Boche might think they've got the upper hand, but they've reckoned without us. We'll give them a run for their money, you'll see. Like de Gaulle said, we won't ever give in, not until France is free again. Now, tell me where you think we should put this barn?" Henri stopped suddenly. "Why don't we make the building a sort of shop as well? A joint venture between our two farms? Then it would be perfectly reasonable for one of us to be there every day and we would have more produce to sell. If I can persuade my parents, it won't cost you so much to build, because we can contribute half the costs. What do you think?"

Louis looked dubious and Henri hastened to explain, his face alight as he planned out loud. "We can sell any surplus the Germans don't take. We can also buy from other farmers and sell for them, taking a tiny profit of course. Our mothers and the other women around here make excellent cheeses, jams and preserves: we could sell those too."

Louis nodded. Although Marie had some savings, Louis didn't want to use them all up, in case they needed money later. In the back of his mind, he had been mulling over the idea of sorting out some fake papers for himself and Marie, so if they had to flee they would be able to do so. He hadn't thought about where they would go yet, but once the escape line was up and running, he would have a much better idea of his options and he could then plan accordingly. Marie's pregnancy was unexpected but did not present an insurmountable problem. If anything, a young baby might help their disguise. But that was a problem for the future. For now, he needed to find a way of getting Patrick on his way and it looked as though Henri might have a solution. He hoped so, because he would much rather put the plans together without the added pressure of hiding an allied airman at the same time.

"Right, let me go home and draw up some plans. By the time they're ready, I may also have news about ways out of the occupied zone. I'll let you know." Henri shook Louis' hand and left deep in thought.

Louis walked back to the farmhouse and explained the new plans to Marie. She was enthusiastic and immediately set to work, seeing how they could produce enough goods to make a shop viable.

****

Aldershot, England

"Marcel!" Charles' voice echoed loudly through the tent making him jump. "I've just bumped into someone who knows your brother, Louis." An expression of delight crossed Marcel's face, quickly replaced by trepidation as he realised he was almost afraid to ask about his brother. However, Charles hastily reassured him: "He's fine, well at least he was a month ago. He's back home on your farm. Because he's the only adult male there, the Germans haven't carted him off to any of the labour camps in Germany. He…" Charles stopped, stunned by the look on Marcel's face. "What's the matter?" he asked.

"You said he was the only adult male there. What about my father?"

Charles shook his head. "Sorry, he didn't mention him, just said your mum was alright and, although Louis was a bit thin, he was fit and working the farm with your mother and still seeing his girlfriend… Brigitte, I think he said?"

"Where is this man? I have to speak to him."

"You'll have to be quick then, he was amongst the latest lot to be shipped out. Does anyone have any idea what's going on?" Charles changed the subject and looked at Paul.

"See, I told you something was happening!" But Marcel was no longer listening. He raced across the camp towards the exit but was just in time to see the last of the trucks pull out and, by the time he reached the gate, they had disappeared around the corner and out of sight.

Panting heavily, he put his hands on his hips and shook his head in despair. He turned to the sentry and said, more in hope than in any real expectation of an answer, "Do you know when they'll be back?"

The sentry shrugged and looked at Marcel as if he was mad. Marcel turned round disconsolately and started to head slowly back towards his tent. Although he was deep in thought, his brain still registered that the camp was half empty, the vacant tents looking almost ghostlike in their silence. Like the others, he was curious about where everyone had gone, but foremost in his thoughts was his worry about his father. Why hadn't he been mentioned? Was he ill again, or…? He couldn't bear to even consider he might be dead, so he quashed the thought and tried to think of some other explanation.

****

La Couture, Northern France

Time dragged by slowly and Louis found it hard to conceal his growing agitation. Things seemed to be taking so long. They still hadn't found a way of getting Patrick away and every day he stayed there increased the risk. He knew Marie was enjoying his company, but she too was becoming increasingly concerned at the length of time they were having to hide him. Eventually, to his relief, Henri arrived at the back door looking pleased with himself.

"The first thing we need to do is to take some photos of your airman and then, when I have the papers, I'll come back and take him. It's better you don't know anything about where he's going or who with. That's my job. Now, the shop…" He looked at their expectant faces and grinned. "My parents like the idea and, no, I haven't said anything other than it's a shop and also somewhere to keep the Boche's share of our goods, so they don't have to keep bothering us. It's much safer that way. The only people who will know what we're really doing will be the three of us. We will move the airmen at night when there is no-one about and we will blindfold them, so they have no idea where they are being hidden. I am looking into some kind of insulation to provide a way of blocking sounds and then I will line the underground room, so the danger of discovery is reduced." He stopped. "Is there anything else we haven't thought of? Can you think of any other precautions we could take?"

Louis and Marie looked at each other and thought hard. Marie was the first to speak. "I can't think of anything at all. Unfortunately any problems are likely to come to light when we are actually using the room, so I think we should prepare to be flexible and make adjustments when necessary."

Louis looked at his mother. "I'm not sure you should be involved in…"

Marie interrupted. "For goodness sake, Louis. How can I not be involved? Do you think if you are arrested they will leave me alone? They will assume I am as guilty as you are, whether I am or not. At least if I'm going to die, let me do something to warrant it!"

Louis opened his mouth to argue but then realised what his mother said was perfectly true. They were both in this together and assuming the Nazis would leave his mother alone just because she was a women was wishful thinking.

****

Glasgow, Scotland

The man in the long trench coat climbed into his car and glanced at his map. He had a long journey ahead of him but he was a salesman and used to travelling around the country.

The network of 'friends', as they were known, stretched across the country. Some were middle aged women in positions where they had access to low level information which helped the Germans build up a picture of everyday life in the enemy's country. Others were men and women of all ages who needed money, for whatever reason. His job was to periodically check up on the ones on his list, to make sure the security services hadn't taken them over, thus compromising the intelligence. He wasn't expecting any problems.

Hopefully the trip would be straightforward and he would only need to stay a couple of days in each place. Just enough time to make sure nothing was wrong.

****

La Couture, Northern France

A few days later Henri arrived to take Patrick out of the yard and across the fields. Marie was surprised by just how sad she was to see him go and, although she was relieved they were no longer in danger, she knew she was going to miss him. She said a silent prayer he would make it safely back to his wife and child and wished she could hear some word from Marcel, letting her know he was all right.

Louis breathed a sigh of relief. Much as he liked defying the Germans, he wanted it to be on his terms. Any other way was sheer lunacy and much too risky. Closing the door, he looked at his mother. "Well that's the first one, finally! I think we should celebrate. Can you have a glass of wine?"

Marie smiled. "One glass will be very therapeutic."

Louis went to the small cupboard where they kept the few bottles the Germans had overlooked on their original search, and found a bottle of red wine. He poured them each a glass, handing one to his mother. "This was one of Dad's favourite wines." he said. "You do think he'd approve of what we're planning to do, don't you?"

Marie smiled and unconsciously put her hand on her stomach. "He would be really proud of you, Louis. You've grown up so much. And yes, he would definitely approve."

Louis relaxed. "Here's to success with our new venture!"

Part Two

September - October 1940

Chapter Twelve

La Couture, Northern France

"Louis! Louis!"

Louis turned around in astonishment. His face lit up when he saw Brigitte, then fell again as he glanced quickly around again to make sure no one had seen her. He hurried across the field to the road and led her towards a hedge so they couldn't be seen from the farmhouse.

"What are you doing here?"

Brigitte pouted. "I thought you'd be pleased to see me. I can always go again."

She made to walk back into the field but Louis grabbed her and pulled her close. "Don't be silly, Brigitte. Of course I'm pleased to see you."

He began kissing her while he tried to work out what to do. He couldn't let his mother see her; not when he'd lied about seeing Brigitte. Her body felt wonderful, her hair smelt of flowers and his hands strayed to her breasts. He wondered if she would object to a quick tumble on the grass by the hedge. Then no one was likely to see her and, when they were finished, she would probably go home.

He undid her blouse and, when she made no attempt to stop him, he continued onto her bra. Brigitte began groaning in the way she knew he liked and his hands snaked down to her skirt.

"I've missed you." He spoke softly and lay down on the ground pulling her on top of him. She straddled him while he struggled to unbutton his fly and then he was free, his erection standing proud. Brigitte lowered herself on top of him, her eyes fixed on his face. He could see her breasts swinging gently while she began to move up and down and he gasped with pleasure.

He reached for her nipples but she pushed his hands away, forcing his arms back above his head. Her face was inches from his and she bent and kissed him, her tongue darting around his mouth in time with the rhythm of her body. Louis closed his eyes and gave himself up to pleasure, all worries about being seen forgotten.

****

Catford, London

"There's a dance at the local hall tonight, Peggy. Do you want to come?" Helen squinted, shading her eyes from the early evening sun. Helen's dad was away for a couple of days and she had invited Peggy round for a late tea. Helen lived in Catford and Peggy was enjoying the opportunity to sit in the garden and relax.

"I'd love to."

Helen was surprised. She was half expecting Peggy to make an excuse not to come. Peggy smiled and was about to say more when the air raid siren sounded. Used to the numerous daylight raids with bombers heading towards the air fields surrounding London, neither Peggy nor Helen bothered to move.

Within minutes, the familiar droning noise could be heard in the distance and gradually grew louder. Peggy felt the first stirrings of unease. She glanced at Helen but her friend was already gazing skyward. Looking up, Peggy was astonished to see hundreds of German bombers flying over. There were so many, the sky was black and the noise was deafening. They watched, transfixed, while the aircraft passed over. A few seconds later, they saw the bomb doors opening. Plane after plane flew over, dropping hundreds of tons of incendiaries and bombs on the city below and the evening sky took on an ominous red glow.

About to thank God they were on the south side of the Thames, their relief was short lived. An enormous crash reverberated through the street, shaking the ground and the house, and showering them in dust. Peggy screamed and Helen cried out as falling roof tiles catapulted to the ground, missing them both by inches.

"Are you alright?" Helen's voice was barely audible above the tremendous noise all around.

Peggy nodded and tried to joke. "Yes, they missed! What about you?"

Helen nodded. "I'm not sure other people have been so lucky, though." They began to brush the dust from their clothes, keeping a wary eye out for more falling debris.

"Come on, let's see if we can help." Helen's voice broke into the cacophony of sound around her and, grateful for something to do, Peggy followed her out into the street. Although the target seemed to be the East End, stray bombs had hit the end of the road, where buildings had collapsed and fires were raging.

The air was filled with thick black smoke and dust and debris were raining down all around. Possessions were strewn everywhere and bodies could be clearly seen, their limbs visible amid the rubble; the remains of what, five minutes earlier, had been a normal suburban family enjoying their early evening meal.

****

La Couture, Northern France

"I'd better get back to work." Louis leant over and kissed her. He was feeling sated and would liked to have lain there a little longer but, now he had satisfied himself, he wanted to get rid of Brigitte before his mother saw her.

"Oh, I thought we could spend some time together. I didn't come all this way just for sex, you know." Brigitte pouted and Louis sighed.

"I can't think of anything I would rather do, my love, but I have to finish the watering or the crops will die. A farmer's work is never done."

"Then, perhaps we should move south, like you suggested. Or have you forgotten?" Her mouth was an angry line and Louis hastened to reassure her. He didn't want to upset her, or she would stop seeing him. He just didn't want her hanging around the farm.

"I haven't forgotten. Let's see what happens, shall we? We don't know what the Boche are going to do yet. There's no point going south if they're going to carry on advancing. And I can't just leave Mama, not now." He felt Brigitte stiffen beside him and he hurried on. "She's pregnant, Brigitte. I can't go until she's had the baby. Maybe then."

She turned to him in surprise. "Isn't she a bit old to be having a baby?"

Louis shrugged. He had no idea. "Obviously not, or she wouldn't be, would she?" He snapped, annoyed by her attitude. Brigitte realised she had gone too far and she snuggled up against him, her hand reaching for his penis. But Louis had had enough and he pushed her hand away, stood up and glanced around quickly to make sure they were still unobserved.

"I'm sorry, Louis. I didn't mean anything. Of course you have to stay here. I understand, I won't ask again."

Louis helped her to her feet and kissed the top of her forehead. "Don't worry, I'm not cross." He glanced up at the sky. It was getting late. "You'd better go. I'll try and come down to see you tomorrow evening, alright?"

Brigitte plastered a smile on her face and kissed him passionately on the lips. "See you tomorrow, then."

She turned and climbed on her bike and rode off. Louis watched her go with relief and, when she was out of sight, he went back to work.

****

Catford, London

It was late evening when Olive heard the knock on the door. The sirens had finally fallen silent and things appeared to be returning to some sense of normality. Olive had been staring into space trying to work out what to do about Tom when the bombs began falling.

For a moment, she wished one would land on her flat, but then she brushed the thought away and followed her neighbours out into the streets. In the distance, she could see the explosions and fires and she shivered. This was what Kurt had worried about: her being injured or killed by his countrymen, while he was powerless to protect her. She thought back to his last letter but the usual comfort his words gave her was no longer there. She hadn't answered him yet, mainly because she had no idea what to say.

Her gaze alighted on the box. The container was where Tom had left it, in the corner near the small bathroom. She had made no attempt to look inside. The box disgusted her, reminding her of every detail of that terrible night. She tried to force herself to think of something else, but inevitably all she could think of was how to kill Tom.

When she heard the knock at the door, she panicked. Surely he couldn't be back again? He had already been back several times since the first night. Then she remembered her fears were groundless. Tom had taken her key and made himself a copy. He wouldn't bother to knock. He took delight in just walking in whenever he felt like it, realising this added to her fear, because she never knew when he would appear. She opened the door and peered out cautiously.

"Yes?" Olive looked pale and distracted and Peggy frowned.

"I just came round to make sure you were alright after the bombing."

Olive made an effort to smile. She had almost forgotten she and Peggy were supposed to be friends now. She still hadn't heard back from Kurt with information about where Joe was and somehow her plan to gloat over Joe's whereabouts didn't seem important any more. She stood aside. "Come in. Sorry, I was just a bit shocked. I can't believe they would bomb us, can you?"

Peggy shook her head. She sat down at Olive's table. "I was at my friend's house and some bombs fell in her street. Oh, Olive, it was awful. So frightening."

Olive forced herself to look concerned. Peggy had no idea what real fear was like. She should be in Olive's shoes, having to deal with Tom. "Goodness, Peggy, are you alright? I had no idea you were in danger. I assumed you were at home."

Peggy smiled. "You weren't to know, Olive. I'm fine, just shocked really." There was a brief silence.

"Have you heard anything about Joe yet?"

Peggy's face fell. "No, nothing. But no news is good news, or so everyone keeps telling me."

"I'm sure he is absolutely fine and you're worrying about nothing." Olive spoke with confidence and Peggy laughed.

"I'm so pleased we're friends now. It's much nicer than being enemies."

Somehow Olive managed to smile. "Me too." She glanced at the clock. The pubs would be closing soon. She felt sick. What would happen if Tom came round and Peggy was there? She couldn't take the chance. She stood up, taking Peggy by surprise.

"I don't mean to be rude, but we've both got work tomorrow and it's been a particularly difficult day…"

"Of course, like I said I just wanted to make sure you were alright." Peggy stood up too. "Goodnight, Olive. Sleep well." She hesitated, wondering if she should hug her cousin goodbye, but it didn't seem appropriate, so she headed towards the door.

Olive breathed a sigh of relief. She would wait another half an hour then she should be safe to go to bed.

****

Simonsdorf, Poland

The weather had changed. Gone were the warm, balmy days in which they had longed for a respite from the heat, replaced instead by biting winds and torrential rain, a foretaste of what was to come.

"They're sending us all back to Thorn," Mitchell said cheerfully while Joe threw himself disconsolately on his bed.

"Right, of course they are. And who told you? The Commandant?"

"No, Carter in hut five heard the guards talking while he was taking the slops out." Mitchell was irritated Joe wasn't taking him seriously.

"Yeah, well I'll believe that when it happens. This place is full or rumours, most of them untrue."

"So what's eating you?" Mitchell decided to change the subject.

"Nothing. I'm really happy. Having the best time of my life," Joe snapped.

"Great, me too. I'd always wanted to see Europe. But at least we're alive, eh?" Mitchell turned his back. He understood why Joe was depressed, and knew it was probably better to let him get over his mood in his own time.

"Atchoo!" Pete's sneeze was enough to wake the entire hut, if they'd been asleep, and was followed swiftly by two more.

"Bless you," Joe said grudgingly, feeling rather mean for having snapped Mitchell's head off.

"He needs more than blessing, mate." Bert looked up from the book he was trying to read. "Hope you're not going to spread your filthy germs all around the hut."

"Thanks. Your sympathy is gratefully accepted." Pete felt really awful. His throat was sore, his eyes were running and his nose was blocked. "What I need is a hot toddy," he croaked.

"What's a hot toddy?" Mitchell looked interested.

"Its hot water with a little drop of whisky in, sometimes honey too," Bert answered.

"And that works?"

"Sometimes, but if you put enough whisky in, you don't care!" Bert laughed.

"Well if I see any whisky about, I'll bear it in mind," Mitchell responded. "Seriously, Pete, you really don't look good. Perhaps you should go sick?"

Joe eased himself off his bunk, his self-pity forgotten and peered at Pete. "He's right. You look dreadful. If you should go sick; they might give you something."

"I'll see how I feel in the morning. I'm going to try and get some sleep." Pete turned over and, within minutes, was snoring loudly. Normally this would have provoked a storm of protests from the others but, aware he was ill, they tried to ignore him.

The nights were drawing in and, with the wind howling outside, the hut felt damp and miserable. The bare floor boards were only covered in a light layer of sawdust, so the wind and cold seeped up into the hut and no amount of heating, even if they'd had any, would have made any difference. The one small burner at the other end of the hut was rarely lit, because there was no fuel to burn. There had been discussions about whether they should burn bits of the hut to keep warm but this had been rejected, because they belatedly realised the Germans would have just let them sleep outside if they dismantled the hut. Unfortunately, they only came to this conclusion after they had removed some of the bare floorboards and burnt the wood, leaving empty spaces which let in even more cold wind and the dampness from the long grass under the huts.

****

La Couture, Northern France

Louis was delighted to see Henri waiting when he got in from work. He could tell by Marie's expression that his friend had some news. "Have you drawn up the plans yet?"

Henri laughed. "Yes, here they are." He laid a large sheet of paper out on the table and pointed to where the underground room would be and how it would be concealed. "The room will only be accessible from the storage area where we'll keep their goods. The floor will be wooden and covered with straw. But, not just one floor, it is actually two floors with two layers of overlapping wood so, if they should find the trapdoor, all they will see is a cellar with some wine in. The real room will be hidden under the wine racks and insulated from below. Unless they move the wine racks, they will not find the room. They will only do that if they already suspect and, quite frankly, if they've got that far, we're finished anyway because they'll probably already know. If they stumble on the wine cellar by accident, they are more likely to just confiscate the wine and arrest us for trying to hide goods. We could still get prosecuted but the penalties for hiding drink are obviously a lot less than for hiding allied airmen."

He stopped and waited for comments. Marie smiled at him. "Henri, you've worked really hard. Well done. How long will it take to build?"

"If we get going now? Possibly by the end of the month. Dad's very enthusiastic at the prospect of earning some extra money from the shop, so he's going to give me a hand." He smiled at Louis' expression. "Don't worry, I'll let him help with the main store and the wine cellar and you can help me build the underground room in the evenings and at night."

"Yes, of course. It's brilliant, Henri. Mum's right. Well done. When do we start?"

"Tomorrow morning. Marie, I think you should come down to have a chat with Dad about the produce and management side of the shop and leave the rest to Louis and me."

****

En route to Scotland

As the countryside sped past, Pam closed her eyes and fell into a light sleep. Her leave at home had passed quickly and there had been no more news about Tony, other than a brief phone call congratulating her on her new job with the FANY. She recalled the conversation with a certain amount of amusement. Tony obviously didn't really believe her when she said this was the perfect job for her. However, she was sure he was keeping the conversation fixed on her and deliberately deflecting any questions about himself. She knew he was unable to talk about the war, but they had always been very close, like twins, and had often been able to read each other's thoughts. Just like he knew she was not being entirely truthful, so she knew there were things he wasn't saying.

Pam twisted in her seat to get more comfortable. She'd been lucky to get a seat. All the compartments were filled to capacity, with soldiers, sailors, airmen and people in various uniforms crammed in to every available space. Even the corridors were full of passengers sitting on the floor or standing by the windows. The train slowed down and they pulled into a station. She had no idea where they were, because all the station names had been removed, but she thought they must be somewhere in the Midlands.

The train pulled out again and rumbled on. The light gradually began to fade. Fast asleep, Pam was suddenly jolted awake by one of the soldiers pulling down the blackout curtain. "Sorry, miss. I didn't mean to make you jump."

"Don't worry. I need to wake up anyway. Do you know where we are?"

"Just coming into Glasgow, I think."

Pam jumped up and began straightening her clothes. She took her case from the luggage rack and placed it on the floor and, within minutes, they were pulling into Glasgow. Hurrying off the train, she found herself in a busy bustling station milling with people, all speaking nineteen to the dozen, in an accent she found difficult to understand. There was half an hour before her next train, so she took herself off to the canteen and bought a mug of tea and a large Chelsea bun. She found an empty table and sat down facing the door. The bun was stale but she was hungry, so she washed it down with the tea, which was surprisingly good. Once finished, she went to the cloakroom where she queued for the toilet and then she made her way to platform three to wait for the next train. It was completely dark outside and decidedly colder than London and she shivered. What would the temperature be like as they went even further north?

****

Bethune, Northern France

"I haven't seen Louis here for a while. Is he alright?" Brigitte stared at her father. It was so unlike him to show an interest in her life, she was confused.

"As far as I know." She shrugged.

"Is he coming over to see you tonight?"

Brigitte shook her head. "No, he's got other things to do." She walked off, leaving Fabian staring after her. He shook his head and walked back into the bar.

"Good evening." Rolf saluted Fabian, making him jump. The Frenchman resisted the temptation to punch the German officer and instead he forced himself to smile and answer politely.

"Leutnant, can I get you a drink?"

"No, thank you. I've come to see your daughter."

Fabian shrugged and pointed upstairs. Rolf smiled and disappeared up the stairs, leaving Fabian fuming at the bottom.

"You can't come in, I'm getting dressed…" Brigitte's voice tailed off when she realised it was Rolf at her door. "Hello." She suddenly felt shy. "Sorry, I thought you were my father."

"Get dressed into something nice and put on your coat. We're going out." She winced at his tone. "I'll be waiting downstairs. You have ten minutes." He turned around and left, shutting the door quietly behind him.

****

Catford, London

"Another drink, Olive?" Tom poured some more whisky into his glass and topped hers up. Olive watched him with resignation. There was no point refusing, so she sipped slowly. Maybe she should get drunk before he forced himself on her again, then she might not remember it the next day.

She glanced at the clock. He had been in the flat for half an hour now and he hadn't made any attempt to touch her. Perhaps he was losing interest. Kurt was late tonight. Olive had begun seeing the bombers as Kurt's way of saving her from Tom's attentions after the air raid sirens had rescued her from him twice in the past week.

He was eyeing her speculatively.

"So, what's in the handbag?"

The question caught her completely by surprise and she flinched. "Nothing." The denial was too quick. Tom smiled. Kath was right, then. Olive was hiding something. Perhaps he should have concentrated on that, rather than getting his leg over. Still, no time like the present. He held out his hand. "Let's have a look then."

Olive shook her head. "There's nothing in my bag. Why don't you go before the bombers come over. They'll be here soon." She tried to sound concerned and failed miserably.

Tom grinned. "Olive, I didn't know you cared."

She flushed and took a gulp of her drink. Getting drunk was starting to seem like a good idea.

"Tell you what. Let's have some fun and then I'll go." He saw the look on her face and laughed. "Only this time you've got to pretend you're really enjoying yourself, instead of lying there like a plank of wood."

The air raid siren started up and Olive breathed a sigh of relief, but Tom made no attempt to move. " I'm not going anywhere, not till I take a look in the bag." He leered at her, enjoying her discomfort. "You know you're going to give it to me eventually, so why not stop messing about." He downed his drink and replaced the glass on the table.

Olive shook her head, frantically trying to think of a way out.

Tom sighed. "Alright, how about we do a trade?"

Olive frowned "What do you mean?"

"You let me look at you in that sexy underwear you've got stashed in your drawer and I'll forget all about the bag. What d'you say? You could do a nice striptease for me." His words were slurred and he was already undoing the buttons on his trousers.

Something inside Olive snapped. The corset and knickers had been given to her by Kurt.

"Get out." The words were quiet to start with, then she spoke louder: "I said, get out!"

Tom laughed and, realising he wasn't going, Olive knew she had to escape.

****

Toulouse, Southern France

Gabriel glanced at the pile of files on his desk and sighed. He was working late to try and catch up on some paperwork but he couldn't concentrate. His thoughts kept wandering to Jeanne and then back to his fiancée, Isabelle. If it wasn't for her, he could ask Jeanne out properly instead of just driving her home and being the perfect gentleman. Perhaps he should break off his engagement? He shuddered. Isabelle was ruthless and, if he dumped her to go out with Jeanne, she would make trouble for them. Of course, she could only do so if there was something for her to use. He frowned. He had never bothered to try and find out what Jeanne was hiding and, to be honest, he didn't really care now. But perhaps he should, especially if he was thinking of asking her out. The problem was, he didn't want to spy on her. Investigating her would make him feel like a Nazi. On the other hand, she'd never given him any indication she saw him as anything other than a friend, so maybe he should just leave well alone.

His other problem was what to do about his conscience. He was already turning a blind eye to reports of sabotage and occasionally went out of his way to warn cells they were about to be raided, but he wanted to take things one step further and he wasn't sure how to go about it.

****

Scotland

The small train to Arisaig on the virtually deserted western coast of Inverness-shire arrived on time. There were far fewer people onboard and Pam took a seat in one of the open carriages. Most passengers were in civilian clothes, although there were a few in uniform. The blackout curtains were drawn, so she took out the latest copy of Vogue which her mother had given her. Since France had fallen, America had become the fashion leader and most of the clothes had an American look to them. After a few moments of idly flicking through the pages, she realised she was bored.

"Good magazine?" Pam stared into Richard's sparkling blue eyes. He had sat down so quietly, she hadn't noticed him.

"Not really. I was just thinking how boring it was! Thank you." She took the offered cigarette and was about to ask him what he was doing there when she realised that would probably be unprofessional. "I wasn't expecting to see you here."

"I thought you might like some company," he replied equally blandly and she had a sudden vision of them having years of meaningless conversations, neither really saying what they meant. She couldn't help smiling and he raised an inquisitive eyebrow. "I was just thinking what exciting conversations we have," she said dryly, forestalling the question she could see forming on his lips.

He laughed. "It's the nature of the business, I'm afraid, at least in public." He glanced around to check there was no one in earshot. But they were alone, apart from a man further down the carriage who was reading a book.

"How long before we arrive?"

"About two hours on here and then another half an hour by road. Did you have a good leave?"

"Yes I did, although the days went very quickly."

"How's your brother?"

Pam frowned. "I don't know, to be honest. He says he's alright, but you saw him." She stopped abruptly, wondering if she had said too much. Unable to think of anything else to say that wasn't likely to incriminate her, she looked away and then suggested, "Do you fancy a game of cards?"

Richard nodded and they whiled away the rest of the journey playing Newmarket for matches. Richard was a good player and Pam had to concentrate to hold her own. Before long, the train slowed and pulled into Inverness station.

The imposing granite walls of the town impressed themselves on her memory while the car, a small saloon, sped through the wet streets and out into the country. The driver obviously knew the roads, or at least Pam hoped he did, because he did not make many allowances for the blackout and the lack of lights, speeding along at a breakneck pace, rarely slowing down for the numerous bends in the country lanes.

Eventually, the car skidded to a halt outside a large imposing house, silhouetted against the dark barren mountains standing sentry behind.

They were greeted by a tall, burly sergeant with a large bottle of whisky in one hand and the keys to their rooms in the other. He indicated an open door to their left and they followed him into a drawing room with a roaring fire in the hearth. Gratefully, they sat down in the two arm chairs either side of the fire and took the glasses he was offering in which he had poured them both a generous measure of the golden coloured whisky. The fire was throwing out plenty of heat and Pam relaxed. About to close her eyes and savour the whisky and the warmth, Pam heard a gentle cough. The sergeant was standing by the side of the chairs. Richard smiled. "I think we should go up. You've got a busy day tomorrow. Thank you, Sergeant, for the whisky. It's excellent."

They downed their drinks and followed the soldier back into the hall, where he gave them their keys. Pam was in number fifteen and, without ceremony she was ushered to the stairs and told breakfast was in the dining room to their left and was served sharply at seven o'clock. She would be given the tour and her kit in the morning. Saying goodnight to Richard, she easily found her room and the toilet which was several doors down the dimly lit corridor, unpacked her clothes quickly, washed in cold water because there didn't appear to be any hot, and climbed wearily into bed. Although she was tired after her journey, she still couldn't sleep. The room was freezing and the bedclothes felt cold and damp and she couldn't get warm. Her feet were like ice and, eventually, she got up and put on some socks. Then, carefully laying her coat on top of the bedclothes, she got back into bed.

****

Catford, London

"No?" Tom grinned. He was enjoying making her squirm. He ignored his steadily growing erection and tried to concentrate on the matter in hand. "So, the handbag it is then. We'll save the striptease for later." He stood up. "Where is it?"

Olive shook her head. There was a red mist swimming before her eyes and she was having trouble focusing. She lunged for the door but he was too quick. He caught her arm, swinging her towards him. She crashed into the table, knocking it against the cupboard. The ancient wireless juddered and then fell to the floor and went quiet. Tom grabbed her shoulders and began shaking her. Terrified, she kneed him hard in the groin and he yelled in pain and let her go. Olive tried to squeeze past him but she lost her balance and fell back on the table. This time, the bottle fell over, soaking everything in whisky, but Tom didn't notice. He moved towards her, his eyes filled with fury and slapped her hard across the face. Before she could recover, he put his hands around her throat.

"Tell me where the bag is." His voice was low and menacing, his fingers tightening, and she started to feel dizzy.

"No, please. You've taken everything else. Not that, please." Olive was gasping for breath and sobbing and, for a split second, Tom hesitated. He loosened his grip. It was enough. Her hands scrabbled across the table behind her looking for anything that could save her.

They alighted on the bottle and her fingers grasped the neck before smashing it hard over his head. He froze, his eyes staring at her, glazed and unfocused but he was still standing over her and his hands were still around her neck. She hit him again; still he wouldn't go down, despite the blood running in rivulets down his face, splashing on her cardigan. Terrified, she swung the bottle with more force and, this time, his grip loosened and he crumpled, first to his knees and then finally he fell forward, face down on the floor. Olive stared at him for several moments, waiting for him to get up. He didn't move and tentatively she put out her hand feeling for a pulse. There wasn't one. Olive sank back on her haunches and began sobbing uncontrollably. Then the lights went out and the bombs began falling.

****

Outside Bethune, Northern France

The house was set back from the road. Rolf drew up outside and the door opened. It had been a few days since she'd seen him and he'd said nothing on the journey, failing to even notice her new dress. She was uncertain whether to feel nervous, disappointed or excited, but settled on a mixture of all three. He climbed out, walked round and opened her door. She took his hand and allowed him to lead her into the house, through the ornate hallway and into a large drawing room on the left.

The room was full of men in uniform who all turned towards her when she entered. They had drinks in their hands but no one offered her one and, for the first time, she felt uneasy. In the centre of the room was a solitary chair. Rolf grabbed her arm and pulled her towards the chair, sat down and, without warning, pulled her across his lap.

Brigitte began to struggle but then one of the men came forward and held her arms, another took her legs, holding them slightly apart. Rolf lifted her dress, pulled down her dainty silk knickers and began spanking her hard. She could hear the laughter and then applause, tears beginning to form in her eyes.

Eventually Rolf finished, straightened her dress and told her to stand up.

"How many times do we have to do this? I've told you over and over I will punish you if you do not follow my instructions and now, on top of everything else, I hear you've been laughing with one of my men in the street. When will you learn not to disobey me? I have eyes and ears everywhere. I always know what you are doing. Do I make myself clear?" His voice echoed around the room.

Totally humiliated, Brigitte nodded. Rolf took her hand and led her towards a large table covered with food and drink.

"What would you like?" His tone was so normal, Brigitte wondered if she was dreaming. Without waiting for an answer, he poured her some wine and handed her a plate. "Help yourself. I'll be over there. Come and join me when you've finished."

Brigitte took her time. She could feel the men watching her and she wanted the floor to open up and swallow her, but nothing happened. Eventually, terrified Rolf might repeat his punishment if she didn't obey, she made her way towards him.

To her surprise, he introduced her to his companions, making no reference to what had happened earlier. His friends treated her with respect and she began to relax.

The evening finally finished and gradually the men left. The chair was still in the middle of the room and Brigitte glanced towards it nervously. But Rolf took her hand and led her upstairs to a large bedroom. She gazed around, wondering what the catch was. Sensing she was still nervous, he hastened to reassure her.

"Come to bed. I want to spend the night making love to you. I'm sorry I had to punish you earlier but I did warn you not to keep disobeying me. I don't like hurting you, but you must stop making me look foolish by sleeping with all and sundry the moment my back is turned."

He climbed into bed and Brigitte followed him. She was about to argue that laughing with someone was not the same as sleeping with him, but she thought better of it. What if he knew about Louis? What if that was really what this was about?

"I'm sorry, I won't do it again," she whispered.

"Good, then put your pretty lips to good use and suck me." He pushed her head down under the covers and she took him in her mouth.

****

Simonsdorf, Poland

The next morning was no warmer and outside felt bitterly cold, the biting wind going straight through their thin clothes. Having spent a restless night unable to get warm and wary of going into too deep a sleep in case they were bitten by the marauding rats, they paraded outside for roll call and the interminable counting commenced.

"I'm not sure what's worse," Joe said miserably. "The heat, sunburn and itchy shirts, or those bloody rats and this cold."

"This is nothing – it gets really freezing out here in the winter." Mitchell didn't seem bothered.

Joe gave him a withering look. "Thanks. I'll look forward to that, then."

"Nah, the war'll be over by then." Mitchell still sounded cheerful.

"You could well be right, but who's going to win?" Pete croaked.

"You really should go sick, you know." Joe was seriously concerned for his friend.

"I'm alright." Pete refused to acknowledge just how ill he felt. He was scared to report sick, in case they separated him from the others, so he was hoping he would get better without intervention. He had also heard rumours that, sometimes, no matter how ill you were, the doctor would say you were refusing to work and this would leave him open to some kind of arbitrary punishment. Punishments normally consisted of twenty eight days in solitary confinement with just basic rations, which were even less than he was getting now, but occasionally they consisted of public or private beatings, some of which he'd heard had ended by laughing guards defecating and urinating on the humiliated prisoner. On balance, he would take his chances and hope for the best.

****

Scotland

Pam finally fell into a fitful sleep, only to be woken by a loud siren at six o'clock. The sun was shining brightly through the window and, in the light of day, the room didn't seem quite so sparse. There was a large oak wardrobe and bedside table, a washstand with a jug of cold water and a towel hanging on a rail under the window. She washed and dressed quickly and hurried downstairs; it was much too cold to hang about. She could hear voices even before she reached the dining room and she followed her ears. The dining room was heated by a large roaring coal fire at one end and she stood in front of the hearth, enjoying the warmth on her legs.

"Welcome to the frozen north." Richard looked up from where he was sitting and indicated a seat at the large table. "Come and meet your fellow sufferers. As before, we speak in French at all times and only use code names."

Feeling slightly warmer, Pam looked at the other people sitting at the table. There were about ten people seated there, some of the men she didn't know, but to her delight, Giselle was there and Ricardo, Christophe, Felix and Claude. There was no sign of Irène. Pam wondered briefly if she'd been the female spy, or maybe she'd just not passed the selection tests.

After helping herself to some of the excellent food available: kippers, bacon, eggs, sausages, cereal and fruit juice and pots of hot coffee and tea, she sat down while Richard introduced her to some of the others. She ate quickly and, by eight o'clock, she was lined up with the others in warm sports clothes and they were sent for a ten mile run up and down the mountainous terrain backing onto the house. Even though Pam was reasonably fit, she still struggled up the steep mountains and was panting heavily by the time she got back to the house.

****

Lewisham Council Offices, London

The council was very busy dealing with all the people displaced by the bombing but Olive hardly noticed. She was expecting the police to arrive at any moment to arrest her, so she was surprised to find the day was almost over and nothing had happened.

The events of the previous night were still a blur, but she vaguely remembered Tom's lifeless body lying on her floor, the lights going out and the bombs falling all around. She had no idea how long she'd sat there but eventually she had realised her best chance of getting rid of the body was to try and make it look like he'd been killed in the bombing.

His body was too heavy to lift, so she'd rolled him up in the carpet and then opened the door to check there was no one around. Thanks to the bombers, her nosy neighbour had gone to the shelter much earlier. She looked out of the window. There was no one on the streets and the only light was coming from untended fires and the flashes of the incendiaries.

She wiped the sweat from her brow, took a deep breath and began dragging the carpet through the door towards the stairs. He was so heavy that, to start with, she couldn't move him at all and she began to panic. Taking another deep breath, she pulled with all her might and the carpet finally began to move. She had no idea how she reached the stairs but suddenly she was there. She hesitated. Perhaps she could just shove the carpet down the stairs, but then it might unravel and she would end up with blood everywhere. No, she would have to drag him down, step by step. Her arms were aching and she could feel the strain in her back, but she had no option; she had to keep going.

The body jolted her muscles every time she bounced him down a step but she ignored the pain, fear lending her strength. Somehow, she managed to get him into the street. Then she stopped, sweat dripping from her forehead and she tried to work out what to do with him. Her heart was racing. She couldn't stand there with a dead body for much longer. Despite the intensity of the bombing, someone was bound to come along eventually. She cursed herself for not thinking things through properly. She should have worked out where to dump the corpse first, before moving it.

In desperation she looked up. Searchlights trawled across the sky, occasionally picking out a bomber or his fighter escort and she spotted one directly above. Her own problems momentarily forgotten, she watched mesmerised while the bomb door opened and then she realised the bombs were heading straight for her. She looked around for somewhere to shelter but there was nowhere to go. The first explosion shook the street further down, the second hit the building opposite. The blast threw Olive off her feet and as she shook her head free of dust and debris, she realised she couldn't hear a thing. But even in her debilitated state, she knew this was a chance she couldn't afford to miss. Within moments, she was dragging the body across the road and unravelling it into the large hole that had miraculously appeared. She glanced around for some debris and found some broken timbers, then pushed the wood on top of Tom and stood back. She was panting from the exertion, but she also felt exhilarated. Kurt still loved her and he had rescued her once again.

Chapter Thirteen

Outside Bethune, Northern France

Brigitte was floating on a cloud. Rolf had been so tender and loving after her humiliation, she was convinced he was in love with her and she was also sure she loved him. He was now treating her much better, reserving their games for the times they were alone. She hadn't seen Louis for a few days but she didn't mind. She didn't want to upset Rolf again and, if she was honest, she wasn't really missing Louis anymore. Rolf had just taken her shopping and bought her some new underwear. He had chosen exactly the type he wanted her to wear and, although the corset was rather uncomfortable, pushing her breasts up and pulling her waist in very tight, Brigitte would not have thought of complaining.

"I'll pick you up at eight. Wear something nice... perhaps that new dress I bought you and don't forget your corset. I can't wait to see you in it." Rolf smiled at her and squeezed her leg. That was the other change. Although he was still paying her, he was also buying her clothes and jewellery.

Brigitte smiled back at him and then gazed out of the window. The weather was growing worse. She was grateful she was in a warm car. She would have hated to be walking outside in the cold easterly wind. She was just about to comment on this when she saw Louis. He was in the field to her right and he was staring straight at her, his face a mask of fury.

****

Toulouse, Southern France

Jeanne stared at yet another pile of anonymous letters denouncing Jews. She would have liked to just throw the letters away, but the system for sorting the post made that impossible and so she had no option but to file them neatly into folders and take them upstairs to the officer who was responsible for investigating the accusations.

This was one part of her job she hated. She had no time for Monsieur Plombière, the policeman to whom she sometimes had to deliver the letters. He was a short, rather squat man with piggy eyes and a way of looking her up and down which made her feel dirty. She also had the uncomfortable feeling he could see right through her and he knew she was Jewish and was just waiting for a chance to unmask her. Aware of just how dangerous her position was, she always took great care to be scrupulously polite to him, ignoring his leers and sexually loaded remarks. There was a certain amount of gossip amongst the female staff, which made her even more wary of ever being on her own with him. She always made a point of leaving the door open and appearing as though she was in a great hurry and was expected back downstairs immediately.

Eve was conscious of the rumours and usually tried to ensure Jeanne did not have to take the correspondence up to him. However, the front reception was often busy and she couldn't always leave Jeanne on her own to deal with the numerous enquiries, some of which she didn't yet have the knowledge or ability to deal with.

"I'm sorry, Jeanne, can you take the letters upstairs today, please? There's some for Black Market, but the rest are for Anti-Jewish Affairs. I am waiting for an important phone call, otherwise I'd go myself. Will you be alright?"

Jeanne nodded. She wasn't particularly happy but, if she was quick, she shouldn't have a problem. She took the two folders and began the laborious walk up the three flights of stairs to the Black Market and

Anti-Jewish Affairs offices which were located at the top of the building. The third floor was quiet and she realised many of the staff had gone to lunch. She hadn't noticed it was that time already. She felt the first stirrings of unease but she ignored her instincts, knowing she only had to deliver the letters and she could go back downstairs.

****

Simonsdorf, Poland

The cold made them clumsy. Joe couldn't believe anyone would have deliberately tried to sabotage the line after what had happened before. They were trying to raise some sleepers off the ground when there was a terrific crash from behind and the air was filled with thick dust, soil and debris.

Rushing to see what had happened, Joe was horrified to see two trains had derailed and several of the men were caught under the wreckage. One of the men had his leg trapped under the heavy engine and, by the time Joe arrived, others were trying desperately to pull him out.

The guards were shouting orders no one could hear above the screams of the injured and the prisoners yelling instructions at each other in various languages. Eventually, using only their own strength and sleepers as levers, they managed to free the man. He was unconscious, which Joe considered to be a blessing. The man's foot was completely crushed, the bones and sinews sticking out through mangled flesh covered in blood.

"I think they'll have to amputate his leg." One of the men nearest Joe was speaking. "Poor bastard." Joe was unable to think of anything to say. He was grateful it hadn't been him and then he felt guilty. "That's if they bother to take him to hospital. They'll probably just leave him there to die," the man continued.

Joe stared at him in disbelief. "Surely they can't be so callous?"

The man checked the guards weren't within earshot. "They've done it before." And he went back to work, leaving Joe speechless.

Time wore on, the man drifted in and out of consciousness and the cries of pain reduced to whimpers. Joe looked around him helplessly and, eventually deciding he had to do something, he put down his shovel with the intention of approaching one of the guards.

"What the hell are you doing, Price?" Mitchell's urgent whisper stopped him in his tracks.

"I'm going to see if I can get one of the guards to help him."

"Don't be bloody stupid. The mood they're in, you're likely to get shot."

"But I can't just do nothing," Joe replied, anguish written all over his face. Then he stopped. Another prisoner was approaching a guard. He had chosen carefully, waiting for one of the older men, a less fanatical soldier than his younger comrades. Joe could tell by the body language he wasn't getting anywhere and then he caught his breath. One of the more brutish and violent guards who seemed to delight in humiliating the prisoners, was heading towards them. Despite his fear, Joe continued to walk nearer. He knew exactly what was going to happen, but he was still trying to prevent the inevitable violence he knew would follow.

"Leave it, pal." Mitchell grabbed hold of his arm.

Joe struggled to free himself but he was too late. The German casually raised his rifle and shot the prisoner who was arguing.

Joe stopped struggling, glad Mitchell had intervened and, with a heavy heart, turned back to pick up his shovel. There was no sound from the injured man now and Joe assumed he must be either unconscious or dead. Either way, he realised he had to accept there was nothing anyone could do for him.

****

La Couture, Northern France

Louis stared in disbelief while the German staff car drove past him. In the front seat, bold as brass, was Brigitte. He had no doubts it was her:

she looked straight at him. Louis clenched his fists and wondered how long she had been playing him for a fool. Well, not any longer. Not only was he no longer prepared to be treated like a mug, he had too much to lose now. He couldn't afford to have a relationship with a girl who was sleeping with the enemy, not when he was hiding airmen. His eyes filled with sudden tears and he turned away from the road. He had really loved her, otherwise he would never have given her another chance.

He couldn't even talk to his friends or his mother about how devastated he felt, because they all thought he'd finished with her ages ago. Well, enough was enough. He hardened his heart and put her out of his mind. He had more important things to do than moon over a girl who obviously didn't care about him at all. Even worse, his mother and his friends, everyone except him, could see what she was like. He would be very careful next time he met a girl. No one would ever treat him like this again.

****

Toulouse, Southern France

The office for Investigation into the Black Market was empty, the small staff either out working or at lunch. Jeanne left the files in the in-tray and, closing the door behind her, she headed towards the office for Anti-Jewish Affairs. She walked along the corridor, in her mind already wondering what she could cook for tea. There was no answer to her knock, and she breathed a sigh of relief as she entered. The office was empty, so she walked over to the desk and placed the folder in the filing tray marked 'in'. She turned and stifled a gasp. Monsieur Plombière had come in quietly behind her. He closed the door and stood, barring her way, his arms folded and an unpleasant expression on his face.

"You're always in such a hurry, Jeanne." She was startled he knew her name. She took a breath and tried hard to still her pounding heart.

"I have to deliver these and then go to lunch." She cursed herself; much better to have said they were busy in reception.

"I'm sure you can spare me a little of your precious time." He leered and took a step closer. Even from a distance, she could smell the garlic on his breath and she tried unsuccessfully to control her fear, realising instinctively this was only arousing him more.

"I really do have to go. Eve is very busy on reception and there were lots of people waiting when I came up, so I have to hurry back down or the queues will get even longer." Jeanne knew she was gabbling but she couldn't help herself.

He made no attempt to move, enjoying her discomfort. Desperate to get out of there, she tried to squeeze past him, then realised too late she had done exactly what he wanted her to. She was now within touching distance of him and, to her horror, he lost no time in taking advantage of her naïveté.

One arm grasped her wrist while the other grabbed her chin and brought her face towards his. She tried to wriggle away but he was much too strong and, when she opened her mouth to scream, he spun her round, forced her arm up her back and put a large, dirty hand across her mouth, successfully stifling her efforts to make any noise.

"Mmm, so much nicer when you fight against me, you know." His breath rasped across her nostrils making her feel sick and she struggled even more. Before she could really take in what was happening, he had half dragged, half pushed her across the room, away from the door and safety. She found herself face down across his desk, the weight of his body forcing her hard against its paper-strewn surface, bruising her ribs and making her gasp in pain. His hand was still across her mouth, making it impossible for her to scream and summon help and, while she struggled feebly, he inserted his knee in between her legs and forced them apart.

His left hand was reaching under her body, trying to rip open her blouse. To her horror, she heard the buttons popping and, when the material came away in his hand, he pulled hard, exposing her bra. He lifted her body towards him, away from the desk just enough to insert his left hand into her bra, freeing her breast and squeezing her nipple hard. Jeanne squealed and he laughed.

His right hand was still across her mouth, preventing her from breathing properly, she began to feel dizzy and there was a rushing sound in her head. Her resistance grew more feeble and she began to lose consciousness. She was only dimly aware of his left hand forcing her skirt up and squeezing her buttocks through the cotton of her knickers.

She made one last effort, raising her head, but he slammed it hard into the desk, before letting go of her mouth and undoing the buttons on his trousers.

His movements were so quick and practised, Jeanne was sure this wasn't the first time he had done this. Taking in a gulp of air, anger overcame her and she shoved back with all her might. For a split second the pressure eased, but then he forced her back down and began taunting her, his hoarse voice loud in her ear. "Good girl, keep struggling. Come on, fight me; you know you love it." His voice was alternately rasping and cajoling and his breathing became ragged while his desire rose. He pressed her head into the desk with one hand, while the other ripped away what was left of her knickers exposing her to his erect penis. With a cry of delight, he thrust forward and Jeanne instinctively moved slightly, causing him to stab her buttocks.

"You bitch!" he shouted. He hand pressing her head into the desk now grabbed hold of her hair and yanked back hard whilst he repositioned himself, ready to thrust again.

Chapter Fourteen

Outside Bethune, Northern France

Brigitte was horrified. Although she was no longer in love with Louis, she hadn't wanted to alienate him. She might need him in the future. She thought about the look on his face. He'd seemed so sad and angry. Perhaps he really had loved her. She half twisted in her seat but the car had moved round a bend and she could no longer see him.

"I asked about your dress?" Rolf had slowed the car, taken his eyes off the road and was staring at her. She pulled herself together. Louis was in the past; Rolf was her future.

"Yes, of course. It's such a beautiful dress; you have really good taste." She fluttered her eyelashes and smiled, and Rolf returned his attention to the road.

Brigitte made a supreme effort to get Louis' face out of her mind and concentrate on the coming evening. They were going to a ball at a large country house somewhere on the way to Paris and would be staying the night. She had been really looking forward to the dance until she saw Louis. Now she felt awful. She glanced out of the window and recalled their last meeting. She would have gone away with him; she'd begged him to take her somewhere else, but he preferred to stay with his mother. So be it. She hardened her heart. Louis'd had his chance. She would not allow him to ruin the night for her, or the rest of her life. "Goodbye Louis," she muttered to herself.

"Sorry, I didn't hear you?" Rolf was particularly attentive today and Brigitte smiled at him.

"Nothing, I was just thinking how lucky I am to have met you."

Rolf smiled to himself. He could have had the farm boy deported to some German labour camp but manipulating Brigitte was more fun, so he had decided the best way to get rid of his rival was to let him see the two of them together. Having driven past the property a few times, he had timed their journey in the hope Louis would see Brigitte in the car with him. Judging by the expression on Brigitte's face, his plan had been totally successful. Brigitte would no longer run back to Louis if things weren't going her way. She only had him and her father now. Time to start putting the next part of his plan together.

****

Toulouse, Southern France

Suddenly his hand was gone, the pressure eased completely and Jeanne could feel the air on her exposed body. She was vaguely aware of shouting and what sounded like a struggle and then felt a gentle arm on her shoulder and heard Gabriel's voice softly saying her name.

Shaking with relief, she eased herself off the desk and allowed herself to be enveloped in his safe embracing hug, oblivious to her near naked state.

"Are you alright, Jeanne? He didn't hurt you?" Gabriel was looking at her with tender concern, but there was also another expression on his face which she couldn't immediately fathom. Then she realised she had never seen him angry before. She nodded, her body still shaking with fear and her brain still numb from what had so nearly happened.

"Yes, I think so. I... he..." She stopped, unable to express what had happened or how she felt.

"It's alright, you don't need to explain. It's not the first time he's done this." Gabriel stopped, realising he'd said too much. Looking deep into her eyes he continued, "You must never be alone with him again.

Do you understand?" She nodded, the fear returning. He hugged her close and continued softly, "You have made a bad enemy there; you will need to be careful now, Jeanne. Even if you do nothing against the law, these are strange times and you do not need to be guilty of anything to end up in a camp or even disappear." Seeing the frightened expression on her face, he tried to lighten his words slightly. "I will do my utmost to look after you."

Gabriel resisted the urge to take her in his arms and kiss her. Jeanne had been subject to one assault already today. Just because he liked her, there was no reason to assume she felt the same. The sudden realisation about how he felt made him dizzy, but he was more certain of these feelings than he had ever been. The only thing that had ever come close to this degree of certainty was his determination, while he was growing up, that he wanted to be a policeman.

He had always known he didn't love his fiancée; not really. Isabelle had good connections, he was an ambitious man and he had allowed himself to be dragged along on the crest of the wave of her enthusiasm.

Until he met Jeanne, he'd been quite content to drift along and let fate take its course. But now he realised Isabelle's humour was actually scathing and sarcastic and was always aimed at belittling people. Her 'sense of fun' was the same and she was shallow and selfish; her only topic of conversation was herself. She had no compassion or sympathy. He felt uncomfortable. For him not to have seen this must mean he was the same. The real attraction was her body and her sexual prowess, but even these were beginning to pall and he had already found himself making excuses not to make love to her. Meeting Jeanne had opened his eyes in ways he could not have imagined and he knew he couldn't base his marriage purely on sexual attraction; there had to be more. The war had been a godsend; at least it had prevented him from setting a wedding date and making the biggest mistake of his life.

"Come on, I'll take you home." With reluctance, he withdrew his arms and took off his jacket, giving the coat to Jeanne to cover her blouse which was ripped beyond repair. She was still in shock, so he put his arm around her, guided her down the stairs and out to his car, making no attempt to break the companionable silence.

They pulled away from the kerb and Jeanne spoke quietly. "I don't want to go home yet. Can we go somewhere while I pull myself together? I don't want Angel and Papa to see me like this."

"Of course." Gabriel swung the car away from the police headquarters and headed for the road leading out of the town and towards the hills. They drove along in silence and Jeanne looked out of the open window, feeling the breeze blowing away the strain and stress of the last hour. The road seemed vaguely familiar to Jeanne and she recognised it as the one they had first taken into Toulouse, a lifetime ago. Her mother had been alive then and she began to sob silently, gradually releasing the grief she had struggled so hard not to give in to since she had first known her mother was dying.

****

Simonsdorf, Poland

By the end of the shift, Joe was exhausted, his back aching and his eyes itching from the dust and the cold wind blowing relentlessly through them. One of the other prisoners had grabbed an opportunity to take a look at the badly injured man and came away shaking his head. The other prisoners who had been injured had struggled manfully on through the rest of the day, knowing medical help was not going to be forthcoming until they returned to camp. Joe was increasingly concerned about Pete, whose cough became much worse during the afternoon. By the end of the shift, he could hardly stand.

"You are definitely going sick, even if we have to drag you there," Joe said and Bert and Mitchell nodded in agreement, concerned about Pete's pallor and the hacking cough.

Pete said nothing. He no longer had the strength to argue and felt so ill, he didn't care what the Germans would do to him. Once back on the camp, they frogmarched an uncomplaining Pete to the sick hut where they were told by a surly guard to come back in the morning. No amount of persuasion, gesticulation or shouting had any effect on the guard who just kept repeating they should come back the next day.

Eventually, they gave up and half dragged, half carried Pete back to their hut, where they helped him onto his bunk.

"Here, have my blanket." Joe was horrified by the way Pete was shaking and shivering and by the wild look in his eyes.

"Yeah, have mine too, mate." Mitchell and Bert added theirs to the growing pile covering him.

"Come on, let's leave him to sleep. There's not much else we can do." Bert guided Joe away to his side of the hut and they sat on his bunk in silence, feeling useless.

"Your friend, he not well?" Joe looked up in surprise to see a Polish soldier standing in front of him. He nodded, not sure what else to say. "I have medicine," the man continued.

Joe looked at him warily, wondering what the catch was. Seeing his expression, the man smiled and introduced himself. "I am Corporal Aleksander Kubis, of the Polish Cavalry. Put this in hot water and get your friend to drink slowly." He handed Joe a small piece of paper which Joe carefully unwrapped. Inside was some powder.

"What is that?" Mitchell asked curiously.

"Willow bark." The answer came from a tall lanky soldier who everyone called 'Beanpole'. "It's what they used before aspirin was invented, you know in the middle ages or something. It's really good… worked for me." He smiled at Aleksander. "I was very ill. Honestly, give it a try."

Joe looked at the others and then shrugged. What had they got to lose?

"Thank you." Mitchell went to scrounge some hot water. He was only gone a few minutes before returning with a steaming mug into which Joe sprinkled the powder. They sat Pete up and persuaded him to sip the liquid. He pulled faces but otherwise was docile and uncomplaining. Once he was finished, he lay back down and they covered him with the blankets again.

"Give him this in night." Aleksander handed them some more powder and, smiling broadly, left.

Joe stared at the others. "How did he know?" Then he looked at Beanpole. "Thanks, mate."

"Nothing to do with me." Beanpole looked up from his book. "Spooky is Alek. He always knows when someone's ill, but he's a bloody good doctor, much better than the German quack." He went back to his book, leaving Joe and the others to look at each other in confusion.

****

Toulouse, Southern France

Gabriel pulled off the road into a large lay-by overlooking the city. In the distance, the warm azure blue of the River Garonne could be seen snaking its way lazily through the city and, beyond, shone the smaller, darker blue lines of the Canal du Midi.

"Are you alright? You look… strange." Jeanne had looked up to find Gabriel staring at her, an odd expression on his face.

The question took Gabriel by surprise. He had been unable to stop himself watching her and he realised the expression on his face puzzling her so much was the turmoil going on within him as he fought to stop himself reaching out to her.

"I'm sorry. I…" He looked down in amazement as her hand crept towards his.

She twisted in her seat so she could look deep into his eyes and he could no longer stop himself. He put his arm round her and pulled her gently towards him until her face was inches from his own. She made no move to stop him and exultantly he touched his lips to hers, gently at first and then more insistently, delighted to feel her returning the kiss with passion.

"I'm sorry, Jeanne, I never meant for that to happen." He hesitated. "I know you have a boyfriend and I have a fiancée, but I've liked you for ages and seeing that man…" He stopped. The words sounded lame, even to him. He tried again. "I wanted to kill him for hurting you but what he did made me realise I have feelings for you." He wondered if he was going too fast but she was smiling.

"You've been so kind to me since Mama died, you've been there for me when I needed a shoulder to cry on but I thought you felt sorry for me. I never dreamt you really liked me." Jeanne was staring at him in amazement. Although her thoughts were full of him, she'd presumed he was just being nice and she was being silly to imagine he could find her attractive and interesting. Everything she'd heard about Isabelle from Eve and the other policemen pointed to Isabelle being a beautiful and clever lady, even if she wasn't particularly well liked by them. How could she possibly compete? She was a nobody; how could he prefer her to his accomplished fiancée?

Jeanne searched his face for signs he was lying. But all she could see was tenderness as he confirmed his feelings. "You are silly, Jeanne. How could I not like you? You are beautiful, funny, kind and thoughtful." *Everything Isabelle is not.* He didn't voice the last thought. Instead he put his arms around her and they sat in silence for a while. Eventually, Gabriel drew back. "Do you think your father would object if I took you out?"

"No, I don't think so. He'll be pleased I'm happy." Jeanne crossed her fingers. The only objection she could think her father would have, apart from the fact she was Jewish and he was a policeman working for a fiercely anti-Semitic regime, was her age and, of course, the fact Gabriel was engaged, something she had only just mentioned to her father. She was only seventeen and would not be eighteen until the following January. "What about your fiancée?" A frown appeared on her face when she remembered what Eve had said about her.

"Don't worry about Isabelle. Leave her to me. Everything will be fine," Gabriel replied with a confidence he didn't feel. He had a horrible feeling Isabelle would be very vindictive and he suddenly shivered. The old saying about someone walking over his grave came unbidden into his mind but he pushed it away. She would just have to accept his decision; after all, what could she do? He was going to take Jeanne out and that was the end of it.

Chapter Fifteen

Scotland

Richard had become increasingly fond of Pam. Having followed her to Scotland with the express purpose of spending more time with her and getting to know her better, he realised within hours what a bad idea that was. All agents were told repeatedly of the danger of allowing themselves to become emotionally involved with anyone they worked with, in case it clouded their judgement and put the mission in danger. He had allowed himself to fall into the trap he spent most of his time preaching to his students about and had become too attached. Richard cursed under his breath. He had no idea whether she felt the same way as him and he couldn't ask her. He would have to do the sensible thing for both of them. Reluctantly, he took himself back to London on the pretext of having some urgent work to do. In reality, he needed to put some distance between them, both physically and emotionally.

Pam was disappointed but, although she missed him, she was so busy, she had little time to worry about the reason for his sudden departure.

****

Aldershot, England

Much to Marcel's delight, they had finally been given orders to be ready to deploy. Although they were given no more information, this only served to fire their imaginations even more.

They were issued with complete sets of British tropical dress to go with their battledress, including a rather large, lozenge-shaped enamelled tricolour shield which was supposed to go on the tropical helmet. Marcel looked at the shield in delight and proudly sewed the sign into place. He finished and glanced around. He was the only one to have done so. Charles answered his unspoken query. "The shield will make us stick out like a sore thumb and make us a visible target. I'd dump it if I were you. I bet you don't see the Foreign Legion chaps wearing them."

Marcel realised Charles was speaking the truth. The shield was highly visible and would probably stand out, even at night. He blushed. There were so many things he didn't know yet and, although he was of a similar age to his friends, in experience he was years behind. Feeling dejected, he removed the shield and wondered if he would ever be their equal.

Pierre smiled. "Don't worry, Marcel, after a week on the front line, you'll know all the tricks we do. So, if we're not going to France, where are we going? Obviously somewhere hot."

This fuelled more speculation and discussion but, still feeling slightly stupid after his blunder, Marcel busied himself in packing up his kit and trying to ignore his building nerves.

"I think you're all wasting your time. It's much more likely to be another training exercise." Antoine yawned. Having come in late the night before, he looked like he'd not had much sleep. However, Antoine was always pessimistic and invariably looked tired, so no one took much notice, except Paul who was determined to have the last word.

"So why give us all the tropical kit, then?" he asked, but Antoine was no longer paying attention. He was hunting for bits of his uniform he had lost. After disrupting most of their kit bags looking for a pair of socks he was sure he had misplaced, he eventually found them tucked under his bedroll, much to everyone's amusement.

"I hope you're going to wash those before we leave," Charles said as the ripe smell of sweaty feet reached them.

"Sorry, no time." Antoine smiled and packed the dirty socks in amongst his clean ones to groans of disgust from Marcel. With the others laughing, they left the tents that had been their home for the past few weeks and paraded in the square. Marcel was surprised to see virtually everyone in the camp was lined up ready to go. They stood waiting patiently until they heard the sound of trucks pulling into the camp.

Pierre muttered to Marcel out of the side of his mouth, "Looks like we're off then. Action at last."

Marcel nodded, too excited and nervous to answer.

****

Lambeth Hospital, London

"If you stand there much longer, you'll fall asleep." Peggy smiled at the sound of the familiar voice and turned around to find Chris standing close behind her.

"I found myself thinking about how things are so different from last year and forgot what I came in here for." She yawned. "Sorry, I've never been this tired. I was hoping eventually I might get used to no sleep, but it hasn't happened yet."

Chris gave a sympathetic smile. "It's surprising what punishment the human body can stand." He changed the subject. "Perhaps you were looking for clean sheets?"

Peggy blushed. "Yes, I'm sure that's what I came up here for!" She took the ones he was holding out to her and, turning to leave the laundry cupboard, she bumped straight into Helen who had come to look for her.

"I wondered where you'd got to. Sister's about to have a fit; she thinks you've gone missing."

"I didn't realise I'd been gone so long." Peggy was horrified. "Maybe I did fall asleep."

"Don't worry, Peggy. We're all exhausted and in danger of making mistakes." Chris glanced at his watch and the smile disappeared. "Talking of which, I'd better go. I was due on the surgical ward about ten minutes ago. Bye girls," he finished with a quick smile and left them staring at each other in amusement.

"He is rather nice, isn't he?" Helen watched to see if Peggy would blush, which she did.

"I don't know, I hadn't noticed.'" Peggy's reply was rather too abrupt and she turned away, so Helen couldn't see the red stain deepening on her cheeks.

****

Toulouse, Southern France

They sat making plans until the sun began to set and Jeanne said guiltily, "Goodness, I must get home. Papa will be worried sick about me. I didn't notice the time. I'm so happy, I just want to stay here forever and not have to return to the real world." She smiled. "I know how silly that sounds."

"No, I know how you feel. But the sooner I tell Isabelle and I speak to your father to ask his permission to take you out, the quicker we can start seeing each other." Reluctantly, Jeanne nodded and Gabriel turned the car round and they headed back to the city.

Jean-Paul was waiting anxiously on the small balcony when she arrived home and when the couple went indoors and he saw her clothes, his look of concern turned to one of horror. "What on earth happened to you?" He listened to Gabriel's explanation and his face grew dark. "Will this man be prosecuted?" He could barely manage to contain his anger.

Gabriel shook his head. "Plombière has friends in high places. It's best not to rock the boat too much. Like I said to Jeanne, these are not normal times and its best not to antagonise too many people. I'm sorry, there's nothing I would like better, but I do think it's safer to do nothing, at least for now."

Jean-Paul stared at Jeanne. "Is this what you want, chérie?"

Jeanne nodded and glanced at Gabriel. "There's something else."

Jean-Paul watched them, an expression of concern on his face.

Gabriel cleared his throat. "I would like your permission to start walking out with your daughter, sir. I know we have not known each other very long and we have probably not followed any of the normal customs but, like I said before, these are not normal times." He stopped and, before Jean-Paul could answer, he smiled at Jeanne. "I like your daughter very much. I think I've known this for a while, but today made me realise I needed to do and say something about how I feel."

"I thought you already had a fiancée? How will she take the news you have found someone else?"

Gabriel wondered how much he should say. Something told him he should be totally honest with Jeanne's father. "This is going to sound awful, but I never felt about Isabelle the way I feel about Jeanne. I think I just went along with her because it was politically expedient and would probably help my career." He shrugged uncomfortably, not liking this unexpected glimpse into his flawed personality, even less having to admit it in front of Jeanne.

Jean-Paul knew the truth when he heard it. "And will she just accept your decision?"

"I don't know, to be honest. She can be very malicious and vindictive when she wants to and I don't mind admitting I am not particularly looking forward to telling her."

"Maybe you should finish with your fiancée first and then wait a while before you start to go out with Jeanne officially?" Jean-Paul stared into his eyes. "I have no objection to Jeanne walking out with you but I do not wish her to be subject to gossip or worse at the hands of your spurned fiancée and I'm sure you feel the same." His expression softened. "I know it's hard to wait, especially when you are young but, given the circumstances, it might be sensible. She may still suspect you were together before you broke things off with her, but at least this way she won't be publicly humiliated."

There was silence and then Jeanne spoke. "He's right, Gabriel. We must stop seeing each other for a few weeks, maybe longer. You have to tell her straight away, because the sooner you tell her, the quicker we can be together." She let go of his hand and turned away, so he couldn't see how difficult it had been for her to say those words. She couldn't risk him arguing or she would weaken. There was no guarantee keeping things quiet would lessen the antagonism Isabelle would feel towards them, but it couldn't hurt.

"Jeanne…" Gabriel stopped. He knew what they said made sense. "I would love to argue with you both but I know you are right. We will stop seeing each other outside of work until at least Christmas. That should be long enough, I think." He looked at Jeanne and her father, hoping they would not insist on longer. To his relief they both nodded. Trying to ignore the anguish on Jeanne's face, he kissed her gently. "We could start to see each other officially just before the Christmas holidays. I could ask you out at work, in front of Eve and then we could take things from there. What do you think?" Jeanne nodded. Gabriel looked into her eyes, trying to print the image of her face in his mind and, not trusting himself to speak anymore, kissed her once more. He closed his eyes, savouring the feel of her lips on his and the smell of her hair and then reluctantly turned and left the flat.

Jeanne threw herself into Jean-Paul's arms and sobbed her heart out. Hearing the noise, Angel came rushing in from her room, her eyes wide in fear. "What's happened? Are you hurt Jeanne?" Her voice sounded hoarse but, otherwise, perfectly normal.

Jeanne flung her arms around the little girl. "Angel! You're speaking. Oh, I'm so pleased to hear your voice again. No, I'm fine, honestly." Jeanne hastily wiped away her tears, concerned she didn't cause Angel to lapse back into silence. "Would you like some hot milk and a story?" she asked and was rewarded with a beaming smile.

"Yes, please. Are there any sweets?" They burst out laughing and Jeanne suddenly remembered her mother's saying: *every cloud has a silver lining*. She smiled, feeling her mother was very close.

****

A House on the Road to Paris

The ball was in full swing by the time they arrived. Brigitte felt uncomfortable. The room was full of men in uniform and she was reminded of the last time he'd bought her to a similar gathering. But her fears were groundless. This time there were also women present, wearing elegant dresses and fur stoles. Rolf took her hand, guided her to a group of men and began introducing her. Some were with their wives, but most had girlfriends and she wondered how many wives were back in Germany waiting for their errant husbands. She wondered briefly whether Rolf was married; she'd never thought to ask him. Not that it mattered: he was unlikely to tell her the truth anyway.

The waiter came past with a tray of drinks and Rolf took one, handing the glass to her with a smile. The women were friendly and Brigitte began to relax.

The conversation flowed around her, mostly in German so she spent the time savouring the atmosphere and answering the occasional question in French from one of the officers. They all treated her with respect and Brigitte started to enjoy herself. Rolf asked her to dance and held her close while they waltzed around the floor.

"I have a surprise for you." Brigitte paled but he smiled. "I've booked us two days in Paris. I know I should probably have told you before, but you can buy anything you need when we get there and we can spend the days walking around the city seeing the sights and the nights enjoying ourselves."

Brigitte stared at him in astonishment and then threw her arms around him.

"Thank you so much. I've never been to Paris. I can't wait."

He laughed. "We'll stay here tonight and then drive on tomorrow. You can telephone your father tomorrow morning before we leave and tell him, so he doesn't worry."

Brigitte could hardly believe her ears. Rolf was turning into everything she could ever want in a man. For the first time in her life, Brigitte was head over heels in love.

****

England

The journey northwards seemed interminable. The trucks careered around bends, screeching to a halt at junctions and, several times, they had to retrace their route because the drivers got lost. The lack of signposts hindered their progress because of the drivers' unfamiliarity with English roads. At least twice, they suffered near collisions because they were driving on the wrong side of the road, much to frustration of irate farmers who nearly ended up in the ditches running either side of the narrow country lanes.

Eventually they arrived in Liverpool and were hurried aboard one of two large troopships. Fascinated, Marcel noted the name of theirs was the *Westernland*.

Marcel followed the others down to the lower deck and made himself as comfortable as he could, given the amount of equipment and the close proximity of the other soldiers, many of whom were obviously more experienced than him. Glancing around, he saw several had closed their eyes and were already asleep. Taking a deep breath, Marcel tried to follow suit.

****

Catford, London

The box was still in the corner where Tom had left it. She would have to get rid of whatever was inside, but first Olive just wanted to savour the feeling of being safe. There had been nothing in the newspapers, no police had turned up at work and she was beginning to think she might have got away with Tom's murder.

She glanced down at Kurt's letter and smiled. For the first time in ages, she could sit and read in peace without worrying.

My darling Olive,

I hope this letter finds you well. The young man you asked about is in a prison camp in Poland, so you can tell your cousin he is away from any fighting. Providing he does not try to escape or do anything stupid, he will be safe there until the end of the war, which hopefully will be soon.

I'm not sure how you can give her this information but at least you know he is alright.

I am really worried about you now. There are pictures in German newspapers showing the destruction in London and I have no idea what I can do to keep you safe. People must be very scared and confused seeing their city destroyed, especially as the RAF does not appear to be able to stop German bombers. Perhaps your government will soon see reason and sign an armistice with us, like the French have done. They don't have to worry about Paris being destroyed and Germans and French are getting on very well together. I am sure the same could be true in Britain if only your politicians would see sense.

I'm sorry, my love. I don't mean to go on, I am just so frustrated at not being with you. Please let me know whether the bombing has reached you, or whether you are outside the danger area. I imagine all sorts of things happening to you and I hear food is becoming scarce again, because so many of your ships are being sunk in the Atlantic.

Please write and reassure me you are safe, my beloved. And when you go to bed tonight, put on your corset for me and think of me caressing you and making love to you…

Olive stopped reading. She could never wear the underwear he'd bought her again because it would remind her of that night. Even thinking of sex made her feel sick. All she could see were Tom's hands exploring her body, touching her and making her do things she didn't want to do. He had spoilt everything and, even though he was dead, things would never be the same again.

****

Simonsdorf, Poland

"Where have you been, Joe?" Pete looked up. He was already looking better, much to Joe's relief. "Are you alright? You look a bit shocked."

"Yes, I'm fine. I went to see that fortune teller chap in hut four." He ignored their shouts of derision and continued, "Honestly, it's really scary how much he knew. You want to try him. He's good." Joe found himself unable to express just how incredible he had found the experience, even if it had given him a few things to think about.

"It's all a con, Joe. How much did he swizzle you out of?" Pete was looking at him with something akin to pity on his face.

"Nothing. He didn't charge." Joe was gratified to see the look of surprise on Pete's face.

"No, he's right, Pete. My Mom went to see one back home and she was absolutely amazing. I think there is definitely something in all that stuff. What's his name, Joe, I think I'll go and see him myself." Mitchell was looking at him with enthusiasm and, grateful to have some support in the face of the other's scepticism, Joe gave him the man's name.

"Well, I think you're both mad," Bert said, shutting his book and pulling his blanket around him in an attempt to block out the cold draft circulating the hut.

Joe lay down but he couldn't sleep. The fortune teller had been rather vague about Peggy and, when he did eventually fall into a restless sleep, his dreams were punctuated with images of her. However, every time he tried to get close, she seemed to move further away from him.

****

Toulouse, Southern France

The conversation with Isabelle had gone exactly as Gabriel had expected. She immediately accused him of finding someone else and, despite his vehement denials, he was sure she was not convinced. After the accusations had come tears and, when they had failed to move him, threats. Although he'd tried to shrug these off as the empty threats of a spurned woman, something inside warned him to be careful. He was reasonably certain she could not affect his career or his safety, but Jeanne was another matter.

He thought back to when he'd first met Jeanne, how she had intrigued him and the instinctive feeling he'd had she was hiding something. But, once he grew closer to her, his interest in whatever she was keeping secret had diminished. He knew she was the one Isabelle would target and the only way to protect her was to cut off all contact for a while. In fact, he was seriously considering waiting until after Christmas before taking her out officially, just to be on the safe side. The thought made him sad but it was probably better to wait just a bit longer than to rush in and risk losing her completely. The incident with Plombière had only increased the danger and he was almost tempted to suggest she look for alternative employment away from the police station. But the thought of not being able to at least see her and exchange the occasional pleasantry, was too much for him to bear, so he convinced himself his fears were unfounded.

Chapter Sixteen

Paris

The city was everything Brigitte could have hoped. Rolf was the perfect gentleman, taking her to see the Eiffel Tower, Notre Dame, the Bastille, art galleries and museums. They strolled along the banks of the Seine holding hands, like any other lovers and he spent a fortune buying her several new outfits from various fashion houses. Brigitte gasped at the prices.

"Nothing's too good for my Brigitte!" He smiled when he saw her shocked expression. He was like a different person, taking her to expensive restaurants and even explaining the wine menu. From barely talking to her unless he was barking orders at her, Rolf had suddenly become a witty conversationalist with a stream of funny stories and even the patience to explain politics to her; something she'd never been interested in before. Louis was completely forgotten while she basked in Rolf's open admiration, trying on her new clothes for him and dressing up to go to night clubs where they watched the floor shows together and then danced the night away.

****

En Route to Dakar

The ship had become just like another campsite and Marcel no longer felt excited. The hours wore on and, like the others, he became increasingly bored, uncomfortable and fed up climbing over bodies every time he wanted to go to the toilet and having to fight his way to the canteen. He was grateful he didn't suffer with sea-sickness but wondered where they were going and when they would arrive. On leaving British waters, they were joined by other ships and Marcel was overwhelmed by the size of the convoy.

"It's called *M Force*, which apparently stands for Operation Menace," Paul informed him at the end of the second day.

Marcel looked at him with a certain amount of admiration; Paul always seemed to know what was happening. Meanwhile he looked out to sea where Paul was pointing.

"The battleship over there is the *Barnham*. The cruiser *Devonshire* is the Flagship. Apparently all the commanders are on that one except De Gaulle of course, who's on here." He pointed over to the other side. "The battleship is the *Resolution* and the aircraft carrier you can see is the *Ark Royal*. On board there are apparently twenty five Swordfish torpedo bombers and twenty one Skua fighters.

"Look behind us, those are the British transport ships." He squinted into the light. "And there's a Polish ship the *Sobieski*." He patted Marcel heartily on the back. "A true international force. Those French traitors will surrender to us no problem when they see us outside their harbour. You watch."

Marcel stood watching for ages as the ships powered their way slowly southwards, then reluctantly joined the others on the main deck for their first briefing. To his surprise, the great man himself was there watching and Marcel was fascinated by the sight of General De Gaulle leaning on the rails watching and listening as the officers explained their task.

However, they still had some way to go and, while they travelled further south the atmosphere on the *Westernland* took on a picnic-like quality. Despite the hot clammy heat, lack of cooled water and questionable state of their food rations, which didn't seem to adapt to the tropical heat very well, spirits were high and there were lots of things happening to keep them entertained. At times, Marcel almost forgot they were going to war. He spent his time washing his clothes and hanging them to dry in the gentle breeze on lines strung along the deck, watching the boxing exhibitions, joining in the sing songs and concerts and happily parading up and down at the behest of the French officers. He had soon adapted to the pitching and turning of the ship and, before long, he was hardly aware he was at sea.

There were about a dozen French and English nurses, assistant nurses and ambulance drivers on board and all were members of the Free French Forces. Antoine was particularly smitten by one; a petite girl with dark auburn curly hair and a very engaging smile. Unfortunately, unbeknown to Antoine, she was already involved in a rather torrid relationship with one of the officers and Antoine was more of a minor distraction than the love of her life. She had been trying to persuade the officer to marry her for some time and, with Antoine's unwitting help, she finally succeeded when the officer became predictably jealous of Antoine's advances towards his long-term girlfriend. Realising he stood no chance, Antoine gracefully withdrew from the contest. "There are plenty more fish in the sea," he said, philosophically. "Or should I say nurses in wartime, especially for a handsome brave man like me."

Marcel smiled but he was beginning to get bored. The only excitement had been the mooring alongside of the *Devonshire* in brilliant moonlight in the middle of the month when some other senior officers had come aboard for what Marcel presumed was a meeting with De Gaulle. Other than that, nothing had really happened. He was longing to either stretch his legs or see some action, so he was delighted when the African coast finally came into view.

Their target was to secure the port of Dakar, the capital of Senegal, currently in the hands of Vichy France. The general explained he was optimistic the Vichy forces would surrender and join the fight against the Germans. On arrival, he would send emissaries ashore under the flag of truce so bloodshed could be avoided. If this was unsuccessful, then they would take the capital by force. Marcel felt the stirrings of excitement as he realised all his training had been leading up to this moment. Glancing around at the others, he could see they felt the same. The excitement was crackling between them like electricity and he suddenly couldn't wait to be clambering ashore and joining his fellow countrymen in the fight for the freedom of his country.

****

Simonsdorf, Poland

The skies were leaden and overcast. Joe shivered while they stood in line and the Germans counted the men three times. Then the Commandant appeared, ordered a recount and began making a speech. Joe switched off; he had absolutely no interest in what was being said. He was cold and hungry and, if it was anything important, the others would tell him. He glanced at Pete who had his eyes closed and then at Mitchell, who was surreptitiously reading his book. Perhaps he should listen after all, obviously the others weren't paying any attention either. He sighed and was just wondering whether they would get any more blankets for the winter – he wouldn't put it past the Krauts to let their prisoners freeze to death – when a huge roar of derision went round the gathered men. Startled, he glanced at Bert, the only one who was listening.

Seeing Joe's expression, he grinned. "They're recruiting for the German army." Joe stared at him in disbelief while Bert continued, "Apparently we get extra rations and a uniform that says we're Hitler's Freikorps! How about that for an offer you *can* refuse."

Joe shook his head in disgust but was gratified to see no one had taken the Commandant up on his offer.

"They must be mad, thinking we'd volunteer."

"Nah, they're just so arrogant and blinkered, they can't understand why we wouldn't all jump at the chance." Bert was also disgusted, although there was also a ghost of a smile on his face when he listened to the catcalls and hoots while the men called out their opinions on the wonderful opportunity being offered them. This went on for some time until the senior NCO called the men to order. "I think, Herr Commandant, you've probably had your answer." He saluted smartly, turned back to the men and, without waiting for permission, dismissed them.

****

Scotland

A few days after Richard's abrupt departure, Pam was woken early, given no breakfast and, together with her fellow students, piled into a large covered truck. They were driven for several hours around the country lanes, during which time many went back to sleep. Eventually, the truck stopped and the sergeant major came round to the back and lifted up the flap. He pointed to Claude, who happened to be sitting near the entrance and told him to get out. The flap came down again and they could hear nothing. They exchanged glances, wondering what was happening and then the truck jolted forward and slowly drove off without Claude. They gradually picked up speed before stopping again and the same thing happened. Their numbers steadily reduced. Both Giselle and Pam had survived this far but, when the truck gradually disgorged its passengers one by one leaving only Pam and two of the men, she began to worry this was the end of the line. The truck pulled up and she was ordered out.

She stepped on to the grass and glanced around. It was unexpectedly cold away from the warmth of the truck and the rain was lashing down, stinging her face. She shivered and, while she pulled up her hood, she tried to get her bearings. She had absolutely no idea where she was. The sergeant major handed her a map and a piece of paper containing two sets of co-ordinates.

"Right, Lassie; this is where you are now." He pointed to the top set of co-ordinates. "And in three days, by eighteen hundred hours, you should be back at the house, which is the second set of co-ordinates. Is that clear?" His Scottish brogue sounded even stronger out on the desolate hillside.

Pam nodded. "But I don't have any food or money or…" She tailed off, realising by the grin on his face that the whole point was for her to manage without any of those things.

"By the way…" He was just about to climb back in to the cab of the lorry. "Don't get caught stealing. That's an automatic fail." He slammed the door shut and the truck drove off, leaving her alone on the side of the mountainous road in the freezing cold and pouring rain.

****

La Couture, Northern France

After an early breakfast, Marie and Louis met with Henri's father at the proposed location of the shop. Although Didier, Henri's father, was nothing like Henri to look at, having spoken to him for a few minutes, Marie could see where Henri got his shrewd intellect from. The meeting was quick and amicable and, after his father had left, Henri confirmed that he would be starting work on the new building the next day.

****

Scotland

When the truck drove off, Pam's first reaction was panic. She had no idea where she was; it was cold and wet and visibility was dreadful. Then, common sense and her training kicked in and she headed to the top of the hill to get a better view and establish which way she needed to go. Visibility from the summit was not much better, so she studied the map and, having made her decision, strode confidently in what she considered to be the right direction.

She made good time, stopping only to fill her flask from a stream and pick some late blackberries to eat. Once she was moving, she felt less cold and she determined to keep moving, only stopping for short breaks so her body temperature did not drop too much. For the first few hours, she saw no signs of habitation and she started to feel as though she was the only person in the world, but when evening approached, she spotted a thin stream of smoke winding its way slowly up towards the sky. Assuming the fire was coming from an isolated croft, she began to walk towards the source.

****

Honor Oak Park, London

"Your new hair style suits you!"

Peggy spun round to see Chris standing behind her in the queue. Having decided to spend her afternoon off catching up on her reading, she'd popped to the library.

"Chris! What on earth are you doing here?" She tried to ignore the racing of her heart.

"Annie told me you'd be here. I thought you might like to come to a dance with me on Saturday." Before she could turn him down, he added quickly, "It's in a good cause: they're collecting for a Spitfire."

"Well, I suppose can hardly say no then, can I?" Peggy laughed, although she felt guilty at accepting so quickly. "That's if I can stay awake, of course. Where is it?"

"In my shelter, believe it or not." Chris had a twinkle in his eye and Peggy smiled.

"Sounds very sensible. Yes, I'd love to, thanks." She cursed herself for appearing so eager: he was bound to get the wrong idea.

"Are you working Saturday?"

"Yes, worse luck."

"Then take your party dress to work and we can go straight from there. It's less dangerous than driving around the streets!"

****

Scotland

The light suddenly faded and Pam found herself in complete darkness. For a little while she struggled to see the smoke, but finally she caught glimpses of a small light flickering through the trees. Realising it was an indoor light, she smiled and headed purposefully towards the source. Obviously, black out regulations were not too tightly enforced up here. She was within a few hundred yards of the small croft when the light disappeared and a dog began to bark.

Pam dived flat on the wet ground and waited, her heart racing, wondering if she had been seen. But after a few minutes, she heard an angry voice shouting at the dog and a few seconds later, everything was quiet. Keeping low, she carried on towards the croft and was rewarded by the discovery of an open window at one end. She couldn't hear the dog at all, but just inside the window she saw a large pie and some cheese. Obviously this was the larder, hence the open window. She felt guilty stealing from people who probably had very little, but she salved her conscience by resolving to compensate the crofters once she arrived back at Arisaig. She would just have to make sure she could find this place again.

She helped herself to the pie and the cheese and left hurriedly, just as the dog began to bark again. Her heart raced as she headed back towards the woods and she reached the cover of the trees just as the moon came out from behind the clouds. She glanced back at the croft. It was still in darkness. She stared around her, trying to mentally imprint the location on her memory. Then, using the moon to read the compass, she headed in what she hoped was the right direction.

She ate while she walked, saving most of the food for the next day and only eating enough to stave off the feelings of starvation. If she could make the pie and cheese last the whole time, she wouldn't have to steal again. She walked through most of the night and, as dawn broke, she estimated she was about a day's walk away from the house. Exhausted, cold and wet, she found a large bush, crawled into the centre and fell asleep.

****

Honor Oak Park, London

"Hello, Peggy." Olive forced herself to smile at her cousin.

"Olive, this is a nice surprise. How are you?" Peggy didn't wait for an answer. "We're about to go down to the shelter, do you want to come?"

Olive shook her head. "No, thanks. I'm going to hurry home before the bombing starts, but I just wanted to see if you'd had a letter from Joe yet?"

Peggy's face fell and Olive experienced a thrill of happiness. Somehow, she managed to her keep her expression suitably sombre.

"No, nothing. But everyone keeps telling me I might have to wait ages to actually hear from him." Her face lit up. "I don't expect it will be long now."

Olive nodded. "Yes, dear, I'm sure you're right." She searched for something she could say to wipe the hopeful expression off Peggy's face, but nothing came to mind. "Well, I'd better be off, otherwise I'll get caught out." She started to turn away when the words came to her. "If you do get bad news, dear, you know you can always talk to me, don't you?" Olive was gratified to see the expression on Peggy's face. She reached out and patted her hand. "But of course, I'm sure that won't happen." Olive's sympathetic expression had the desired effect. Peggy now felt she was stupid to hold on to false hope.

Olive walked off down the path, leaving Peggy confused. Had her cousin been offering her help or had she just come round to upset her?

Chapter Seventeen

Paris

The time passed much too quickly and Brigitte wished they could stay there forever.

"What's the matter, Brigitte? You look sad."

"I was just thinking how much I've enjoyed myself and I don't want to go home again in case things change." She glanced at him, a wary expression on her face. She was terrified the old Rolf would reappear if she did or said something to upset him.

"Why should anything change?" Rolf looked surprised, then he smiled. "I have an idea." Brigitte waited. "Why don't you move in with me, then we can be together like this all the time?"

Brigitte stared in astonishment, then flung her arms around him. "Are you asking me to marry you?"

Rolf shook his head. "No Brigitte, marriage would be too difficult because of our different nationalities. But if we live together, you will be treated like my wife by all my friends. Marriage is just a piece of paper, after all. Then we can have lots of weekends away. I will support you and you can spend your days making yourself beautiful for me."

Brigitte couldn't think of anything she wanted more. Delighted, she reached over and kissed him on the cheek. "I'd love to."

****

Scotland

When Pam woke, the sun was shining and, although her clothes were damp and uncomfortable, she felt quite warm. She finished her water and, after checking the compass, she began walking again, studiously ignoring the blister she could feel rubbing on the heel of her left foot. The countryside was still totally deserted; there was no sign of any habitation at all, which she was beginning to find disconcerting. Pam shook her head and, ignoring the feelings of isolation threatening to overwhelm her, she made herself concentrate on her objective: to pass the course and move onto the next stage.

She pressed on over seemingly endless hills and down through valleys, across streams and over tracks, her thoughts focused on how she would feel when she finally reached her destination. She ate the remains of the meat pie and, as she wrapped the rest of the cheese, she suddenly recognised where she was. They had come this way on one of their cross country runs. She stood still trying to get her bearings and then she remembered. They had gone out in a truck and, after an hour or so or driving round the winding country lanes, they'd stopped, climbed out and done some intensive map reading for a couple of hours before climbing back on the truck. The certainty the house wasn't far away gave her a second wind and she strode purposefully ahead, only stopping when she finally entered the courtyard and the door opened.

To her delight, Richard stood there, a big smile on his face. Pam smiled, despite her exhaustion.

"Richard! I wasn't expecting to see you."

He grinned. "I had to see how my favourite pupil was doing. Well done! I'm sure you could do with a bath and something to eat?"

She nodded, suddenly unable to speak as exhaustion kicked in with a vengeance, leaving her struggling to stay upright. The thought briefly crossed her mind that she must look and smell awful, but she was too tired to care. She couldn't remember much about the bath or the meal that followed it and her first real memory was of the next morning when she insisted Richard drive her back out to find where the croft was. It took them some considerable time to find the dwelling but, eventually, she was sure she had the right one and she made a note of the address so she could send some money.

****

Honor Oak Park, London

"Here's the address, Peggy." Pauline handed Peggy a piece of paper with Joe's address printed on it. "I'm so sorry I haven't brought it round before, but with all this bombing, it's not been safe to go out. I've been scared out of my wits, to be honest. You do forgive me don't you?"

Pauline looked so ashamed, Peggy hugged her. "Of course I do. The main thing is, he's safe and we know where he is."

"Do you want to read his letter?" Pauline asked.

Peggy nodded, unable to believe Pauline finally knew where Joe was. Life was so strange. It was only the previous night Olive had been round and then, the very next morning, along came Pauline with Joe's letter. She read quickly and then handed the paper back to Pauline. "I'll write to him straight away. Most of the letters I've written are out of date, but maybe I'll send them all anyway. It will be a bit like a diary for him then, won't it?"

Pauline nodded, pleased to see Peggy looking so happy. "I wrote a quick note as soon as I got his letter and explained about the bombing, so he knows there might be a delay in hearing from you. I explained we got his message as well. I'll let you write something to him next, then I'll put pen to paper again later, when I can think of other news to give him."

"I'm so excited!" Peggy flung her arms around Pauline and the older woman hugged her back. Peggy made a mental note to let Olive know Joe was safe. After all, her cousin had been so sympathetic, even coming all the way over when the streets were so dangerous.

****

Poland

At first Joe was quite happy at the thought of returning to Thorn, because it would mean a chance to see all his friends again. He would miss Pete but he was pleased Mitchell was going with him. He had grown quite close to the laconic American with his dry sense of humour and Mitchell didn't think he was mad for seeing the fortune teller, which had reinforced the bond between the two men.

Joe tried to take an interest in the countryside but there was surprisingly little to see other than vast expanses of fields, woodland and scrub. Whereas in England, the fields were punctuated with houses, roads or other farm buildings, here there was just mile upon mile of nothingness. There were very few people about and those they did see seemed to be very poor, their clothes old and tattered and pulled tight to protect against the cold. Most had their heads bent into the wind and paid scant attention while they tried to scratch their meagre living from the land.

"You'd think the countryside would be the same wherever you were, wouldn't you?" Mitchell surprised him by saying what he had been thinking.

Joe agreed. "This looks nothing like England though, or America, I bet."

Mitchell nodded. "The one thing I noticed when I came to England and Europe was how small everything seemed and how close together things are. I'm not criticising, honestly." He sensed Joe was about to take offence. "America's not necessarily better, just a lot bigger."

They lapsed into silence. The weather deteriorated as they travelled north; the wind became stronger, the threat of rain increased and Joe was relieved when they finally arrived.

They alighted from the truck and were made to stand in two rows while the guards counted them. Standing in the open, the wind was even colder, cutting through their clothes and leaving them shivering and irritable.

"For God's sake, don't they think they might have noticed if one of us had gone missing on the way!" Mitchell earned himself a shout of abuse from one of the camp guards who then proceeded to start the count again. This was too much for some of the other men who, hungry, cold and tired after their journey, began heckling.

"You make sure they haven't lost any, Adolf, before you sign for us, or you'll be joining us."

"Didn't they teach you to count at school?"

"You didn't count me last time, you'd better start again."

The guards shouted at the men to be quiet and, realising they were only prolonging things, they lapsed into a sullen silence. The clouds had steadily darkened while they were standing in the open and the wind had also strengthened. Joe hoped the gale would be strong enough to blow the rain away before it had a chance to soak them. Eventually, satisfied they were all there, the men were herded away from the main subterranean structures of the fort towards an area of the camp Joe didn't recognise. Relieved to be moving again and to feel the circulation returning to their cold arms and legs, the men marched at double quick pace, taking the German escort by surprise and leaving them hurrying to keep up. Finally the guards pointed to a couple of huts near the perimeter and Joe followed the others through the door, relieved to escape the biting wind. He rubbed his hands together in an attempt to get some feeling back and glanced around.

At the far end of the hut he could see a small wood burning stove, a faint glow indicating it was alight. Huddled around the fire, a few men were chatting quietly. He followed Mitchell, making his way through the hut towards the heater. Seeing the bunks nearest the wood burner were already taken, Mitchell quickly grabbed the first vacant bottom bunk as near as he could get. Joe took the top one, pleased, because heat rose so he would be marginally warmer and the lice and cockroaches often fell onto the bunks beneath. There was a flattish pillow and a single blanket on the mattress and, before Joe stretched out and pulled the blanket round him, he went through a painstaking search of all the seams of the meagre bedding and the wooden boards of the bunk, squashing the lice when he found them. Eventually, satisfied he had found most, he wrapped the blanket around him and lay there shivering. If the hut was this cold now, what would happen when the snow came?

****

Dakar, Senegal

Dakar was situated on a small peninsula jutting out from the African mainland. The whole bay was heavily defended by fixed coastal batteries, searchlights, anti-submarine and anti-torpedo booms, not to mention seaplanes, squadrons of fighters and bombers and five regiments of troops. There were also a battleship, two cruisers, three super cruisers, a destroyer and two submarines. But Marcel and his friends were completely unaware of the possible opposition, having been lulled into a false sense of security by the optimistic promises that Dakar was just waiting to come over to the Free French.

Dawn was not until half past five in the morning, so they waited eagerly on deck for their first glimpse of their objective but when daylight appeared, they received their first set back. They were shrouded in a dank, dripping, wet, tropical fog which obscured their view, sapped their energy and which worsened as the sun rose higher in the sky.

Paul gave a cynical laugh. "Ha! So much for waking up to the glorious sight of the Free French forces arriving to liberate them! I doubt whether they even know we're here."

The next half an hour passed uneventfully.

"What are we waiting for?" Marcel asked Pierre.

"I should think they're trying to get our fellow countrymen to surrender. It could take some time; I'd sit down and take a rest, if I were you."

Just as he finished speaking, the Free French sloop came into view, heading for the harbour. Because the boat looked like the Vichy ships, no one tried to stop them. Then, three miles south of the boom, just within the range of their vision, the sloop stopped and lowered two unarmed motor boats which headed towards the harbour, flying large Tricolours with the Cross of Lorraine and the white flags of truce. The first boat carried de Gaulle's emissaries, thirteen officers and ratings in French uniforms. On the second was a security detachment of a dozen men.

Marcel and his friends watched while the first boat approached the harbour and tied up. The second waited some distance off. They could hear the engines idling. Then, puffs of white smoke rose lazily into the sky and they could hear gunfire. The French authorities had opened fire on the unarmed men. The emissaries managed to get aboard their boat and, together with the security detachment, hastened back towards the sloop, chased by an old tug which was also firing. The gun post at the extreme end of the southern jetty also opened fire. Fortunately, the fog thickened again and the boats reached the safety of the sloop, which hurriedly withdrew back to the fleet.

****

Bethune, Northern France

"Are you sure you want to live with him?" Fabian was horrified by the idea, but he could see no way of stopping his wayward daughter. If he objected, the German would probably just take her by force.

"Of course, Papa. I've had a wonderful time in Paris and he loves me. We would get married but it's too complicated because he's German and I'm French, so this is the next best thing."

Fabian shook his head. Brigitte was quite obviously too besotted with the man to see he was just using her and she was much too stubborn to listen to him. He tried to look for something good in the situation and eventually decided it might be useful to have his daughter living with a German if things became difficult. The Germans were behaving themselves at the moment but he couldn't see that lasting much longer. Eventually they would show their true colours. He only hoped he would be around to rescue Brigitte if things went wrong.

"I'm only living a few kilometres away, I'll come and see you and you can always visit me." She couldn't wait to show off the new house Rolf had found. There were three bedrooms and a large living room, kitchen and bathroom. One of the bedrooms was to be Rolf's office and the biggest one would be theirs, with a spare one if anyone came to visit.

She finished packing and turned to leave. For a moment she felt sad to be leaving, but the thought of her new life soon banished her gloom. "Au revoir, Papa."

Fabian said nothing. He hugged his daughter and wished he could turn back the clock and do everything differently.

****

Lewisham Council Offices, London

Kath stared at the switchboard, ignored the buzzing lines and wondered where Tom was. He'd completely disappeared. She was sure he hadn't been arrested or she would have heard. So where on earth was he? She glanced across at Olive who was busy typing something and didn't look up. Kath stared at her for several moments, trying to see if there was any difference in her demeanour.

Maybe Tom had run off with whatever money he'd got from her. She frowned. Or maybe he'd finally managed to get a look in the old girl's handbag and, to keep him quiet, she had given him enough to start a new life. Kath shook her head. That was ridiculous. If Olive had that much money, she'd hardly be working in the council offices.

She sighed. Tom had been acting rather strangely, though, before he went missing. He seemed obsessed with Olive, and not in a nice way. She stared at Olive again and this time Olive looked up. Their eyes met and Kath had the weirdest feeling Olive was laughing at her. She held the older woman's gaze for several seconds before looking away. Something wasn't right and Kath had no intention of letting her supervisor off the hook.

****

Dakar, Senegal

After a shocked silence, the men on the ship all began talking at once.

"The boat's unarmed."

"What do they think they're doing?"

"They were under the flag of truce."

Marcel looked at his friends, the disbelief on his own face echoed on theirs. "What's going to happen now?"

"I don't know, but De Gaulle can't let them get away with that." Antoine was, for once, wide awake and paying attention. "I would say we should get ready to go ashore!"

The sloop returned slowly to the ship and the wounded were transferred to another vessel, the rumour quickly circulating that at least two men were seriously injured. In the meantime, other boats had approached the boom and tried to land troops but the fog had lifted and they too were fired on and had to withdraw.

"Looks like the battle's going well then!" Antoine muttered while they watched the boats heading back. Now the fog had cleared, they had a perfect view of the harbour, but the Vichy French forces could also see them. The guns of Cape Manuel opened up and the British ships began firing back.

The sound was deafening and Marcel was immediately transported back to the roads in France when he and Jeanne had been fleeing from the advancing Germans.

At first, the defending shells fell wide but they soon found their mark and hit two of the destroyers. The shore batteries continued to fire on the ships whose guns who were no match for them. One shell hit the cruiser *Cumberland*, piercing the port side over the armour belt, and burst just above the lower deck. Marcel watched in horror as smoke began to billow into the blue, cloudless sky. He felt like he was watching a film. He could hear the noise and see the action but they were not part of the fight.

By midday, the fog had come down again, even thicker than before and they couldn't see anything. Then, the engines started up and the ship began to move.

"Are we giving up?" Marcel asked.

Pierre shrugged and didn't answer. Paul looked thoughtful. "I wouldn't think so. Must have cost a fortune to get us here. I'm sure we won't just give up that easily." But to Marcel's ears Paul didn't sound particularly confident. Marcel wasn't sure whether to be pleased they hadn't gone ashore, or not. Part of him was relieved he hadn't had to fight, whilst another part of him was disappointed.

Seeing his expression, Paul grinned. "Don't worry, Marcel. I'm sure there'll be plenty of time for you to get stuck in and kill a few Germans. This war's got a long way to go yet, you mark my words."

****

Stalag XXA, Poland

"What time's grub?" Mitchell asked one of the men on the adjacent bunk, who, having watched their lice checks with amusement for a while, had lost interest and gone back to reading.

"About an hour and a half." The man glanced up from his book. "Although, if you're expecting a banquet, you've come to the wrong place."

"It's okay, we're used to the Kraut's hospitality. I'm going somewhere else for my holiday next time!" Mitchell's response made the man smile and he put down his book.

"So where've you come from?"

"We've just left Simonsdorf but before, we were both at Calais. I'm 60th Rifles and Joe's Rifle Brigade. Joe was here before he went to Simonsdorf. What about you?"

The man had sat upright at the mention of Calais but his attention was focused on Joe.

"I'm Rifle Brigade too. A Company."

Joe stared at him. "'I thought you looked vaguely familiar. I'm from B Company. We were in Needham Market together. You were a friend of Chalky's brother." There was a brief silence while Joe remembered his friend.

"Yeah, where is he? Is he with you?" He saw the expression on Joe's face and stopped. "Bought it, did he?"

Joe nodded, unable to reply for a moment.

"Sorry. I'm Cyril Green and it's been sixteen weeks and one day and several hours since I was last a free man. Dick?" he called to the man in the bunk above him. "You're outnumbered. Here's another Rifle Brigade man."

Dick gave a theatrical groan. "Oh God, not more of you. I'll never get any peace now. It'll be *the Rifle Brigade this and the Rifle Brigade that*, on and on and on and on…"

Joe laughed and successfully managed to put the last image of his best friend Chalky out of his head. "Joe Price. Any more of us here?"

"A few," Cyril replied. "Although none are in this hut. The Krauts like to split regiments and units up, as I'm sure you've noticed."

Joe nodded and then, unable to contain his hope, asked, "Is Rob still here? Frank Roberts."

"Yeah. He's in hut five. A proper laugh he is. Gets the Jerries right at it, he does."

Joe breathed a sigh of relief. He would have hated to have got back there only to find Rob had been moved somewhere else. "Will I be able to see him at tea?" Joe wasn't sure whether they would all eat together.

"Yeah. Oh no, hold on a minute." Cyril hesitated for a moment and Joe looked at him, suddenly fearing the worst. Cyril glanced at Dick. "Normally we all eat together, but we've had a diphtheria epidemic. More than two hundred blokes have died. Hut five is still quarantined."

Chapter Eighteen

Dakar, Senegal

By the late afternoon, they were moored up again, this time off Cape Rouge, about seven miles from Rufisque. They were joined by two other ships and a contingent of marines. To Marcel's delight, he and some of the men, including Paul, Pierre, Antoine and Charles, were given a quick briefing and told they had been selected to go ashore with the marines.

Marcel hadn't had time to feel nervous on the ship, but once they transferred to the landing craft about three-quarters of a mile from the beach, he found himself much closer to the water. He did his best to ignore the butterflies in his stomach while they approached the shore, but they had not gone far when the guns at the foot of the lighthouse opened fire. They were also fired on by troops who were lining the shore with machine guns. Although the sea itself was quite calm, the shelling caused massive waves which threatened to sink them.

The landing craft in front of Marcel's was hit by a shell and disintegrated into small pieces, throwing men and equipment into the water. What remained of the boat sank beneath the surface and Marcel could see the bodies of several men floating past. He looked away and then, hearing a man shouting, he glanced back. To the left of where he was crouched, he could see a hand surfacing and then disappearing beneath the frothing waves.

"There's someone in trouble," he yelled to Antoine who was nearest to him. "I'm going to try and reach him."

Without waiting for an answer, his nerves forgotten, Marcel pulled off his backpack and, before Antoine could stop him, he dived into the swirling waters. Although they were not far from the beach, the water was colder and deeper than he expected and he sank beneath the waves. He surfaced but was unable to see anyone, so he dived back under the water searching for some sign of the man. Then, just when he was about to run out of air, he spotted him.

The combination of the cold water and the weight of his clothes began to drag Marcel down but, somehow, finding a last vestige of strength, he swam forwards to where he had last seen the man, reaching him just as he was about to sink beneath the waves again. Grabbing him under his arms Marcel began the long swim back to his landing craft, which was now some distance away.

****

Stalag XXA, Poland

Joe and Mitchell stared at him in horror. Cyril saw their reactions and hastened to reassure them. "Don't worry. Looks like it's pretty much over now; no one's been carted off sick for about three days. But I wouldn't drink the water in the bathhouse if I were you, although it's alright for washing in. The standpipe's out the front, along with the latrines. Don't expect a torrent of water, though. Damn thing barely drips out at the best of times."

"And Rob?" Joe wasn't listening to the rest of the conversation, he was only interested in what had happened to his friend.

"He's alright. Well, he was the last time I saw him. We can speak to them through the wire, just don't go too close; you know, close enough to pick up anything."

Joe nodded, not in the least reassured. Maybe they had been better off in Simonsdorf after all. Thorn was just as bad as he remembered.

The living conditions had not improved; they had just added more huts to cope with the increased number of prisoners. The conditions inside the fort were even worse than when he'd left, if Cyril was to be believed.

Joe was grateful he was in one of the outside huts. Although they were poorly constructed with little insulation and no facilities, at least the fresh air would be more healthy. Then he remembered what the fortune teller had told him; he would survive, although others around him would die. He closed his eyes for a moment and offered up a silent prayer Rob would survive too. Hadn't he seen enough death, destruction and cruelty to last him a lifetime? Hadn't he lost enough of his friends? Did he really need to lose any more? For the first time in his life, Joe began to question his faith. How could God allow this kind of mindless destruction to happen? His initial feelings of contentment at being warmer, meeting a 'friend of a friend' and knowing Rob was still alive began to recede, leaving him feeling depressed again.

He realised Mitchell was shaking the bunk. "Come on, Joe. Don't tell me you're not hungry? That's got to be a first."

Making a big effort to shake off his feelings of despair, Joe made himself laugh. "Nah, not me, mate. I'm starving; could eat a horse and probably the saddle as well!"

****

Lewisham, London

The man in the long trench coat watched Olive leave the building. Kurt's description made her easy to spot and soon he was following her at a safe distance. He yawned. He'd been on the road for a while now and he couldn't wait to get back to Scotland. A life-long communist, he'd been slightly uneasy when Stalin and Hitler had signed a pact, but if that put him on the side of the Nazis, then so be it. He couldn't stand the English and was glad to see they were getting a good pasting from the Luftwaffe, although he would prefer not to be killed while he was in London.

He grinned. Kurt must have a strong stomach. Some of the women he'd picked up looked pretty awful. He couldn't have fucked them, although he quite enjoyed writing the letters. Mind you, he would have to forget what they looked like when he got home, or he'd never be able to write the filth he was instructed to put in. He was still chuckling to himself when he felt the hair on the back of his neck begin to stand up: a definite sign of trouble.

He stepped aside and pretended to be doing up his shoelace. Sure enough, there was someone else watching Olive. The blackout made things very dark but she appeared to be a young, fairly attractive, red haired woman. He frowned. What on earth was going on here? The young woman was obviously an amateur and not the security services; she didn't appear to have seen him at all. Her eyes were fixed on Olive, who seemed to have no idea anyone was following her.

****

Dakar, Senegal

The man was thrashing about wildly and Marcel didn't have the strength to fight him and swim. Without thinking, he hit the man hard on the chin and the struggling ceased. Almost at the end of his strength, he continued swimming towards the craft which miraculously seemed to be heading back towards him. Shells were still falling all around and each time one hit the sea, the waves grew in size, hindering his progress. The noise of shells hitting the water mingled with the pinging of the machine gun bullets as they skimmed off the surface and hurt his ears. He could hear men shouting and crying out and cordite and smoke filled his nostrils. Marcel tried to block out the sounds and smells around him and concentrate solely on his own battle to survive. He could feel his strength ebbing away; every stroke was agony and then, suddenly, the pressure eased and he felt himself being dragged out of the water. He was dimly aware he was back on the boat and he lay gasping for breath.

"You bloody fool." Paul's voice seemed to be coming from a long way away. "What on earth were you thinking?"

"He wasn't thinking!" The big grin on Pierre's face belied the harshness of his words and the gruff tone of his voice.

Marcel gave a tired smile and eased himself up onto one elbow. "Is he alright?"

Charles appeared in front of him, holding onto the pitching craft when yet another shell hit the water, showering them with water and making the boat rock alarmingly. "Yeah. He's swallowed some water but he'll live to fight another day!"

"Good job it's still so hot, despite the fog. Your clothes'll only take a few hours to dry out. Here's your kit." Antoine handed him his bag. "If you'd wanted a swim, I'm sure we could have found somewhere a bit safer!" He punched Marcel on the arm playfully and Marcel felt his spirits rise. For once, he felt an equal with his friends and, although he was tired, he couldn't help feeling elated.

Behind them, their guns opened fire and when they destroyed the lighthouse, a wave of delighted celebration went up from the men, Marcel included. However, their orders were to try and avoid bloodshed if they could, so they moved further south. Looking ahead, Marcel watched the beach coming closer and, after making a quick sign of the cross, he got ready to clamber out and make his way ashore.

But when they were about three hundred yards from the beach, some isolated shots were heard and, to his intense disappointment, the attack was called off.

****

Stalag XXA, Poland

Cyril was right. The occupants of hut five did not appear at dinner that evening. However, when Joe returned to the hut, depressed and worried about Rob, he was surprised to hear his name called out. He spun around to find a corporal holding out a letter for him. Judging from the crossed out addresses, the letter had gone to Simonsdorf and then been redirected to Stalag XXA Thorn.

The writing looked very familiar, so he quickly turned the letter over to see who it was from. To his delight, his mother's name and address were written clearly on the back. The letter had been opened, presumably by the censor, but he didn't care. If she was writing to him, then she knew he was alive, but then his heart sank and he hesitated. What if she was ashamed of him because they had surrendered and been captured? He sat there looking at the letter for several minutes, trying to decide whether or not to read it, until eventually curiosity got the better of him and he turned the letter back over and carefully took it out of the envelope.

****

Catford, London

Olive caught the bus home, oblivious of the two people following her. She entered the block of flats and glanced across the road at the bombed-out building. The property had been empty for some time and, as far she knew, no one had bothered to check for casualties after the air raid. The chances were, Tom's body was probably still there, under the rubble, where she'd buried him. The thought that he was so close made her feel slightly uncomfortable, but she didn't believe in ghosts. Tom could no longer hurt her and she needed to put him out of her mind and try to get on with her life.

Having made the decision not to think about him anymore, her next task was to open the box, which was still by the bathroom door where Tom had placed it, and get rid of the contents. She made herself some sardines on toast and a cup of tea and stared at the container, wondering why she was putting off the inevitable. Brushing away the crumbs from her jumper, she stood up and, taking her scissors, began cutting through the tape. She pulled back the cardboard lid and peered inside. The first layer consisted entirely of bars of chocolate. Olive removed these to find a layer of cigarettes. Under the cigarettes were several bottles of Irish whiskey. Olive sat back and stared, her mind racing.

The sensible thing to do would be to take the whole lot across the road and bury them with Tom; then, if anyone found him and was suspicious, they would think he had been killed because of his black market activities. However, she loved chocolate and she could never bring herself to throw away so many bars. As for the cigarettes and whiskey, they were very hard to get now and people were paying good money for both items. If she sold some, she could recoup the money Tom had stolen from her.

But how would she sell whiskey and cigarettes? She couldn't just walk into the nearest pub and she didn't know anyone she could ask. The only people she ever mixed with were at work and trying to sell the stuff there would be stupid.

She decided not to do anything hasty. She counted the chocolate. There were one hundred bars of her favourite Cadbury's Dairy Milk. Whatever else she did, the chocolate was staying. She sorted the bars into smaller piles, left one on the table and began hiding the rest around the flat amongst other items. She put the cigarettes back in the box and pushed the container into the bathroom, behind the door, out of sight.

Returning to the main room, she opened a bar of chocolate and tried to work out what to do about the rest of the illicit goods.

****

Outside Bethune, Northern France

Brigitte loved her new house and she busied herself with making it clean and tidy and dressing up for Rolf.

He was bringing a couple of friends home for dinner and she had hired someone to cook. She looked in the wardrobe and decided to wear one of the dresses Rolf had bought her in Paris. She stared in the mirror and admired herself. Rolf would be home soon. She couldn't wait.

She dressed and then looked around for something to amuse herself with. The cook was due in about half an hour. Until then there was absolutely nothing to do.

****

Catford, London

Kath stood on the corner of the road where she could see the flats. Olive had disappeared inside and Kath had no idea what to do next. She couldn't stand there all night on the off-chance Tom would appear and, even if he did, she could hardly barge into Olive's flat to see what was going on. She peered at her watch and decided to wait a little longer. Then the siren went off, followed almost immediately by the ominous drone of the German bombers in the distance. Kath hesitated for a few seconds then made up her mind. Tom was not likely to be wandering around in the middle of an air raid, so unless he was hiding in Olive's flat for some reason, she was wasting her time. If she hurried, she could reach the nearest underground station before the bombs started dropping.

****

Outside Bethune, Northern France

The meal had been fun, his friends treating her like their equal. Brigitte was in seventh heaven and Louis was long forgotten.

"Well, have you enjoyed your first day in our house?" Rolf smiled at her.

Brigitte conveniently forgot he had commandeered the house and smiled back. "I've had a wonderful day. I'm really happy. And I enjoyed the meal too."

"Good. So, you are grateful to me then for rescuing you from your life of boredom and drudgery?"

"Of course I am." Brigitte wasn't sure her life before Rolf had been quite as terrible as he was making it sound, but she didn't want to spoil the mood by arguing.

"How grateful?" Rolf was already undoing his trousers and Brigitte couldn't wait to show him.

****

Lambeth, London

Although the bombs were crashing down outside, for once, Peggy didn't notice. Chris was holding her waist and they were dancing the hokey cokey in the small shelter. There wasn't really enough room, but this made the whole thing funnier when they fell over people's feet and bags. They were singing at the tops of their voices and she didn't feel at all scared. The drink was flowing and even Peggy had drunk some sherry, which had gone straight to her head. She felt very merry and was enjoying the feel of Chris's arms around her.

The music finished and he spun her to face him.

"Are you glad you came?" he shouted above the general noise.

"Yes. Going into the shelter will never be the same again. I wish mine was like this every night!" Peggy knew she was slightly drunk but she didn't care. Joe was safe, she could stop worrying about him and relax after the stress of the past few months.

Feeling surprisingly happy, she'd changed into her long-sleeved evening dress, pulled her warm winter coat tight and allowed Chris to drive her to the shelter. She still felt slightly awkward in his company, so said little on the journey but when she arrived at the underground cellar, the mood was so jolly, she was soon into the swing of things.

The small band began playing, *We'll Meet Again* and Chris took her in his arms holding her close as they swayed on the spot, the small space full of people dancing, their eyes closed while they listened to the lyrics. Peggy found the movement hypnotic and she allowed herself to relax. She moved closer and soon his body was pressing up against her. She moved her head and, suddenly, he was kissing her and she responded, her tongue probing his until the music finished.

Peggy sprang back as if scalded, a horrified expression on her face. Chris made to speak but she was already turning away.

"Peggy, I'm sorry."

"I want to go home."

"You can't, the all clear hasn't sounded yet." Distraught, he searched frantically for something to make her stay. "Look, sit down and I promise not to come too close. I really didn't mean to spoil our evening. It won't happen again."

He looked so sad, Peggy relented. "I can't kiss you again, Chris. It's not fair on Joe. I know he's safe, but he is a prisoner and he's probably not having a very nice time. I shouldn't really be here." She sounded desolate. Chris nodded but he couldn't forget the feel of her body next to his or her tongue in his mouth. If he was going to succeed in making her his girlfriend, he would just have to take things slower.

****

Catford, London

The man in the long trench coat sat in his car making notes. When the air raid siren went off, the girl who had been watching walked off, presumably to find somewhere a little safer than the street corner. But Olive did not appear, even though an elderly lady had shuffled out and headed in what he assumed was the direction of the nearest shelter. The man frowned. Perhaps Olive didn't bother. Great, that meant he had to sit in his car while the Luftwaffe dropped their bombs. On cue, the explosions began and he cursed. *Stupid woman.* She was likely to get them both killed. He could hardly go and sit in the shelter if she was still in her flat; he might miss something.

He winced as several explosions followed, the car shook violently and a house further down the road took a direct hit. What the hell was the matter with the woman? Did she have a death wish? He was about to curse her some more when he saw the main door open and Olive peered out. She glanced up and down the road and disappeared back inside. A few seconds later she came out carrying a shopping bag. She looked around again, then crept out. Her behaviour was very suspicious and he sighed. What on earth was she doing? He watched her cross the road to the bombed out building opposite and vanish into the darkness. He hesitated and then climbed out of the car and followed her.

****

Dakar, Senegal

After much posturing and increasing levels of threats, the battleships of the convoy and the shore batteries entered into a fierce battle with each firing barrages at the other. General de Gaulle was on their ship, so they were situated just outside of the range of the powerful shore batteries.

"General de Gaulle's keen we aren't seen to be firing on our own countrymen," Paul informed Marcel rather cynically, when he asked why the French were not more involved. "He's still hoping they will surrender, which obviously they won't, but he doesn't want to give Vichy too much of a propaganda victory."

Marcel sighed and resumed watching the battle. The fog had lifted and they could see Dakar in the distance, although the smoke of the guns was causing its own smog.

The battle continued with neither side seemingly winning or gaining any advantage. Once he adjusted to the noise, Marcel began to find the whole battle quite boring and eventually allowed Pierre to distract him with a game of cards. "It's alright to be bored, Marcel. It's not like we can do anything. Might as well make the most of the quiet and relax!"

Marcel finally agreed and settled down on deck to enjoy the game. Gradually, the noise around them abated and then, suddenly, the battle was all over and the rumour spread rapidly through the ship that they were withdrawing.

Marcel glanced at the others. They heard the engines fire up and they began to steam back towards Freetown. The attempt to land at Dakar was over, the first Free French endeavour ending without success.

****

Stalag XXA, Poland

Joe began to read, the tension flowing out of him. It was all he could do to stop himself crying with relief.

My darling son,
Thank God you are alive and unhurt. It was so good to know you had survived so soon, even though I wasn't officially notified until September.

His initial relief turned to puzzlement. What did she mean about knowing so soon even though she wasn't notified officially? Then it hit him like a ton of bricks. The note must have reached her. The Frenchman to whom he'd handed the piece of paper, by the side of the road must have managed to get to England after all. He was absolutely stunned his message had travelled all the way from an occupied country back to his mum in South London. He closed his eyes for a moment, then opened them and re-read the first paragraph again to make sure he hadn't made a mistake. He realised his mother was being careful with her words, but he was sure that was what she was saying. The next paragraph confirmed his suspicions.

Peggy was also over the moon you were still alive. She had been so worried about you. She said of course she will wait for you, as if she would even consider doing anything else.

Joe smiled at both the news and at the confirmation his hastily scribbled missive had reached home. He had asked Peggy to wait for him in the message but not in any of the letters he had sent since he had been able to write officially, so that proved it beyond a shadow of a doubt. The next few words had been blacked out by the censor, followed by:

… so Peggy probably won't be able to write for a while. Don't worry about us, though. We're all doing fine.

He frowned, wondering what could be the problem and why it could mean that Peggy would be unable to write. He hoped she wasn't ill. Confused, he carried on reading:

I promise, we are all well here, although we are missing you of course. But the most important thing is, you are alive and soon you will be home. I saw your dad the other day, he sends his love and will write soon when he has time.

Joe took this to confirm his dad had got home safely from Dunkirk and was unhurt and had therefore rejoined his unit. Obviously, there were lots of things his mum couldn't say because of the war. He would have to become very adept at reading between the lines.

Fred is now known to all and sundry as 'Joe' since the firm insisted on calling him after you, which is a great compliment, don't you think? He's so proud to be called after you, I think he's forgotten his real name is Fred!
We had a lovely Harvest Supper at the church last week. Everyone was there and asking about you. They all send their love and now they have an address, you should get some letters from them. The Pastor said some prayers for you and we had a collection to buy some extra goodies to put in a parcel for you. I will be posting it next week, although I'm not sure how long it will take to get to you.

The next bit was blanked out again with the heavy black block of the censor and Joe was unable to decipher any of the writing. He tried holding the letter up to the light and from different angles but it was no good.

"Wasting your time, mate." Dick had been watching his attempts with some amusement. "We've all tried. There's no way to read the stuff the censor has blocked off."

"Who's censored it? The Germans?"

'Nah. More likely our own side, in case they give away any important information about the war. That's why we can't see through the black lines. If we could, so could the Krauts."

Joe nodded. Although he understood what Dick was saying, he was bitterly disappointed because he suddenly desperately wanted to know what was under the thick black lines, even though it was probably something he would consider quite innocuous. He sighed and continued reading. Conscious he was almost finished, he tried to make the letter last as long as he could:

Well, I'm starting to run out of paper and there's so much news, you'll have to wait until you come home which, God willing, won't be long. Look after yourself and remember we are all so proud of you and can't wait for you to come safely home to us.

With all my love, Mum.

PS. Fred says he will write to you too, although I wouldn't hold your breath. You know what he's like!

Not wanting the others to see how emotional he was, Joe turned over in his bunk and closed his eyes.

Chapter Nineteen

Honor Oak Park, London

Yet again, the deafening noise of the air raid siren woke Peggy with a start. Bleary-eyed, she peered at the clock on her bedside cupboard and groaned. The raids had been going on every night for weeks without a break. She dragged herself wearily out of bed, grateful she had long since stopped wearing nightdresses in favour of heavier, but unflattering, pyjamas. At least they were warmer and the last thing she was worried about when she made her way to the shelter, night after night, was what she looked like.

Still struggling to see in the dark and feeling a sense of urgency, she scrabbled around on the floor to find her shoes, which seemed to have disappeared. Eventually, she retrieved them from under the bed and put them on her feet which, despite the warm socks she had started wearing in bed, were already feeling cold. She knew Joe would have teased her unmercifully about wearing something so old fashioned as socks in bed. Almost as if she could hear him, she said aloud, "You wouldn't laugh if you were here and had to keep going down to the wretched shelter in the middle of the night!"

Reluctantly, she pulled on her clothes over her pyjamas, finishing with her winter coat. Once dressed, she grabbed her shelter bag and Joe's picture and opened her bedroom door just as Annie called her.

"I'm here, Annie. Goodness its cold."

In the darkness, she could just make out Annie's head nodding in affirmation. "I know, you'd think I would feel warmer with all this extra padding." She patted her protruding stomach protectively.

"How do you feel?" Peggy asked, her own discomfort forgotten.

"I'm fine, honestly. At least I don't have to go to work so I can catch up with my sleep during the day." In the distance they could hear the familiar sounds of the approaching bombers. Peggy hurriedly locked the front door. The irony she was locking the door to protect against looters, her own countrymen, was not lost on her.

The streets were full of people in their bedclothes with their outside clothes on over the top, all making their way to the shelter. A few were wearing dual purpose capes which protected them from the rain during the day and doubled up as a temporary mattress at night during the raids. Others had their own home-made shelter satchels with pockets for books, knitting, playing cards, first aid dressings and the government-issued rubber ear plugs. She greeted a few people but the camaraderie of the early days, brought on by the novelty of the situation, had soon worn off and most people were too tired and bleary eyed to want to chat. Most just wanted to get a decent night's sleep and many had taken to sleeping in the shelter from early evening, leading to fights over the limited spaces. Peggy made her way through the wet streets and decided she should do the same. At least she might get some sleep and she would be guaranteed a bunk rather than having to sit on the cold floor.

****

Toulouse, Southern France

Conditions in Vichy France were deteriorating. The ideals proclaimed by Marshal Pétain of Work; Family; Country had been altered by de Gaulle to Work – unobtainable; Family – Scattered; Country – Humiliated and could often be seen scrawled defiantly on walls. The BBC broadcast the slogan regularly and Gabriel smiled to himself every time he saw the words, although he was careful to keep his feelings to himself.

The previous night, whilst drinking in his favourite bar, he had been approached by a 'friend of a friend' who had spent some time trying to find out where his loyalties lay. He was extremely wary of saying too much, especially since he still had Isabelle's threats ringing in his ears. With her vindictive nature and the connections to back up her venom, he was only too aware of the danger she could pose to him and the last thing he needed was to give her any ammunition. She would have little difficulty in arranging a trap for him, so he would have to be on his guard.

He intended to check out the man who had made the approach, although, his instinctive feeling was this was probably genuine and he tried to temper his growing excitement with common sense. Joining any group would mean committing himself to something extremely dangerous and would give his enemies the perfect opportunity to plot his downfall.

His other problem was Jeanne. He couldn't let her know what he was going to do, because the fewer people who knew, the safer he would be, but the last thing he wanted to do was to start their relationship with a lie and add to the danger they were already in.

****

Outside Bethune, Northern France

Brigitte stared out of the window and yawned. She'd never been so bored in all her life. The house was spotless and Rolf was away until the following day, meaning she would be on her own until he returned. She thought about going to visit her father, but sitting in the café wasn't very exciting and, in any case, German soldiers frequented her father's bar and she didn't want to run the risk of upsetting Rolf. The thought briefly crossed her mind that perhaps she should get on her bicycle and go to La Couture to see Louis. She knew he probably wouldn't want to speak to her, but they'd fallen out before and she'd always been able to talk him around. Then she realised that was a ridiculous idea. If she was worried about Rolf's reaction to her mixing with soldiers in her father's café, what on earth would he do if he found out she'd gone to see her ex-boyfriend? Maybe the answer was to ask Rolf if she could go and work in the café during the day. That way she wouldn't be bored and he would know where she was. Pleased with her idea, Brigitte began to work out the best way to get Rolf to agree to her plan.

****

Stalag XXA, Poland

Feeling better the following morning, Joe was dying to tell someone about his message. "I wrote a note on a signals pad I found when they were marching us here and gave the piece of paper to a Frenchman in one of the villages and it got home to my mum before she was told officially I was alright. How about that, then?"

Dick looked at him in amazement. "Crikey, that's incredible. I wonder if the Frenchman passed the note on, or took it to England himself?"

"No idea. Pretty amazing though, isn't it?"

"What's that?" Cyril looked very pleased with himself.

Joe repeated the story but was disappointed by Cyril's reaction, until he explained his wife had just written to tell him she had given birth to a bouncing baby boy, named Cyril, after him. "Apparently, he looks just like me!" Cyril finished proudly.

"Poor sod!" Dick ducked when a pillow came flying through the air towards him.

Joe laughed, pleased he had made some new friends.

"Joe!" Mitchell was calling him from the door. "They've relaxed the quarantine regulations. You should be able to get to hut five now. Come on! What're you waiting for?"

Joe headed towards the door and across the camp.

"Joe!" Rob's cry greeted him before he got there. Joe looked up and, there in front of him, standing by the door looking much thinner and older, but smiling with obvious delight, was Rob.

"Bad pennies always turn up." Joe was slightly embarrassed by just how pleased he was to see Rob again.

"You look older!" They both spoke at the same time and then burst out laughing, their awkwardness forgotten. "So, what've you been doing?" Rob continued before Joe could say anything else. "Come on in and warm up. It's safe now, or we can go to yours if you like? It's too bloody cold to stand around out here."

Joe nodded while Rob explained he had been moved out of the cellar and put into the hut shortly after Joe left. They were keeping the main buildings for the new arrivals. Starved of war news, Joe was disappointed by the little Rob was able to tell him. Most of the news was bad, although the Germans had not succeeded in invading England yet.

"Work parties are the same. All work, no extra rations and bad tempered Kraut guards, but other than that…" Rob shrugged and listened while Joe told him about the shooting of the Polish worker and the constant rumours of infiltrators that had plagued Simonsdorf.

He was just about to ask Rob whether he had heard from Lizzie when the sound of a commotion outside interrupted them. Joe looked up alarmed, but Rob shrugged. "Happens all the time. They suddenly decide they want us all for another roll call. God knows where they think we're going to escape to."

He'd barely finished speaking when the hut door was flung open and several German guards with dogs, barking furiously and straining at their leashes, burst in.

"RAUS, RAUS!" Joe and Rob followed the others out onto the bitterly cold parade ground. The wind had grown in strength and Joe shivered. Nothing appeared to be happening and the men started to grumble bitterly at having to stand out in the cold for no apparent reason. Just when the heckling started to grow louder, there were the sounds of a commotion over to the left of the camp. They fidgeted and strained their heads to see what was happening and saw several guards rush into one of the other huts. The sound of banging and crashing grew louder and was accompanied by shouting.

Joe glanced at Rob who was staring ahead studiously as if nothing was happening and, seeing the other men were also now motionless and silent, Joe decided to take his cue from them. Realising belatedly he should probably have lined up with the members of his own hut, he wondered whether he should make his way over to them. He looked around quickly. The guards were not watching him; their attention was fixed on the source of the commotion. Taking a deep breath, he started to tell Rob where he was going but, before he could utter a word, the sound of shots rang out. Nervously, he looked towards where the sound had come from and realised two men had somehow managed to get through the first barbed wire fence but not the second outer fence. They were caught between the two.

They were wearing British uniforms and his heart sank. The shots had hit one of the men squarely in his back, the force throwing him face down across the second fence. The second had his hands raised high in the air and was shouting loudly in poor German, "Schiessen sie nicht."

The guard raised his rifle and took aim. Closing his mind to what was about to happen, knowing he could do nothing to prevent it, Joe took the opportunity to try and make his way back to where he should have been.

"HALT!"

Joe froze and, as two shots rang out behind him, he found himself looking down the barrel of a rifle.

****

London

The train jolted sharply, shuddering to a halt yet again and the sound of bombs dropping in the surrounding countryside grew louder. Pam threw herself on the floor with the rest of the passengers, her nose inches from the highly polished boots of a soldier who had not bothered to leave his seat. They were just outside London and this was the second time the train had stopped.

"Aren't you going to bother?" she said, feeling slightly stupid lying on the dirty floor when the soldier was still seated.

"Nah. If it's got my name on it, lying on the floor won't make any difference. I'd rather die in comfort wouldn't you?" His impish grin restored Pam's own sense of humour and she sat herself back down on her seat. Most people in the south were used to the constant bombing, some, like the soldier, treating the raids with total disdain. The air raids had come as a complete shock to her. Wandering around the Scottish moors for days in isolation, she had been totally out of touch and the training centre was so remote anyway, most of the time she had hardly known there was a war at all. This left her completely unprepared for what she saw when she arrived back in London.

Her next shock was when the train pulled into Kings Cross station and she saw the large craters everywhere. But that was just the beginning. She left the main station and headed down into the underground, intending to catch the circle line tube to Bayswater. It was still early in the morning and those who had been sheltering in the underground stations had not yet left. Everywhere she looked, there were people sleeping, on the platforms, on the elevators and the corridors and even the toilets. Most of those she could see were women and children and, although there were a few bunks at one end of the platform, the majority were just lying on the floor, covered with blankets and using their clothes for pillows. The scene was made even more surreal by the sight of commuters on their way to work, soldiers on route to their latest deployment and general passengers stepping over this seething mass of humanity while they went about their business. Even worse was the dreadful smell that greeted her, the smell of overflowing toilets and buckets mingling with the more general smell of stale air and unwashed bodies. Pam made a concerted effort not to gasp at the sights and smells assaulting her, realising she was the one who was out of step with normal everyday life in the capital.

Despite the disruption, the underground ran smoothly and, within minutes, she arrived at Bayswater. She made her way to the surface and gasped. She couldn't believe the devastation all around her and, instead of going straight home, she decided to go for a walk first. She headed towards Oxford Street, but the familiar landmarks that would normally have greeted her were altered beyond recognition and she had to resist the temptation to pinch herself to check she wasn't dreaming.

John Lewis, Bourne and Hollingsworth and DH Evans had all been hit, as had Peter Robinson's at Oxford Circus. The once familiar buildings were empty hollow shells and some were still smouldering, surrounded by exhausted firemen trying their best to damp them down and put out the remaining fires. Even Selfridges had sustained considerable damage, although the store did at least appear to be open.

She stared around with a growing sense of unreality; everywhere she looked, shop and business staff were beginning to clear up, some whistling cheerfully, others silent and grimly determined to reopen as soon as possible. She was about to offer to help when she suddenly panicked. What about her own house and her parents? Fearing the worst, she turned around and headed home, her heart in her mouth, stopping only to buy a selection of newspapers. Much to her relief, the house appeared to be untouched, its sandbags serenely in place, the crisscross of blast-proof tape across its windows strangely comforting.

There was no one in, but that wasn't surprising; her father would be at work and her mother had numerous 'good works' keeping her occupied for a considerable amount of time.

She spent her first hour at home drinking coffee and reading through the papers, all thoughts of soaking in a nice hot bath completely forgotten. Having a better idea of what had been happening whilst she had been away, she rang Tony only to find out he had been transferred further north now the Germans had moved their attentions from the airfields to the cities. Her first thought was one of relief when she realised this was just what he needed; time to recuperate and recover from the murderous onslaught they had been facing. But when she thought about the horror stories in the papers and listened to the news on the wireless, she began to wonder at the price the civilians of Britain, particularly London, Liverpool and the South Coast were paying, so the RAF and their airfields could recover. She also wondered how Peggy was getting on. According to the papers, several of the hospitals had been hit and at one hospital, several nurses had been killed. But, in line with national security measures, the name of the hospital wasn't revealed.

****

Toulouse, Southern France

Jeanne was still worrying about Isabelle's reaction, but consoled herself that although they would have to be extremely careful now that Gabriel had broken off the engagement, eventually, they would be able to meet in the open. Rather than focus on missing him, she made herself think about how much she was looking forward to Christmas and to being able see him again.

The news Gabriel had broken off his engagement had gone round the police station like wildfire. Although Gabriel had not said anything to anyone other than Jeanne, the unexpected appearance of Isabelle a few days later soon ended any idea he had of keeping the end of the relationship quiet and personal.

Jeanne had been trying to answer a query from one of the detectives when she saw Isabelle enter the building and head for Gabriel's office. She tried hard not to pay any attention but her heart was beating wildly, because at any moment she expected Isabelle to come back down and accuse her of stealing her fiancé. Trying hard not to shake, she quickly found the information the detective was looking for. Normally, she would have stood and chatted with him, as this was the more interesting part of her job and often they would tell her what they were doing. Much to his surprise, she couldn't get rid of him quickly enough.

Not long after he had gone, the sound of shouting filled the large entrance hall. Although not all the words could be heard, there was enough for people to be able to make out what was happening. Jeanne glanced round nervously. She was petrified her name would come out and, not for the first time in her life, she thanked her father for his wisdom and foresight in making them keep their relationship a secret. The voices grew louder and then suddenly became much clearer when Isabelle flung open the door

"... Don't think you've heard the end of this. I know there's someone else and when I find out who she is, you and she will wish you'd never been born! No one makes a fool of me and gets away with it."

"The only one making a fool of you is you, Isabelle. I keep telling you, there's no one else. I've just realised I'm not in love with you, which is not fair on either of us. Why can't you just accept that gracefully, instead of behaving like a fishwife?" Gabriel's voice sounded calm and reasonable after Isabelle's shrieking but Jeanne still winced. Calling his ex-fiancée a 'fishwife' was hardly likely to diffuse the situation. A strange noise at her side made her jump and, looking round, she was astonished to see Eve, hand pressed hard against her mouth, trying frantically not to laugh.

Jeanne looked at her in amazement and Eve whispered softly, "Sorry, I know I shouldn't laugh, but it's about time he told her what's what. He's always been too good for her. She's a really nasty bit of work."

"Then surely, that's all the more reason not to antagonise her?" Jeanne was becoming even more alarmed.

Eve shrugged, but after a couple of minutes' thought, nodded soberly. "You could be right. Maybe he should be a bit more careful. I wonder who the mystery woman is?"

"You heard him, he says there isn't anyone." Jeanne tone was slightly too sharp but Eve didn't seem to notice.

"I said he was too good for her, I didn't say he was a saint. There's bound to be another woman; he's a man isn't he?" Eve stopped suddenly and looked closely at Jeanne. "You've been spending a lot of time with him lately." Jeanne could feel her face beginning to flush while Eve continued, "Has he said anything to you?"

Unable to believe her luck, Jeanne frantically tried to compose herself. "No, he's not mentioned anyone and, anyway, I haven't seen much of him," she added forcefully… Too forcefully. Realisation slowly dawned on Eve's face. She looked round to make sure no one could hear and then turned back to Jeanne.

"It's you, isn't it?"

Chapter Twenty

Stalag XXA, Poland

Total silence followed the shooting, then all hell broke loose. Yelling in anger and shock, the men launched themselves towards the wire and the German who had fired the shots. Distracted by the sudden commotion, the guard, whose rifle was so perilously close to Joe's head, glanced away to see what was happening and Joe took the opportunity to disappear into the melée of angry men. When the guard looked back, Joe had gone and, having more important things to worry about, he pushed his way through the crowds of furious men towards the riot now taking place behind him. Joe allowed himself to be swallowed up by the crowds; he was shaking violently and he knew he had been lucky.

Unable to control the situation by weight of numbers or rescue the German who had fired the fatal shots, the other guards began firing into the air, the bullets whistling only inches above the prisoners' heads. Finally, with the help of the senior British NCO, who was concerned other men would be shot, order was gradually restored. Joe was now back where he should have been and, with the others, he watched silently while the Germans carried the severely beaten guard towards the Guard Room. Having vented their anger on the culprit, the men waited nervously, wondering how the Germans would deal with their attempted insurrection. The tension in the air was palpable and the senior British NCO watched warily as the remaining guards repeatedly threatened the prisoners, trying to goad them into reacting.

"Just ignore them, lads!" he shouted when someone looked about to retaliate. To his relief, the man's companions seemed to have more sense and managed to restrain him before things got out of hand.

"I think we should've just carried on. Bloody NCO's always interfering; we might've got out," a voice muttered angrily behind Joe.

"And gone where? We're God knows how many thousands of miles away from home. The Krauts would have been so angry if we'd all tried to escape, we'd probably all have been shot out of hand. I don't know about you, but I intend to go home at the end of this stinking war and I'm not going to give the bastards the slightest excuse to shoot me."

Joe privately thought the second man was probably right. He would have loved to have escaped and gone home but the chances of succeeding were pretty remote, given where they were. He glanced up and realised it was snowing. There were just a few tiny flakes at first but then they grew bigger and heavier until the snow began to swirl round them, settling on their boots and clothes and gradually covering the ground. They were all shivering violently, their clothing no match for the icy wind.

It was the snow that finally saved them. Unable to resist the temptation to make snowmen with their feet in an attempt to keep warm, the tension gradually dissipated and the guards, thoroughly fed up and needing their own warm waterproof winter clothing, decided to send the men back to their huts.

"Christ, I'm cold." Mitchell lowered his voice as they hurried towards the relative warmth of their hut. "That was a close one, pal. Want on earth were you doing?"

"Trying to get back to the right line," Joe answered. "I thought there'd be trouble if I was caught in the wrong place."

"You nearly ended up in the same place as those poor suckers caught between the wires. How could the bastard just shoot him when he had his hands up? Want sort of mindless cretins are they?" The fury in Mitchell's voice was echoed by many of the men, the air full of angry comments while they discussed what had happened and more than one climbed onto his bunk planning revenge.

****

Toulouse, Southern France

Unable to lie to the woman who had been so good to her, Jeanne nodded, anguish written all across her face. "You won't say anything, will you?" she pleaded.

"Of course I won't, you silly girl! Stop looking so worried, you'll only draw attention to yourself. For what it's worth, I'm glad. I think you'll be very good for each other, if Isabelle doesn't have you both deported to the Third Reich for some spurious reason first… You'll have to be very careful for a while, you know that don't you?"

Before Jeanne could answer, Isabelle appeared at the top of the stairs, swung her fur stole carelessly over her left shoulder, swept haughtily down the steps and out of the building without giving them a second glance. Jeanne realised she had been holding her breath.

"You'll have to get better at hiding your feelings. The gossip mill will be working overtime now, while everyone tries to find the mystery woman."

"But why? This has nothing to do with anyone else."

"That won't stop them, Jeanne. We're at war, even though it might not seem like it here. And make no mistake, we're occupied, even though it might look like a French government is in charge. People get nervous and do things they wouldn't normally. Having friends in high places is a good way of finding some security. Isabelle has very powerful connections and she would no doubt be very grateful to anyone who could tell her who her fiancé had dumped her for. Then she could wreak her revenge. I like you, Jeanne, very much and I'd hate to see anything happen to you." She was about to say more when she caught a movement out of the corner of her eye. "Hello, Theo. How are you this morning?"

"Better than the boss!" He grinned, indicating upstairs. He glanced around. "Better off without her, no doubt about that. Let's hope she finds someone new to get her claws into quickly, then she'll leave the boss alone." He collected the post and headed towards the stairs.

****

Lambeth Hospital, London

Pam made her way across the Thames to Lambeth and was relieved to see the hospital was still standing and relatively unscathed, despite the devastation surrounding it. She wondered which shift Peggy was likely to be on and decided the best way to find out was to ask someone. She headed for the emergency department, guessing this was where Peggy was likely to be.

The department was chaotic; there were injured people everywhere, some on stretchers in the corridors, all the available chairs were full and people were even sitting on the floors. Many of those waiting were in shock, their clothes filthy and in shreds, or they were wrapped in blankets, their eyes unfocused. Pam wondered whether this was a good time to be bothering Peggy. If she was here, she would probably have her hands full. She turned away

"Pam? Pam, are you injured?"

She spun around. "Hello, Peggy. No, I came to see if you were alright. I've been away and I didn't know what had been happening…" She stopped.

Peggy looked completely exhausted, her eyes were red rimmed with dark bags underneath. Her face was streaked with dirt and her uniform was less than spotless, but she was smiling. "Sorry. I look a bit of a mess. It's been a bit hectic over the last few weeks, but today's a little quieter, thank goodness."

Pam's heart sank. If this was a quiet day, what on earth was a busy one like?

"When do you finish? I'll take you to dinner." Peggy opened her mouth to argue, to say all she really wanted was to go to bed and sleep for a week, but she could see the familiar stubborn look on Pam's face and gave in with a good grace.

"I finish in about an hour and I've got tomorrow off, thank goodness."

"Then that's settled. I'll wait and you can come back with me for the night. The West End seems safer than the rest of London, so you can sleep at my place; all day if you want. I've only got a few days, Peggy and then I've got to go away again. Please, let me help?"

Peggy was too tired to argue and the thought of sleeping in a bed all night and possibly all day too, without having to go to the shelter, was too good to turn down. She would have to go home and change first and tell Annie where she was going, but she was already feeling better at the thought of an uninterrupted night's sleep. She smiled at Pam and then called to the next person in line. Pam hesitated and then followed Peggy into the emergency ward. Peggy's patient was a girl of about twelve with dried blood caked to the side of her head and Peggy began the task of trying to remove the blood carefully whilst getting some details from the girl about who she was and where her family might be. Fortunately, the girl was quite chatty, unlike some who were so traumatised they couldn't even speak.

Pam walked along the length of the curtained cubicles until she found a harassed looking doctor busily writing some notes. He glanced up and then carried on writing. "You'll have to wait your turn, I'm afraid."

"I don't need help. I trained here for two years and I'm with the FANY now. I wanted to see if there was anything I could do to help while I wait for my friend to finish her shift."

"Who's your friend?"

The doctor seemed marginally more interested now and, encouraged, Pam continued, "Nurse Cooper."

"Oh, Peggy! No problem." The doctor's attitude changed completely and he pointed to the corridor where she had come in. "If you could try and get some details from them... you know, who they are, where they live or lived and, if they're young, try and find out where the rest of the family is and if they're still alive. There's some notebooks in the cupboard over there. Thanks. It'll be a great help." He went back to filling in his forms.

Pam headed over to where he had pointed and took out a notebook, relieved he hadn't asked her to do anything else. She had become so used to her cover story, she'd almost forgotten she hadn't actually done any nursing for two years. More intriguing was the way the young doctor's face lit up when she mentioned Peggy. He was rather good looking too! She would have to tease Peggy about him later, she mused to herself and then, faced with her first patient, the doctor was forgotten while she began to hear first-hand just how bad the bombing was.

****

Stalag XXA, Poland

Joe climbed onto his bunk and pulled his thin blanket round him. He was still shivering, although whether from the cold or shock, he wasn't sure. But the incident was not quite over. Within minutes the hut door was flung open again and one of the guards stood there, his rifle raised menacingly. He shouted for the hut interpreter to come forward, a young man with glasses and a nervous stutter known by all as 'the professor' or 'Prof' for short because of his university degree and his ability to speak both French and German.

The guard began shouting and 'Prof' did his best to keep up.

"Put all your blankets here, now. You can have them back when the Commandant says so. If you think you can get away with assaulting a German guard going about his lawful business, you can think again. You're lucky you're not all dead."

Joe had an idea the original version had not been quite so polite, but the meaning was certainly clear enough and, like the others, he immediately protested loudly. But the guard was in no mood for any objections and to prove it, he fired his rifle into the wooden ceiling of the hut. The men threw themselves on the floor or ducked frantically under their bunks. Eventually, after much grumbling and moaning, the blankets were piled up by the door and the guard picked out two prisoners to carry them. As they opened the door and left the hut, the temperature plummeted, causing those closest to the door to yell insults at the departing guard and the accompanying prisoners.

"Christ, we'll be lucky if we don't freeze to death in this weather." Mitchell pulled his coat over him. "I'm sure they're not allowed to do this."

"I agree and I think you should go and tell the Commandant. I think we should elect you the hut spokesmen. What do you think, chaps?" Cyril said loudly, sarcasm dripping from every word.

"There's no need to start on me." Mitchell began to climb off his bunk, anger showing on his face

"Come on, lads, it's not worth arguing over," Joe interrupted hastily. "We're all angry and you're probably right, they shouldn't take away our blankets, but there's loads of other things they shouldn't do as well, like starving us, using our Red Cross parcels to feed us and shooting unarmed men, to mention a few. But there's nothing we can do and fighting amongst ourselves is not going to help."

"Well said, 'Joe the peacemaker'," Dick responded from his bunk. "Obviously they do teach you something in the Rifle Brigade!"

Cyril immediately forgot the argument with Mitchell and turned his attention to Dick, intending to defend the honour of the regiment. However, Dick was grinning at him and he sat down again just as quickly, realising he was being ragged.

"Yeah, sorry and all that," he said sheepishly to Mitchell who shrugged.

"No problem. I'm just frustrated because we can't do anything."

"Oh, I don't know," Dick said without looking up from his book.

Mitchell, Joe and Cyril looked at him expectantly, waiting for him to elaborate. After a few minutes, Mitchell said, "Well, come on then, Dick. What do you mean?"

"Just that if we find out where the blankets are, we can go and get them back again."

Mitchell turned over in disgust. "Yeah, right! That's a sure good way to get ourselves killed."

Dick seemed unconcerned by the criticism. "Not if we do things right. We just give it a couple of days until the heat's died down and, if they don't return the blankets, we'll go and get them."

Joe looked dubiously at Cyril and Mitchell, who were shaking their heads in disbelief.

He was about to say something when the door of the hut opened and the two men who had carried the blankets reappeared, looking frozen and covered in a dusting of snow. Before he could speak, Dick had scrambled down from his bunk and, crossing the short distance to the two men in double quick time, had engaged them in conversation.

"If I'd known he could move that quick, I'd have recommended him for the Rifle Brigade," Cyril said sarcastically.

Joe grinned but didn't answer, his eyes still fixed firmly on Dick and the two men. They were totally engrossed in a deep conversation, their heads close together, any sound muffled by the other noises in the hut. Unable to make out what they were saying, he sighed and gave up, climbing back up on to his bunk.

****

London

They had a tasty stew with plenty of meat, vegetables and potatoes, followed by apple pie. Peggy was surprised by how much she was able to eat, especially when she hadn't felt hungry before the food was dished up.

"So who's the dishy doctor, then?" Pam was surprised to see Peggy blush.

"He's just a friend. His name's Chris. He's from Wales." Realising she sounded defensive Peggy followed up her statement with a large yawn and Pam hid a smile. It looked as though Peggy might have taken her advice not to put her life on hold after all. Peggy was a hopeless liar and the fact she didn't want to talk about Chris only confirmed Pam's suspicions that there was more than friendship between them.

Not wanting to embarrass her friend, she changed the subject and, when Peggy had finished her meal, Pam ushered her upstairs.

"I'm not having any arguments. Go to bed and we can catch up in the morning when you're not so tired."

Peggy washed and undressed quickly and climbed under the crisp white sheets and fresh smelling blankets. Within minutes, she was fast asleep.

Pam went back downstairs and poured herself a whisky, grateful for once that her father 'had connections.' She sat in the comfortable armchair in front of the roaring fire and closed her eyes.

"Penny for your thoughts?" Pam started awake, surprised to see her father smiling down at her.

"Goodness, I must have fallen asleep. Peggy is upstairs by the way. I gave her the spare room." She gave her father a brief summary of the day's events by way of explanation.

"Good. Now, how are you?" She had lost some weight but, apart from looking slightly tired, she appeared very fit and healthy. If he didn't know better, he would've thought she'd been on some kind of intensive physical training course. Perhaps the FANY did physical training now, he mused, although why they would need to was a mystery to him. There was also something else he couldn't quite put his finger on; an alertness that hadn't been there before. Oh well, whatever she was up to seemed to be doing her good. He'd never seen her looking so contented before. "How long have you got?"

"Two days." She yawned and, sensing he might be about to ask some awkward questions, she carried on quickly, "I think I'd better go up now before I fall asleep here again." She stood up and, kissing him on the cheek, said softly, "Goodnight, Pops." The use of her childhood name for him distracted him briefly, as she'd known it would, and she left the room before he realised she'd not said where she'd been or where she was going.

Part Three

November - December 1940

Chapter Twenty-one

La Couture, Northern France

"It's finished." Henri put his head round the door, a big smile on his face. Louis appeared beside him. "Would you like to come and have a look?"

Marie was already standing up, delight written on her face. "That didn't take long." Marie tied her scarf under her chin and pulled her winter coat around her.

"Come on then!" she called to Georges who came running up, wagging his tail.

Georges was their new Border Collie puppy and Marie thought he was wonderful. She had never had a dog before and Louis had to work hard to stop her treating him like another child. He slept outside and made the perfect guard dog, along with the half dozen geese that had mysteriously appeared with him. Henri wouldn't say how he had managed to get Giraud to part with them as well, but with the geese and Georges to warn them if anyone came near the farmhouse, Marie felt a lot safer.

The weather was bitterly cold and Marie glanced up anxiously at the leaden skies. "Looks like snow."

Louis nodded. "Yes, I'll bring the cows into the barn tonight and make sure the chickens are safely in their pen when we get back. I'm going to sit up for a while anyway. I'd like to shoot the fox before he has any more of the chickens."

"What about the geese?"

"I'd feel sorry for any fox trying to get in amongst them! I'll let Georges sleep in the barn too, if he wants." He looked at Henri and shook his head; honestly, women! If his mother had her way, Georges would not only be sleeping in the farmhouse, but probably in his mother's bedroom, on her bed.

The temperature was dropping rapidly and, before long, they could feel the air freezing around them and even the mud became more solid under their feet.

The new structure looked quite impressive from a distance. Henri showed them round, trying hard to hide his pride in his workmanship and Marie could understand why. From both the outside and inside, the building looked exactly what it claimed to be, a farm shop selling surplus produce.

The floor was covered with dried straw and there was a small counter spanning three quarters of the length of the back wall. Along the sides were several shelves with space in between for small sacks of items, like potatoes. The door to the storeroom was on the left hand side of the counter. Positioned directly opposite the door into the shop, the opening offered a direct invitation into the storeroom, clearly stating there was nothing to hide. Marie walked through the door into the storeroom holding her breath, expecting to see something to indicate its true purpose. But there was nothing, other than a bare room with straw on the floor, in fact it looked so boringly normal that, for a moment, she wondered if they had changed their mind and hidden the room somewhere else. However, a quick look at Henri's face confirmed they were in the right place and, after asking Louis to keep a look out, he walked over to the corner and cleared the straw, revealing a small trapdoor built into the floor. He lifted the trap carefully and Marie could see steps going down into the darkness.

"Are you alright to go down?" he asked, but Marie was already lowering herself carefully through the small space.

Henri followed her and lit the gas lamp on the wall. The room was exactly the same size and very much like the one above, only darker, without the benefit of the natural light that came through the one tiny window that lit the shop. The room contained several empty wine racks, some against the walls, others in rows in the middle. Once again, the floor was covered with straw and the general impression was of clutter and an almost timeless permanence, as though it had always been there.

Henri smiled at her. "What do you think so far?"

Marie was impressed. But before she answered, she began to make her way around the room, carefully squeezing between the racks looking for any sign of another entrance or something out of the ordinary. Henri watched patiently, saying nothing. This was the first test. Once Marie knew exactly where the entrance was, she would automatically see it when she came in here. He needed her to look for the hidden room without knowing where, very much like the Germans would if they suspected anything.

Eventually, finding nothing out of the ordinary, she gave up. "I can't see anything that shouldn't be here. Come on, don't keep me in suspense!"

****

Outside Bethune, Northern France

"Are you doing anything exciting?" Brigitte wandered into Rolf's study. It was the first time in ages he'd been around long enough for her to speak to him. She hadn't wanted to bother him while he was busy, so she'd waited until things seemed to have quietened down and he was in a good mood. He closed the file he was looking at and smiled.

"No, just boring work, nothing that would interest your pretty little head." He reached out for her. "Why don't you come and sit on my lap and tell me what you've been doing all day."

Brigitte sat down, put her arms around his neck and then pouted. "I haven't been doing anything. To be honest, I'm really bored." She kissed him and then fluttered her eyelashes at him. "Would you mind if I helped my father out during the day? I know he's quite busy and would appreciated the help."

Rolf pretended to consider her request. He'd wondered how long she would survive with nothing to do. She'd held out longer than he'd expected. "Of course I don't mind." He hugged her and rubbed his fingers across her nipples in the way he knew she liked. "I've got a favour to ask too, if you don't mind?"

Delighted he'd agreed so quickly, Brigitte nodded. "Of course, anything." She thought he wanted sex, so she was surprised when he spun the chair around and reached for a file. Her heart beat a little faster. She couldn't believe he was about to share his work with her. Her father was wrong: he did love her.

"There have been some thefts of German alcohol. My superiors think the culprit comes from Bethune. I have been ordered to search the town sometime in the next few days." He stared into her eyes. "That will mean locking up anyone who sells alcohol in the hope one of them will talk. I don't want to arrest your father but I will have no option. If you could ask around, I might be able to find the real culprit and leave everyone else alone." He held his breath, wondering if he had made his move too soon.

Brigitte stared back at him. She didn't want her father arrested and, in any case, if someone was selling stolen liquor, her father would be losing money. She couldn't see any harm in helping Rolf.

"Alright, I'll ask around for you while I'm working. If I hear anything, I'll tell you."

"Thank you, darling." Rolf buried his face in her breasts, not wanting her to see the look of triumph in his eyes. He undid the buttons on the back of her dress and slipped the garment off her shoulders. While she took off her bra, he slid his hand up her leg until he felt the bare skin at the top of her stockings. While his fingers snaked upwards, he reflected just how easy it was to manipulate her.

****

La Couture, Northern France

"Here, take my hand." Henri led her to the wall furthest away from the trapdoor and carefully moved one of the wine racks. Marie stared, but she still couldn't see anything. Henri cleared the straw, revealing what looked like the outline to another trapdoor, but this one was completely flush to the floor and there was no visible means of opening it. Marie frowned and gingerly put her foot on the trapdoor and trod down as she shifted her weight. Nothing happened and she frowned, still not entirely sure this was where the hidden room was.

"How on earth do you open the door?"

Henri walked across to another wine rack and reached behind the shelves. As if by magic, the trapdoor opened and Marie peered down into the darkness. Her eyes adjusted and she could see a ladder leading down. She stopped at the edge of the open space and gazed down. "That's amazing, Henri. How does it work?"

"There's a small button attached to the back of the wine rack. Look." He showed her, but she could see nothing.

He put his finger over one of the nodules in the wood of the rack frame and pressed gently. The trapdoor closed and she gasped in astonishment. "Amazing. Unless you're looking, you'd never find anything. It's ingenious, perfectly camouflaged. Henri you've worked so hard."

Henri was serious. "This is not a game we're playing, so I've tried to think of everything. The idea is, if they find this room they'll assume we were trying to hide the wine and won't look any further. Although the penalties are quite severe, there's a chance they'll just confiscate the alcohol and threaten us. Especially if we make a point of being reasonably friendly. Not too friendly, mind, or they'll smell a rat, but not blatantly rude either. At the very worst, they'll lock us up for a few months and then, hopefully, let us go. If we get caught hiding airmen, they'll shoot us."

Marie nodded as he continued, "When we bring the men here, we'll blindfold them and the same when they leave. One of my biggest problems was trying to work out how to get air in. Obviously the room is sealed, and without air they would die. Eventually I came up with the idea of a pipe. It runs down the corner of both rooms and the shop itself but is actually hidden in the brickwork so can't be seen. It's quite thick and goes up to the roof and emerges in the guttering. I've had a good look and I can't see anything from the ground. Obviously, if they go up on the roof for any reason…" He stopped and shrugged. If they were up on the roof, then they would probably already be suspicious of something anyway. He turned his attention back to Marie. "We can put thick straw on the floor and plenty of blankets to keep the men warm, a small stock of food and water if for any reason we can't get here every day and a bucket for a toilet behind a small screen."

He hesitated. "My main worry was they can't open the door from inside. We thought long and hard but we can't risk anyone coming out at the wrong time."

Marie looked at him with concern. "But what if there is an emergency, or a fire or we are arrested and can't get here to let them out?"

Henri smiled and pointed to the far corner of the small room. Marie could just make out a metal grille. She looked at Henri, puzzled, and he smiled again. "It's a tunnel; not the biggest and possibly not particularly safe, but it's an emergency escape route which comes out in the woods about three hundred metres away and the entrance is well hidden from the road."

Marie was silent for a while. "What if someone stumbles on the other end by accident?"

Henri shook his head. "The other end is not completed. I have dug most of the way up, there's about fifty centimetres of soil left to dig through. Above is a board to stop people falling through, covered with another thirty centimetres of soil. I have left a pick and shovel at the far end, as well as a pick and shovel in here, so, if they get trapped here and have to use the emergency exit, they can dig themselves out. All they have to do is crawl to the end and dig straight up and they will exit into the woods."

Marie smiled at him in admiration. "You've thought of everything."

Henri relaxed. "I'm glad you're pleased. The fact you couldn't see any sign of the room means it must be reasonably secure; let's hope so anyway, for all our sakes," he finished quietly under his breath as he replaced the straw and the wine rack against the wall.

Chapter Twenty-two

Toulouse, Southern France

Jeanne still hadn't mentioned Isabelle's threats towards Gabriel to her father because she didn't want to worry him. She also knew he had problems of his own. Angel was getting on very well at school and seemed to be recovering from the traumatic events that had brought them all together in the first place. However, occasionally she would refer to Jean-Paul by his first name instead of 'Papa'. He usually managed to explain this away as the harmless behaviour of a young girl who had been quite traumatised by the things they had experienced on their travels south, and by the death of her mother. But that wasn't his biggest concern.

Angel had soon made friends and, once the news of Claudette's tragic death spread, he had been grateful for the extra help and support offered to him. He was unable to be at the school every night to pick her up, so some of the other mothers offered to take Angel home with their children until he had finished work and was able to collect her from their house. Mourning the love of his life, he accepted the offers in the spirit most of them were offered: support for a widowed man and his young daughter.

However, as the time passed and he began to pay more attention to the world again, he started to have some doubts about the reasons behind the help. Most men of working and military age were either prisoners in Germany and Poland or employed in labour camps. Many of the women whose daughters and sons were the same age as Angel were young and had been apart from their men for a long time. They were lonely. Often they had no idea whether their husbands were even alive or when they would be back. Although some were already going out with the German or Italian soldiers, who were present in the unoccupied zone in great numbers, the community as a whole frowned on this type of fraternisation, thus the only alternative was to look for those in reserved occupations or older men who, for whatever reason, had escaped the forced labour deportations.

Whilst he was immensely flattered these attractive young women could be interested in him, the pain of Claudette's death was much too raw for him to consider starting a relationship with any of them. Furthermore, his position as a Jew hiding in fiercely anti-Semitic Vichy made it much too dangerous to start any kind of liaison. His primary concern was to protect Jeanne and Angel and he could only do so if he was careful.

"Papa, can I go to Marianne's to play after school tonight? Her mother said I could." Angel's voice broke into his thoughts as they arrived at the school gates.

"Of course, chère." He smiled, despite his misgivings about Marianne's mother and some of the people he had seen her with. He had also heard Marianne say things he did not approve of, but as she was only expressing the sentiments of the government, there was little he could do. He couldn't even chastise Angel when she repeated some of the more extreme anti-Semitic comments, in case she repeated his views at school. "I'll pick you up when I finish work. Have a lovely day." He turned and walked off, trying unsuccessfully to silence the anxious voice in his head.

"Good morning, Monsieur Coultard." The voice was loud and grated on his ears. Sighing inwardly, he composed his face into a smile and turned to greet Marianne's mother, who was heading towards him, an ingratiating smile plastered on her rather vacuous face. Chastising himself for being so judgmental, he made more of an effort than he really wanted to.

"How are you this morning?" Without giving him time to answer, she continued, "As Angel is coming to play with Marianne after school, why don't you both eat with us? We could get something quite nice if we pooled our rations. I'm sure your older daughter can manage on her own for once. A good looking girl like her, I'm surprised she doesn't have the men falling over themselves to take her out." This time her smile held more than a hint of lasciviousness and Jean-Paul shuddered inwardly, although outwardly he did his best to maintain his composure

"Thank you, *Madame* Fourier." He emphasised the 'Madame' as if to remind her she was a married woman. "That's very kind of you, but we have already made arrangements for tonight. Another time, perhaps?" He glanced at his watch and said regretfully, "You'll have to excuse me, I'm afraid. I really have to get to work. I can't afford to be late. I'll see you later when I come to collect Angel and thank you again for your kind offer and for picking up Angel from school." He was already walking off while he finished speaking, giving her no opportunity to respond.

He strode briskly away, knowing he would have to do something about this situation. Perhaps he could ask Jeanne to collect Angel in the evenings. But that was only a very short term solution and might cause even more problems. He would still have to see Madame Fourier tomorrow morning, because he could hardly expect Jeanne to take Angel to school for him. Maybe the best thing would be to acknowledge her obvious overtures and explain he really wasn't ready for another relationship, because it was much too soon after his wife's death. He wondered though whether that would be enough. He had a nasty feeling, if he left any room for doubt, she would insist on waiting until he was ready. Lost in his thoughts, he did not see the woman in front of him until it was too late and he had bumped into her.

"Goodness, please forgive me." He began to apologise profusely but the woman laughed

"It was as much my fault as yours, honestly. I wasn't looking where I was going either; too busy thinking of things I can do nothing about." She smiled at him and Jean-Paul looked at her more closely.

She was an attractive woman of about thirty-five or so, and his overwhelming impression was one of warmth and fun.

"I insist on taking all the blame, really. Perhaps by way of an apology, I can buy you coffee?" The words were out of his mouth before he could stop them and then he remembered he was supposed to be at work and he couldn't believe how let down he felt.

"I would love to, but I am already late for work. Perhaps later? I work in the Town Hall. Suzanne Siémens." She held out her hand. "I finish at four today."

Jean-Paul shook her outstretched hand. "Jean-Paul Coultard. I'm a teacher, so I finish about the same time. Can I meet you outside the Town Hall at about quarter past?"

Suzanne smiled. "I will look forward to it. And now I really must go, Monsieur Coultard. Au revoir."

"Au revoir." Jean-Paul resisted the temptation to watch her walking away and headed off towards the school. All of a sudden, he felt like a young school boy about to go on his first date and he couldn't help smiling to himself, his previous worries about Marianne's mother completely forgotten, as he contemplated his date with the delightful Suzanne.

****

Lewisham, London

Kath hurried along the road unable to believe she had overslept. 'The old cow', as she always referred to Olive, would have a field day. She was about to cross the road when two men stepped in front of her, barring her way.

"Excuse me..." Her voice dried up when she realised who they were. "Sorry, Mr Dickson, I didn't realise it was you." She cleared her throat, but neither man moved and she started to feel uneasy.

"Hello, Kath. You're looking very well." Bernard Dickson was tall and well-built, with a boxer's face, the nose slightly crooked, the lips puffy, the eyes veined red. His companion was small and wiry with a sparse beard and shifty eyes. He reminded Kath of a weasel. Dickson was the local villain and Kath wondered what on earth he wanted with her.

"Thank you." She couldn't think of anything else to say.

He stared at her for several seconds before speaking again. "I'm looking for Tom. Have you seen him?"

Kath began to relax. "No. I was getting worried about him to be honest. I haven't seen him for ages."

Dickson didn't answer and Kath's nerves began to return. "Honestly, Mr Dickson, I'm telling you the truth. I really haven't seen him. I'd tell you if I had."

"I do hope so, my dear." He continued to stare at her and Kath's legs turned to water. She was just about to repeat her denial when he spoke. "You and he've been seen together a lot. What've you been up to?"

For a split second, Kath thought about lying and saying they were seeing each other, then she changed her mind. "He's blackmailing someone I know," she blurted out.

Dickson smiled, but it wasn't a pleasant smile. "Really? Do tell me more."

"I need to get to work, Mr Dickson. I'm already late and it's a long story," Kath pleaded and, to her surprise, he stood aside.

"I'll see you down the Red Lion, seven o'clock. Don't be late, Kath. I'd hate to have to come looking for you." He tipped his hat and moved away, leaving Kath shaking. She hurried off, trying to resist the temptation to turn around and make sure he wasn't coming after her. At least she had a full day to work out what to tell him, although given his reputation, perhaps she should just tell him the whole truth and leave him to sort Olive out.

****

Bethune, Northern France

"You're sure?" Brigitte asked the thin faced man sitting at the bar in her father's café. He nodded, drank the rest of his wine and left. Brigitte was surprised just how easy it had been to find the name Rolf wanted. Raul Germain hadn't restricted his activities to stealing from the Germans and most people she spoke to, including her father, seemed quite happy to moan to her about him. He was also suspected of being an informer, because he appeared to be getting away with his crimes.

Of course, they had no idea what she was intending to do with the information, but she couldn't see how they could complain. They obviously wanted something done about him and she was just obliging them. Delighted she would be able to please Rolf, Brigitte asked her father if she could finish early. She couldn't wait to get home and tell him.

"You've only been here five minutes!" Fabian grumbled. He stared at his daughter. Her face was flushed; she was definitely up to something.

****

Toulouse, Southern France

"So, how long have you lived in Toulouse?" Suzanne sipped her coffee and smiled across the table at Jean-Paul.

"We came here after France surrendered." Suzanne raised her eyebrows and Jean-Paul explained, "My wife, she died not long after we arrived, and my two daughters, Jeanne and Angel. What about you?"

"I've always lived here. Very boring really and, before you ask, no, I've never been married. There was someone, but…" An expression he couldn't quite fathom crossed her face and she changed the subject. "How old are your daughters?"

"Jeanne is nearly eighteen and Angel's five. She's just started school. I'm a history teacher, by the way. What do you do?"

"I'm just a clerk at the Town Hall. Well, general dogsbody really. I've been working there for about six years now and, to be honest, I'm very bored, but a job's a job, especially in these troubling times." Again the same strange expression crossed her face, but was gone so quickly, Jean-Paul wasn't sure if he was imagining things.

"You'll have to let me buy you dinner one evening…" The words were out of his mouth before Jean-Paul could stop himself. There was something about this woman he couldn't explain; maybe, like him, she had a secret? He found her very attractive and, to his surprise, he realised he wanted to get to know her better. He stopped, unable to believe he was thinking such a thing and then Claudette's dying words floated into his mind and he relaxed and smiled gently to himself.

****

Lewisham, London

"And that's everything?" Dickson's eyes bore into Kath's and she nodded.

Her first inclination after their meeting that morning had been to try and protect Olive if she could, or at least warn her. However, she'd soon changed her mind after she'd walked through the door and Olive had summoned her to the supervisor's office, given her a black mark for being late and informed her that her lateness, for the second time in two weeks, would go on her record. Kath had immediately begun to argue that the previous time had not been her fault. There had been an unexploded bomb and the bus had been unable to get through, so the passengers had to walk. Olive ignored her protests, her beady eyes behind the thick glasses making little attempt to hide her pleasure. Any pity Kath felt instantly disappeared and she resolved to throw Olive to Dickson without a second thought.

"And you both thought she'd killed Mary?" Dickson seemed unable to take in what she was telling him and Kath nodded.

"Over losing her job?" He sounded incredulous.

"She wouldn't have paid, would she, if she hadn't?"

He shook his head. "Quite so. Well thank you, Kath. You've been very helpful. Very much appreciated."

The conversation was obviously at an end and, with considerable relief, Kath stood up, headed towards the bar and ordered a double gin.

****

La Couture, Northern France

Louis was struggling to sleep. Only a few months ago he thought the Boche had won. But now he had found a way to hit back. He alternated between excitement, fear, nerves, satisfaction and anticipation and finally fell into a deep sleep, a big smile on his face.

Marie was also finding sleep difficult. The baby was very active tonight. Maybe she had her dates wrong? But no, she knew when the baby had been conceived. Perhaps she was just anxious to get here and pay her part in getting rid of the Germans. Marie was sure the child was a girl and had begun referring to the baby as *she*. The thought made her smile and, as she said goodnight to Marcel, something she did every night, she too fell asleep with a smile on her face.

The sound of the geese shrieking loudly and Georges barking excitedly woke them both in the early hours of the morning. Louis jumped out of bed, instantly awake, and reached for his shotgun which he now kept permanently under the bed.

He knew he was taking a risk keeping a shotgun, but he had to have some means of defending them and, if the Germans were searching the house, then they were probably already suspicious. The gun was very old and Louis hoped if it was found, he could argue he only used the ancient weapon to keep foxes down.

His father had stopped using the old gun when he had bought his new one. Louis had found the weapon on his return, half hidden under some straw in the barn, long forgotten by all the family. Somehow the

Germans who'd killed his father had failed to find the weapon and he'd taken it to Gerald's father who had carefully restored the gun so it could be used again.

By the time he had reached the landing, Marie was also out of bed, her heart pounding uncomfortably against her rib cage.

"Stay in your room while I take a look." Louis nodded back towards her bedroom and hurried down the stairs.

"Be careful!" Marie's words of caution followed him as he disappeared into the darkness and out of sight. She was unable to make out anything above the sounds of the geese and the constant barking, so after several minutes and being unable to bear the tension of not knowing what was happening, she made her way carefully down to the kitchen. The hall and landing were freezing and she shivered violently, as much from fear as from the cold.

The geese were now quiet, Georges had finally stopped barking and she could hear muffled voices. Marie's heart sank as she realised they were German. She forced herself to carry on. Louis had no patience with the enemy and she didn't want him antagonising them. Then she wondered why she was worrying. At the moment, they had done nothing wrong; they were only planning something and, surely the Germans couldn't read minds? Feeling slightly more confident, she took another step towards the kitchen. Then she froze again. What about the English airman? What if they had picked him up at some point and the trail had led them back to the farm? What if they'd arrested Henri and he'd told them everything? Her heart began racing as her mind ran through the possibilities and she started to feel dizzy. Concern she was about to faint overrode everything else and Marie rushed down the last few steps and pushed open the door.

****

Southern England

The man in the trench coat drove along the road, his mind still on the events in Catford. He had continued on his planned route and was now travelling along the south coast, but he was worried. Perhaps he should cancel the rest of his visits and go back later. There were no concerns about the remaining 'friends', at the moment so they could probably wait a little longer. He didn't want to risk using the telephone, so perhaps the best thing to do was to drive back to Glasgow and speak to his German master in person. He had no idea what was going on with the Cooper woman, but whatever she was involved in could affect their whole operation and he needed some advice.

He pulled up, turned the car around, lit himself a cigarette and shook his head. His old mum had always said the quiet women were the ones to watch and, given what he'd found in Catford, she was probably right.

****

La Couture, Northern France

Ignoring the surprised looks on the Germans' faces and the worried expression of her son, Marie headed straight for the settee and sat down heavily, praying the light-headedness would pass so she could think straight.

"Mama, are you alright?" Louis turned his back on the tall German officer and his companion and went straight to her.

Marie nodded, although her hands were shaking. "I'm fine, Louis. I just got out of bed a little too quickly, I think."

"You are unwell, madame?" The guttural, but accurate French came from the taller of the two men. Marie quickly took in the upright stance of what she assumed was a Prussian officer. He was about her age with a square face, a firm jaw, even features and rather gentle blue eyes. The normal arrogance she associated with the enemy was absent and all she could see in his face was concern, which she found extremely disconcerting.

Pulling herself together and trying to ignore the sound of her pulse pounding loudly in her head, Marie shook her head and pointed to her large stomach and said more abruptly than she'd intended, "I'm pregnant. It makes you light headed sometimes." Before he could say anything else she continued, "What brings you here at this hour?"

"I am sorry to have woken you, madame, but we have received reports of British soldiers hiding in this area."

Marie stared at him as if he was mad. "British soldiers? What on earth are you talking about? It's months since they all ran away home and left us to our fate."

Fortunately, both the Germans had their backs to Louis because he had trouble hiding the smile that was threatening to break out. With one sentence, his mother had firmly established herself and the farm as a most unlikely refuge for anyone escaping from the Germans.

But, despite his friendly demeanour, the officer was not put off quite so easily and continued politely. "So you have not seen anything… suspicious. Anyone hanging around? No food has gone missing?"

Marie got up slowly from the settee and stood facing him. "If I had seen anyone, Louis would have either chased them off or reported them to you lot." Not giving him any time to speak, she continued, "Thanks to you, we have little enough food here, so we would certainly have noticed if anything had gone missing. In any case, why would I help soldiers? You and the British with your stupid wars killed my husband, leaving me to bring up my child alone, so don't you think I have enough to concern me, without giving myself more worry?" By now her fear had gone and she was genuinely angry. "If you've finished, perhaps I can go back to bed, or do you want to search the house as well?" Without waiting for his reply, she carried on, "If so, can you hurry up, because its cold and I'm really not feeling too well."

The officer stared at her for several minutes. Despite her advanced pregnancy, or perhaps because of it, Marie was an attractive woman. Her eyes, a deep rich blue, flashed with anger as she answered him and he found himself entranced by her fiery manner and her mane of thick blonde glossy hair, full lips and curvaceous figure. Totally unaware of his thoughts, Marie glared back at him. Now she had said her piece, her anger had subsided and she was starting to feel scared again. Somehow, she managed to hold his gaze whilst rubbing her swollen stomach in an attempt to quieten down the baby who was doing somersaults inside her. Eventually, he gave a genuine smile, taking her completely by surprise

"We will not trouble you anymore, madame. I wish you well with your baby and bid you goodnight." Saluting smartly, he replaced his cap, clicked his heels together loudly and, speaking quickly to his companion, they left, slamming the door behind them.

Louis stared at his mother in admiration and Marie gave him a tired smile. "Come on, let's get a drink. I'm too unsettled to sleep but make sure the curtains are well drawn. We don't want them coming back and finding us still up."

While Louis made a drink, Marie replayed the conversation over and over in her mind. She couldn't see how the Germans could suspect them of anything, so the officer was probably speaking the truth and it was just coincidence they should arrive so soon after the cellar was completed.

"Perhaps you should go back to bed, Mama? It's still very early and I can manage this morning."

"Don't worry about me, Louis. I'm fine, honestly. I was just a bit shocked finding Germans here. The problem is, even if you haven't done anything, you find yourself feeling terrified and your mind starts to imagine all sorts of things. I had found us both guilty, tried and convicted before I even opened the door!"

Louis grinned. "Me too. I was convinced they knew everything and had come to arrest us. We have to find some way of stopping our imaginations from doing that, or we could end up talking ourselves into trouble, or looking so guilty they arrest us anyway because they think we must have done something."

"I'm not sure how we can. The only good thing is, most people probably react the same way, even if they haven't done anything. They're probably used to it!" Marie yawned. "I think you're right. I will go back to bed, while I still can. Once the baby is here, there'll be no time to do that. Did the officer give you his name?"

"Major Heinz Klug, I think he said. Why?"

"No reason." Marie answered quickly. "He just seemed quite reasonable for a German. Might be useful to have his name. You never know when it could come in handy."

****

Bethune, Northern France

"Did you tell that bloody German about Germain?" Fabian sounded furious and Brigitte flushed.

"Well, what if I did?" She was defiant. "You all wanted something done about him. You even said you thought he was some kind of informer, so I did you all a favour."

Fabian stared at her. "Telling the Boche makes you just as bad as him. Can't you see that?"

Brigitte pouted. "Whatever I do is wrong. He was costing you money, stealing things from your friends and God knows what else. He's hardly a loss to the community. You're such a hypocrite!"

Fabian raised his hand and she moved out of the way, thinking he was going to slap her.

"I'm going home. If you want me to come back, you need to stop treating me like dirt. I don't have to help you out. I thought you'd like me here but all you ever do is moan at me." She flounced out into the street, leaving Fabian staring after her.

She stormed up the road, tears streaming down her face. Rolf had been so pleased with her, he'd bought her a beautiful bracelet, told her how wonderful she was and then they had drunk champagne and made love in the bath. How dare her father try to ruin things?

"Brigitte! What on earth's the matter?" Lost in her thoughts she hadn't noticed Rolf driving past. In between sobs, she told him of her father's harsh words. Rolf held her close. "Don't let him worry you.

You have me and our life together. You don't need him anymore, do you?"

Enjoying his comforting arms around her, Brigitte considered his words. He was right. She had Rolf now, she didn't need anyone else.

Rolf smiled: mission accomplished.

Chapter Twenty-three

La Couture, Northern France

"What's the matter, Georges?" Marie started awake, her heart thudding. She had dozed off on the settee listening to the wireless and Georges' barking and pawing at the back door made her jump. Louis came running down the stairs and, after checking there was nothing incriminating lying around, he opened the door. Standing there were three men, their clothes worn and pain and hunger etched on their faces.

Marie shouted at Louis to turn off the light. She had no idea whether there were any Germans in the vicinity and, although she was sure Georges would have let her know if anyone else was outside, she did not want to take any chances. Once the room was in darkness, she quickly ushered the men in, closed the door and Louis put the light back on.

"We're very sorry to have disturbed you," the man spoke in accurate but heavily accented French.

"They're English," Louis said in astonishment.

One appeared to be injured and was being supported by the other two. Marie took charge and began issuing Louis with instructions.

"Go and get me some hot water and the first aid box and some clean clothes from Marcel's room. Only one seems to be hurt, so take the other two upstairs to the bathroom. Get what's left of their clothes and put them into the fire. We can't afford to leave anything lying around.

When you've done that, go and heat up what's left of the stew. Good thing I made enough for tomorrow as well. They look like they are in need of some nourishment."

While Louis headed off to get the water, she spoke slowly using some of the English Patrick had taught her. "You speak French?"

"A little," the one who had spoken earlier answered.

"I speak a little English," she said, "so we try, yes?"

He smiled and then paled. Fearing he was about to faint from hunger, she spoke quickly in French. "I will tend to your friend's injury. Sit him down on this chair and go with my son. He will let you wash and give you clean clothes. Then you can eat." She hoped he could understand.

He nodded and spoke rapidly to the others. They helped the injured man onto the chair and, when Louis returned with the water and bandages, they followed him upstairs where he pointed to the bathroom and some clean clothes. The first man shook his hand gratefully and Louis left them to take off their filthy rags. The smell of the stew wafted upstairs, filling the air with the inviting fragrance of herbs and they both hurried back down to where their companion was already eating. He was no longer wearing his rags either and instead was dressed in some trousers and a jumper that was slightly too big. Marie pointed to his leg, a bowl of water and some strange looking concoction they assumed was some kind of cream and then bandages indicating she had dressed his wound.

"Is he badly hurt?"

"No, but he needs rest."

Relieved the injury did not appear too serious, the other two began to relax, enjoying the warm food which was the first meal they had eaten in weeks.

****

Glasgow, Scotland

The man in the trench coat waited for his superior to speak.

"You're quite sure about this?"

He nodded. "I waited until she'd finished and then I went and dug through the rubble. Together with the whiskey and cigarettes, there was the body of a man. He'd been there a while and, no, I've no idea who he is."

"Well, it doesn't sound like the security services. Maybe she's mixed up with the black market or something?" The German accent sounded stronger now. He thought for a few moments. "What about the girl?"

The man shrugged. "She didn't come back and I had no means of knowing where she'd come from, or who she was so I couldn't follow her. Do you want me to go back down and see if I can find her?"

The German thought for a moment and then shook his head. "No, I don't think so, not yet anyway. Keep writing the letters and we'll see what Miss Cooper says. If we sense there is any problem you can go back but, at the moment, I need you here."

The man in the trench coat left and the German stared into space, his thoughts on Olive Cooper and her mysterious activities. Providing they didn't threaten his operation, he would not interfere but if there was any danger of MI5 or anyone else getting involved, he would send the man in the trench coat to deal with her.

****

Lambeth Hospital, London

"You can't keep avoiding me forever." Peggy jumped. Chris was right behind her.

"I'm not." She moved away. "I've been busy, that's all."

Chris took her hand and she made no attempt to pull away. "I'm really sorry, Peggy. I don't know how many more times I can tell you. I give you my word I won't kiss you again." He was about to add *"not without your permission"*, but decided that probably wasn't such a good idea, not if he wanted her to talk to him again.

Peggy stared at him and then relented. She'd missed talking to him. Perhaps she should forgive him. The problem was, she'd wanted to kiss him and she'd enjoyed the experience, otherwise she wouldn't have been so annoyed.

"How's Connie? Has she heard anything yet from her young man?"

Chris shook his head, relieved she was talking to him again. "No, he's not turned up anywhere, so Connie thinks he's probably dead. Unfortunately he was an orphan, so she can't even contact his family for information."

"I'm sorry. You must be really worried about her."

"Well Da's taking care of her and Ma's decided her daughter being pregnant is probably not the worst thing that could happen to her, given we're at war, so things have improved at home. We're more worried about Simon to be honest." He saw her confusion. "My youngest brother."

"Oh, the one who ran away to sea?"

"Yes, we've just discovered he's on the Atlantic convoys, but we still can't find out which ship."

Peggy frowned. "Surely the Merchant Navy must know what ship he's on?"

"He'd managed to get hold of same false identity papers. God knows how. That's why it's taken us so long to find him. Have you heard from Joe?"

Peggy's face lit up then fell. "Yes, I had another letter yesterday."

"Is he alright?"

"Yes, I think so. He just sounded a bit aloof. But, perhaps that's because it's been so long since I've seen him." Peggy didn't want to say any more, but Joe's letters were a complete disappointment. He hadn't said anything about missing her and they seemed stilted.

"Maybe it's because of the censorship? Can't be easy saying what you want to, when you know someone else is going to read your words."

Peggy nodded. "Yes, maybe you're right." She was surprised Chris was defending Joe. Perhaps she had been wrong about him and he genuinely wanted to be friends. She smiled. "I'd better get on, or I'll be in trouble."

Chris nodded. "Yes of course."

"Goodbye."

They spoke at the same time and she hurried away. He watched her go, feeling much happier. At least they were speaking. Perhaps it was a good job he hadn't asked her to go out with him again. Next time would be easier. He was just going to have to learn more patience.

****

Freetown, Sierra Leone

"If we don't leave here soon, we'll all die of Malaria or some other tropical bug," Pierre angrily brushed off another fly.

At first, they had been delighted to reach Freetown. Except for the brief spell of fighting, this was the first time they had been allowed off the ships, since they had left England. But they'd been here for ages, had several trips ashore and, other than several men dying from diseases, nothing had happened. There had been no news about their officer training and, as far as they were concerned, the war seemed to have ground to a temporary halt.

Marcel had been fascinated by his first real experience of Africa but soon became bored. He hadn't risked everything escaping from France to die of a tropical disease.

He still missed Jeanne and Angel but, much as he hated to admit to himself, he sometimes had trouble seeing them clearly in his mind. He wondered if this was because he still felt guilty about Lilly, even though there was no reason for Jeanne to ever know. He'd been lonely and Lilly had been available. The thought crossed his mind that Jeanne might also meet someone, especially as she had no idea where he was, but he quickly pushed it away.

"… I said, have you been bitten as badly as me?" Pierre shouted loudly in his ear making him jump.

"Sorry, Pierre. No, I've been lucky. They don't seem to like the taste of my skin."

"Probably because you don't wash enough." Paul ducked behind the cupboard next to the wall before Marcel could reach him.

Marcel smiled. Even though he was bored, he still enjoyed the friendly banter between the men. "Well, it works for me!" He shrugged as they all groaned and added various uncomplimentary remarks.

"Guess what? We're moving out." Charles burst into the cabin looking animated for the first time in ages.

"Yeah? Who says so?" Paul looked at him suspiciously.

"I do. I've volunteered us for a mission." He looked around waiting for their enthusiastic responses. After several seconds, he realised perhaps they weren't quite as keen.

"Haven't you learnt anything?" Paul said disgustedly. "You never volunteer for anything, you moron."

"What's the mission?" Marcel showed slightly more interest. "Anything's got to be better than sitting around here."

Charles sat down heavily on his bed. "I don't know yet. We've got to report to the harbour at 06:00 hours with all our kit."

Despite their negative reactions, Paul and Pierre began packing up immediately and, for the first time in a week, there was a spark back in Pierre's eyes.

"Well, thanks, Charles." Marcel realised no one else was going to say thank you. "Hadn't we better go and find Antoine?"

Paul sighed. "Yeah, come on then. I suppose we'd better start with the brothels and then work our way out to the bars."

"Better bring some money, I guess," Pierre added, his eyes shining. Marcel groaned inwardly. He really couldn't see the attraction of the local brothels. Most were filthy and the girls were none to clean either. He wouldn't have minded finding a nice woman to make love to but he drew the line at one who was likely to give him some horrible disease. He still remembered the films they had been shown in England and he wasn't about to take the risk.

He quickly turned his thoughts to the prospect of getting drunk, but that didn't really appeal to him either. He had done that on his first night in port and had taken two days to get over the hangover. He also had no idea what he had done when he was drunk which was even more worrying. He could only hope he hadn't visited one of the brothels or, if he had, he'd been too drunk to do anything. Realising he had no option but to go along with his friends, he stood up and followed them out of the cabin. At least he could keep an eye on them and make sure they all got back safely.

The ship was tied up in the harbour and they were not confined on board, so they had no trouble finding someone to row the short distance ashore.

"Going to have some fun, lads?" the sailor asked winking lasciviously at them.

"Yeah, that's right," Paul answered quickly before anyone could say anything differently and the rest of the short trip was spent listening to the sailor's recommendations as to the best bars and brothels.

****

La Couture, Northern France

"We don't want to get you into any trouble. If you want to give us up to the Boche, you can."

Louis grinned. "We're not allowed to call the Krauts that anymore. They don't like it! If they hear us use that word, they can shoot us apparently. On the other hand, there are so many things we can be shot for, it becomes quite hard to remember them all!" He laughed, taking his visitors by surprise.

The Englishman translated this in his head and then grinned. He turned to his companions and repeated the conversation. Within seconds, the remaining tension drained away and the one who spoke French held out his hand. "I'm James Gilbert, this is Gordon and the clumsy sod who got himself shot is Arthur."

Marie and Louis smiled and introduced themselves. Marie made a mental note to talk to Louis about just how much information they should give out in future but, for the moment, they had other pressing concerns.

The men could not remain seated in the kitchen much longer. It was too dangerous.

"We need to work out what to do." Marie watched the soldiers wolfing down their stew. "They can't stay in the house, but we can't take them to…" She hesitated, even though she knew they did not speak enough French to understand and then continued more quietly, "Well, you know where, until they've had some rest. I don't think the wounded man would make it at the moment."

"They'll have to stay here." Louis thought for a moment. "They can go up into the loft, and we move them later. I'll go and see Henri and we can work out the best way to do that."

Marie frowned. "Alright, the loft it is then. They'll have to be quiet though."

"I would think the biggest danger will be if they all start snoring," Louis replied. "They look like they'll fall asleep at the table if we don't move them soon. Come on," he continued to James. "We'll go upstairs to the loft and move you somewhere else tonight."

They followed Louis out of the kitchen, having first thanked Marie for the food and bandaging their friend's wound. She breathed a sigh of relief and began to work out what they would need to take with them to the hiding place. She had no idea how long the men would be there and they didn't want to make unnecessary trips to the shop which might draw attention. She packed some tinned food, a can opener, a small tilly lamp, some petrol, coffee, water and blankets in some bags. There was no means of heating the hiding place yet, so they would need the blankets or they would freeze. Despite her worries, she was suddenly very relieved the soldiers were safe inside her loft instead of taking their chances in the frozen fields.

****

Freetown, Sierra Leone

Although it was night time, the streets were full of people in colourful clothes and the market stalls were crammed with tantalisingly exotic-looking food and drink. Although the French influence was obvious, there was a primitive element that added something erotic and foreign, which Marcel couldn't completely identify. It wasn't just that the air smelled and tasted different from the France he was used to, the very atmosphere was charged with an air of electricity and he couldn't help the excitement that rose in the pit of his stomach every time he set foot ashore. This frisson of excitement increased whenever he travelled to the outskirts and stood gazing at the African bush that formed the backdrop to the port. He would have loved to go and explore further, but they were not allowed to leave the port area, so the most he had been able to do was to gaze at the inhospitable landscape from the safety of the town.

They arrived at the harbour steps and he followed the others into the town. Marcel would have been happy standing still and watching the inhabitants while they went about their business, but Paul caught hold of his arm and dragged him towards one of the side streets. Marcel sighed. This particular street led to a rather notorious brothel which he thought was out of bounds. He was about to say something when, to his relief, Pierre suddenly spotted Antoine emerge, blinking, from a door in the shadows into the scorching hot sunlight. On his arm was an attractive, scantily clad African girl who watched their approach warily.

"Have I been that long?" Antoine said, astonished to see them all.

"No, we're mobilising." Paul indicated the girl. "How much?"

Antoine smiled at him lazily. "More than you can afford, my friend. Why would she want to go for anything so inferior when she has experienced the best?"

"Ten francs." She smiled seductively at Paul, hastily removing her arm from Antoine's.

Paul followed her back inside, leaving Antoine shrugging. "There's no accounting for taste, is there?"

"Great! Now we have to wait for him." Pierre glanced at the others. "I can't possibly imagine what we could do to amuse ourselves. Any ideas?"

Marcel shook his head resignedly and followed Pierre, Charles and Antoine through the door.

"So, what's this about being mobilised?" Antoine asked Marcel once they had purchased some drinks and were seated in a small alcove. Pierre and Charles had followed Paul and were now nowhere to be seen.

Marcel shook his head. "We don't know exactly. Charles volunteered us for something, although he didn't know what and we leave first thing tomorrow."

"Ah well, better than sitting around here for weeks on end."

"That's what I thought and, although Paul moaned at him, I think he was quite pleased too."

They drank in companionable silence for a while and then Antoine indicated the back room. "Are you sure you don't want to go and have some fun? I don't mind waiting in here on my own. I'm quite used to that."

Marcel shook his head. "No, thanks. I'm really not interested in…" He hesitated, not wanting to offend Antoine.

"Sleeping with whores?" Antoine finished for him with a gleam in his eye.

"Do you think there's something wrong with me?" As soon as the words were out of his mouth, Marcel could have bitten off his tongue. Although he had thought about this quite a lot, he hadn't meant to express his concerns.

"No, we're all different," Antoine reassured him. "You are in love, so you feel too guilty to really let yourself go," he added, hitting the nail on the head. There was silence. "It's nothing to do with me, Marcel, and you should make up your own mind, but we're fighting a war. You could be dead tomorrow, so could your girlfriend. Perhaps you should decide that, what happens now and until you find her again, doesn't count. It's not like normal life, so you don't have to behave like you normally would. You can save that for when you find her and then, if you both still feel the same, you can get married and settle down together."

Marcel digested his words and realised they made a lot of sense and would also save him from feeling guilty about what had happened with Lilly. As Antoine said, he could save himself for Jeanne and never find her again. She could be dead or she could have given up on him and found someone else. The time had come to be realistic. He finished his drink and sat back for a moment, suddenly feeling much happier. Watching the conflicting emotions crossing Marcel's face, Antoine could see he had come to a decision. This was confirmed when he suddenly stood up and headed towards the door leading into the back room.

****

Catford, London

Olive couldn't sleep. She was still terrified. After she'd buried the illicit goods, she'd thought her problems were over and then those two horrible men had come knocking on her door.

They had threatened her from the start, telling her they knew about Mary and her involvement with Tom and they wanted to know where he was.

Olive denied any knowledge of his whereabouts, all the time struggling not to glance towards the derelict building across the street. They wouldn't believe her and the smaller man slapped her hard before slamming her up against the wall and punching her in the stomach. They had timed their visit well. The bombs were falling outside and she knew her neighbour wasn't going to come to her aid because she would have gone to the shelter. The building was empty.

Olive crumpled to the floor and began to tell the two men the truth. To start with, they didn't believe her. The small man grabbed her left hand and bent back her little finger until she finally lost her temper, yelling at them to go and look for themselves. He went, leaving the tall man helping himself to what was left of her sherry.

When the man came back and confirmed her story, the tall man laughed and then, leaning down, his face inches from hers, he told her he would be collecting instead and her first payment was due the next day.

The two men left and, now lying in bed, Olive stared at the ceiling, feeling hopeless. She was back where she started.

Chapter Twenty-four

Freetown, Sierra Leone

At exactly half past five the following morning, Pierre woke Marcel up by shouting loudly in his ear. Deeply asleep, Marcel started awake and, sitting up too quickly, fell out of his hammock and banged his head on the floor.

"Merde; merde; merde," he muttered, easing himself gently into a sitting position and holding his head in his hands, groaning. He could not believe how ill he felt; his head was pounding, he felt sick and he had a dreadful taste in his mouth. He ignored the muffled laughter he could hear coming from the others and, carefully standing up, he headed quickly for the showers, praying desperately they would be working. As he made his way along the corridor, the floor seemed to be swaying and moving and he wondered just how ill he really was. What if he had poisoned himself?

He couldn't remember much of the previous evening at all but, when he stood under the stream of cold water in the shower room, his head began to clear and everything started to come back. Remembering the two girls he had spent some time with, he smiled and, reliving the whole evening again, he forgot his hangover completely. Feeling much better, even though his head was pounding and the ship seemed to be moving underneath his feet, he headed back to his cabin where he was surprised to see his friends all still lying in their hammocks.

"Shouldn't you be getting ready?" He looked confused and then even more bemused as they collapsed into helpless laughter.

"Did you enjoy yourself last night?" Pierre asked him and, to his horror Marcel began to blush.

"Yes." He was embarrassed and then he put his head up. "Yes I did, it was wonderful! I didn't think sex could ever be like that."

"Good." Pierre glanced around at the others. "Then, you won't mind if we tell you we er… tricked you, will you?"

"Tricked me?" Marcel was totally bewildered

"We knew we were being mobilised, we found out yesterday while you were lying on your hammock daydreaming, and we thought it would do you good to go ashore and let your hair down."

Charles continued, "But we knew you would refuse unless there was a good reason. So we arranged for Antoine to be 'missing', because we knew you wouldn't refuse to come and look for him."

There was an uneasy silence. "So the ship really is moving and the engines are pounding? I thought it was my hangover!"

Relieved he had not taken offence, they all laughed and, after a few seconds, Marcel joined in.

****

La Couture, Northern France

"I need to speak to Gerald. I think he has contacts who can get people across the demarcation line. I don't need details but I would like to have two options so I'm not relying on Henri." Seeing Marie's puzzled expression, Louis explained, "If anything happens to Henri, we could be left stranded. I'm just trying to plan ahead. However, I need to ask in such a way Gerald doesn't know what I am doing."

"Well the first thing is not to tell Gerald you are hiding anyone at all. Perhaps you should just let him think you are a middleman, you know, speaking for someone else. If he has a way to cross into the south, you can then find a way of taking the men to him." Marie hesitated. "Are you sure you want to involve someone else?"

"Not really, but I want a back-up plan and this is the best I can think of. Don't worry, I'll be careful. I'm just going to sound him out to start with." He frowned. "We also need to find a way of letting allied soldiers and downed airmen know we are here to help them, if needed, but at the same time we have to keep everything totally secret and I'm blowed if I know how."

Marie shook her head. "No, I don't either. Perhaps that's something you should discuss with Henri?"

Louis nodded. "You're right. I'll talk to him after I speak to Gerald." He kissed her on the cheek and headed out the door. As he walked across the fields, he thought how quickly the war had changed things. A few months ago, he would have trusted Henri and Gerald with his life. Now he couldn't afford to because he wasn't just gambling with his life; there was his mother's and the baby's as well, not to mention the lives of the English soldiers.

Gerald was just setting out for work and he looked at Louis in surprise. "Everything alright, Louis?" he asked.

"What?" Louis looked puzzled and then gave a nervous smile. "Oh, yes. There's nothing wrong. I just wanted to ask your advice, really."

"Oh?" Gerald looked pleased. "Go on then."

Louis looked around cautiously but there was no one in sight, so he took a deep breath and said carefully, "How's Josephine?"

Josephine was Gerald's girlfriend. Gerald looked suspicious. "Why do you ask?"

"This bloody war." Louis' outburst caught his friend by surprise but he had no time to say anything as Louis continued, "It's making everyone so suspicious. Look at us. We're best friends, yet we're tiptoeing round each other like we'd just met."

Gerald smiled ruefully. "I know what you mean, but life's too dangerous now not to take some precautions."

He sounded so serious, Louis looked at him in some astonishment. He was amazed just how much his friends had grown up, but then so had he.

He nodded and then, feeling considerably more confident continued, "I heard you managed to get Josephine across the demarcation line after the riots in Paris. I need to get some people to the south and wondered if you could help."

****

Hampshire, England

Although Pam was tired and her brain felt like bursting, she finally began to feel she was getting somewhere. Thanks to the French clothes they were wearing and the French cuisine served to them morning, noon and night, she felt she fitted right in to the SOE French house in Hampshire, and she had almost finished her training. As before, the conversation was only in French and she found herself easily picking up the various dialects and slang used by the genuine French members of the group.

"You pick up accents very well," Ricardo said to her as they were finishing their coffee by the fire one evening. "That's quite a gift and may end up saving your life."

Pam looked at him quizzically and he hastened to explain, "Sorry, I just meant if you had to disappear, all you would need to do would be to change your appearance and your accent and it would be very difficult for the Germans to identify you. Unless you speak a language fluently or have a very good ear, it's hard to identify different dialects. But you are so good, I think even the French police would struggle to be sure you were the person they were looking for. The trick is to be able to keep the accent up for long periods of time of course. Do you find picking up the dialects in your own country easy too?"

Pam smiled wryly. "Yes, I only have to live somewhere for a few days and I start talking like a local. I used to think it was a curse but, like you say, it could actually be very useful in the field."

They sat in companionable silence for a while, gazing into the fire whilst lost in their own thoughts. Being unable to ask personal questions meant conversations between the prospective agents were often stilted and unnatural as they took pains to avoid sensitive subjects or to ask for prohibited information.

In the distance, they could hear the continuous dull thuds of the high explosive shells landing on the nearby towns.

"Sounds like Portsmouth's copping it again tonight," Pam sighed. "I think I'll get some fresh air." She stood up and walked to the front door, carefully moved aside the heavy blackout curtain and stepped out into the cold night air. Outside, the noise was much louder and, in the distance, she could see a faint orange glow lighting up the sky where she thought Portsmouth was and to the right a much brighter glow which she was sure was over Southampton.

"Penny for them?" She looked round to see Richard standing quietly beside her.

"I didn't hear you. Doesn't say much for my skills." She turned to face him. "But it is good to see you on your own again." Although she had seen him occasionally when he delivered lectures, she had not been alone with him since their time in Scotland and she was surprised by just how much she had missed him.

Richard smiled down at her and, unable to resist, although he knew it was against all the rules of common sense, he found himself bending down towards her upturned face, his lips urgently seeking hers. There was no resistance and, to his delight, she returned his kiss with a passion equalling his own. Eventually, he pulled back and looked at her.

"I'm sorry. I shouldn't have done that." But the look in his eyes belied his apology and Pam put her fingers on his lips and shook her head.

"I think we both knew it was going to happen, the only question was when."

"It's against all the regulations, though, and I should have known better." A frown appeared on his brow.

Pam shrugged. "We could be dead tomorrow or next week or next month. Aren't we entitled to some happiness? In any case, we're not 'in the field'. You're not coming to France with me, are you? I could understand it would be seriously dangerous to get emotionally involved whilst on an operation; but here…?"

Richard sighed and put his arm around her, pulling her close to him. Eventually Pam pulled away and, taking his hand, said softly, "Come on, its cold out here, let's go upstairs."

Richard smiled. "I don't think that's such a good idea, do you? We wouldn't be a secret for more than a few seconds. Let's wait until you've finished your training and then we can meet in London properly."

"I didn't actually mean that." Pam blushed furiously, mortified he had misunderstood her. What on earth must he think of her? "I meant we ought to go in, because it was getting late and we should go to our *separate* beds!"

Richard grinned. "Wishful thinking on my part, then! Sorry."

"I'm not saying no, never, just no, not at the moment. You do understand, don't you?"

Richard pulled her close. "Of course I do." He pushed her away slightly and, taking her chin in his hand, he looked into her eyes. "I think I'm falling in love with you, Pam. I didn't mean to, but I can't help myself."

"Good, because I think I feel the same." They held each other tight before Richard reluctantly opened the door and they went back inside. The house was quiet; most of their companions had already gone to bed.

"Goodnight." Pam ran quickly up the stairs to her room before he could answer.

Richard watched her go up the stairs and then went into the sitting room and poured himself a large whisky.

"Not good to get too involved." Giselle was sitting quietly by the fire and was so still Richard, preoccupied by his thoughts, hadn't noticed her.

"I know. You don't have to tell me. I didn't choose to. It just happened."

"Well, just be careful and make the most of your time together."

He didn't need to ask her what she meant; he already knew.

Chapter Twenty-five

Toulouse, Southern France

Jeanne looked nervously over her shoulder. She couldn't shake off the feeling she was being followed. She knew she was being ridiculous. Why would anyone want to follow her? She was a nobody who worked at the police station. She hadn't done anything wrong, well other than being Jewish and using false identity papers, of course, but no one knew about that. She was aware there was a growing resistance movement in Toulouse. She had seen some of the police reports. Their main role seemed to be helping allied soldiers and airmen who had escaped from the occupied zone get back to England, but she had no connections to anyone who was in the movement, as far as she knew, so the whole idea of someone following her was ludicrous. But although she couldn't see anyone, the niggling voice in the back of her head wouldn't go away, so by the time she arrived at work she was trembling. She quickly buried herself in her work, hoping that would dispel the sense of fear she felt.

Finding they were out of envelopes, she made her way to the store room to get some more.

"What on earth's the matter, Jeanne?"

She had not seen Eve come into the store room, nor had she heard her shut the door quietly behind her and she jumped violently.

"Jeanne?" Eve was looking even more concerned. "You haven't been yourself since you got here this morning and now, look at you, you're shaking like a leaf."

"You just made me jump." Jeanne tried to calm herself down, not wanting to admit her fears, which would sound even more ridiculous if she spoke them out loud.

Eve folded her arms. "You can trust me, Jeanne. I know something is worrying you. Please tell me. You never know, I might be able to help you."

There was a silence as Jeanne tried to decide whether to tell her or not and then the dam burst. "This is going to sound crazy, but I keep thinking someone's watching me and I'm being followed. I have no idea why and I can't see anyone but… I'm sure they're there," she tailed off, unable to think of anything else to say.

To her surprise, Eve did not dismiss her fears immediately. Instead, she said nothing for a few seconds. "Have you told Gabriel?"

Jeanne shook her head.

"Or your father?" Eve had met Jeanne's father once and had been very impressed with the quietly spoken man who was obviously intelligent and missed very little. The type of man you could rely on in a crisis, Eve had thought at the time.

Jeanne shook her head again. "I thought you'd tell me I was being stupid."

"We live in dangerous times, Jeanne." Eve was looking very serious and Jeanne felt the fear return. "People disappear for the most trivial of reasons or for no reason at all. If Isabelle has found out about your relationship with Gabriel, that would be more than enough reason for both you and your family to disappear. You need to tell your father and Gabriel and you need to do it quickly."

"Alright, I will tell my father tonight but I don't know how I can tell Gabriel. We agreed to keep away from each other for a few months, as we both thought that would be safer."

"I'll tell him for you. I'll be glad to help in any way I can. I couldn't stand that snooty cow Isabelle, so it'll be my pleasure. Anyway I like you and your father and I wouldn't want anything to happen to you."

****

Stalag XXA, Poland

The snow had arrived in regular flurries, blown into small piles by an icy cold north wind. Rob had been shipped out to one of the labour camps and Joe was missing him. Although he had other friends, Rob was the man he'd fought with and being separated from him was hard, especially as he had no idea if he would ever see him again. The Germans had still not returned their khaki blankets, despite the senior NCO making several complaints and the cold damp conditions, coupled with the lack of sufficient bed clothes and their already weakened condition, was giving rise to serious concern. It was the increasing illness amongst the men, which Joe and the others were convinced finally persuaded the Germans to give the prisoners back their blankets, that and an impending visit from the Red Cross inspectors which, strangely enough, coincided with the long awaited distribution of their Red Cross parcels.

Having long since run out of leaves, which, given the sound of his cough was probably a blessing in disguise; Joe pounced eagerly on the tobacco and rolled his first decent cigarette for several weeks. While he was smoking contentedly, the guards arrived and hustled them outside into the courtyard. It was freezing cold and the snow was falling so heavily that at first they didn't realise what was happening. In front of them, on the wet ground, were piles of brand new clothes. The Germans indicated the garments and began shouting.

Initially confused by this sudden unexpected generosity, Joe, Mitchell, Pete, Cyril and Dick soon caught up with the others and, before long, they had changed out of the tattered remnants of their uniforms and were luxuriating in the slightly damp warmth and cleanliness of the unexpected new uniforms.

"I wouldn't get too used to them." The voice came from McMahon, a wily rugged Scotsman who was amongst those who had been there the longest. "There must be a Red Cross inspection due. As soon as they leave the camp, the Krauts'll have these off you until next time and they'll give you back your old ones." He glanced around to make sure no one was listening and then carried on, his voice so quiet they had to bend closer to catch what he was saying. "If I were you, I'd try and find an opportunity to hide some. Take more than you need and then you can wear the new clothes under your old stuff."

As one of the guards approached, he backed away. They checked no one was watching and grabbed some extra socks and trousers, hastily pulling them over the ones they had already put on. Spotting some thick army jumpers, Joe nudged Mitchell but the guard was on his way back. Quick as a flash, Cyril started an argument with Dick, the two men threatening each other with punches and gradually distancing themselves from the piles of new clothing. Distracted by the fight, the guard's eyes followed the action, whilst Joe and Mitchell pulled on two extra jumpers each. They would have pulled on more but they were beginning to look rather overweight and the last thing they wanted to do was to draw attention to themselves. Glancing round, Joe realised his fellow prisoners all suddenly looked much better fed than they had an hour ago and, taking his cue from the others, he waddled carefully back to his hut, unable to believe the guards hadn't spotted what they were doing.

Joe was still laughing when a thought came to him and he began hunting frantically for his makeshift calendar.

"What's the matter, Joe?" Cyril was watching him with concern.

"Nothing," Joe responded cheerfully after consulting his calendar. "Today's my 22nd birthday."

"*Happy Birthday to you!*" Cyril and the others chorused loudly and were soon joined by the rest of the hut.

Beginning to wish he hadn't said anything, Joe looked suitably embarrassed, but when he looked at all the cheerful smiling faces around him, all belting out *Happy Birthday*, he decided they should celebrate, after all they might not be at home with those they loved, but at least they were all still alive.

****

Honor Oak Park, London

Peggy and Pauline also toasted Joe's health. Peggy spent much of the day thinking about him and wondering how he was spending his birthday and, not for the first time, she wished he could be home safe with her. She had decided Chris was right. Joe was probably concerned about censorship, hence the reason his letters were so stiff and formal. She resolved to write to him again when she returned from church. She didn't care who read her letter. She would tell him she loved him and would wait for him, however long the war lasted. She would also seek Chris out the next day and thank him for his advice. He had been a really good friend to her; the least she could do would be to support him with his family worries.

Later, she sat down and began to write to Joe all about Sally's wedding the previous Saturday and how lovely the service had been. Peggy still smiled when she thought about the contented expression on her friend's face when she said her vows, her eyes fixed lovingly on Peter's face. Peter seemed equally happy. Having recovered after his leg amputation, he had quickly volunteered as a fire watcher and was so efficient he had soon been employed permanently training others. There was barely any sign of a limp and Peggy was delighted the injury had not affected their relationship. Although she tried not to be envious, it was hard not to be when Joe was so far away and the war showed no signs of finishing in the near future. Sally had worn a beautiful white silk dress she and Annie had made from one of her mother's evening dresses. They had enough material to make a veil and had found some matching gloves at one of the more expensive shops in the West End.

Peggy had worn a long purple and white bridesmaid's dress made from the material from a couple of her Aunt Maud's smart, rather expensive dresses which she assured Peggy she no longer needed. Everyone had said how much the colour suited her. Not used to so many compliments, she had blushed furiously and wished Joe could have been with her to share such a lovely day.

****

Toulouse, Southern France

Jeanne did not have a chance to speak to Eve again for the remainder of the day, so she had no idea whether she had managed to talk to Gabriel. The clock finally chimed out the hour to go home, but Eve was nowhere in sight. Jeanne hesitated. Should she wait to speak to her, or just go home? Exhaustion won and she reached for her coat and hat, relieved the day had finally finished. Although the weather was not really cold in Toulouse, certainly not like she had been used to in Northern France, there was a chill in the air in the evenings. She wished Christmas would hurry up and come and then her relationship with Gabriel would be out in the open and she wouldn't feel so alone. Not being able to speak to him, other than in front of other people, was very testing and he was so good an actor, sometimes she wondered if perhaps she had dreamt the whole thing. But then, she would catch him watching her when he thought no one was looking and the strength of his love was so apparent, she wondered how on earth she could ever have doubted him.

She set out through the door, down the steps and out into the town. A few moments later Eve reappeared. She had been trying yet again to find Gabriel but he was not in the building, so she would have to wait until tomorrow. Finding Jeanne had already gone, Eve hurried towards the door with a certain amount of apprehension. Something told her Jeanne really was in danger and the sooner she told someone, the better. Telling Jeanne's father was one thing, but it was much more important Gabriel knew. He was probably the only one in a position to do something.

She hurried out of the door and scanned the horizon for Jeanne, eventually spotting her, several metres in the distance, heading away from the Place du Capitole. Her head was down and she was leaning into the slight wind that had sprung up and did not look back. Eve hesitated, wondering whether to run after her or… the idea of following Jeanne suddenly came into her head. If she was behind

Jeanne, perhaps she could see if there was anyone watching her.

Her position on top of the steps gave her quite a good vantage point, so she stood still and began looking at the various people going about their business, trying to identify anyone who looked suspicious. The problem was, she had no real idea what to look out for. She wished she'd managed to find Gabriel. He would know what to do, whereas she had no idea. If only Jeanne would stop walking or change direction, it might be easier, but her road home was quite straight, at least until she left the square, and there were so many people about, it was impossible to tell if anyone was paying her particular attention. Eve tied her brightly patterned scarf round her head and stepped down into the street. There was nothing for it but to follow her friend. At least then, she would know Jeanne had reached home safely.

By now, Jeanne had almost crossed the square. She was totally unaware of Eve watching her, her thoughts firmly fixed on Gabriel and how good it would be once they could be together properly. Although she still felt as if someone was following her, she had resolved to put the matter out of her mind, at least until she had spoken to her father.

Lost in her thoughts, she carried on walking briskly, totally unaware of what was happening behind her.

****

Hampshire, England

Pam had been lying there all day, her orders to watch the farm in the far corner of the field running adjacent to the woods. It had been a beautiful crisp winter's day with the sun shining brightly in a crystal clear blue sky. The trees were bare, their branches stark against the skyline, the path and surrounding undergrowth covered by fallen leaves, their brown crisp shapes crunching whenever anything disturbed them.

Pam sighed quietly and resisted the temptation to yawn. It was really beautiful here, even if she was very cold. In fact, now the sun was going down, she couldn't feel her feet at all, despite the healthy covering of leaves and her left arm was starting to cramp. Carefully, she changed position, making sure her movements were slow and measured and taking extra care not to disturb the leaves and evergreen foliage she was using to camouflage her position. She raised the binoculars to her eyes again and focused her attention back on the farmhouse and surrounding outbuildings. There was no movement at all, although she was sure she could hear a dog barking somewhere in the distance.

She shivered and tried to re-focus her attention on the job in hand but there was still no activity and her mind moved restlessly on, looking for something to keep her from nodding off, which would be a cardinal sin and liable to end up in her being sent back to be a hostess at charity functions. That thought had the desired effect and she instantly lost the urge to sleep.

A faint crunching noise in the distance caught her attention and, carefully turning her head, she looked warily in the direction from which the noise had come. She couldn't see anything but she was sure she'd heard something. Of course, it might just be a rabbit or a fox or even a New Forest pony but for some reason, she didn't think so. She held her breath. Yes, there it was again. She was sure the noise wasn't an animal. She would have bet her life on that. There was something too deliberate, too careful, as if someone was trying not to be heard.

The noise came closer but she still couldn't see anything. Her attention was now so firmly fixed on the direction the noise was coming from, she almost failed to notice there was a sudden rush of activity at the farm. It was only the flash of rapidly fading sunlight reflecting on the barrel of the shotgun that made her look back. Damn! She had almost missed what she had been waiting for. She cursed her stupidity but she was still uneasy. She hadn't yet identified the noise and, until she had, she wouldn't be able to settle to just watching the farm. Deciding to use her eyes to watch the farm and her ears to listen, she lay completely still and waited. Three men had appeared by the gate of the farm and they were heading out towards the road in the opposite direction to where she was waiting. Her colleagues were covering the other side so, breathing a sigh of relief she made a note of the time and turned her attention back to the noise which now appeared to have ceased all together.

She turned round carefully and almost screamed. Standing right in front of her was a man with a gun pointed firmly at her head.

Chapter Twenty-six

La Couture, Northern France

Evening seemed to have come earlier than usual thanks to the leaden skies and steadily falling snow. Marie thought about the three men hiding in the cellar of the shop. She hoped they were warm enough, not that there was much she could do if they weren't. In any case, they were leaving soon. She didn't know all the details of their departure, because it was safer that way, but she did know Louis would collect the men, take them to an agreed place in the woods and then leave them for Gerald's friends to collect and take south. The little Louis had said implied they would be passed from one courier to another, each of whom would take the men one step further to their destination. None of the couriers would see each other as they would hand the men a sealed envelope before leaving them. This would have instructions as to where to meet the next courier and a password or phrase for the courier to identify him or herself. By having cut-off points, everyone was protected as much as possible, although there was no guarantee things wouldn't go wrong. The most dangerous part was when the men were on their own and travelling between couriers, but the distances were deliberately short and the places carefully chosen to minimise the chances of anything going wrong.

Marie shivered and crossed herself. Although she had gone into this with her eyes open, only now was she really beginning to appreciate that she, Louis and her unborn baby would be in continual danger until the Germans were finally defeated. The alternative, that they would never leave, she wouldn't even bear to contemplate.

****

Outside Bethune, Northern France

Brigitte let herself into Rolf's office. He wasn't there, so she sat down and waited. After a few moments she was bored, so she stood up and glanced at the papers on his desk. She frowned. Some of the documents looked like exit papers to cross the Demarcation Line. They reminded her of Louis and their plans to move south and she felt sad. Then she shook her head, banishing him from her mind. She hadn't seen him since the day she and Rolf had driven past him, which was probably good. She didn't need a scene or anything that might annoy Rolf, especially when he was being so nice to her.

She wondered where he was. He had told her to meet him here at six o'clock and he was very particular about punctuality. It wasn't like him to be late. She would wait a little longer, then leave him a note. She turned away from the desk and heard a strange sound coming from the door to her left.

Brigitte stared at the door and then took a step closer. The noise was definitely coming from the other side. Brigitte had been in the small room once before; there was nothing there except a table and a couple of chairs. She hesitated and was about to walk off when the noise came again. Curiosity got the better of her. She stepped forward and opened the door… and immediately wished she hadn't.

****

Catford, London

"Hello, Peggy." Olive was not pleased to see her cousin who was obviously on her way home from work, but she forced a smile onto her face. "Come in. What can I do for you?"

"I just came round to find out how you are. I haven't seen you for ages."

"Oh, well... now I've been promoted I'm quite busy." Olive couldn't think of any other excuse. She could hardly tell Peggy what was really going on in her life. "So, have you heard any more from Joe?" Olive wasn't really interested but she felt obliged to ask.

"Yes, I've had a couple of letters now." Peggy had pushed aside her earlier misgivings and was now genuinely grateful to have heard from him.

Olive was relieved her face was turned away while Peggy walked past her into the flat, because she couldn't keep the fury off her face. By the time Peggy had turned towards her, Olive was smiling again, her brain frantically trying to think of something to wipe the smug expression off Peggy's face.

"That's good." Olive searched for something else to say. For some reason Kurt's letters popped into her mind. "No doubt his letters are full of how much he is missing you and how he can't wait to be back home again?"

Peggy looked uncomfortable. "No, not really. He's a bit distant to be honest. I think it's because he knows someone else is likely to be reading his letters first."

Sensing a chink in her armour, Olive pounced. "Oh, you do surprise me. I thought they'd be all lovey dovey. Aren't you worried?"

Peggy shook her head, although her earlier doubts were beginning to resurface.

Olive carried on, "Well, he's a long way away and it's ages since you've seen each other, perhaps he's worried you might have found someone else. I know that's ridiculous, but you know what men are like." She was astonished to see Peggy blush and her curiosity was piqued.

"I'd never cheat on Joe." Peggy looked horrified.

Olive patted her hand and nodded. "Of course you wouldn't, Peggy. You're not like that at all." She changed the subject. "I was just about to have a drink and some chocolate; would you like to join me?"

"I'd love a cup of tea, thanks and I can't believe you've managed to find some more chocolate. You must know the right people," Peggy joked. Olive spun round in horror but Peggy was smiling and Olive relaxed. She didn't know Olive's secret, she was just being funny. Olive waited for the kettle to boil and, when she was sure Peggy wasn't watching added a small amount of whiskey to her cup. Her original intention had been to bury all the alcohol, but she had changed her mind at the last moment and hidden a couple of bottles under the bed. After the visit from the villains, she had started having a small glass at night to help her sleep.

They sat there drinking their tea in silence. Peggy was feeling guilty about her friendship with Chris and wondering if her cousin knew somehow. Olive was pondering Peggy's strange reaction to her statement about her finding someone else. She'd not expected to succeed in dampening her cousin's enthusiasm quite so easily. Olive was intrigued and vowed to find out more. If nothing else, trying to dig up some dirt on her precious cousin would take her mind off her own problems.

****

Toulouse, Southern France

The man soon realised he was being followed himself. His training was good, as were his instincts and the person behind him was an amateur; he was sure of that within minutes of sensing their presence. He moved towards the shops at the edge of the square and gazed into one of the larger windows, using the glass as a mirror. The question was whether the person was following him, or his target. He never called the people he spied on by name, because the work was never personal for him. He was a professional. A private detective before the war, he worked for whoever paid him, he wasn't fussy and he had no interest in politics. He smiled. Ah, there she was, a matronly, middle-aged woman with a rather garish scarf on her head.

He risked a quick glance, but she was intent on the target and failed to notice him. There was nothing startling about her, other than the bright yellow leaf-patterned scarf, which annoyed him for some reason he couldn't quite fathom, and the fact she was intruding in his business. He turned back to the window, waited until she had gone past, then he headed swiftly back to the main part of the road and fell in behind her. She seemed completely unaware of him so, unless she was much better than he was giving her credit for, she must be following his target. He wondered why. Perhaps his client didn't trust him and had employed someone else. But that didn't make much sense. If they didn't trust him, they would have just terminated his contract. In any case she didn't seem like a professional. He watched her a little longer and then made up his mind. She was obviously an amateur but that made no difference. She was in the way and that made her dangerous.

They had reached the Rue Peyrolieres and he turned his attention back to the two women. His instructions were to follow the target and report on who she met and where she went. He had been following her for several days and she was extremely boring. She didn't do anything, other than go to work and return back home to her father and sister. At the weekend, they had gone for a couple of walks together, done some shopping and returned home. Either she knew he was there, in which case she was a very accomplished actress, or she was genuinely innocent of whatever they thought she was doing.

****

Outside Bethune, Northern France

"Come in. I thought you were going to be late." Rolf smiled up at her. He was seated on a chair and a naked girl was on her knees in front of him, sucking his penis. "Grab a glass of wine and come and give me a kiss."

Brigitte stared at him and shook her head.

"Don't be silly and do as you're told." His voice was still calm but she could hear an edge to it. She hesitated. The girl who was sucking him turned towards her. She looked vaguely familiar. Her eyes were full of amusement and Rolf reached down and slapped her hard. She returned her attention to him but Brigitte was sure the girl was laughing at her.

Brigitte made up her mind. She couldn't bear the thought of the girl thinking she hadn't known about this. Even worse was the thought of Rolf punishing her in front of the girl. It would be much better if she thought Brigitte was part of the entertainment, so she walked over to the table and poured herself some wine. She took a deep drink then stepped towards him and kissed him. He reached up and began undoing her blouse. He had specifically requested she wear the corset with cut outs for her nipples and now she knew why. She closed her eyes while he squeezed her nipples and then began sucking and biting them. He groaned and, with one hand, began pushing the girl's head up and down, faster and faster. With his free hand he reached under Brigitte's skirt and slid his fingers inside her. Despite herself, Brigitte was beginning to feel aroused and then, abruptly, he stopped. "I thought you might like to watch for a change, rather than be on the receiving end, so I hired her for the next hour." He indicated the chair by the table. "Go and sit down and you can tell me if I'm doing everything right."

Brigitte was still stunned but she was so used to doing what he told her, she did as he said.

He waited until she was seated and then pushed the girl away. Brigitte watched in a trance while he shouted orders at her and then put her across his knee and spanked her. Despite her horror that he was doing this to another girl, a part of her was enjoying the whole thing, although she was reluctant to let him see that.

He finished eventually, told the girl to dress and sent her away. Once she had gone, he smiled at Brigitte who was still sitting in the chair. "You needn't worry. I saved some for you." He pointed at his erect penis. "Come on then, what are you waiting for?"

****

Hampshire

Now the light was almost gone it took a full second for Pam to realise the man was Richard and, although he was pointing a gun at her head, there was a broad smile on his face.

"You bastard!" she whispered, her heart pounding wildly, although whether from fear or pleasure at seeing Richard again, she wasn't entirely sure.

"You look wonderful when you're covered in leaves, you know!"

Despite herself, Pam smiled at him and then frowned. "Does this mean I've failed?"

"What did you see at the farm?"

Pam repeated what she had seen.

"Not bad. You just need to be aware that not all the action may be where you're looking. You obviously heard me coming, because I saw you turn round and glance in my direction. You would have done better to register my presence in your head and not move. That way your ears would have told you when I was closer and you wouldn't have given your own position away."

He smiled at her crestfallen face. "Don't look so worried. You're here to learn, aren't you? Come on, I'll walk back with you." When she made no attempt to move, he grinned. "You've done as well, if not better, than the others, so cheer up! Come on. I don't know about you but all this creeping around in the woods gives me an appetite!"

As they walked slowly through the forest back to the house, she looked at him shyly, remembering the last time they had been alone and recalling their long lingering kiss.

Almost as if he had read her mind, Richard suddenly stopped and, pulling her behind a large sturdy oak tree, he crushed his lips to hers, relieved when she kissed him back just as greedily. As he kissed her, his hands began to wander over her body and, pulling away she stopped him, her face flushed.

"Not here. We agreed to wait. Anyway it's cold and damp!"

Reluctantly Richard pulled back and offered her a cigarette. "Sorry, it's very difficult to resist you." His eyes were twinkling and Pam took the offered cigarette and drew the smoke deeply into her lungs, trying to still the frantic beating of her own heart.

"So, how much more have I to learn before I know whether I've been accepted? Or can't you tell me?"

Richard shook his head. "It's not up to me, it's up to your trainers. You've got a couple more things to learn and then, if you pass them satisfactorily, you'll get some leave before you go to France."

He was silent, not wanting to think about her being dropped into occupied territory where he could no longer protect her. They finished their cigarettes in silence and then walked on back to the house. Even though they both knew the outcome was always going to be that she would go to France, the likelihood of her going soon had suddenly become real and created an invisible barrier between them.

****

Toulouse, Southern France

Eve was still following Jeanne, even though she was beginning to feel slightly stupid. What if Jeanne turned round and saw her? She'd wonder what on earth was going on. She smiled. Jeanne would probably laugh, but Eve was sure she would appreciate her concern. She glanced up and saw Jeanne was approaching the side road into which she would turn.

Jeanne turned off and disappeared from sight. Eve slowed down so she could watch properly and realised she had been so intent on her thoughts, she hadn't noticed the sun had sunk below the headland and she was now in the dark. It was now much easier to see if anyone was behaving suspiciously because this part of town was quieter with fewer people about. In fact, there was hardly anyone around except Jeanne, herself and… she frowned. Someone was behind her. She hadn't noticed before and she wondered how long they'd been there.

Eve suddenly felt very uneasy. Maybe she shouldn't be doing this; she was putting herself in danger and… she never finished the thought as, without warning, a large hand covered her mouth and she was dragged soundlessly into an alleyway separating two shops. She was vaguely aware he had slammed her up against the wall and she began to struggle, but she was much too late. He was considerably stronger than she was and he already had his hands round her throat. He squeezed tighter and tighter and she felt the life draining out of her as he slowly choked her to death. Her last conscious thoughts were: she had failed Jeanne, she'd never warned Gabriel. Then everything went black and she sank slowly, almost gracefully, to the floor at the feet of her attacker.

Breathing hard from the exertion, the man bent down and checked her neck for a pulse. Nothing. He turned her head slightly and it slumped lifelessly onto her chest. He quickly searched her pockets looking for her ID card. When he found the document, he was even more confused. She worked for the police, so what was she doing following his target? He stood for a moment wondering if this would cause him a problem. He'd better get rid of the body. The shops here backed onto the Garonne River. It was only a short walk down the alley and he would be at the river's edge. He strained his ears but he could hear nothing. Making his decision, he dragged the body quickly towards the far end of the alley. This took him hardly any time at all and, within minutes, he had shoved her body over the edge into the water below and was walking briskly away towards the room he had rented across the street from Jeanne's apartment.

Chapter Twenty-seven

La Couture, Northern France

Louis arrived at the cellar an hour before the time he was due to hand the airmen over and swiftly gave them the winter coats Marie had sorted out for him.

They set out, picking their way across the frozen ground which was covered in a shining layer of frozen snow several centimetres thick. Their breath filled the air with clouds of white steam; the sky was cloudless and they found the light from the half moon and the stars lit their path quite well. No one spoke and the only sound was their feet crunching across the frozen rutted snow on the edges of the fields as they kept close to the hedges so they couldn't be seen.

After a relatively short period, they reached the beginning of the woods. The trees soon blocked out the little light and their progress slowed down considerably. The problem now was not the crunching of the frozen snow but the sound of branches breaking and twigs snapping because they were unable to see where they were putting their feet. Each twig or branch sounded like a gun shot in the frozen darkness of the woods and Louis quickly called a halt while they all adopted a way of walking to minimise the sound. But this slowed their progress so much Louis began to worry about time.

He was about to increase his pace when he heard the sound of a branch snapping somewhere ahead. Instantly he froze, his hand raised to halt the others even though they couldn't see his arm in the dark.

But they too had heard the noise and were waiting motionless, trying to discern who or what was ahead.

The silence lengthened and Louis wondered what he should do. He needed to reach the rendezvous at the right time, or they would have to start again another night.

Several more moments passed and Louis knew he needed to make a decision. The noise had not been repeated but that did not fill him with confidence. If it was innocent, then the noise would probably have carried on…

Whatever he was going to think next went straight out of his head as he realised someone was striding towards him.

****

Catford, London

Olive glanced at the latest letter from Kurt and sighed. She'd been sitting there for hours staring at the note and wishing she could tell him what was going on. Outside, the bombs were still raining down and the night was punctuated with the usual sounds of the Blitz. Olive had never been to the local shelter and had no intention of doing so now. If she was going to die, she'd do so in the privacy of her own home.

She poured herself another small glass of whiskey and stared at the wireless. Drinking didn't provide her with any answers, but did help her forget her problems. She was surprised by how much she had drunk; soon this bottle would be empty, leaving only one and then what would she do? The answer came immediately and she gave a wry smile. Of course, she could ask the two bastards who were blackmailing her. She was still ruminating on this when there was a knock on the door. She stood up, surprised to find she was slightly unsteady on her feet. She glanced around, hid the bottle under the cushions on the settee and stepped towards the door. She wasn't expecting anyone, especially during an air raid. Obviously someone else couldn't care less about the bombing, which probably ruled out the villains, gutless bastards. Olive found this quite funny and she was still laughing when she opened the door.

"Hello, Olive. Pleased to see me, are you?" Dickson tipped his hat and his sidekick giggled.

"Looks like she's drunk, boss!"

Olive said nothing. She stood back, indicating they should come in and shut the door behind her. "What do you want?"

Dickson smiled and leant forward. "You surprise me, Olive. I really didn't think you were the type to drink alone."

Olive shrugged. "If it wasn't for people like you, I wouldn't have to." The alcohol had loosened her tongue and she stopped abruptly.

Dickson laughed. "Get out the bottle, then. Let's all have a glass. I've got a proposition for you."

Olive paled, remembering the last time those words had been said but Dickson didn't appear to notice her discomfort. He was looking for the bottle.

"Well come on, Olive. I haven't got all day, chop chop."

Olive jumped and made her way towards the sofa, pulled out the bottle and looked around for some more glasses. She realised belatedly she'd left hers in plain sight on the table.

"Don't worry." Dickson opened the bottle and took a swig before pouring some in her glass. He indicated the other man. "He doesn't drink when he's on duty, bit like the police." He laughed loudly at his own joke. "Drink up!"

Olive's feeling that she was in a recurring nightmare was not helped by his next words.

"You're not a rich woman are you, Olive? So it seems a bit mean to keep taking your savings." He watched her eyes light up and grinned. "So, how about you work for me instead?"

Olive frowned. She must be more drunk than she thought.

****

Honor Oak Park, London

"For Gawd's sake, will you stop running around!" The exasperated voice broke into Peggy's thoughts and she pulled her blanket over her face in an attempt to block out the noise and the smell.

"I'm not going to tell you again." The voice was very loud and was followed by a slap. The child in question burst into noisy tears which Peggy found more irritating than him running around. But who was she to judge? For the first time since Joe had been captured, Peggy was grateful she hadn't married him before he went away. If she had, she might have had a child by now. She would have hated having to worry about a child of her own, as well as everything else.

"I'm really sorry, love." The voice was a bit quieter this time but close to Peggy's ear. She opened her eyes with reluctance and saw a young woman, a little older than her, with short brown hair and a tired exhaustion-lined face. She was indicating Peggy's bag which was poking out from under the blanket. There was some kind of stain spreading across the side and Peggy realised the child had spilt something on the bag which was why the mother had slapped him.

"Don't worry, really. The bag's not new and it can't be easy for him being stuck in here. Or for you either."

Relieved Peggy wasn't making more out of the accident, the girl gave a weary smile and held out her hand.

"It's really nice of you to be so understanding, thank you. I'm Jane Harrison by the way. And the horror is Alf." She glanced to where Alf was sitting, a sulky expression on his face. He was somewhere between two and three with short blond hair, deep blue eyes and long curling eyelashes. He was watching Peggy from under them, his thumb firmly in his mouth.

Unable to resist his cheeky face, Peggy smiled and was rewarded with an enormous grin in return.

"His Dad's..." Jane stopped and put her hand over her mouth. "Well, you know... He's away."

"You must miss him terribly, especially with a small child to look after?"

Surprised and pleased to have found what might be a new 'shelter friend', Jane smiled. "Not much I can do though, so I'll just have to grin and bear it."

We're gonna hang out the washing on the Siegfried Line – always a popular air-raid song because it was loud, jolly and defiant – echoed round the confines of the shelter, accompanied by a man on a harmonica. Giving up any idea of sleep or further conversation, Peggy shrugged and joined in. Jane beckoned to Alf and patted her knee. He came and sat on her lap while she bounced him in time to the music. They were in full voice when an enormous explosion rocked the shelter, filling the small space with dust and debris and the lights flickered and went out. Alf shrieked loudly as darkness suddenly engulfed them and then the lights came back on again.

"Sshh." Jane gently rocked him, trying to hide her own fear, although she was shaking violently, but he was sobbing softly and seemed unaware of her gentle crooning.

Peggy took a deep breath and looked to where Annie was sitting. To her relief, Annie smiled serenely, her hands resting comfortably on her 'bump', as she called it.

The shelter had filled with dust, the familiar smell of burst sewage pipes and seeping gas, mixed with the normal rancid shelter smells.

"The buckets have gone over, I'm afraid ladies and gentlemen, so we'll have to wait awhile before we can use them." The resigned voice of the ARP warden went some way to calming the atmosphere, although his words were greeted with good natured moans and groans. Most people were just grateful they were still alive and unhurt, although a good number, including Peggy, were wondering whether they still had a home to go to. The man with the harmonica, who obviously had a sense of humour began playing *The Sun has got its hat on, hip hip hip hooray!* and everyone was soon singing along. If nothing else, the singing drowned out the sounds of the bombs, the continual ack-ack fire and the constant jangling of the fire engines' bells as they rushed to put out the fires being ignited by the incendiaries.

Run Rabbit Run replaced the previous song and Peggy joined in. Alf was now fast asleep in Jane's arms, and she smiled ruefully. "Chance'd be a fine thing. I haven't seen any rabbit on sale for ages."

Before Peggy could answer, the woman sitting on the other side of Jane butted in, "Nor me, although I think there's some to be had on the black market, if you know where to look." She winked and carried on singing. This sounded so much like something from one of the Ministry of Information films, Peggy looked at Jane and the two girls burst into laughter, frantically trying to cover their fit of the giggles by singing extra loudly. Unfortunately, this woke Alf, who glared at them both with such a ferocious look before falling back into a deep sleep that they laughed even more.

****

La Couture, Northern France

Louis made out a shape and then heard the sound of a dog growling softly.

"Shh!" The hissed whisper caught him by surprise and he found himself face to face with what he assumed was a man completely muffled up in winter clothes, carrying a couple of rabbits over his shoulder, his dog padding along quietly behind him.

"Christ, you gave me a fright." The man peered at Louis. "What the…?" Then he saw the other men cowering behind Louis and he nodded. "Ah… Good on you, son," he muttered, and he was gone almost as suddenly as he had appeared.

Louis breathed a sigh of relief, wiped the sweat off his brow and upper lip and started to move forward again. They were almost at the rendezvous site now. Once there, he would leave the men and head back to the farm. The courier would collect them when he was out of sight.

The last few hundred yards were uneventful and they soon reached the clearing. Louis stopped and indicated they should wait while he'd checked the area was safe. Having made his way round the edge of the clearing carefully, he decided everything was secure.

He returned to the waiting men and took them to the edge of the clearing. "This is where I leave you." Marie had been coaching him so he could say the next few words in English. "Your password is *'It will soon be light'*. You say this and they will reply *'When the war is won'*. You have this?"

"Thank you." The men quickly shook his hand and stepped back into the trees to wait for the next courier.

Louis said one last goodbye and then turned and left. The temptation to look back was almost overwhelming but he resisted. Their fate was no longer in his hands.

Chapter Twenty-eight

Honor Oak Park, London

The all clear sounded at around five in the morning. Peggy stood up and stretched as much as she could in the restricted space. She helped Annie up and rubbed her back, which was sore from being stuck in the same position for so long.

"Ah well, see you tomorrow night, I suppose," Jane said as they emerged into the street, Alf fast asleep in her arms, his head resting on her shoulder. She hesitated. "Perhaps we could go to the pictures one night. I could get a babysitter. *Rebecca*'s on this week. The book was brilliant and I'd love to see the film."

Peggy smiled. "That sounds like a good idea. What do you think, Annie? I was thinking about going to see *Rebecca* myself and it'll be nice to all go together. Might as well make the most of your freedom before the little one's born."

They stood enjoying the fresh air. After the foetid stench of the shelter, the air in the street felt cold and infinitely fresher, despite the heavy pall of smoke and dust swirling around. Amongst the other odours, Peggy could clearly smell gas again and she could hear ARP wardens busy warning people not to light cigarettes, which probably meant there would be no gas at home as the main was probably fractured again. She turned back to Jane to ask if she was coming to the WRVS mobile canteen to get some tea and hot food.

"No, thanks anyway, but I think I'm going to get him home to bed and have a nice sit down and rest before he wakes up and starts driving me mad again! I live just over there." She pointed over her shoulder without looking. "See you tonight and we can arrange something?" Smiling, she turned away, heading in the opposite direction. But she had only taken a couple of steps when she stopped, a look of confusion on her face.

"Are you alright?" Peggy was watching her new friend.

Jane didn't answer. Instead she was staring blankly ahead.

"What's the matter, Jane?" Even in the darkness, Peggy could see Jane had gone as white as a ghost and was clearly in deep shock.

Jane turned towards Peggy. Her eyes, previously so full of life, despite her obvious exhaustion, were now dull and lifeless and wordlessly she pointed to a large crater in the street backing onto the road where Peggy's house was. Only two walls remained, joined down one edge. Their crumbling bricks were cut off abruptly just below the roof and the far ends tapered away sharply into nothing. Despite the darkness, they could just make out the flowery wallpaper and a picture of an idyllic rural scene, hanging lopsidedly from a hook, that had remarkably survived the bomb which had destroyed the rest of the properties. They could see the remains of possessions strewn amongst the rubble and fallen masonry. Clothes, toys, photos and books were mixed up with bits of broken furniture, all covered in the contents of the tins and other food from the larder. This was obviously where the bomb that had shaken the shelter so badly had fallen and Peggy looked at Annie in horror as understanding gradually dawned.

"Oh my God… Was that your house?"

Jane nodded and slowly sank to her knees. "All our things, all my photos, Alf's toys… Our home, mine and Mick's…"

Peggy was shocked and couldn't think of anything to say. Jane began to cry softly and then raised her tearstained face to Peggy and said pitifully. "If the house isn't there, he'll have nothing to come home to; he won't be able to find us, will he?" Before Peggy could answer, her expression changed. "He'll be ever so cross about the house. He asked me to look after it, but this wasn't my fault, was it?"

"Of course not and he won't be cross." Peggy said briskly, her arm round Jane's shoulder. "He'll be so grateful you and Alf are alright, he won't worry at all about the house. You'll see. As to him being able to find you, they have systems set up to deal with this, so you don't need to worry. The most important thing is both you and Alf are safe." She had no idea whether the authorities did have ways of notifying people about bombed-out relatives but she assumed they must have, so she spoke confidently.

Her nurse's training took over and she helped Jane to stand up, speaking firmly but gently. "Come on, let's get some hot sweet tea inside you." After taking the sleeping Alf from her arms, she gently steered Jane towards the WRVS canteen where they gave her a hot mug of sweet tea.

The drink did the trick and Jane gradually become more aware of her surroundings. "Thank you. I'm sorry. I just didn't know… don't know what to do." She stared sightlessly into the distance, as if that would hold the answer.

"If you go to the Town Hall, luvvie, they'll sort you out. You know, find you and your little boy somewhere to stay and get you some clothes and rations." The WRVS lady was smiling kindly at her; she had become used to making the same speech with minor variations.

"No, don't bother," Peggy interrupted and, looking at Annie for agreement, she said clearly, "Come on, Jane, you can come home with us. We have a spare room you can have; at least we did before we came to the shelter tonight… You can stay with us until you find somewhere else."

****

Toulouse, Southern France

The day started badly. Jeanne arrived at work, only to find that, for once, Eve was not there. It was unusual for Eve to be late, but Jeanne was not unduly concerned at first. However, as the day wore on and there was still no sign of her, she grew increasingly worried. It was not like Eve to not come to work; in all the time Jeanne had been there, Eve had never missed a day, but even more worrying was she had not sent any message to explain her absence. Jeanne became so concerned, she spoke to one of the detectives when he came to collect the post. At first he was inclined to dismiss her fears but, seeing how worried she was and acknowledging it was strange there had been no message from Eve, he agreed to investigate.

****

Lewisham Council Offices, London

The switchboard was busy. Olive stared out at the girls and wished she could turn back the clock to the time before the war, when she felt she had everything. When Dickson had suggested she work for him, she'd thought she'd misheard. Seeing her bemused expression, he'd hastened to explain all she had to do was to hide some of his merchandise in her flat and he would stop taking her money. Instead he would pay her a small percentage of the profit on anything she looked after for him. Olive had stared at him for several moments and then nodded. What choice did she have? At least this way she could afford to buy some more whisky when she ran out.

Her thoughts turned to Peggy. She'd not had time to visit her cousin for a few days. Maybe she'd pop round to see her when the bombing was less severe and see if she could find out why Peggy had looked so guilty when she'd mentioned being unfaithful to Joe. Perhaps there was someone else after all. She'd love to have something on her cousin.

She would write to Kurt tonight. It was nearly two weeks since her last letter. He would be getting worried if she didn't reply soon. She frowned. She would have to think of something to tell him. Most of what was happening in her life she couldn't write down. Olive reached down into her handbag and, after making sure no one was watching, took a small swig from the silver flask she'd treated herself to. A wry smile crossed her face: if she couldn't think of anything to write, she could always make something up.

****

Toulouse, Southern France

Jeanne spent the next few hours awaiting news and wondering whether something really had happened to Eve. If she had gone missing a few days earlier, Jeanne would have dismissed her fears as stupid but when she thought about their conversation yesterday, she wasn't so sure. Then she told herself not to be so stupid. If Gabriel had been worried after Eve spoke to him, he would have told her, but she hadn't seen him. Having made several mistakes in her work and realising she had almost thrown away the latest post instead of the scrap paper, she decided to put her fears aside, at least while she was at work. So, for the rest of the day, she concentrated on what she was doing. She had hoped the detective would have called in again to tell her whether he had found anything but there was no sign of him and eventually it was time to go home.

When she'd arrived home the previous night, she'd waited until they'd finished supper and Angel had gone to bed before mentioning anything to her father. Jean-Paul immediately told her not to look round or give any indication she was aware she was being followed. He was relieved Eve had told Gabriel and felt if there was anything serious, Gabriel would have let them know. After careful consideration, he decided the best thing was to do nothing and wait for Gabriel to contact them. He tried to ignore the niggling voice in the back of his mind which asked why Gabriel had not already been in contact. He must know Jeanne would be worried.

Chapter Twenty-nine

En Route to Gabon

The ship was awash with rumours and Marcel had no idea what to believe. First they were told there would be no need for fighting, as Gabon had declared its allegiance to the Free French, but no sooner had that rumour travelled round than another began, stating the exact opposite. Having berthed at Douala in the Cameroon, they waited impatiently to find out what would happen next.

"God, I'm fed up." Pierre was standing on deck leaning on the rail of the ship and looking longingly at the lights of Douala. The fierce heat made it too hot to stay in their cabins unless they absolutely had to, so they spent as much time as possible up on deck. It was early evening and the sea was relatively calm. The sun had descended into the sea a little while earlier, a fiery red ball, its energy quenched by the waters of the ocean, providing yet another spectacular sunset, and they were enjoying the cooler evening air. They had been berthed outside the port for several days now and, much to their disgust, had not been allowed to go ashore.

"What do you think's happening?" Marcel asked, not for the first time that day and Paul threw a mock punch at him.

"Goodness Marcel, you're worse than a child. We know no more than you do. Just relax and enjoy the evening. I reckon we'll soon be in the thick of the fighting, so let's make the most of this."

Marcel stared up at the stars filling the sky above him. The one thing he still couldn't get used to was seeing so many stars all at once. Everywhere he looked, there were stars stretching into infinity. They reminded him of Jeanne and Angel and he wondered how they were and what they were doing. He was convinced they were still alive somewhere and he wished he could at least write to them.

He sat down and closed his eyes. This was always the best time to sleep as it was warm and pleasantly comfortable on deck, unlike the close confines of their cramped cabin. They seemed to have been on ships forever and he was beginning to forget what dry land was like. He had just begun to doze off when Pierre nudged him, none too gently, in the ribs.

"Look! Something's happening."

Instantly awake, Marcel stood up and looked to where Pierre was pointing. In the gloom, he could just make out a small boat coming to a stop by the steps which had been lowered and someone climbing up onto the ship. He couldn't see who it was but the man must have been quite important as the crew nearest to the steps saluted. Marcel squinted into the darkness but the man had vanished from sight and, after several minutes of intense watching, he gave up and sat back down on the deck again. Nothing else happened for a couple of hours and then the ship suddenly became a hive of activity as the crew rushed around preparing to leave.

The piercing whistle that signalled they should all parade on deck suddenly broke into their thoughts and they hurried eagerly to comply. At last some news.

As soon as they were all assembled, they were told the garrison at Lambarene had surrendered to the Free French and they were on their way to Libreville, the capital of Gabon.

****

Stalag XXA, Poland

"So, Joe, are you going to help with our concert, or not?" Dick was laying on his bunk busy drawing up some designs for a stage set. Unfortunately any mention of putting on a concert always brought back unwelcome memories of the Germans shooting the two Polish men in the other camp. Joe shut off the memory and glanced up from his book, a look of resignation on his face. "Go on then; what do you want me to do? I'm not dressing up as a woman."

Dick grinned. "Nah, we've got plenty of people who want to do that, which, come to think of it is rather worrying! No, you're a carpenter, so I thought you could give me a hand with making some of this stuff for the background."

"Well, I'll have to see if I can fit you into my busy timetable." Joe winked at Cyril who was watching the exchange with amusement. He knew Joe was dying to get involved; he was just goading Dick for fun, which he had to admit wasn't hard. Even now, after months here, he was still terribly gullible and had a kind of naivety that would get him killed if he wasn't careful. Cyril still smiled when he thought about the stupid idea he'd had to get back their blankets after the Krauts had confiscated them. Good job they'd stopped him and finally managed to make him see sense. It would have been all the more difficult though, if McMahon hadn't told them about the Red Cross trick. Even now, it made him laugh to think about how they had stolen all those clothes from right under the Krauts' noses. Even funnier was the thought of all the floorboards they had removed to make hiding places for the extra clothing, not to mention the clothes hidden in the loft and under the stove. And, of course, the floorboards had provided some much needed extra heat as they burned away merrily in the stove. Bit of a shame they hadn't been able to save the wood for another time, but there wasn't anywhere to hide such large pieces, so they'd had no option but to burn them immediately. Still, the hut had been lovely and warm and they'd all slept really well that night.

It wasn't a bad haul at the end of the day. They'd all managed to get at least one thick army jumper, a new pair of trousers and some underwear, so all in all, a rather profitable day. He was surprised the Krauts hadn't noticed, but they'd been too preoccupied trying to oversee exactly what the Red Cross were doing and making sure no one got to talk to the officials without a guard being present. The Red Cross, on the other hand, had been just as determined they were going to talk to some people on their own, so it had been quite a tussle of wills and he'd been pleased to see it hadn't all gone the Krauts' way.

"Sorry?" Cyril realised Dick was asking him something.

"I said are you going to do anything for the concert?"

"Nah, I'm not good at things like that, but I'm going to be watching!"

"You'll enjoy my act," Mitchell said cheerfully. "I'm going to sing some American songs."

"What are they about? How to avoid going to war, despite talking the good fight?" The voice belonged to Carstairs, a tall thin Geordie, who didn't particularly like Mitchell and never could resist the opportunity to rile him.

"I agree entirely. That's why I risked imprisonment and death to join up and fight with you," Mitchell replied patiently. He'd had this conversation several times with Carstairs and others and he was becoming slightly bored. He would have felt the same if the positions had been reversed. But why have a go at him? Not only was he risking his life but also his liberty twice over. If his country didn't get involved, he wouldn't be able to go home without risking being locked up there as well.

He was about to point this out when Joe joined in, "Shut up, Carstairs. You should be thanking him, not moaning at him."

"What's it got to do with you, Price?"

"He's my mate and he joined up, like the rest of us, to fight the ruddy Germans, not each other."

"Hear, hear." Dick applauded from his bunk. "Come on, chaps, lets' stop arguing amongst ourselves and plan the concert, eh?" Dick was annoyed the conversation had been hijacked by Carstairs, who he couldn't stand.

"As I said, you can count me in," Mitchell said cheerfully, turning his attention back to Dick.

"Let's have a look at what you want and we'll see what's possible." Joe took the plan from Dick's outstretched hand and began to study the piece of paper. "You don't want much, do you? The biggest problem's going to be the materials. I can't see the Krauts giving us this stuff and I'm not sure we'll be able to scrounge everything either."

"You leave the scrounging to me," Cyril joined in. "Just tell me exactly what you need and I'll have a go. What about costumes, Dick?"

"Jeffries is organising that. He used to be a tailor in civvy street so he reckons he can make anything we want. So, can you do it then, Joe?"

Joe shrugged. "If Cyril can get the materials, I'll have a go; that's the best I can do, alright?"

Chapter Thirty

Lambeth Hospital, London

Peggy yawned. It was her first week back on nights and she wasn't completely used to the shift pattern yet. The best thing about working nights was she was managing to get some sleep. Raids during the day were very few and far between and Alf was very well behaved, so he rarely disturbed her. After six days of proper sleep, she was starting to feel like herself again.

Nights at the hospital, however, were busier than ever. Not only was the hospital housing a sizeable number of homeless families, but the bombing continued unabated.

The sirens heralded the beginning of another raid and a large number of incendiaries began landing on the roof of the hospital. Peggy and Helen were dispatched with others to start evacuating patients from the most threatened wards and, as they hurried through the hospital, they could hear shrapnel and other bomb debris raining down on and ricocheting off the tiles.

"They must be targeting this area." Peggy sounded breathless as they tried to hurry those patients who could be moved, out of their beds and into wheelchairs.

"I went to see *Go to Blazes* a few weeks ago. I can't believe I thought the film was funny," Helen grumbled as the sound of yet more incendiaries could be heard whistling through the air.

"Peggy, I was worried when they said you'd come up here. Are you alright?" Chris had failed to notice Helen and he stopped in embarrassment.

Peggy stared back at him, her cheeks scarlet.

"Sorry," he flustered. " I mean… I saw you both come up and I was concerned for your safety." Chris ignored the furious expression on Peggy's face and began to help the girls move the patients.

Helen said nothing until he'd gone and then she grabbed Peggy's arm. "Come on then, tell me everything."

Peggy pulled away, her face a mixture of anger and embarrassment. "There's nothing to tell. We're just good friends."

"So, why are you keeping him such a big secret?" Helen persisted.

"Because people like you would get the wrong idea." Peggy faced Helen. "Joe's a prisoner. There's not much I can do about that, but I don't want him hearing from anyone I've taken up with another man, especially as it isn't true. We really are just friends." Even as she said the last few words, the memory of their kiss flooded her mind and she turned away.

****

Bethune, Northern France

Brigitte had no idea what was going on. Rolf still treated her well but the only time they had sex was when other girls were there. To start with, he reserved his punishments for the other girls and she watched. Gradually, she found herself joining in, until she too was being chastised and then having sex with the other girls while Rolf watched. Brigitte did not find the other girls attractive and she longed for the time when it had been just her and Rolf. Each morning, she resolved to tell him she no longer wanted to participate, but he seemed to think she was enjoying the sex as well, so she kept finding excuses not to say anything. She was also terrified that, if she complained, he would throw her out and she had nowhere to go. Her father had made it quite clear he no longer wanted her back after their argument and she hadn't spoken to Louis in ages.

The previous evening had been particularly horrible and Brigitte wasn't sure how much more she could take. She would have to save up some more money and leave. But that was no longer simple. She would need exit permits to cross the Demarcation Line to go south and, even if she went to Paris, she would need papers. Then a thought crossed her mind. She'd seen some documents in Rolf's office. Perhaps she could steal some and use them. She would hang on a bit longer and see if things improved. If they didn't, she would help herself to the exit papers and disappear. Maybe Louis would be interested in coming with her. He must hate living under the Germans. She would even be prepared for Marie to come as well, if that was the only way Louis would leave.

"Come back to bed, darling…"

Brigitte sighed, plastered an expression of pleasure on her face and turned back to Rolf and his latest girl, a large breasted dark haired girl with a big nose and sharp teeth.

****

Toulouse, Southern France

Madame Fournier, or Adele, as she insisted he call her, was proving extremely persistent. Jean-Paul had explained it was much too soon after his wife's death for him to become involved with anyone else, but that seemed to have made things worse. Part of him was tempted to bed her and be done with the matter, but common sense told him that would not be a very good idea. If she was like this now when he had given her no encouragement, what on earth would she be like if he did give her reason to hope there might be a future for them?

His thoughts turned to Suzanne and he found himself smiling. Suzanne was intelligent, sophisticated and good looking. She dressed her age, with style and was wonderful company. He'd finally taken his courage in both hands and invited her to dinner with Jeanne and Angel. He had no idea how they would react so he was very nervous, but he needn't have been. Angel adored her and even Jeanne liked her. If he was ever going to settle down with anyone else, Suzanne would be the one. But therein lay the problem. Could he really settle down with someone who did not know the truth? What kind of relationship could they have based on such a big lie and, in any case, once they were all living together it would be impossible to keep their secret from her. That meant telling her the truth before committing to anything and, apart from the obvious risks to himself and his family, that meant putting her in danger as well: not something you did to people you cared about. Jean-Paul sighed heavily.

"Come on, Angel, or we'll be late." Angel came running out and was soon chattering to one of her friends, Clara, who lived close by. Jean-Paul took turns with Clara's mother, Sian, to walk the girls to school, an arrangement that suited both parties. Sian was delightful and, even better, had no designs on him at all which made their relationship a pleasure as far as Jean-Paul was concerned. In fact, Sian found Adele's overtures towards him highly amusing and often made him laugh about them. Her husband was also a POW but, whereas Adele seemed happy to forget her husband, Sian talked about hers constantly as though he was still there with her. Jean-Paul found this incredibly touching and he always made a point of asking if she had heard from him.

He watched Angel skipping along the street. She seemed really happy at the school and the only downside was that her best friend was Marianne, Adele's daughter. He groaned. It was like he'd conjured her up; Adele was walking towards him. Fortunately, they were at the school gates now and, hastily taking his leave from Angel and Clara, Jean-Paul waved vaguely in her direction, smartly turned on his heel and headed in the other direction. He could hear her rather coarse, high pitched voice calling him but he pretended not to hear. He had enough on his mind this morning without having to cope with her as well. Sian was collecting the girls tonight, so he wouldn't have to see Adele at all today.

As he hurried away, he was sure he could hear Claudette laughing at his cowardice and he found himself smiling slightly as he spoke tenderly to her in his mind. *"If you were still here, I wouldn't have to do this at all!"*

****

Gabon

"So help me God, I am not going to teach you any more games." Paul flung the cards down in disgust, having lost yet more money to Marcel, who grinned. For some reason, he was very lucky and, once he understood how to play, he had turned the tables on his friends to the extent that none of them would play cards with him at all because he always won.

"Well, you did only teach me to play so you had someone you could beat." He moved swiftly to one side as Paul kicked out. The others laughed, knowing what Marcel said was partly true. However, they had also taught him to play so he felt more at home with them. They just hadn't expected him to learn quite so quickly.

"Well it's all very nice being on this cruise ship, you know permanent blue skies, continual sunshine, even though the service is not great, but I am really bored," Pierre complained, squinting up into the cloudless blue sky. They were all perspiring profusely despite the cooling sea breeze which rippled through their uniforms and the underwear they had hung out to dry on the rails alongside the deck.

"Look!" Paul's voice broke into their thoughts and they looked to where he was pointing. "Isn't that land?"

Marcel peered eagerly into the distance. "Yes, yes, I think it is. Surely if we can see land, we must be coming close to where we're going?"

By now they had been joined by other soldiers, all leaning on the rails, pointing and talking excitedly and, as they watched, the land gradually came closer.

****

Stalag XXA, Poland

"Raus, Raus! Aufstehen schnell!"

Reluctantly, Joe climbed down from his bunk and joined the others lining up on the parade ground. The wind howled and the snow that had been falling intermittently began to settle around their boots. Joe shivered, wondering how long they were likely to have to stand there.

As time wore slowly on and the men became colder, the verbal heckling of the guards became louder and more aggressive until, eventually, they began threatening the men with their rifles. Just as the situation seemed likely to get out of hand, the Commandant appeared and, behind him, they could see what appeared to be a sergeant major from The Queen's Regiment, escorted by two grim-faced guards.

"This man has attempted to steal food from the cookhouse." The Commandant ignored the yells of encouragement and ragged cheering from the ranks. "This behaviour will not be tolerated." The two guards escorted the man towards the main building. They disappeared inside and the men glanced at each other warily. There was silence among the prisoners, although the guards were nudging each other and laughing.

Joe looked at Cyril. "What's going on?"

"I should think the bastards have been sent to give him a good pasting." He spat on the ground, the only way he could show his contempt. Joe closed his eyes and offered up a silent prayer for the unfortunate man and then opened them again in surprise as a roar of laughter, and applause shattered the silence. Joe looked towards the building and saw why everyone was cheering. The two guards had staggered out, covered in blood and looking more than the worse for wear. There was total pandemonium as the men continued to cheer and laugh and the guards went berserk, threatening to shoot the jeering men. Order was only restored when the guards began firing their rifles just above the heads of the prisoners, who threw themselves flat into the snow covering the parade ground.

"Enough lads. Give it a rest or we'll all get shot." The NCO's voice rang out clearly, silence was restored and the guards stopped firing.

Others were sent in to finish the punishment and the men stood sullenly in silence, waiting. Eventually, they reappeared, dragging the lifeless body of the sergeant major and propped him up by the wire fence. The guards lined up in front of him and aimed their rifles at the prone body, ready to fire. Joe closed his eyes in horror. There was no doubting what was about to happen and he really didn't want to watch.

Several shots rang out and the body jumped convulsively before coming to rest in an unnatural heap. Joe made the sign of the cross. The tension and hatred in the air was palpable and they listened sullenly while the Commandant threatened them again with similar treatment if they broke any more rules. Sickened, the men returned silently to their huts. The cold was forgotten as they wondered whether they had been indirectly responsible for their companion's death by their goading of the guards or whether they had always intended to shoot him as an example.

****

Gabon

The sun gradually began its slow descent into the ocean, night fell and the ship came to a stop, weighing anchor some distance off the coast. Marcel could feel his heart pounding against his chest. Although he had been waiting for this moment, he was concerned he still had to prove himself and he licked his parched lips with a mixture of fear and anticipation. He fought hard to still the compulsion to check he had everything he needed. He had already done this at least three times and he knew he had remembered everything. The ship rolled and pitched gently as the wind got up and he almost stumbled. He'd forgotten to compensate for the large pack he was carrying.

"You'll be fine, Marcel. Stop worrying." Pierre spoke softly, making sure the others would not hear. He had no doubt about Marcel's ability; it was only Marcel who doubted himself. Once they saw some action, Marcel would stop worrying.

The order to disembark into the small boats came and Marcel followed Pierre over the side and down the rope ladders into the boats. Once seated, he peered out into the darkness in the direction he thought land was, but he could see nothing.

"Do you know where we are?" he asked Paul who was sitting next to him.

"Would it make any difference if you knew?" Paul replied and Marcel could see the flash of his white teeth, grinning at him in the darkness. "Actually I think we're at a place called Pointe La Mondah, wherever that is!"

"Oh, well that's alright then," Marcel replied pleased to have the opportunity to joke around a bit. "I thought we might be somewhere else!"

"I hope you remembered to bring the money you won off me," Paul muttered as the boat set off into the darkness. "The first round is on you, don't forget."

"You haven't got money with you, have you?" Pierre whispered in disbelief.

"Don't worry, it's safe enough." Marcel changed the subject. "Do you think they'll be waiting for us when we land?"

"No idea. It sounds quiet enough…" Pierre started to say.

"They'll definitely be waiting if you lot don't shut up." The sergeant's urgent whisper interrupted him and, grinning, they all sat back and lapsed into silence, lost in their own thoughts as the boats crept closer and closer to the shore.

****

Toulouse, Southern France

They had just finished their evening meal and Angel was in bed. The knock at the door made Jeanne jump and she rushed to answer it.

Gabriel took her hands and led her into the small sitting room where Jean-Paul was waiting. "Come and sit down, my love." He waited until she was seated before speaking. "I'm so sorry to have to tell you this, Jeanne, but Eve is dead."

Jeanne stared at him in horror.

"What do you mean? Was she ill? Or was there an accident?' Jean-Paul asked more sharply than he'd intended.

Gabriel shook his head and turned back to Jeanne. "I'm sorry, Jeanne. There's no easy way to say this. But if I don't tell you, someone else will, or you will read about it in the papers. She was strangled and her body thrown into the River Garonne."

Jeanne gasped. "But who would…?" Words failed her and she stopped, unable to believe her friend, kind, gentle, Eve had been murdered.

There was a long silence.

"Do you think it's something to do with the person who is following Jeanne?" Jean-Paul asked.

Gabriel looked at him in astonishment. "What's this?"

"Don't you know?" Jean-Paul was even more concerned now.

Jeanne spoke slowly. "I told Eve the last time I saw her that I thought someone was following me. She said I should tell my father and she would tell you."

"I haven't been in the office much the last few days and I certainly haven't seen Eve." He paused for a few moments. "This changes everything." Seeing Jeanne's distressed face and the concern in Jean-Paul's, he hastened to reassure them. "There's nothing to say this isn't just a coincidence." However his instincts told him the two things were linked, although how, he had no idea.

His brain was racing with unanswered questions. Who was having Jeanne followed and why? When Eve had been unable to find him, had she mentioned the matter to someone else? Was that why she had been killed?

Gabriel was suddenly aware of Jeanne and Jean-Paul watching him closely and, raising her hand to his lips, he kissed it gently and smiled at her.

"Take tomorrow off…" He sensed she was about to argue and raised his hand to forestall her. "Eve's death has been a shock for you and no one would expect you to come in to work. You'll be safe here?" He looked questioningly at Jean-Paul.

"I'll let the school know and I will stay home with her tomorrow. But what about when she does go back to work?"

"I'll arrange for her to be picked up by a police car for a while, at least until we've found whoever did this." For the first time since he'd arrived, Gabriel relaxed slightly. "If the person who is following you did do this, then at least we can make it harder for them to track you for the next few weeks… I have to go now, sweetheart. If I stay too long, it will look suspicious. It is entirely normal I would come to tell you about Eve's death, but after asking you questions, I would then leave." Seeing her forlorn expression, he smiled again. "Not much longer now. Be brave." He kissed her tenderly and, after shaking Jean-Paul's hand, he left the apartment. As he went down the stairs, he put Jeanne firmly out of his mind and began to concentrate on the various strands of the puzzle he had been handed.

Somehow he had to find out who was following Jeanne at the same time as investigating Eve's death. Until he knew the answer to the first question he had no idea whether the two events were related. But at the same time he could not tell the rest of his team about Jeanne, because he would have to give them a reason why someone should be following her. That meant either telling them about his relationship with her or telling them what happened with Plombière, neither of which he was prepared to do. Telling other people about either could put Jeanne in even more danger, so he would just have to solve the mystery himself.

****

La Couture, Northern France

The baby kicked hard and changed position for the umpteenth time that day and Marie smiled. She was very large now, considering she still had two months to go and, if she wasn't so sure when she'd conceived, she would have wondered if she got her dates wrong. She had said as much to the doctor, especially as she was much larger than she had been with either of the boys but the doctor had said that was just her age and she had no reason not to believe him. It certainly wasn't from eating too much. She and Louis were reasonably well off as far as food was concerned, even with the extra mouths they had to feed, but she had heard rumours of shortages in the cities. These would probably be made worse by the unseasonably early cold weather and frozen ground which was preventing the farmers from digging up many of the root vegetables. She couldn't remember the snow coming quite as early as it had this year and she hoped the bad weather wasn't a portent of things to come.

****

Toulouse, Southern France

In the apartment across the road, the man watched Gabriel leave with interest. He recognised him immediately and his curiosity was piqued. Why would the deputy commissioner be visiting his target? His employer would be extremely interested in this snippet of information, hopefully interested enough to ignore any trouble he might have caused by killing that woman. He pulled up a chair so he had a good view of the rooms opposite, positioned the small occasional table by his side and placed the bottle of cognac and a glass on top. He sat down carefully and reached for the bottle, pouring himself another glass of the rich velvety brown liquid. He swirled the alcohol around the glass for a while, admiring the texture and allowing time for the alcohol to warm in his hand. Then he drank deeply. Replacing the glass on the table, he took his small black notebook and pencil out of his waistcoat pocket and began writing laboriously, his spidery writing covering two pages before he finally snapped the book shut and replaced it in his pocket.

Night had fallen but the flat opposite was lit. Although the curtains were drawn, he could make out shadows moving around behind them and then the light went out, plunging the flat into darkness. The man waited patiently. This was the best part of this job. He licked his lips lasciviously; he could feel himself growing hard in anticipation and, just when he thought he couldn't wait any longer, the light came on in the room with the small balcony overlooking the street. Although the curtains were drawn, he could make out the contours of her body as she slowly undressed. The fact she was totally unaware of him watching made everything all the more sensuous. His breathing came in short sharp bursts and he groaned loudly as he reached the point of no return, his orgasm shaking the table and making the glass rattle against the side of the bottle.

****

Stalag XXA, Poland

"Joe!" He looked up startled. "God Joe, where were you? I've been calling you for ages, well twice actually. There's a letter for you."

Joe sat up eagerly and almost snatched the letter from Cyril's hand.

He recognised the writing immediately. It was from Peggy. Joe settled back down onto his pillow and began reading. Before long he was confused. Peggy was talking about someone called Annie who had moved in. Joe frowned, had Ethel or Sally moved out then? No, she said Sally was getting married next month, so it couldn't be her. It must be Ethel then. He checked back in Peggy's earlier letters but he couldn't find any mention that Ethel had moved out. He checked the dates and noticed there was quite a large gap between some of them, so perhaps he was missing some letters. He sighed and wondered what else he didn't know about. Realising there wasn't much he could do about the missing mail other than asking Peggy to clarify things when he next wrote to her, he carried on, frowning when he read the bit about Annie's presence being a secret from her father. He didn't really approve of Peggy keeping such a big secret and he hoped she wouldn't do anything silly. He didn't know Helen and Annie's dad but he didn't sound very nice and he didn't want him coming round and threatening Peggy when he wasn't there to protect her.

He carried on reading, delighted that, amongst the news, there were continual references to how much she missed him. As he read, Joe could feel a glow fill his body, leaving him feeling warm for the first time in ages and he felt almost happy. She was alive and well, as were his family and she loved him and was waiting for him to come home. What could be nicer than that?

****

Honor Oak Park, London

"Thanks for the lift." Peggy climbed out of the car. "Do you want to come in for a cup of tea?"

"That would be lovely, thanks." Chris turned off the engine and followed Peggy up the path.

She unlocked the front door and took him straight into the kitchen. To her surprise, the house was quiet.

"Is everything alright?"

"Sorry, I was just wondering where Jane and Annie are. They must have popped out." Peggy suddenly felt uncomfortable. It was one thing asking Chris into the house when Jane, Annie and Alf were there; another thing entirely if they were to be alone.

Chris grinned. "I promise I won't jump on you!"

Peggy blushed and was about to say she'd not been thinking anything of the sort, when she realised he was joking. "Sorry, I'm just conscious with Joe away, people might get the wrong idea."

"Well, as there's no one here, that's probably not a problem!" Chris was laughing and Peggy joined in. He sat down at the table while she put the kettle on and hunted for some biscuits. She finally found some in a sealed box at the back of the cupboard. "To keep Alf out," she explained seeing Chris' amused expression.

"Well, I'm pleased to say, we've finally found Simon. He was very lucky. The ship he was on was torpedoed, with lots of casualties, but he got picked up by a destroyer. As soon as they realised he was under age, they called Da and he went and picked him up from Plymouth. He's now back on the farm with strict instructions to stay there until he's old enough!"

Peggy smiled. "I'm so pleased. You must be very relieved. Do you think he'll take any notice though?"

Chris sighed. "No, probably not. Da can't be always keeping any eye on him so I would think it's just a matter of time before he goes and tries to join up somewhere else."

"And how's Connie?"

"Getting bigger by the day. The baby's due soon and Ma's finally come round, so everything's looking up at the moment." Chris wanted to add *'including our relationship'* but decided that probably wouldn't be a very good idea.

Unaware of his thoughts, Peggy poured out the tea and sat down with him, her earlier reservations completely forgotten.

Chapter Thirty-one

Mitzic, Gabon

The next two weeks were a constant struggle as they forced their way through the dense rainforest towards the town of Mitzic. The intense humidity left the soldiers sweating profusely and the constant irritation of leeches fastening themselves to any bare flesh drove them to distraction. The forest was so impenetrable, at times, they were not even sure it was daylight, the thick canopy of the trees completely shielding them from the light. For Marcel, the most confusing thing was the lack of variation in the hours of daylight. When he could see light through the forest canopy, he found it odd each day seemed to start at about six o'clock and get dark almost exactly twelve hours later. Used to days and nights varying in length, this left him with the feeling time was standing still, an impression added to by their seeming lack of progress. The forest appeared the same each day and, after a while, he wondered if perhaps they were just reliving the same day again and again.

"I'm sure we've been through here before," Pierre said disconsolately, echoing Marcel's thoughts. They were busy hacking their way through some particularly hefty foliage that seemed intent on entwining itself round their machetes. The forest was thick here and Marcel longed for nothing more than to find some shade, crawl into it and have a long cool drink.

"Maybe we have." Paul also sounded fed up. "Perhaps we're lost and no one's bothered to tell us yet."

"No, we're still headed north," Charles said confidently. "I checked the compass this morning."

Marcel stared at Pierre in surprise. Charles was quite lazy, so doing something that was in any way proactive was quite out of character. Seeing Marcel's expression, Charles looked sheepish. "I thought the same: that we were lost and just wandering round in circles, so I checked. Just in case, of course…' His voice trailed off as he realised no one was really listening.

Although they had been in the forest for nearly two weeks, they were still struggling to acclimatise themselves. They had long since discarded most of their uniforms, preferring to carry their heavier outer clothes. They were down to shorts and vests, long socks and boots, and still they were too hot.

But things were about to change and, to their unutterable relief, the foliage began to thin out. Now they could see the sky, the sun felt even hotter but gradually the humidity decreased and then they were out of the rainforest and the terrain changed to a tropical savanna of rolling grasslands, dotted with isolated trees and bushes. They began the long climb up the hilly slopes towards the town of Mitzic.

Relieved to be out of the physically draining intensity of the rainforest, at first Marcel was vigilant, his senses alert as he expected to be attacked at any moment. But after a while, with no one to be seen, he began to relax. Gradually their pace slowed and, in the distance, he could see lights. The tension began to rise and, using the sparse bushes and trees as cover, they cautiously approached the town. Everything seemed very quiet, so the first hail of small arms fire raking the air around them, caught Marcel by surprise. He threw himself to the ground, rolling towards a large bush which lay fortuitously to his right.

For a short while, they found themselves pinned down. The defenders had the advantage of being at the top of a hill, but gradually the superior numbers and training of the Free French turned the tables. The initial tortuous forward movement soon turned into a full scale rout and, within hours, the fighting was over and Mitzic was under their control.

They walked cautiously into the town and Marcel looked around. People were peering out from their primitive dwellings, watching the invading troops fearfully. A small child, her eyes wide with terror hanging onto her mother's skirts, reminded him forcefully of Angel and he smiled, hoping to reassure her.

"Don't relax just yet." Paul's voice was loud in his ear. "Don't forget this place is a Vichy town." His warning came just in time as a single shot rang out, hitting a soldier further down the line. Marcel swiftly followed the others into the shelter of one of the primitive huts, steeling himself to ignore the terrified screams of its inhabitants.

While Paul watched through the open space that was the window, Marcel sought to calm the residents; an elderly man, a younger woman and two small children.

"We won't hurt you." He spoke quietly at first and then more loudly as his words seemed to be having little effect. Using a mixture of pointing and gesturing with his rifle, Marcel finally managed to herd the family into one corner of the hut and he turned his attention back to Paul.

"What's happening?" he asked as a barrage of shots rang out, followed by silence.

Paul shook his head. "Not sure, but I think they got him."

There was another brief silence then they could hear the sergeant shouting, "Come on, let's go."

They left the hut without a backward glance and carefully re-joined the others. In sight was the colonial barracks, which seemed eerily quiet and they approached with caution, but it seemed any resistance was over and Mitzic was theirs. It was months since Marcel had left France and his first thought was again that it had almost seemed too simple and he felt the same sense of anti-climax he had experienced after the attempt to take Dakar.

Seeing his expression, Pierre grinned. "He won't be happy until we are in a fight to the death." He punched Marcel playfully on the arm.

"Relax and enjoy, Marcel. I wish all our victories would be as easy as this, but I fear they won't, so let's make the most of the ones that are. Now come and have a drink and celebrate with us."

Marcel smiled and, throwing off his doubts, followed the others into the main part of the town.

The next morning, with his head aching and vowing he would never drink so much again, they began the long march to Libreville, just over four hundred kilometres away.

****

Toulouse, Southern France

Gabriel handed over the day-to-day running of the investigation into Eve's murder to his deputy who was extremely competent and, meanwhile, concentrated his own efforts on trying to find out who was following Jeanne and whether the two things were connected.

He had also been contacted again by the person who had originally tried to recruit him to the resistance. He still needed to be cautious and make sure their security was water tight, which was why he had agreed to a meeting, to see just how many people were aware he had been approached. At the present time, he had done nothing to compromise himself and could easily claim it was part of his job to try and infiltrate these groups if it all turned out to be an elaborate trap. He would make his final decision after the meeting and, in the meantime, do his best to ignore the frisson of anticipation simmering just below the surface. Although it was very dangerous, the thought of doing something to strike back was too good to miss and he couldn't help feeling excited at the prospect.

****

Libreville, Gabon

A few days after Marcel left Mitzic, they heard the Free French forces had overseen the surrender of Vichy-French forces at Lambarene.

"Looks like it's finally coming together," Pierre remarked. "The Gabon campaign will give de Gaulle some much needed success which will quieten those who've been moaning about him and we can also use Gabon as a staging point to attack Italian forces in Libya."

"Don't you feel bad about fighting other Frenchmen?" Marcel asked. They were now on the outskirts of Libreville and, according to the officers, they would soon be joining up with the French Legionnaires, Senegalese, and Cameroonian troops, who had landed at Pointe La Mondah near Libreville from garrisons in Equatorial Africa. Most of the heavy shelling they could hear was coming from the seaward side of the city and rumours abounded it was the Free French Navy, although others said it was the British. Marcel didn't care who was doing the shelling, as long as they were winning. In the distance, they could hear the Free French Lysanders flying in from Douala and bombing the airport.

"Yes, but they have a choice too. They could join us and they are also firing on us, don't forget."

An enormous boom shook the ground and they could see the sky light up in the distance.

Twenty minutes later, Paul appeared by their side, the first with the news as usual.

"That noise was the Vichy cruiser *Bougainville* going up in flames. Apparently the British shelled the capital for hours to prepare for the Free French landings."

"How do you know all this?" Although he was reluctant to give Paul any opportunity to brag, Marcel gave in to his curiosity.

Paul grinned. "I have a friend in high places and he keeps me up to date. Apparently the British denied any responsibility for the shelling, but did admit they had forced the ocean-going French submarine *Poncelet* to be scuttled off Gabon."

"Why on earth would the British try to pretend they weren't helping us?" Marcel was confused.

"Because they don't want to give the Germans too much of a propaganda victory like they did when they sank the French fleet. Don't you remember all the hoo-ha then?"

Marcel nodded. It made sense now, although he couldn't really understand why the British didn't just come right out and say they were supporting the Free French. Surely they were all on the same side?

Seeing his expression and guessing what he was thinking, Pierre chipped in. "Politics, my dear Marcel. The scourge of armies everywhere." He stood up. "Come on, let's move out. We haven't got much farther to go, I can smell the fighting from here!"

As they came closer to the city, they heard Koenig's legionnaires had finally broken Vichy resistance at the aerodrome and they had surrendered. Resistance was gradually tailing off and it was beginning to look as though, yet again, Marcel would fail to find the real fighting he craved to prove himself. Then, to his delight, he and his friends were sent to join some Legionnaires who were busy attacking the garrison. Marcel's initial nervousness at being placed with such iconic legends of French folklore soon dissipated and he concentrated on the job in hand.

With bullets ricocheting round him and with the smoke of grenades and explosions filling the air, Marcel soon forgot his concerns that he was fighting other Frenchmen. They were, after all, trying to kill him.

"Cover me, Marcel." Paul's face was filthy and covered in dirt and cordite. Marcel began firing in the direction of the garrison wall where some Vichy Frenchmen were stubbornly refusing to give up, despite the continuous bombardment going on all around them. Paul crawled slowly forward on his stomach, keeping low so he was not in the line of fire. Marcel continued to shoot, making sure the defenders were unable to raise their heads above the wall and waited for Paul to get close enough to throw a grenade. When Paul was within striking distance of the wall, Marcel intensified his fire, raising the arc slightly so he would not hit his friend by mistake. Now hidden in the shadow of the wall, Paul turned back and raised his hand and Marcel stopped firing. Paul pulled the pin and waited. Marcel knew he was waiting until the last second before lobbing the grenade over the wall, so there was no time for the defenders to throw it back but, even so, the wait seemed interminable. Just as Marcel thought he had waited too long, Paul lobbed the explosive over the wall and threw himself flat on the ground.

****

Honor Oak Park, London

Annie was sitting at the bottom of the stairs, her face pale and etched with pain.

"What the matter?" Peggy hurried down the last few steps.

"Nothing, just a very strong kick, I think. He's probably going to be a footballer!"

"You're definitely sure the baby's a boy then?"

"I have no idea, really. Up until a few months ago I would have said it was much better to be born a boy, at least he wouldn't have people trying to tell him what to do for the rest of his life, but now I'm not so sure. If it's a boy, he might have to go and fight."

"I'm sure the war'll be over long before he or she grows up." Peggy was horrified at the thought the war might go on that long.

Annie shrugged, the gloom descending again and then suddenly she doubled up, gasping in pain.

Peggy waited for the contraction to subside. "Has Jane gone to the shelter yet or is she still here?"

Annie shook her head, taking deep breaths. "No, she's in the kitchen."

"Jane! Jane!" Peggy called and Jane appeared in a rush, looking flustered.

"What's up, Peggy? Are you alright?"

"I'm fine, but the baby's coming. Can you go and fetch the midwife. I'll keep an eye on Alf. Where is he?"

"He's in the kitchen." Jane was already taking off her apron and grabbing her coat and hat from the hall stand.

"Alf, I've got to go out for a minute, you stay with Peggy and Annie. I'll only be two ticks."

Alf appeared at the door, looking worried and opened his mouth to object.

Annie spoke gently. "Don't worry, Alf. She won't be a minute, honestly. Go and get your nursery rhyme book and come and sit by me and we'll read together."

Alf went to fetch his book while Jane slipped quickly out of the front door and headed towards the telephone box at the bottom of the road. The air was bitterly cold and the icy fog swirled around her, reducing visibility to almost nil and muffling any noise.

She sent up a silent prayer that the telephone was still connected, otherwise the next nearest phone was several streets away. Her footsteps echoed on the pavement and she thought about how much her life had changed in the past few weeks. After the shock of finding her home had been demolished in the bombing raid, she had not expected it to be quite so easy to start again. One of her biggest fears, other than losing her husband or Alf, had been to lose her home. Her parents had died when she was a child so she had no family she could go and live with, and Mick was also an orphan. They had been so proud of their home, but in one night everything they had worked for had gone, obliterated by one high explosive bomb. Then, in the moment of her deepest despair, Peggy and Annie had been there for her and, in the space of a few weeks, had become like a family to her. Until she had moved in with her new friends, she had not realised how lonely she had been since Mick had been called up, or how much she had withdrawn into herself.

****

London

Being back in London was almost an anti-climax, although Pam was relieved to see the bombing seemed to have eased slightly, probably due to the poor weather conditions. She had not heard from Richard at all, despite his promise to contact her and she couldn't make up her mind whether that was a good or a bad thing. She wouldn't admit she missed him, so instead she convinced herself she didn't care. That worked well, until he phoned and then she forgot all her good intentions and immediately agreed to have dinner with him.

She spent all day trying to ignore the growing excitement within her but to no avail and eventually decided she might just as well admit she was really looking forward to seeing him again. She thought carefully about whether she should go in her uniform or whether she should throw caution to the winds and wear something long and flowing and reminiscent of happier times. Her desire to attract him finally won out over her practical side and, proud as she was of her uniform, she chose a long black silk dress, low cut and alluring, with long black gloves. The outfit was one of her favourites and a reminder of a time when all she had to worry about was whether she was wearing the latest fashion and how she looked.

The ringing of the door bell startled her and she hurried downstairs. Richard too had elected to wear civilian clothes. He looked at her appreciatively and smiled. "You look very nice." The understatement made her smile. She could see his real feelings in his eyes. She quickly grabbed her fur coat from the hall stand and left the house, her arm firmly wrapped round his and a growing feeling of excitement in the pit of her stomach.

"I thought we'd go to the Dorchester, if that's alright with you?"

"Sounds perfect." She snuggled up to him. Despite the warmth of her fur coat, the night air was surprisingly cold and her breath made clouds of steam as they walked briskly to his car, a 1935 Daimler, its sleek outline just visible in the unlit streets.

"Aren't you worried Göring might bomb such a beautiful car?" she asked, a mischievous expression on her face. "It would be a terrible shame if he did." She ran her hands over its shiny bodywork loving its rich, opulent feel.

"It's only a car." Richard was amused at the look of horror that came over her face.

"Don't you ever let a car enthusiast hear you say that!" He could see a glint of amusement in her eyes. "They'll probably lynch you."

"So, are you going to get in or are you going to stand here in the cold admiring the car all night? If I'd known, I would have arranged a picnic."

Pam laughed and climbed in through the passenger door he had opened for her. The inside was just as luxurious, the dashboard made of walnut and the seats very expensive leather, which she sank into as if they were made for her.

The car sped smoothly along the dark streets and Pam was surprised the searchlights weren't in action. "Do you think the Germans have stopped bombing London?"

"No, very unlikely. They've been turning their attention to other cities after their success in Coventry. Liverpool, Sheffield, Portsmouth, Southampton: they've all had a pounding over the last few weeks. I think they are hoping to demoralise people in other places, because the plan doesn't seem to be working too well in London. They're also going after industry, now much of it has moved north. On the other hand, they might think there are less defences in other cities, or they aren't so well prepared. The RAF have pretty much stopped all but the odd stray bomber getting through in daylight, which is why all their concentrated attacks are at night now."

"Then if we can survive until the spring, the hours they can bomb us will be reduced."

"It's a big 'if'. People are beginning to adjust, so the fear the authorities had in the beginning, that morale would collapse seems to have receded, but we're not out of the woods yet."

"We will win eventually, won't we?" Pam was suddenly afraid that, after all this, they could still lose.

"We have to. The alternative is not worth thinking about ."

She nodded and then changed the subject. "So, is the food at the Dorchester as good as it used to be?"

Richard laughed. "Yes. They've moved indoors so there's no dining in the restaurant overlooking Park Lane now. But from what I've heard, its very much business as usual."

Pam laughed uncertainly, not sure whether she had correctly identified a touch of sarcasm in his voice, but as they swept down the stairs to the inner elegant oval ballroom that was now the restaurant, she realised exactly what he meant. The ballroom was protected by the whole of the reinforced concrete structure of the hotel and was like a different world; one without a war. An elegant waiter led them to their table and she glanced around. The place was full of the same crowd of people who used to come here before the war: the monocled men and the cigar smoking women, the only difference appeared to be the prevalence of uniforms. Although many people were in civilian clothes, there were a lot more in uniform and, for an instant, Pam wished she had worn hers. Standing there, she felt just like she had before joining SOE, a social butterfly who had no real purpose.

Richard took her elbow and guided her to a seat. "Most of the uniforms are for show, so don't let them bother you. What you're going to be doing is far more important than anything this lot are contributing to the war effort, believe me."

She smiled up at him gratefully, her confidence restored. She glanced at the menus and wine lists which seemed to have changed little and suddenly felt guilty. People were being bombed in their houses and she was sitting in elegant surroundings, drinking expensive wine and eating luxurious food. Although customers were rationed to three lumps of sugar per meal, there was still granulated sugar in the silver topped shakers and this seemed to be freely flowing.

Richard called the waiter over, ordered a bottle of wine and, seeing her reluctance, took the menu from her. "Would you like me to order for you?"

"Yes please, but not too much. I'm suddenly not very hungry." She stared at him across the immaculate table cloth.

He reached over and checked no one was within earshot. "Enjoy yourself while you can. Soon you will be living off your nerves and this will be just a distant memory."

She smiled. He was right of course. Feeling guilty would only spoil their evening together and wouldn't make a jot of difference to anyone else here. The waiter poured out their wine and she picked up her glass, waited until he had gone and said softly, "A toast to the future and to success."

They clinked glasses, and while Pam looked forward with anticipation, Richard tried to ignore his growing misgivings that the woman he was falling in love with was about to be catapulted into danger and he would not be able to do anything to protect her.

****

Honor Oak Park, London

Annie took a deep breath and closed her eyes as the next contraction passed through her body in a wave of intense pain.

"Are you sick?" Alf was looking frightened and Peggy hastened to reassure him.

"She's alright, honestly, Alf. She's going to have a baby, that's all. Your mum's gone, to fetch the midwife."

Alf watched Annie in silence and then said thoughtfully, "So where's the baby then? I can't see it."

"Oh dear," Peggy muttered. "How am I going to explain this one?" But she was saved by Jane's return, the cold December air coming in through the front door as she rushed in to try and prevent any light showing.

"The phone box in the next street was still connected, so I rang her from there. She'll be here in about an hour or so, depending on the roads and the Germans," she added as the siren began to wail.

"We can't move her, but you take Alf to the shelter. We'll be fine here, honestly. There's no point you risking staying here too."

Peggy sounded quite decisive and, although Jane hesitated for a moment, the thought of putting Alf in danger made up her mind for her. "If you're sure?"

"We'll both be quite safe. With a bit of luck, this'll be another light raid. Anyway, if we go to the shelter, the midwife won't be able to find us. Go on, off you go and we'll see you in the morning."

As Jane and Alf left hurriedly for the shelter, Peggy smiled confidently at Annie and offered up a silent prayer that Hitler would drop his bombs somewhere else tonight. She knew that sounded very selfish, and she wasn't wishing death and destruction on anyone else; she just wanted Annie's baby to be born into a world that didn't sound like it was about to come to an end at any minute.

"Shall I get the wireless?" she suggested. "It'll give us something to listen to."

Annie nodded and then her face contorted as yet another contraction swept through her. Peggy glanced surreptitiously at her watch. The contractions were coming quite fast now which was unusual for a first baby. They normally took hours, but Annie's baby was obviously in a tearing hurry to be born. Peggy gave a wry smile. Perhaps the baby had heard the bombers coming and wanted to get here before they arrived, she thought as she went to get the wireless.

"Too late then," she muttered to herself, hearing the dull thud of the bombs dropping some distance away and she began to count. Then the aircraft were overhead, the building shaking as bombs dropped all around.

"I'll go and boil some water, while the gas is still on," she said, but Annie grabbed her hand.

"No, don't leave me, Peggy." Annie squeezed Peggy's fingers hard and Peggy was about to gently release her hand when there was an enormous crash and a whooshing sound and the lights went out, leaving them in darkness.

Chapter Thirty-two

Libreville, Gabon

The explosion was almost instantaneous. Marcel scrambled up and followed Paul through the gap left by the grenade, where he found himself surrounded by thick black smoke. He couldn't see anything and in panic he pushed his way forward.

"Over here." He heard Paul calling him but still couldn't see anything.

"I'm here." The voice close to his right ear made him jump and then the smoke cleared and he could see Paul's grinning face. "Best to look before leaping, boy." He grinned even more at Marcel's shamefaced expression. "Never mind, no harm done and you'll know next time." He patted him on the back. They were joined by the rest of the company and, nodding he was alright, Marcel followed Paul and the others as they slowly overran the last of the defenders on their side of the garrison.

The fighting continued unabated and Marcel soon forgot everything except staying alert and learning from his friends. He was used to the smell of cordite by now and the constant rattle of gunfire; his face was streaked with sweat and the grime and dirt of the battle, and his uniform was tattered. He had even become immune to the bodies mounting around them. His main concern was that his water bottle was empty; he was extremely thirsty and his head was beginning to pound.

"You alright, Marcel?" He jumped, astonished to find Pierre by his side. Seeing his surprised expression, Pierre handed him a fresh water bottle. "Thought you might be needing this." He saw Marcel's questioning face and shook his head. "You don't need to know where it comes from, just drink."

Marcel hesitated and then took the bottle gratefully. He unscrewed the top and drank deeply from the flask, feeling the surprisingly cool water run down his parched throat.

"Don't drink too much too quickly." Pierre put his hand on top of the flask to prevent him drinking any more. "Just put some in your mouth and wet your lips to stop them cracking." He waited while Marcel did as he said and then patted him on the back. "Come on."

Marcel followed him carefully across the garrison square towards the main building. Gunfire was sporadic but was still dangerous. They thought the last of the Vichy French were holed up in the main building but, just because everything appeared quiet didn't mean it was. They were halfway across when the guns opened up. Marcel didn't hesitate, he shoved Pierre hard in the back, knocking him to the ground and fired at the building. He had no idea what he was shooting at, just that he needed to make the enemy keep their heads down to give them time to get out of the firing line.

Pierre rolled over and was also firing. "Get down, Marcel, you bloody fool," he shouted, aware Marcel was still standing, making himself a rather large target.

Marcel threw himself flat on the ground and began rolling in the direction of the nearest building while Pierre covered him. Once there, he took over and, within seconds, Pierre was beside him.

The firing continued for a few minutes and then they were joined by other members of the company. With the heat off, Pierre turned to Marcel and said, "Thank you – I owe you my life."

Marcel looked embarrassed but Pierre could also see underneath he was pleased and he understood. Marcel had finally proved to himself he was their equal. He was about to say something else when a shout went up and the firing stopped. There was silence and then a cheer. Marcel looked at Pierre questioningly.

"I think they've surrendered." He was rewarded by Marcel's smile. "Honestly?"

"Yes. Well done, Marcel. You now have as much experience as us!" He held out his hand for Marcel to shake.

To Marcel's surprise, there were fewer bodies than he had expected and the damage was less than anticipated. Feeling better now he had experienced and survived what he considered to be a real battle, Marcel was in a good mood.

"You must be our lucky charm, Marcel," Charles said cheerfully as they arrived at the harbour. "Perhaps we can go through the whole war arriving just when the fighting is finishing."

"What do you mean?" Marcel was aghast. "We have been fighting."

"That was nothing, my friend," Charles replied. He was very fond of Marcel, but the boy was so easy to tease, it almost wasn't any fun at all. "That was a walk in the park compared to the fighting in France."

Seeing Marcel's downcast face, Pierre quickly stepped in. "Stop teasing the boy, Charles. He did well. He saved my life and, when we do face heavier fighting, I for one will be proud to have him at my side."

"I'm only teasing, Marcel." Charles suddenly felt rather mean. "You are more than our equal, believe me. In fact, I'd rather have you at my side than any of this lot of wasters."

"There's no need to overdo it," Marcel said, trying hard to keep the gleam out of his eye.

Charles opened his mouth to argue and then realised Marcel had neatly turned the tables. "Ha, very good." He clapped him on the back.

"Don't worry, Marcel. I have a feeling this is just the beginning and there will be plenty of time for you to get involved in really heavy fighting." Paul realised his comment hadn't helped at all, so he added, "Pierre's right. You did really well."

"What will happen to the Vichy French soldiers and their general?" Marcel had been puzzling over this for some time.

Paul shrugged. "They'll probably be offered the chance to fight for the Free French and, if they don't want to, they'll become prisoners of war, I suppose. There's a camp in Brazzaville, in the Congo, I think."

"So what happens now?" Marcel asked.

"Goodness, boy, are you so eager to fight again that you can't even enjoy this victory?" Antoine had been listening to the conversation with amusement. He put his arm round Marcel. "What happens next is we go into town and find ourselves a nice bar with some very friendly girls and enjoy ourselves while we can."

****

Toulouse, Southern France

Gabriel was getting nowhere in investigating the identity of Jeanne's mysterious follower. If Eve had not been murdered, he might have thought it was the 'morality police'. He was a public figure and a 'guardian of the nation's morals', so it was quite normal under the Pétain regime for his behaviour outside the police to be monitored and this would also include Jeanne if they had somehow linked her to him. He just hoped this wasn't something instigated by Isabelle, because that would imply she had found out about Jeanne. Not that things would be any better if it was Plombière who was having her followed. He wasn't sure which was worse. Although Plombière had a certain amount of power, Isabelle, through her influential friends, wielded considerably more and, on balance, was probably the more dangerous enemy of the two.

He gave a rueful smile and glanced at his watch. As if he didn't have enough problems, he was also about to join the resistance. The message had been to go to a small warehouse on the outskirts of the city. Gabriel checked his pistol was in his shoulder holster yet again. He couldn't afford to take any chances.

He was still thinking about this when he sat up suddenly. If Isabelle was behind everything, she would probably be having him followed too and he was sure no one was tailing him. He felt a vague sense of unease. Plombière rarely did anything without a good reason. As much as Gabriel couldn't stand him, he nevertheless respected his ability as a policeman. If he was having Jeanne followed, the question remained – why?

When he had first met Jeanne, he'd felt she and her family were hiding something but, when he'd grown to love her, he'd suppressed his policeman's instincts and forgotten all about his initial doubts. But, what if they were hiding something, something which could get them all killed? Gabriel frowned. Perhaps he should ask her. *'Ask her what?'* the voice in his head argued. *'Ask her whether she's hiding some big dramatic secret?'* He would not only look a complete idiot, he was likely to wreck his relationship with Jeanne, and for what? An unfounded suspicion, that may or may not have any basis of truth.

He was still wrestling with the problem when he left to go to his meeting.

****

Outside Bethune, Northern France

"But I don't want to." Brigitte stared at Rolf in confusion. She'd gone along with his desire to share their bed with other women, but this was a step too far. Although she was terrified of losing him and being on her own, she couldn't do what he was asking.

"He's a very high ranking officer, Brigitte. He can do my career a lot of good." Rolf was pleading with her; something she'd never seen before. Her expression softened. Rolf saw she was wavering and immediately pressed home his advantage. "If I get promoted, we could be sent somewhere nice, like Paris or even Rome. You'd love that wouldn't you?"

"Why me? Can't you get one of your whores to do it instead?" Brigitte was not about to be won over quite so easily. When she'd moved in with Rolf, she had thought things would change and she would be a respectable lady with one man in her life. She didn't understand why Rolf was suddenly asking her to sleep with this officer. Hadn't he humiliated her in front of all those men just for laughing with a soldier in the street? "I thought you didn't like me sleeping with other men?"

Rolf shook his head. "I don't, but this is different." He didn't explain why. "He asked specifically for you and, to be honest, Brigitte, I daren't turn him down. He could also see to it I was sent home or somewhere else a long way from you."

Brigitte was horrified. She couldn't bear him to be sent away. "Alright, I'll sleep with him." The reply was grudging and she was not watching Rolf, so she missed the look of triumph that crossed his face.

****

Honor Oak Park, London

"Oh God, please not the lights," Peggy pleaded. The bulbs flickered and then came back on properly. "Thank you." Peggy breathed a sigh of relief.

"Maybe you should get some candles?" Annie suggested

"What if there's any fractured gas mains? We wouldn't know unless we smelt gas and by then it might be too late. We'll just have to trust to God."

Annie started to reply and then stopped as her body was again wracked with pain. Peggy waited until the contraction had subsided and then helped her into a more upright position

"Is that better?"

"Yes, thanks. What a time to have a baby!"

"Well, just think of all the stories you can tell him or her about their birth," Peggy said, sounding much more cheerful than she was feeling. Where was the midwife? The contractions were terribly close together now. If she didn't come soon, Peggy would have to deliver the baby and she really didn't think she was ready for that just yet.

The lights flickered again, came back on and the wireless crackled back to life. *"Here is the nine o'clock news read tonight by…"* The wireless hissed loudly, drowning out the name of the news reader, went off completely and then came back on in time for them to hear him say.

"Several enemy raiders have already been shot down over London tonight..." The voice of the news reader droned on but at least gave them something to think about other than wondering where the midwife had got to.

"Let's try and find something else," Peggy said, conscious Annie would probably like to listen to some music and, in any case, who wanted to be born to the sounds of the news about people dying?

She fiddled with the dial and tried to retune the radio as yet another contraction shook Annie.

There was a brief lull in the bombing and she heard the sound of a car.

"I think that's the midwife. I'm just going to take a peek."

She switched off the light, moved the blackout curtain, opened the front door and peered out. Despite her anxiety about Annie, she smiled at the sight that met her eyes. The midwife's car, which looked extremely old, appeared to have two mattresses strapped to the roof.

"Are you the midwife?" Peggy asked as a stout woman climbed out of the car and headed swiftly in her direction.

"That's me, dear. Where's the mother to be?"

Peggy pointed inside to Annie who was now groaning loudly.

"Right, dear. You put the kettle on. I've got a terrible thirst and then we'll get on. So what's your name?"

"Peggy. I'm sorry but I've got to ask, why have you got mattresses strapped to the roof of your car?"

The midwife laughed. "Oh, they're to protect against shrapnel, dear. Probably wouldn't be much good against those filthy big bombs but they should protect me against other flying debris. I have to go out in all conditions, you know. Babies don't wait for the bombing to stop. If they're coming, they're coming and that's all there is to it."

Peggy grinned and went to make the tea, relieved the responsibility was out of her hands. She poured the tea into the teapot and took it with the cups through to the hall where Annie was in last stages of labour.

"Ah, thanks love, nectar that is. Good job the water's still on. Do you want to get me some towels and a nice bowl of hot water before 'itler cuts us off."

Peggy nodded obediently and went to do as she was bid. The water took some time to boil again and she returned to the hall just in time to hear the indignant cry of a very small baby who had just been slapped on the bottom.

****

Catford, London

The first consignment had arrived and filled one corner of the flat. No one ever came round except Peggy, so that wasn't a problem. If her cousin did turn up, she would say the boxes belonged to a friend who had been bombed out.

Olive was curious and wondered what was in the containers but they were sealed, and she didn't dare tear them open. Dickson had informed her that her share would be £10. Olive had been amazed. At that rate, she would soon recoup her savings. Dickson had also given her a bottle of whisky. "Goodwill," he'd said, but she wondered if he had an ulterior motive. She was beginning to struggle to not to have a drink every day. From a small glass in the evening, she was now sipping some throughout the day as well. She would have to make a concerted effort to stop, or she would become an old drunk. The thought horrified her. She was much too strong for that to happen. She downed the rest of the glass and vowed not to have any more for two days.

She put the bottle out of sight and decided to write to Kurt. That would take her mind off the drink and then she would have an early night. For the first time in ages, she didn't feel scared. Dickson was a villain but he was only interested in making money, nothing else. Providing she did what he told her to do, she had nothing to worry about.

****

Toulouse, Southern France

Gabriel left his car several roads from the warehouse and made his way on foot to ensure he was not being followed. He walked briskly, stopping suddenly a few times to check no one was behind him. All was quiet; the only sound on the pavement were his own shoes and, when he stopped, the noise also ceased. By the time he reached the warehouse he was sure he was alone, so he concentrated on preparing to meet whoever had invited him.

The warehouse was in total darkness and, for a moment, Gabriel wondered if he was in the wrong place, but then he spotted a small light in the distance, probably coming from a torch. He was about to walk towards it when he heard a slight noise behind him. He began to turn around but stopped abruptly when he felt the gun in his back.

"Good evening, Deputy Commissionaire." The voice was well spoken, calm and unthreatening and, if it hadn't been for the gun, would have sounded quite welcoming. "Just walk slowly towards the light and don't make any sudden moves," the voice continued without giving him time to answer. "You understand we must take precautions. We are not playing games."

Despite the gun in his back, Gabriel felt reassured by the words. He would have done exactly the same himself, so he relaxed slightly and allowed himself to be ushered into the darkness of the warehouse. Once inside, the door shut quietly behind him and then the room was flooded with light, blinding him for a few seconds and he automatically raised his hand to shade his eyes. Immediately the pressure of the gun increased and he lowered his arm

"Sorry, I couldn't see." There was no response so he continued as calmly as he could, "It was a reflex action."

The pressure from the gun decreased again and he breathed out slowly, realising he had been holding his breath.

He could make out a table in front of him and a chair. He could also see he was directly facing a spotlight, hence the intensity of its brightness.

"Go and sit down."

Gabriel moved forward cautiously and did as he was told. He could no longer feel the gun in his back but he was sure the man was still behind him. He focused his attention on the table and could just discern two shadows on the other side.

"As our companion said, we're sorry about this but what we are doing and plan to do in the future is extremely dangerous. For the moment it is safer for all of us if you do not know who we are."

"But you know who I am. How do I know you are who you say you are?"

"That's a fair point." The answer came from the other person behind the table. To Gabriel's surprise the voice was a woman's. "Unfortunately, you are going to have to trust us, the same as we are going to have to trust you."

Without giving him a chance to speak, she turned to her companion and said something Gabriel couldn't hear.

"Are you able to get the papers?" This was from the man behind the table and, after the briefest of hesitations, Gabriel made his decision.

"Yes. Yes, I can, but I will need some notice and we need to find a way of communicating that keeps us all safe. I also need to make sure the papers cannot be traced back to me."

"How long before you can supply them?" The woman was leaning forward. He could see the angle of her head and he made out the outline of her features. He had a brief impression of long thick wavy hair and he wondered briefly if she was Spanish. Then she moved back behind the light.

He thought for a moment. "A week should suffice. How many do you need?"

There was a brief conference in muffled voices and then the man spoke again. This time Gabriel could discern a slight northern accent before he turned his attention to what was being said.

"Fifty sets to start with. There's no point in having more because they keep changing them."

There was a pause and Gabriel felt obliged to say something. "Yes, you're right but it will be safer if we do not meet too often. There are no plans to alter anything for the next few weeks, so maybe I should get you a hundred. If you give me some way of contacting you, I can warn you if anything changes, so you can stop using the papers until I can supply revised ones."

Again the whispered conference and this time the woman spoke.

"We will contact you again in a week's time and arrange the details of how to deliver. If you are not ready, put the following in Thursday's *La Depeche du Midi*: 'For K. Meet at usual place. Love G'. If you have not used the message, you can use the same one to notify us of any changes. We will check the paper every day."

Gabriel repeated the message once and nodded. "Otherwise?"

"If we don't see the message, we will contact you." As the man finished speaking, Gabriel felt the gun in his back again and he got up slowly. The meeting was obviously over. In what seemed like seconds, the warehouse was in darkness and he found himself back in the street, alone.

Chapter Thirty-three

Honor Oak Park, London

"She has a little girl." Annie looked so content Peggy almost envied her. "And a lively one too," the midwife added as she wrapped the baby in one of the towels and handed her to Annie. Mother and baby looked at each other carefully and Peggy began to relax.

"Is everything alright?" Peggy finally pulled herself reluctantly back to reality.

"Yes, everything's tickety boo. Both mother and baby doing well, as they say." The midwife finished the dregs of her tea, which was now nearly cold and stood up, stretching as she did so. "I'll leave you to clear up then, love. I've got another birth due a bit later and I need to get my skates on, or I won't get there in time. Best of luck to you both and you take care of the little one. She's a pretty little thing, make no mistake. Takes after her mum, I've no doubt." And with a big smile, Peggy switched off the hall light and she departed. There was a lull in the bombing and after a few seconds they heard her car start up and disappear down the road.

"Do you want anything?"

Annie shook her head. "No thanks, Peggy. Isn't she amazing? So beautiful and so tiny."

"Have you got a name for her yet?"

Annie had changed her mind about names every few days and there had been so many she had subsequently discarded, Peggy had lost track of the last one that had been in favour. Annie shook her head again. "No, if the baby had been a boy I would have called him John, but I've got no idea at the moment. Plenty of time, anyway. She doesn't need to be registered for a few days." She yawned sleepily. "Goodness, I'm tired. I'd probably better get some rest whilst she's asleep, hadn't I?" Her baby daughter was fast asleep, curled up on her chest and Peggy took her gently while Annie stood up.

"Are you alright to go upstairs, or do you want a bed made up in the sitting room?"

"Oh, that would be lovely, but are you sure it's not too much bother?"

Peggy busied herself making up a bed and brought down the cot from Annie's room. After helping Annie into the sitting room, she went into the kitchen to make some toast. In normal times, she would have popped over to Helen's house to tell her the good news, but it really wasn't a good idea to go out at night unless you had to and, in any case, Annie and Helen's father was likely to be there.

Another bomb crashed into the street and the lights went out completely. She waited for her eyes to adjust to the darkness and then went quietly into the sitting room. There was no sound apart from a gentle snoring, so she assumed Annie and the baby were fast asleep. Tiptoeing across the room, taking care not to walk into anything, she made her way to the window where she carefully opened the heavy blackout curtains. The room was instantly lit by an orange glow and she could smell the smoke from the partly filled oil drums containing old rags they were encouraged to leave at intervals round the streets. The oil drums produced clouds of thick black noxious smoke which helped obscure the light of the numerous fires from the bombers overhead. She could see the arcs of the searchlights as they scanned the sky looking for aeroplanes. Occasionally, she spotted one caught in the light before the aircraft vanished back into the darkness.

****

Toulouse, Southern France

Gabriel stood still for a moment but there was nothing; no sound, no sign anyone had even been there. He turned slowly and began the long walk back to his car. So far, he was impressed with their professionalism and relieved they seemed to take their security so seriously.

He sighed and turned his attention to his next task, which was to make sure any papers he supplied could not be traced back to him. He suddenly had an idea. At first he dismissed it as too audacious and probably foolhardy but the more he thought, the more sensible it appeared. Not only could he protect himself but, with careful planning, perhaps he could also rid Jeanne and himself of a very dangerous enemy. Thinking about Jeanne reminded him of just how much he loved her and he was grateful there was not too much longer until Christmas. He was fed up with all the pretence and not being able to be with the woman he loved. He knew joining the resistance was not the best way to keep her safe, but he would do his best to protect her and he had to do something. He could no longer sit back and watch his country continue to kowtow to the Germans.

Gabriel arrived back at his car and drove sedately back into the city. All thoughts of asking Jeanne whether she had some deep secret had gone as he concentrated on trying to work out exactly how he could frame Plombière.

Two kilometres away, two men and a woman were driving away from the meeting in different directions through the suburbs of Toulouse. In the large black Citroën saloon, the woman, dressed in the skimpy clothes of a cabaret dancer, pulled her fur coat tightly round her and put her hand on the knee of her companion. He was dressed in an expensive evening suit with a stylish black bow tie. They were driving at a sensible pace so as not to draw attention to themselves; a rich man with his mistress at his side, on their way to a secret rendezvous. The disguise had worked well for quite a long time everywhere else they had used it and they had never yet had any trouble from either police or German roadblocks.

In the opposite direction, the other man was driving his rickety lorry filled with empty crates from the warehouse and was on his way back to his farm in the low lying hills outside Toulouse. He had to drive through at least two check points to reach Toulouse from his farm, but he always had the right papers and did the journey regularly twice a week, so the checkpoint guards had got to know him quite well. He made sure by stopping to chat to the soldiers, always offering cigarettes and joking when they searched his lorry, something that only happened very rarely now.

All three were members of a new group, but its three members had already learnt their skills further north and were now expanding southwards, intending to use their knowledge and experience to set up more resistance cells and escape lines across the Pyrenees into Spain. All three were satisfied by the way the meeting had gone and they were sure Gabriel would deliver what he promised.

****

London

The immediacy of the war and its privations receded into the background, helped by the pre-war atmosphere of the Dorchester and their insulation from the sounds and smells of the Blitz continuing unabated outside. For a short while, Pam forgot about the danger and concentrated all her attention on her companion.

Although the portions were slightly smaller than she remembered and the service not quite so efficient, the whole atmosphere was reminiscent of happier times. After they finished their meal, they moved on to the Grosvenor House Hotel where they danced to the Sidney Lipton orchestra until after midnight. Richard was a good dancer and she loved the feeling of his body against hers as they held each other close.

The music finished and people began to collect their coats and look for taxis to take them home. For those who couldn't find a taxi, rooms were available. The thought passed briefly through Pam's mind that it was a shame Richard had driven them there. If he hadn't, they would have had an excuse to spend the night together.

It was cold outside in the street and their breath sent clouds of steam into the cold crisp air. They stood by the Thames, Richard's arms around her and they watched in silence as the beams of the searchlights in the east arched across the sky searching for intruders. They could see the orange glow of the many fires burning in the docks and they could hear the faint jangling of the fire engines as they went about their work. Pam sighed and Richard pulled her closer

"It'll be alright, you'll see. We will win in the end." His voice was reassuring.

"But at what cost?" Pam raised her troubled face to his. The moon chose that moment to come out from behind the clouds and, seeing her upturned face, Richard was unable to prevent his lips reaching for hers. For Pam, the war, the fires, the death and destruction going on all around, vanished. All she was aware of was the urgency of his kiss which she returned with an intensity and passion that was almost overwhelming.

They stayed there for several minutes until, reluctantly, Richard pulled back and looked at her. "Time to take you home, I think." He put his finger gently on her lips to forestall the words he knew she was about to say. "I don't want to rush you, Pam. I know we don't know how much time we have, but I still want to take this slowly. It's too important to rush and I want you to be absolutely sure."

Pam was slightly shaken by the depth of her own feelings and, although a part of her was disappointed, she knew he was right to wait. They walked in silence back to the car, which Pam was grateful to see was unscathed, and Richard opened the door for her. The interior felt cold and she shivered involuntarily.

"It'll soon warm up once we get going. So, what are you doing tomorrow?"

Pam shrugged. "I don't know, to be honest. I hadn't made any plans yet. I want to go and see my friend, Peggy, but she's been on nights.

She's a nurse," she added by way of explanation. "But other than that, I have no idea. Tony doesn't have any leave until Christmas, otherwise I'd go and see him. What about you?"

Richard smiled back. "I've got a few things to do during the day but, how about I pick you up at six? I'll cook you dinner and then we can either stay in or, if you fancy something a little more exciting, we can always go to a night club."

Pam nodded enthusiastically. "Wonderful. I'll look forward to it."

"Good, that's settled then." Richard pulled up in front of her house. He switched the engine off and, turning towards her, he reached across and put his arm around her, pulling her close into his embrace so he could kiss her goodnight. The slow lingering kiss seemed to last forever and this time it was Pam who pulled away first.

****

Toulouse, Southern France

"Yes?" He'd been waiting by the phone and answered it on the first ring.

"The meeting went like clockwork. He's taken the bait. I'll keep you informed."

He replaced the receiver, a big smile on his face. No one ever got the better of him. It might take him a while but he would have his revenge. He lit a cigarette, poured himself a large cognac and reflected on just how easy it was to manipulate people, especially those who considered themselves untouchable.

****

Stalag XXA, Poland

"Raus Raus!" The unexpected shout of the guard woke the prisoners early and, slightly bemused, Joe sat up.

"What's going on now?" he muttered, more to himself than the others. He had been having a wonderful dream. They had just sat down to Christmas dinner, a big fat chicken with the juices running clear into the dish. The bird was surrounded by loads of roast potatoes and parsnips all glistening with fat and cooked to perfection. Next to the plate with the chicken he had been just about to carve, were two large bowls full to the brim with sprouts and carrots and peas and another smaller one with what looked and smelt like stuffing. In the kitchen, he had seen the Christmas pudding simmering in a saucepan and he could smell the mince pies cooking in the oven. Bloody Germans, why couldn't they have waited until he at least tasted some?

"God knows." Cyril was also not best pleased to be woken up just as he was enjoying drinks in some kind of bar with Jane Mansfield and Betty Grable. "I was having a wonderful dream…"

"Me too," Joe interrupted and began telling him about his Christmas dinner.

"Enough, Cooper!" Mitchell yelled as he swung his legs off his bunk. "Have you no mercy?"

"And the potatoes…" Joe stopped abruptly, a big grin on his face and tried to duck but was slightly too slow, as Mitchell's pillow hit him squarely in the face.

"RAUS! RAUS!" The guard, his greatcoat glistening with snow, was level with their bunks, glaring threateningly, his rifle aimed at Mitchell's head.

"Ich komme, ich komme." Mitchell smiled at the guard, demonstrating his intentions by standing upright and preparing to move past him.

The guard glared at him for a moment and then, apparently satisfied, lowered his rifle and moved out of the way to let him pass.

"Perhaps we've won the war and they're going to release us," Dick said optimistically as they headed towards the door, much to the others' scathing amusement.

"Well if that's what it is, I'll eat your hat," Joe muttered. "I'd eat my own, but I'm going to need one on the long walk home." No one was listening; the others were also letting Dick have their views on his comment.

"I think you could be right." Carstairs winked at those closest to him who sniggered. "Why don't you ask the Kraut?" Carstairs voice was louder than the others and before Cyril could stop him, Dick turned to the guard

"Is the war over? Have you surrendered?"

Unfortunately for Dick, the guard understood enough English to follow the questions and, turning quickly, he snarled at him and raised his rifle.

****

Toulouse, Southern France

Gabriel made sure no one was looking then pocketed the resistance pamphlet. The apartment was empty and he gave a wry smile. Obviously his last-minute warning of a raid had reached them in time, but he couldn't afford to do this too often, or someone would get suspicious.

"I'll clear up here." His deputy disappeared into another room and Gabriel pulled out the pamphlet and began scanning through the front page which was all about Libreville.

> *The Governor of Libreville, Georges Pierre Masson, declared for De Gaulle and accompanied our glorious Free French troops hoping to persuade the Vichy forces to surrender peacefully. However, he was quickly replaced by the vice Governor, General Tenu, who immediately declared for Vichy. Having failed and fearing for the future, the brave Masson committed suicide while the traitor General Tenu announced, "Nothing will make us bend our knee". His disgraceful actions meant fighting between the Free French and the traitorous Vichy intensified and caused more sons of France to die unnecessarily whilst fighting each other instead of the enemy. Vichy troops were rushed by sea from Dakar and a naval squadron sailed from Toulon to defend the city. The liberating columns also met determined resistance*

from the garrison of four battalions of Tirailleurs Sénégalais but eventually the two columns of Free French forces linked up around Libreville and finally the city was free. A wonderful victory for our brave men.

Used to a diet of Vichy propaganda, Gabriel would happily have read more but his deputy reappeared. "The rest of the place is empty, sir." He glanced at the leaflet in Gabriel's hands. Gabriel smiled and handed it to him. "More propaganda rubbish. Stick it with anything else you've found and take everything back to the police station. We'll have a proper look through then."

"Yes, sir." The deputy left the room and Gabriel breathed a sigh of relief. There was nothing wrong with him reading the pamphlet, that was his job, but his guilt was playing havoc with his nerves. He smiled. Now he'd privately declared himself for the Free French, it was nice to know he'd picked the winning side. At least he hoped that was what he'd done.

****

Bethune, Northern France

"You said I would only have to do it once." Brigitte glared at Rolf.

He shook his head. "No, I didn't, but you aren't going to argue with me, are you? He paid you well, so what are you complaining about?"

"But you took half of the money."

"Of course. You're not cheap to keep, Brigitte, and I have other expenses. Don't you like this new arrangement?" He didn't give her a chance to answer. "I'm sure I can always find another girl, if you'd like to leave?"

The challenge hung in the air between them and Brigitte backed down. She had nowhere to go and, even if she did, she didn't want to go on her own.

Seeing the defeat in her eyes, Rolf smiled. "Good girl. I knew you would see sense. I will take you to his house again this evening. He's having a party and, although there will be other girls, you are the main attraction."

"So when will you know if you've got the promotion?"

Rolf looked blank then remembered what he'd told her. "Hopefully after tonight. As long as you behave yourself, there shouldn't be any danger of him sending me home and, with a bit of luck, we might be off somewhere nice soon."

Brigitte watched him leave the room and resisted the temptation to cry. She would not allow him to do this much longer. He had gone too far. She would go and see Louis and find out if he still wanted to come with her to the south. Rolf could find someone else to whore for him.

****

Stalag XXA, Poland

Cyril dived in front of Dick and pointed to his head, frantically making gestures to indicate Dick was mad and, eventually, after several fraught seconds, the guard lowered his rifle and a collective sigh of relief went round the hut.

"You are a fucking prick, Carstairs." Cyril spoke softly but made sure he was close enough for Carstairs and those closest to him to hear. "If you do that again, I'll personally swing for you." He turned his attention to the two men either side of Carstairs who had done nothing to stop him. "As for you two wankers... haven't you got any brains at all? We're supposed to be fighting the fucking Germans, not getting each other killed for a bit of light entertainment."

He turned his back in disgust, leaving the two men shamefaced, and followed Joe, Dick and Mitchell outside.

The temperature outside the hut was so cold it took their breath away. The snow was at least nine inches deep and their boots crunched as they walked across the pristine whiteness. The daily thaw had yet to set in and the only good thing about the morning was the sight of the watery sun rising gallantly in the east and the clear blue sky, meaning no more snow, at least for a while.

Once there, the guards lined them up and began the tedious counting routine to the accompaniment of the usual abuse. The guards took little notice of the heckling now, but the men carried on because it made them feel better. Today, however, it seemed to Joe to be more vitriolic than usual, but that was probably just because they were all so cold and standing still was almost painful. His body was frozen and he had stopped shivering. Looking around, he could see the same applied to most of the others. He began to stamp his feet and clap his hands together in an attempt to get some feeling back into his limbs.

"You're wasting your time, Adolf. He hasn't escaped, he's frozen to death," one of the men shouted to sporadic applause when it appeared the guards were about to start the count again.

"Yeah, just like we will if we stand here much longer," another shouted. The guards made a half-hearted attempt to find the culprits and then finally decided the numbers did tally after all.

"I do wish the Third Reich's education system was better," Mitchell said none too quietly to Joe. "If they could count properly, just think how much time they could save."

"Yeah, but what would they do with that time?" Cyril asked.

"Use it invade some other poor sod's country probably," Joe said wryly, to the amusement of those closest to him.

Now the guards were satisfied no one had escaped overnight, the men were marched out of the camp through the snow and down the hill towards the station. The temperature outside was even colder and, within minutes, they were all frozen again.

Cyril glanced at Joe. "I think it's about time we taught the Germans the Rifle Brigade march. What do you think?"

Joe nodded agreement. He was too cold to speak and they began to speed up. The other men immediately followed suit, taking the Germans by surprise and, before long, they had completely outstripped the guards and were opening up a rather large gap.

"Stoppen Sie, oder wir werden schießen!" the guard at the front of the pursuing Germans yelled furiously, his rifle raised menacingly.

"I think he wants us to stop." Cyril looked bemused. "Nicht verstehen," he shouted back, much to the amusement of the others who were marching so quickly, even Cyril and Joe were struggling to keep up.

"Stoppen Sie, oder wir werden schießen." The guard tried again. "Stop or I shoot."

"Too cold!" Joe marched even faster as he mimed rubbing his hands together. "We're trying to keep warm."

"STOPPEN SIE, ODER WIR WERDEN SCHIEßEN!" The guard was almost hysterical as he chased the rapidly marching men down the hill.

What would have happened if they hadn't suddenly slipped on the ice, there was no way of knowing, but one by one, they were caught up in the flailing limbs of others, until eventually most of men were lying in the snow laughing.

The guards came up, shouting abuse. Although they began to get up, it was not quick enough for the guards who, furious at having to chase the prisoners down the frozen hill, began laying into them with their rifles. Eventually, slightly the worse for wear and with several sporting bruises and cuts, they were all back in line and, just to reinforce their authority, the Germans began to count them again, very slowly.

"You're only doing this so you can get your breath back, Adolf." The heckling came from somewhere behind Joe but, other than smiling to himself, he showed no sign of having heard. There was a time when you could get away with having some fun with the guards, but you had to know when to stop, and now was definitely the time to stop. Eventually, they finished counting and started marching again, this time at the pace the Germans dictated.

Joe gritted his teeth, wondering how they were going to survive the winter on such low rations. His stomach was growling with hunger and he felt dizzy and light headed more often than not. They had no coats to wear on top of their uniforms and the last time it had rained when they were out, the water had frozen solid onto the back of his uniform. The resultant clumps of ice had not defrosted until he had been in the hut for almost an hour. He was also wary because they were going towards the station. Although nothing had been said about moving them, he had learned to take nothing for granted.

****

Catford, London

"Her name's Miss Olive Cooper, aged thirty two. She's a spinster who works at Lewisham council, a supervisor on the switchboard. Nothing else known about her. Seems to be of good clean character from what I can see. I've got no idea what Dickson and his crony were doing round there."

"And he didn't take anything in there or leave with anything?" The inspector asked the beat policeman who shook his head. "No, sir. Like I said, I only saw him by accident and wondered what he was doing so far away from his normal haunts."

The inspector re-read the report and shrugged. He had enough to worry about, with looters on the loose, to fret about Dickson. He'd keep.

"Well, don't worry about it for now, but if you see him in the area again, perhaps we'll take a look at this…" He glanced back at the report. "This Miss Olive Cooper."

****

La Couture, Northern France

Marie sighed and wondered what kind of Christmas this year would bring. She had arranged to go to the market with Louis and was feeling sad. Probably because this was normally such a happy time of year and her trip to the December market had always been made in anticipation of the coming celebrations. Now there would just be her and Louis. As if to remind her of its presence, the baby kicked hard and, despite her unhappiness, Marie smiled. "Yes I know, chérie. Next year you will be here and who knows, maybe Marcel will also be home."

Louis stepped inside the door and, seeing her expression, came over and put his arms around her. "You can't change the past, Mama and you owe it to Papa and Marcel to celebrate Christmas for them. They can't be here but wherever Marcel is, he will be thinking of us."

Marie smiled through her tears and, taking Louis' hand, leant her head on his chest. He could be surprisingly perceptive sometimes and he had grown up so much in the past few months, she could hardly remember what he had been like before.

"I know you're right, but it's not easy."

"Come on, let's go or we'll get stuck in the snow and we won't get there at all!"

Petrol was virtually impossible to get hold of, so they had long since abandoned the truck, and went everywhere by cart. Marie had found the cart very relaxing in the autumn but now the weather was cold, she was not particularly looking forward to their journey.

Louis also seemed to be having second thoughts. "Do you really want to go to the market today, Mama? It's very cold out there. Maybe we should wait until next week; the snow may well have gone again by then?"

"And the weather could be worse. No, I have to go and today is as good a day as any."

Louis did not look particularly convinced but he knew better than to argue with her when her mind was made up. "Right, I'll go and harness the horse. Give me a few moments and then come out."

Marie nodded and went to get ready. She was just struggling to put on her boots when she heard the sound of an engine. She frowned and listened again, it seemed to be coming closer. She closed her eyes and said a quick prayer. The only people who had cars were the Germans, so the vehicle must belong to the enemy. The car skidded to a halt in the yard outside and she heard the car doors slam, followed by voices.

Chapter Thirty-four

Stalag XXA, Poland

Having arrived at the station, they were directed to the sidings where there was a goods train full of coal. Relieved they were not being moved to another camp, Joe relaxed. Although it was obvious what they were expected to do, they all stood there for several minutes waiting for the guards to point to the shovels and tell them. When they did eventually start, the work was hard, especially on empty stomachs, but at least it kept them warm.

"We could do with some of this in the hut to run the stove," Dick remarked.

"Don't even think about taking any." Cyril was horrified. "They're bound to search us when we get back to the camp and they'll probably shoot anyone who tries to smuggle coal back in."

Dick looked like he was about to argue, so Joe chipped in too.

"He's right, Dick. It's not worth it, mate."

Dick looked disappointed but didn't continue to argue. Cyril scratched his head and, checking Dick was not in earshot, said softly to Joe, "Thanks. I wonder about him sometimes. Maybe what I said to the Kraut about him being mad isn't so far off the truth after all."

Joe didn't get a chance to answer as a guard approached, rifle raised threateningly, and they put their heads down and concentrated on shovelling coal.

****

La Couture, Northern France

The next moment, the door opened and Louis stood there looking slightly bemused. Behind him was the German officer followed by another soldier who was carrying some bags which appeared to contain food.

"Please forgive my intrusion, madame." The major clicked his heels and inclined his head politely. "I thought you might be having some trouble getting into town with the petrol shortages and the bad weather, so I thought these may be of use to you."

Marie exchanged glances with Louis and then looked back at the officer again. "Er… thank you. I… I don't really know what to say." She could feel herself blushing. Out of the corner of her eye, she could see Louis was about to say something. Fearing he would refuse to accept the food, she spoke quickly. "This is really very kind of you Major…?"

"Major Heinz Krug at your service." He smiled and she found herself responding. "Here, let me help you." He began emptying the bag of tins of fruit and meat, flour, chocolate, nuts, butter, coffee and sugar. Marie and Louis looked on in astonishment.

"I'm not sure we can accept such generosity, Major."

"There's no catch, I promise. I…" He hesitated. "I wanted to do something to help. It can't be easy being…" He faltered again and indicated her stomach.

"Then I thank you for your kindness," Marie said, making up her mind before Louis could say anything. "Would you like some coffee?"

He smiled. "No, thank you. I must be on my way and, anyway, the coffee is for you." He clicked his heels again, saluted smartly and, turning on his heel, headed for the door. His driver opened it for him and then they were gone, leaving Louis and Marie staring at each other in amazement.

"Well, goodness."

"I don't know what to say." Marie and Louis both spoke together and then burst out laughing. This was such an unexpected turn of events, neither knew what to make of it.

Marie recovered first. "Well, the food will help to feed our extra mouths." Amusement shone in her eyes.

Louis nodded. "That was my thought too. I was going to refuse at first but then realised that would be stupid. It would antagonise him and may even make him suspicious."

"Come on, let's put everything away. I think we'll go to market next week after all." Marie was still smiling at their good fortune. She hadn't seen coffee for ages and, even though they did have butter, they always had to be careful of how much they used. Feeding escaping airmen was putting a considerable strain on their rations, leaving them with no option but to start using the food they had put away for emergencies. This would help to replace some of their stores. "Let's put all the tinned food away until we need it. As for the flour and chocolate and nuts I will use that to make us a buche de noël."

"So, you will be getting out the crèche then?" Louis was amused. "Just for the two of us?"

"Yes, you were right. We owe it to Marcel and Jacques to remember and drink a toast to them both. So, on Christmas Eve, we will go to midnight mass and then we will come back and have le reveillon and celebrate that we are both still alive. We have found a way of doing something useful and soon you will have a new brother or sister!"

****

Stalag XXA, Poland

After a little while, they worked out that, by moving the coal to one area and the men there transferring the same lumps to another area, they could move the same pieces around for quite a long time without actually making any headway into the supplies on the train. Although this would not slow the war effort up by much, it made the prisoners feel better to know they were hindering the Germans. This went on for some time before the guards realised very little coal had actually been shifted, despite the hard work going on all around them. After much shouting and gesturing, not to mention the odd rifle butt in the face, the guards began to pay more attention and there were no more opportunities to sabotage the work duty.

"I'm surprised they didn't shoot anyone," Joe said quietly to Cyril a little later.

Cyril grinned. "They didn't realise we were doing it deliberately; they thought we were just stupid!" He checked there was no one looking. "You'll have to improve your German, Joe. You're really missing out, you know!"

Joe grinned and stretched for a moment, trying to relieve the pain in his back. "I'll bear that in mind. I'll have a word with the prof; he's giving lessons isn't he?"

"Yeah, it'll cost you some tobacco, though."

Joe frowned. "I don't think I'll bother then. I need my tobacco, I don't *need* to learn German."

There was a long silence while they shovelled some more coal on to the steadily growing pile in their corner of the shed. Eventually, the guards signalled it was time to stop and, to their surprise, pointed to some bread and what looked like cheese near the entrance of the shed. They could also smell some ersatz coffee steaming in a large tureen by the food. The men did not need telling twice. The fact there was some cheese, even though it was only a small amount, was surprising enough, but then the guards disappeared out of sight, leaving the men completely on their own.

They stopped halfway through dividing the rations and looked around, but the guards had definitely gone.

"What is this? Some kind of trap?" Joe asked warily. "Do they think we're going to try and escape in this weather?"

"Don't know." Cyril shrugged and his eyes went back to the men cutting up the bread. "You make sure you cut the loaf properly."

"You wanna try?" The man was doing his best to cut the bread with the edge of his POW disk in a way that was fair to all.

"Leave him alone, Green, or the Krauts'll be back before we get to eat."

"I was only saying…" Cyril sounded hurt, but just as it appeared a row was likely to break out, they were interrupted.

"They go for coffee." The voice came from the edge of the shed. "We make them coffee and cake to distract."

Joe spun around, startled by the sound of the first female voice he had heard in ages. He could hardly see her, because of the dim light in the shed but he could just make out a female form wearing a long skirt, covered in thick shawls and a head scarf.

"We bring you food. Only a little; we don't have much. Don't let Germans see or they shoot us." She spoke in heavily accented English and then disappeared.

After making sure there were definitely no guards around, the men scrambled across the shed to where she had been hiding and found some more bread, oat cakes and cheese, enough for all of them to supplement the food the Germans had left. Starving hungry and unable to believe their luck, they crammed half the food into their mouths before dividing up the remainder and hiding it amongst their clothes. The guards had still not returned, so they posted a look-out and sat down to finish the food at a more leisurely pace.

"That was wonderful." Joe washed down the last mouthful with the coffee. "Even if I have got stomach ache now."

Cyril nodded and was about to reply when the lookout whistled quickly and disappeared back into the gloom of the shed. Within minutes, the guards returned, also looking satisfied.

"Here." They threw some cake onto the floor, laughing when the men raced to pick it up. Although Joe was reluctant to give them the satisfaction, he joined in, knowing if they hadn't eaten their fill, they would have been so hungry they would have fought over the food, however dirty. To ignore it or refuse to eat would only have drawn attention to the fact they weren't hungry, which might have led to the arrest of the Polish women who had risked their lives to feed them.

****

Lambeth, London

"Peggy! Peggy!"

Peggy stopped in the street by the bus stop and looked round in astonishment. "Pam! What are you doing here?" Her face lit up with pleasure at seeing her friend. "There's nothing wrong, is there?" Her face fell.

Pam hastened to reassure her. "No, no. I've got some leave, so I thought I'd see how you were. Oh, I've also bought you a small gift for Christmas and no I don't want anything from you in return. Just accept the present in the spirit its offered, please."

"Of course I will. What is it?"

Pam laughed. "Oh no, you can't open it until Christmas Day, well at least until you get home, anyway!"

"Can you come for tea tonight or do you have to get back?"

"I can't tonight, but maybe tomorrow?" She didn't mention having dinner with Richard because then she would have to explain where she'd met him which she couldn't do. Rather than tell lots of lies, it was easier to say nothing. "So, tell me what's been happening to you? Have you heard any more from Joe?"

Peggy shook her head. "No, not since I last saw you. I know the post is very slow but it's depressing not hearing anything week after week. I've written several letters now, but because I didn't know whether he had received them or not, I wasn't sure whether I should repeat things or just carry on, assuming he's read them." She grinned. "It must be very confusing if he hasn't, a bit like having a book with missing pages!"

Pam laughed. "What about Annie. Has she had her baby yet?"

"Oh yes. She had a little girl. She's beautiful and Annie's called her Helen after her sister. Anyway, what about you? How's your new job going?"

"Yes, I'm enjoying it but there's not much to tell, really. How's the hospital coping? I hear there are lots of homeless families living there now. I must say you look a lot better than you did the last time I saw you."

"Well, the bombing has eased off a bit, probably because of the weather, but I suppose if you experience something long enough, you adapt. Anyway, enough about the war. What are you doing for Christmas?"

They chattered on until the bus arrived. Pam watched Peggy, wondering what was different about her. There was a glow that hadn't been there before. If she didn't know better, she'd have thought Peggy had a man in her life, but that couldn't be. Joe was thousands of miles away and, although Peggy loved him, he could hardly be responsible for putting a smile on her face from that distance, especially since Peggy had said she hadn't heard from him. Perhaps the dishy doctor was responsible?

As Peggy settled onto the bus, she was also trying to work out why Pam seemed so changed. She couldn't believe just having a job had cheered her friend up so much. Knowing Pam there had to be a man involved somewhere but usually Pam couldn't wait to tell her if she had a new boyfriend. Come to think of it, Pam had become very secretive lately, and not just about her love life.

Chapter Thirty-five

London

To Pam's surprise, Richard had made a game pie for dinner. "Somehow I didn't have you down as a chef." She raised an eyebrow. "It smells delicious," she added.

He dished up and she tucked in. He smiled at the appreciative expression on her face. "I enjoy cooking, I find it very relaxing."

"Well, you can cook for me anytime." Pam responded between mouthfuls.

After the meal, she stretched out on his comfortable sofa, and he suggested a game of chess. "Unless you want to go out?"

Always enjoying the challenge of trying to beat Richard and preferring to spend time alone with him rather than share him with other people, Pam chose the game and was enjoying sparring against him until, while she was busy trying to work out how to escape from the seemingly inescapable 'check' he had her in, he dropped the bombshell:

"I've got to go away tomorrow, for a few days." He spoke with a studied casualness that did not fool her for a moment. Stunned, she stared up at him, all thoughts of the game driven from her mind. Opening her mouth to ask him why, she realised the answer before the words had completely formed in her mind and she looked away suddenly, busying herself in the chess board, so he wouldn't see the tears in her eyes.

He reached across the table and took her chin in his hands, forcing her to look at him. "You knew this would happen at some point, Pam. We have had a wonderful time together and we will again when I come back. This is not the end, to paraphrase our glorious leader, this is just the beginning. I'll be back before you know I'm gone, I promise. Please don't cry, darling."

Making a supreme effort, Pam shook the unshed tears from her eyes and smiled shakily at him. "I know. I'm sorry, I don't mean to be a wimp. It's just a bit of a shock, that's all."

"I didn't want to spoil our time together by telling you earlier; I kept putting it off and also…" His voice trailed off and he looked embarrassed. Pam watched him but said nothing, waiting for him to continue and, after a few seconds he added, "I didn't want you to think I was using my departure as a way of getting you to sleep with me."

He now looked even more embarrassed and then he risked looking at Pam who had buried her face in her hands and was shaking.

"Oh darling, what must you think of me…" he said in horror, thinking she was crying.

Removing her hands from her face, he realised she was shaking so much from laughter she couldn't speak for a moment. "Pam? What are you laughing at?"

Eventually finding her voice, she spluttered, "The 'I could be dead tomorrow' chat up line, you mean?"

Richard looked sheepish, then began laughing almost as much as Pam. Standing up, he crossed the short distance between them and put his arms tightly round her. "I love you so much, you know." He buried his face in her shoulder.

Pam snuggled down into his arms. "I know and I love you too." Then she pulled back slightly and, gazing up at him with a mischievous glint in her eye continued, "Doesn't mean I'm falling for the chat up line though."

****

La Couture, Northern France

Louis was pleased to see his mother looking happier and, for the first time in ages, he felt life was worth living again, even if it was quite nerve racking at times. Breaking up with Brigitte had affected him more than he'd expected. He missed her, but he knew he'd done the right thing. He couldn't trust her and he wasn't prepared to share her with the German.

At least he was doing something constructive to help the war effort and he was also delighted that moving their guests on to the next stage in their journey home had become his responsibility.

To start with, Henri had been quite insistent that Louis was not to be involved in anything to do with the movement of any of the men from the cellar.

"We need to arrange things in different compartments," he'd explained patiently when Louis had objected to being left out. "You are responsible for hiding and feeding the men and letting Gerald know how many you have. I will be responsible for moving them and Gerald will be responsible for making the arrangements for sending them south."

Louis shook his head. "That's stupid, Henri. It would make more sense for me to liaise with Gerald and for you to concentrate on the shop side of things and keeping the Germans happy. You don't need to know about their movement."

Henri finally gave in. "You're right. I'll take you through the arrangements in a moment and then let Gerald know. There's something else you should know, Louis."

Louis waited.

"We need to have some way of vetting our packages in future, to make sure they are who they claim to be."

"I agree, but how on earth are we going to check they are genuine?"

"You'll have to ask new arrivals for certain information. We'll supply the questions, you just have to get us the answers. Once we're satisfied, we'll work to move them on, but in future, no one leaves the cellar until they have been checked."

"And if they're not genuine?"

"They won't be going anywhere." The hard edge to Henri's voice left Louis in no doubt what would happen to those who were suspected of being spies.

****

Stalag XXA, Poland

More snow had fallen overnight and it felt even colder than the day before. There was an icy wind swirling around them, blowing isolated snowflakes onto their frozen bodies while they waited miserably for the endless counting ritual to finish.

They were marched back down the icy, snow laden hill, but this time the guards made sure they couldn't repeat the speedy march of the previous day and so they had little opportunity to warm up. On arrival at the frozen station, Joe was momentarily mesmerised by the hundreds of icicles hanging down from the trucks and the station buildings. All different shapes, sizes and lengths, their glassy stateliness belied the barren situation and he almost forgot the cold while he marvelled that the beauty of nature could reach even this icy, frozen wasteland. Then he felt a rifle butt in his back and the harsh guttural tones of the guard shouting in his ear, pushing him towards the piles of coal.

The morning wore on slowly but eventually, the whistle blew and their lunch arrived, a watery stew, hot but not very nourishing. Again, the guards disappeared. Joe glanced around hoping to see the women again but there was no-one about. He was heading back to the shed entrance when he heard a noise behind him. Two women appeared, each carrying a large parcel of food. They placed them down and the men crowded round immediately.

"You must quiet be!" The woman looked terrified. "They hear!" She turned to her companion and they hurried to the entrance to keep watch.

While they ate, the men discussed their benefactors.

"I think we should do something for the women too," one of the prisoners suggested.

"What could we do?" another asked. "It's not like we have anything we can give them."

The first man indicated the coal lying all round. "How about we each take a piece of coal and drop it in the snow on the way back to camp. It'll be dark, so the Krauts won't notice and they can collect the coal once the Krauts are safely back in camp. We didn't get searched until we got back to camp yesterday, so it's likely to be the same today. They won't expect us to be smuggling coal out just to drop the lumps on the hill."

There was a murmur of approval, although one or two shook their heads.

"If we get caught, we'll get shot."

"So will they for bringing us food!" Joe joined in angrily.

"We'd only be risking our own lives," another man piped up. "If they get caught, the Jerries are likely to shoot all their families too, after they've finished with them."

There was a brooding silence.

"Well, you can always go without the extra food if you don't want to help." This came from Mitchell, who suddenly realised one of the dissenters was Carstairs. "You were quick enough to get your nose in the trough, I noticed." He was glad to get one over on his arch enemy.

"Yeah, he's right." Other voices joined in and Carstairs had no option but to give in.

****

La Couture, Northern France

Louis stared at Brigitte in astonishment. She was thinner than he remembered and there was something else he couldn't put his finger on: a sadness he'd never seen before.

"What on earth are you doing here?"

"I'm going to run away from Rolf, to the south and I wanted to know if you would come with me."

Louis was about to laugh at her audacity when he realised what she'd said. "How are you going to get across the line? Don't you know it's heavily guarded and you need papers?"

"Rolf has some in his office. I was going to take some and fill them in myself. There are loads there; he won't miss one or two. So, are you interested, or not?"

Louis couldn't believe what he was hearing. She had access to the very papers he needed. If he had his own documents, things would be much easier. They wouldn't have to keep waiting for other people to supply them. But he would need to be very careful; he wasn't sure she could be trusted.

"Why are you leaving him?"

Brigitte blushed. "He's not very nice."

Louis waited.

"He's making me sleep with other officers and keeping the money." Brigitte no longer cared what he thought of her. Obviously he wasn't going to come with her. She couldn't blame him. She'd been completely taken in by Rolf. She shuddered when she thought of the things he'd made her do.

Louis was furious. He wasn't in love with her anymore but he still cared enough about her to be angry at the way the Boche were treating her. "There have been rumours you've told him things about people and they've been arrested." Louis' voice was hard.

Brigitte blanched. "Only one, and he was a thief. I thought people would be pleased, not angry."

"So you're going to run away? Do you think Keller will be upset?"

Brigitte shook her head. "No. I'm sure he'll just find someone else. I don't care. I can't get even with him, so what's the point in staying around?"

"Perhaps there's a way you could get back at him and make amends with your father, although no one could know, not until the end of the war, anyway."

Brigitte was confused. "I don't understand. There's nothing I could do to hurt him and, in any case, what does it matter? I'm going to go away from here to somewhere no one knows me."

"You could help other people escape to the south instead. You could be a real heroine." Louis hunted frantically for something else to say to persuade her to help him. "All the time he thinks he's using you, you could be helping the resistance and fighting against the Nazis. What better way of hurting him?"

Brigitte stared at him, a doubtful expression on her face. "What would I have to do?"

"First you would have to promise never to tell anyone of our conversation." Louis grabbed hold of her arm. "Lives depend on it!"

Brigitte nodded. She had no intention of ever telling Rolf anything again and the thought of hurting him was appealing.

"If I asked you to get some blank exit papers, would you be able to?"

She shrugged. "Yes, I suppose so, but only until I leave."

Louis thought quickly. "You could stay a little longer and then, when the war's over, I could make sure people in Bethune knew what you'd done to fight against the Nazis. I would also tell your father once you'd left. He'd have to keep it a secret but he would know how brave you were and just think how proud of you he would be."

Brigitte shivered as the enormity of what he was asking dawned on her. "If Rolf finds out I am even talking to you, let alone stealing documents from his office, he will probably kill me."

"Yes. I can't promise to protect you from him." Louis glanced down at his feet. He knew he was putting her in great danger, but she could help so many people.

Brigitte thought for a few seconds. Rolf had broken her heart; she would derive great pleasure from getting her own back on him.

"Alright. When do you want them and how many?"

****

Stalag XXA, Poland

Joe quickly told one of the women what they were planning to do. She stared at him in astonishment, thanked him profusely and they both disappeared.

The men finished the cheese, bread and oatcakes and then divided the food the Germans had left. For once, it was a struggle to eat everything and the stew tasted even worse than usual.

They sat back and waited for the guards to return. Feeling very full and slightly sick, they hoped the food would have time to go down before they had to start moving heavy shovels full of coal around. Fortunately, this time the guards took a little longer and by the time they returned, everyone felt slightly better. Again, the guards threw some cake on the floor for the men to fight over. The prisoners did what was expected, although most only pretended to eat, instead secreting the bits of cake in their clothes to eat later.

Joe found he was holding his breath as they left the shed. Just because they hadn't searched the prisoners yesterday until they had reached the fort, didn't mean the same thing would happen today. But his fears were groundless. Almost as cold as the men, the guards were in no mood to hang about at the station. After the quickest count Joe could remember, they marched the prisoners back up the hill to the fort as rapidly as they could. They were in such a hurry to get back, they were even less watchful than the previous day, assuming no one in their right mind would attempt to escape in such cold weather. Although the wind had died away, the air was so icy that breathing was painful, and Joe concentrated what energy he did have left on making sure no one observed him dropping his piece of coal into the pristine white snow beneath his feet.

****

Toulouse, Southern France

Angel's face was alight with pleasure. Jean-Paul and Jeanne had taken her into the main square to show her the Christmas market, with its wooden chalet-style stalls adorned in lights and to see the Place du Capitole. This was the first time they had been out together in ages and, for a while, they all forgot the horrors of the past year and enjoyed themselves. Despite the war, the stalls were full of goods and Angel immediately dragged them towards one selling nativity scenes.

"Please, can we have one?" She pointed to a particularly well-crafted crèche with the Holy family, shepherds, several angels and saints as well as the requisite model of Marshal Pétain. The sight of the Marshal side-by-side with the other religious figures was so ludicrous, Jean-Paul wanted to laugh out loud. It was the custom to add local dignitaries to the crèche, but somehow the Marshal did not seem to be in keeping with the sentiment of the occasion.

Jeanne was about to say no, they were not Christians, when she suddenly remembered and, hastily covering up for her mistake, agreed to Angel's request. The lady on the stall placed everything in a small box and paper bag, which she passed to Angel.

"Come on, let's have something to eat and drink." Jean-Paul was smiling. "We can sit in the café and watch all the people buying their goodies for Christmas."

They sat down at the table and Jean-Paul ordered some coffee and biscuits.

"What do you think Marcel is doing?" Angel's question caught them by surprise. She hadn't asked about him for so long, they thought she had forgotten all about him.

Jeanne blushed and felt guilty. Since she'd fallen in love with Gabriel, she'd hardly given Marcel a thought. Seeing her discomfort, Jean-Paul replied for her, "I expect he is somewhere fighting for France." He had lowered his voice, after looking round to make sure no one was close enough to be listening.

"Do you think he still remembers us?" Angel was staring directly at Jeanne.

"I have no idea, Angel. We have no way of contacting him or even knowing if he is safe and he won't be able to find us either so, other than thinking of him in our prayers, I think we should try and forget him."

"But he promised to come back and we said we'd wait for him." Angel raised her voice, her eyes filling with tears.

"Angel, there's no point getting upset," Jeanne snapped, more harshly than she'd intended because Angel's words had made her feel terribly guilty.

"But you did! You said you would wait for him to find you. You did! I heard you…" Angel's voice was loud enough to cause the conversation at nearby tables to cease and Jeanne and Jean-Paul were both conscious they were now the centre of attention.

"I think we should probably go." Jean-Paul hoped if they moved, Angel would stop complaining.

"I don't want to go. I want to know where Marcel is." Angel was becoming hysterical and everyone was staring.

Jean-Paul grabbed hold of Angel's arm, indicated that Jeanne should pay the bill and, whilst apologising to the other patrons, he half dragged, half carried Angel away from the café.

"Enough, Angel or Père Noël will not be coming to visit you!" He shouted as she continued to struggle. The words had an instant effect and Angel stopped. Jean-Paul breathed a sigh of relief. He would explain about Marcel once they were home and away from prying eyes.

He glanced at Jeanne. She was very pale and there were bags under her eyes. The last thing she needed was to be made to feel guilty about Marcel. He understood why Angel was upset; they should have spoken to her before and he realised the whole situation must be very confusing for her. She did not know about Gabriel yet, so in her mind Jeanne was still with Marcel. As they trudged home, he wondered if they were still being followed and, somehow, managed to resist the temptation to check behind them.

****

La Couture, Northern France

The door opened and Henri peered in. "Is it safe to talk?" He lowered his voice.

Louis and Marie nodded and he came in swiftly, closing the door behind him.

"I have been to meet up with some other contacts of mine. I wanted to sort out some way of checking the information we ask the escapees for. The Germans aren't stupid by any means and, before long, they will try infiltrating us. The other problem we have is the backlog of escaping soldiers and airmen being hidden in various places around the countryside, with people like you, who have no idea what to do with them. Somehow we have to make contact with the right people and move the packages on. This is when the danger may arise. Many of the people who are hiding escapees will not have been particularly cautious and there could already be spies in their midst. I have made contact with another resistance group who are better organised. They will gradually check out the people who are currently in hiding and, once they have been approved, we will start moving them. That's where you come in, Louis, Marie…" Henri's face was serious. "Your cellar will be one of the safe houses for those who are about to move south."

"So they will be checked out before they reach us?"

"Yes, although you may have the odd person turn up who hasn't been vetted. If you do, we'll have to take our chances but it might be worth having some kind of plan so we're not caught on the hop. When we have worked out the finer details we may have to… to deal with any of the new packages who do not pass the tests."

There was silence as Louis and Marie took in what he was saying. Louis understood immediately, having already discussed exactly the same thing with Henri, but Marie looked blank.

"What do you mean?"

Henri sighed and Louis answered for him.

"There may be German plants. We can't take the chance of any getting through. They could put hundreds of people in danger, not to mention hamper future efforts to run the escape and evasion lines."

Marie gasped. "You mean you will kill them?"

Henri nodded. "I'm sorry, Marie, but we can't afford to take chances."

"But what if the information is wrong or a mistake is made?"

He shrugged but made no attempt to answer. Marie stared at him for a few moments. "I understand, but I don't like it. I only hope to God it doesn't come to that."

Henri stood up to go. "Your next guests should come via me, so I'll be in touch. If you do have any unexpected arrivals, then you know where I am. Just make sure you blindfold anyone before taking them to the cellar." He leaned across and kissed Marie on the cheek. "Have a good Christmas, both of you. I expect I'll see you at Midnight Mass?"

The change of conversation took Marie by surprise. "Yes, you will. You have a good Christmas too and wish your family the same." Louis followed Henri to the door, leaving Marie on her own, thinking over the conversation.

She knew there was no real alternative to Henri's plan. They could hardly take prisoners and keep them until the end of the war, whenever that was likely to be. She wished Jacques was still alive. Louis had grown up considerably but he was still so young and she also had to think about her unborn baby. In a way, what Henri was telling her was reassuring but she couldn't rid herself of the doubts. What if they executed innocent people? She shook her head. She had made her choice when she had agreed to help Louis run the safe house; there would be plenty of time to worry about her conscience once the war was over.

****

North Africa

Marcel stared in horror at the letter that had just arrived in the post. He'd been so surprised to get a letter, he'd mistakenly assumed it was from his family or even from Jeanne. If only it had been. He re-read the letter again, hoping he had misread the words.

Dear Marcel…

The writing was quite child-like and, at first, he'd had no idea who was writing to him, especially in English, so he had quickly looked at the end of the letter. He frowned. It was from Lilly. Why was she writing to him? They'd hardly parted on good terms and he hadn't heard from her since their argument in the pub, months ago. Even more surprising was how she had known where to contact to him. Curious, he began reading and then the words registered and his heart sank. Seizing on any excuse for the contents not to be true, he wondered if he'd misunderstood, so he started again. It made no difference, the letter still said exactly the same thing.

> *… I hope you are well. There's no easy way to tell you this, so I'll just come out with it. I'm pregnant with your baby. There's no doubt at all, as there's not been anyone else. I'm sorry and I know we argued before you left but I have to do what's best for the child and I think we should put all that behind us now and plan for our future with our baby. I didn't want this to happen and I'm no happier than you probably are, but I'm not the only one to blame and we have to make the best of things. My dad says you'll just ignore this letter and I'm wasting my time writing to you, but I know different. I know you are an honourable man and you would not want your baby growing up without a father.*
>
> *I know there is a war on and it may be some time before you are back in England again, but please write and tell me what you think we should do. The baby is due next May, so there's plenty of time yet and, hopefully, you will be home on leave before then, so we can get married before the baby is born.*
>
> *Look after yourself and I look forward to hearing from you.*
> *Your loving Lilly.*

****

Toulouse, Southern France

They had walked home in silence, Jean-Paul's mind on more pressing problems than Marcel. There was still no news about who had killed Eve. Her body had been dumped in the city's main river and yet the police seemed unable to find the culprit. Jean-Paul was also worried about Gabriel. He was reasonably sure the man loved Jeanne and he wasn't anti-Semitic, but he was a senior police officer and working in the same building as the special department set up specifically to monitor the activities of the large Jewish population. There were several rumours already circulating that the government was getting ready to expel all foreign Jews into the occupied zone. The thought of the knife edge they were all balanced on sometimes made him feel dizzy with fear. He suddenly realised Angel was talking to him

"I'm sorry, Papa. I didn't mean to upset Jeanne but I love Marcel and I want him to be with us."

Jean-Paul sighed and gave her a hug. It was very hard to explain something so complicated to a five year-old. "We all do, Angel, but the problem is we have no idea whether Marcel is alive or dead, or if we will ever see him again. We can't sit around and wait for him to come and find us, when he doesn't know where we are either, or whether *we* are alive or dead." Seeing her tears beginning to fall again, he carried on quickly

"We have to get on with our lives as Marcel will also be doing, wherever he is. Then, when the war is over, we can start thinking about how to find him again. Marcel loved you very much and he would not want you to be sad or to sit around wasting your life on the off-chance we will all find each other again when the war is over. We have no idea how long this war is going to last or what the future holds, so we have to live for today and try to make the best of what we have."

His words were meant as much for Jeanne as for Angel and they seemed to have the desired effect as both girls seemed a little happier.

"Come on, let's plan what we are going to have for Christmas dinner."

****

North Africa

Marcel's first reaction was to screw up the letter and throw it away but he couldn't bring himself to do that. He didn't want to marry Lilly, he didn't even want to see her again. But he had a duty to the baby and his parents would be horrified if they knew he had he just ignored her.

"You could pretend you haven't received the letter," the voice in his head said calmly. *"There's a war on. The letter could have gone anywhere and, anyway, how do you know the baby's yours?"* He shook his head in an attempt to get rid of the niggling voice but failed miserably.

"You alright, Marcel?" Pierre was staring at him. Marcel was the colour of chalk under the rich desert tan they all had, after so many months in Africa.

Marcel looked blank for a moment and then pulled himself together. The last thing he needed was everyone knowing how stupid he'd been.

"Yes, fine thanks. Let's go and eat." Marcel shoved the letter back in his pocket and tried to forget about it.

Chapter Thirty-six

London

Pam yawned and stared out of the window onto the park below. The day was bitterly cold and the wind was howling through the trees. The sky was covered with a layer of thick heavy grey clouds, full of unshed snow waiting to empty their load onto the long suffering population below. The park, normally so beautiful and uplifting, looked bleak and unfriendly and she shivered involuntarily, pulling her clothes tightly around her.

She had fully expected to be overseas, carrying out her first assignment by now. But instead she was working in a building in the city where she spent her time compiling intelligence from those still managing to flee the Germans and decoding messages from those agents who were fortunate enough to be doing something worthwhile.

Most of the intelligence she was decoding and compiling came from Vichy France and she was fast becoming an expert on the conditions there, as well as the problems facing the agents sent into the Free Zone. She could only hope this would be useful when she was finally able to put her training into practice. She would have much preferred to go into Northern France but she was so desperate to do something, she would have happily settled for Vichy, or even Portugal or Spain.

She turned away from the wintry view out of her bedroom window and headed downstairs. She had no idea what she was going to do for the rest of her day off and was pondering just how bored she was when the telephone rang.

As she spoke into the receiver, a big smile crossed her face. "Richard! You're back… from Kent!" she added before he could complain about a lapse of security.

"Hello, darling." She could hear him smiling. "You've missed me then!"

"What on earth makes you think that?" Pam laughed. "Yes, of course I have. You have no idea how much."

"Good, then you'll have dinner with me tonight? At the flat? I'll cook, if you don't mind not going out. I would really like to spend a quiet night with you rather than risk bumping into lots of people."

"Sounds wonderful," Pam replied. She knew her mother had told her not to appear so keen but, quite frankly, given the war, one really couldn't waste time playing silly games.

"See you later then. I'll pick you up at about six?"

"TTFN," Pam responded.

She heard his deep chuckle before he hung up and she smiled again. The day had taken on a whole new meaning and she couldn't wait for the evening.

****

Lewisham Council Offices, London

Olive finished the last of her reports and began some filing. Although she enjoyed the role of supervisor, she missed listening in on the phone calls. The gossip was always useful to write to Kurt and she was having to make things up now, because she couldn't think of anything to say to him. She almost blushed when she thought of her last letter in which she'd said the whole of her street had been bombed and her house was the only one still standing. She'd also told him she hadn't eaten for a few days because the shops had no food in. She'd continued by telling him people were rioting in the streets and threatening to overthrow the government. She had no idea why she was telling him such rubbish. She could just as easily have told him everything was fine but she wanted to punish him for not being there to protect her.

His letters were still full of references to their relationship, but so many things had happened since then, she couldn't really remember anything about the nights they had spent together. Whenever she tried to think about Kurt, all she could see were Tom's hands pawing her, his fingers touching, probing, his repulsive body on top of hers. Olive opened her eyes and blocked off the memory. She glanced at the switchboard but the girls were too busy to be watching her. At least Dickson was polite in his own way and, since he had taken over from Tom, Kath had given her a wide berth. Olive still hated Kath and was determined to get revenge on her for her part in both Tom and Dickson's blackmail schemes, but she hadn't yet thought up a suitable punishment.

No one was watching, so she took a quick nip of whisky and glanced at the clock. She was planning on leaving early tonight. Dickson wanted her to drop off a small package near Honor Oak Park. She would be well paid and the trip would give her the welcome opportunity to call in on Peggy; not because she wanted to see her cousin but in the hope of catching her doing something she shouldn't.

****

Libya

The next few days passed relatively quickly, the preparations for the next raid on the isolated Italian border posts at least keeping Marcel's mind occupied. But every now and then, there was a lull in the activity and, when everything was quiet, his mind returned to the letter burning a hole in his pocket. The more he thought about the contents, the more ridiculous and unfair everything seemed. They had only made love a few times, so how could she possibly be pregnant? The words of the film he'd watched came unbidden into his mind, reminding him it only took one time. He shook his head; he must have misread the letter. Deciding this was the most likely explanation, he clung to that thought until he settled down in his tent later than evening. The light from the small tilly lamp was quite dim but was enough to read by. Taking a deep breath and uttering a small prayer he was wrong, he took the letter out again. No, there was definitely no mistake. Lilly was pregnant; he was the father; he would have to marry her; his life was over.

"So are you going to tell me?" Pierre's face was inches from his and made him jump. "I know you received a letter and ever since, you've been distracted, to say the least. In fact, you've been downright miserable."

Marcel was about to argue, then changed his mind and handed over the letter. They would know soon enough so he might as well get it over with.

There was silence while Pierre read the few lines. His English was better than Marcel's but he wanted to make sure he'd understood before he commented.

"Ah!" He let out a long breath. "Now I understand." He folded up the letter and handed the paper back to Marcel. "So, what are you going to do?"

Marcel shrugged. "I have no idea." He sounded miserable and Pierre looked at him in amazement.

"Surely you are not considering marrying her?"

Marcel didn't answer and Pierre watched with growing concern. "What about Jeanne and Angel and your dreams of a life with them when all this is over?" When Marcel still said nothing, he swore loudly. "Merde… Marcel, this is utter madness! You have no idea whether the child is even yours and yet you are prepared to give up your whole life on the word of some whore."

Marcel winced but said nothing. That was exactly what he was going to do. Not because he wanted to, but because marrying her was the decent thing to do and because he had been brought up to be honourable. He could never go home with his head held high if he abandoned Lilly and his child. Already in his mind he had accepted parentage, knowing he probably was the father. And, if he wasn't, well only time would tell. In the meantime, whatever anyone else said, he knew he had no real option.

"I can't explain it, Pierre. Only I can't ignore this. If I hadn't been meant to know, then the letter would not have arrived. It's a bit like the message from the soldier. He gave the note to me, not Jean-Paul or Jeanne or Claudette, but me. That was why I had to make sure the message was delivered." He looked at Pierre, hoping to see some understanding and compassion in his face but there was nothing. Pierre was staring at him as if he had lost his mind.

"At least wait and see what the others say." Pierre tried a different tack hoping, if nothing else, it would delay Marcel writing back. If they could just prevent him from answering for a while, then maybe they could change his mind. But deep down Pierre knew he had already lost the argument.

One of the things he had always liked most about Marcel was his stubbornness. If he thought he was right, nothing on earth would persuade him to change his mind. Talking to the others would probably only delay the inevitable. He sighed while Marcel replied, "I'll listen to what they have to say but I doubt they can change my mind. You've always said I should do what is right for me and I know, deep down, this is something I have to do." He lay down, turned over and closed his eyes. The conversation was at an end. Once he'd read the letter, he'd never really had a choice.

****

Honor Oak Park, London

"That was a great film. I've wanted to see it for ages, but the war seemed to keep getting in the way!" Chris had taken her to see *Rebecca* with Laurence Olivier and Joan Fontaine on her afternoon off. "Thank you for taking me."

"My pleasure. So, would you help me if I had murdered someone?"

Peggy grinned. "No! Why? Are you planning to?"

Chris laughed. "That would be telling!"

They walked through the streets enjoying each other's company. "Well, at least you'll be home before the bombing starts. Are you going to the shelter?"

Peggy grimaced. "I expect so. I just wonder how much longer they can keep this up."

Chris shook his head and was about to speak when the colour drained from Peggy's face. "Are you alright?"

"Yes, I've just seen someone I'd rather not see." Peggy turned her face the other way but she was too late.

"Peggy?" Olive couldn't believe her luck. She'd seen the couple approaching and thought how lucky they were, their heads tilted towards each other. She was having to face up to her second Christmas without Kurt and was feeling decidedly miserable. "So, are you going to introduce me then?" Olive had planted herself in front of Peggy and was obviously not going to move.

"This is Chris. He's a student doctor at the hospital." Peggy wanted to add he was just a friend but somehow she knew that would make things worse. Although she and Olive were friends now, Peggy still didn't really trust her cousin.

"This is my cousin, Olive." She indicated Chris.

"Hello, Olive." Chris could feel the tension between the two women. "Well, Peggy, I'm glad I bumped into you, it'll save me having to come across to the ward with the message tomorrow. If you'd just let Helen know? Goodnight." He turned towards Olive and tipped his hat. "Goodnight, Olive. Nice to have met you."

Peggy breathed a sigh of relief and turned her attention to Olive, who had a speculative expression on her face. He might have just bumped into Peggy but she'd been watching the two of them for a while and she could have sworn there was more going on.

"So, what are you doing in Honor Oak Park?" Peggy asked.

"I was just on my way round to you to give you this for Christmas." Olive improvised hastily. She reached into her bag and pulled out three bars of chocolate. "I thought you might like to share some with your friends."

"Thank you so much, Olive. We'll love these." Peggy forgot her embarrassment. "Would you like to come in?"

"Not now, thanks. This was only meant to be a flying visit. I'm on my way to a friend." Olive couldn't think of any reason she should be in Peggy's neighbourhood, so she said the first thing that came into her head. A look of surprise crossed Peggy's face. She didn't know Olive had any friends. Olive read her mind and struggled to contain her anger.

"Have a good evening, then. I'll see you soon." She turned away and was disappearing into the distance before Peggy could say anything.

****

Toulouse, Southern France

There was still no news from Gabriel and, although they worked in the same building, Jeanne had not seen him alone to speak to since the night he had come to break the news of Eve's death. On the odd occasion she saw him, she sensed he was distracted, so she made no attempt to ask what he was doing and whether he was any further forward with the investigation, either into Eve's death or the man who was following her.

Christmas week had arrived. Gabriel had said Christmas was a good time for them to get together but he'd made no move to speak to her, so she was beginning to despair of that ever happening.

"You look lost in thought." His voice made her jump and she looked up in surprise. There were several people about, so she just smiled and looked slightly embarrassed. Gabriel smiled back and started to walk off, when suddenly he turned around and headed back to the counter.

"How would you like to have dinner with me?"

Jeanne stared at him in amazement and almost missed the wink.

"Yes, er yes, I would love to," she stammered and, to her astonishment, realised she was blushing furiously.

Gabriel smiled, leant across the counter and whispered, "Well done, the blushing is inspired!" Leaning back he raised his voice. "Good, I'll pick you up this evening about seven-thirty then?"

Jeanne nodded, unable to think of anything to say and watched as he walked across the entrance hall and disappeared up the stairs two at a time. She spent the rest of the day in a daze, unable to believe her greatest wish had finally come true.

****

Catford, London

Olive sat and stared at the piece of paper. It hadn't been hard to get Joe's address from her parents. They had written to him a couple of times and sent him a birthday card. She smiled and wondered what she should say. She drank some more whisky and began to write:

Dear Joe,
I'm so sorry to be the bearer of bad news but I thought it only right you should know. Peggy has been seen out with another man several times. He's not just a friend, as they have been seen kissing in public. I thought you should know what kind of girl you are engaged to.
Yours sincerely,
A well-wisher.

Olive re-read the letter and nodded. Perfect. She put the note in the envelope and wrote the address on the outside. She would make sure she caught the post in the morning.

****

Toulouse, Southern France

Gabriel smiled. Jeanne blushing was a wonderful bonus. Nobody who was watching that performance would think it was anything other than him asking out the girl from reception for the first time. He turned his attention back to the papers he was getting ready for the resistance. There were several sets of documentation and it had taken him some time to make sure they all had genuine stamps and to hide his involvement, so if anyone investigated, the trail would lead eventually to Plombière. He couldn't make the evidence too obvious or it would look suspicious, so he had to leave a series of false trails to confuse the issue even more.

He had left the holding message for the resistance in the newspaper for the past two weeks but finally he was ready, so he just had to wait for them to contact him again. He made sure the papers were hidden in the back of his safe and prepared to lock up for the night. He was looking forward to going out in public with Jeanne at last and the evening couldn't come quickly enough. He was just about to leave the office when the phone rang. He hesitated and then picked up the receiver.

"Hello, darling. Its Katerina here."

Gabriel frowned. The rich melodious voice sounded vaguely familiar but he didn't recognise the name. "I'm sorry. I think you may have the wrong number."

"Oh, darling, don't be so silly. You left a message for me to contact you." The words were followed by peals of laughter, a deep throaty sound he found very attractive.

"Hello, Katerina. I'm sorry I didn't recognise your voice."

"Not a problem, darling. I just wanted to arrange to meet you tonight at the place we met before, same time?"

Gabriel smiled at her caution, if anyone was listening, he could always say she was married and that was why she had been so careful about naming their meeting place. Then he frowned and shook his head, even though she couldn't see him

"It'll have to be earlier, I'm afraid. I have something arranged." Suddenly conscious someone might be listening, he added warmly, "I can't wait to see you, darling, but this is a long standing arrangement and unfortunately I can't get out of it."

"Seven then?"

"That should be alright," Gabriel replied and the phone went dead. He stood for a few moments listening before replacing the receiver carefully back on its cradle. He'd not heard anything on the line, which was a good sign. He smiled. Everything was starting to happen; he could drop off the papers first and then come back and pick up Jeanne.

He felt a thrill of excitement course through his body. The coming year promised to be interesting. He was aware of the risks he was running but the good far outweighed the possible cost to himself, he was sure. He glanced at the clock; time to go. If he hurried, perhaps he could give Jeanne a lift home and tell her he might be a little late. He took the papers from the back of his safe, tucked them inside a police magazine languishing unread in his in-tray, dropped the magazine in his briefcase, grabbed his coat and hat and headed down into reception.

****

Stalag XXA, Poland

Back at the camp, preparations for the concert were firmly underway. Much to everyone's amazement, the Germans had been quite helpful and had supplied paint for the scenery and some old clothing they had handed to Jeffries to adapt for their costumes. Dick was sure this was thanks to the current senior NCO, who had persuaded the Commandant the men were better occupied finding ways to amuse themselves than plotting other things.

Humming away to himself, Joe finished the last of the painting and took a step back to admire his handiwork.

"Not bad, Joe." Mitchell had just appeared in the hut, carrying some clothes and other props.

"What have you got there?"

"Just some clothes from the fat guard over near the main building. You know, the one who's always laughing and joking. He's alright actually and has offered to try and get hold of some other things too. I think he's quite lonely, really. The other guards seem to take the mickey out of him quite a bit."

After checking no one was close enough to overhear, Mitchell lowered his voice. "Come and give me a hand." Without waiting for a response, he walked towards the end of the hut to the small store room they had built. Joe followed and, when they were safely inside and the door closed, Mitchell carefully removed the clothes, revealing a small wireless.

"Christ, Mitchell. Where the hell did you get a radio? If the Krauts see it, you'll get us shot."

"I bartered it from a Polish man yesterday."

"How on earth did you smuggle it in?" Joe asked. "No, on second thoughts, I don't want to know. Where are you going to hide it?"

"I'm not. I was asked to get a wireless and leave it here." He stared at the radio, a look of longing on his face. "I'd love to switch on and have a listen. What do you think?"

"I think we'd do best to go back outside, although I'd love to hear the BBC." Joe weighed up the dangers.

Before he could make a decision, the door burst open, leaving Mitchell only seconds to hide the contraband back under the clothes. A sergeant entered, closing the door carefully behind him. He glanced at Joe and then at Mitchell. He was about to ask whether Mitchell had been successful but he could tell by his ashen face and shaking hands the radio was probably under the pile of clothes he was holding so anxiously.

"Thanks, lad. Well done. Not a word to anyone now."

"Will we be able to listen at all?" Joe asked.

The sergeant shook his head. "No, lad, but we'll make sure everyone is kept up to date with all the news from home." He winked and Joe and Mitchell left, feeling somewhat happier than they had for a while.

At least they would have some idea of what was happening outside now, other than what the Germans chose to tell them.

****

Toulouse, Southern France

He was just in time to catch Jeanne as she walked out through the front entrance

"Jeanne!" She stopped, turned around and smiled as he caught her up. "Come on, I'll give you a lift home."

"Thank you, that would be wonderful. What about the police car?"

Gabriel spoke quickly to the driver who had pulled up to collect her and he nodded and drove off. He turned back to her and, leaning close, whispered, "There you go, now you're all mine!" He resisted the impulse to kiss her and contented himself with murmuring, "I've waited so long to be able to do this."

"Me too. I thought the time would never come." She frowned, suddenly feeling guilty about her own happiness when her best friend was dead, possibly because of her. "Have you found out anything about who killed Eve or who is following me?"

Gabriel shook his head. They had reached his car and he opened the door for her before answering, "No, nothing at all yet, but I've thought of another avenue to pursue, so don't give up on me just yet."

Jeanne waited until he was seated next to her before replying, "Do you think the two things are definitely connected?"

Gabriel didn't want to worry her, nor did he want to lie, so he concentrated on carefully manoeuvring the car out of the rather tight space he had parked in and then answered, "To be honest, I don't know. My instincts tell me they are, but I have no proof." He reached out and took her hand. "Let's try and forget all about this for tonight. Otherwise we'll just go round and round in circles." He squeezed her hand. "I will find out who is responsible, I promise and I will make sure they pay, but for now let's try and enjoy ourselves. If we don't, then whoever is responsible has won, haven't they?"

Jeanne nodded and, satisfied, Gabriel changed the subject. "I'd like you to meet my parents."

Jeanne looked worried. "What if they don't like me?"

Gabriel grinned. "They will love you, darling." He didn't add that, after Isabelle, his parents would have welcomed almost anyone. He knew they would love Jeanne as much as he did and he suddenly couldn't wait to take her home and introduce her. He was about to say more but they had arrived at her apartment and Jeanne climbed out.

Gabriel leaned across the car. "I may be a little late tonight, I have something to do on the other side of town but I will be here, so don't worry."

"Alright. I'll see you when you get here."

"Oh, and don't dress up too much. I won't have time to change so we'll go to a bistro rather than a restaurant."

****

London

Pam's earlier good mood had evaporated by the time Richard arrived to pick her up. They climbed in the car and he drove off.

"You were really happy when I spoke to you earlier. What's the matter?"

"Sorry." She smiled up at him. "I'm pleased to see you. I'm just fed up waiting for an assignment."

There was a brief silence while Richard negotiated a large crater in the road. "How do you fancy going to Spain?"

Pam stared at him in amazement. "I'd love to." She tried to hide her enthusiasm and failed miserably. "When?"

Richard laughed. "Soon, I promise. Now, please can we enjoy the evening and stop talking about work. I've been looking forward to seeing you. In fact, that's what's kept me going over the past few days, so can we please make the most of our time together?"

"Of course we can. What are we going to eat?"

"Now that would be telling! Rest assured, you will enjoy it!" He laughed, refusing to say anymore, despite her attempts to get him to reveal anything else.

She gave up. "So, where have you been? Or are you not allowed to tell me?"

Richard gave wry smile. "No, sorry. And the same will apply to you. Just because we are in the same line of work, doesn't mean we can discuss operations."

He pulled up outside the block of flats and climbed out. Before Pam could let herself out, he opened the door for her and, when she climbed out, he put his arms around her and pulled her close.

"Oh, God. I have missed you so much," he whispered in her ear. Pam hugged him tight, her eyes closed, enjoying the feel of his body against hers. All thoughts of Spain were forgotten as she allowed herself to relax into his arms.

She wasn't sure how long they stood there, oblivious to the bombs dropping elsewhere in the capital. Eventually, he pulled away and, taking her hand, led her through the entrance and up the stairs to his flat. In the distance, the shells fell and the ground trembled from the onslaught. The ack ack guns continued to fire and the sky was lit by the arcs of the searchlights trying to pinpoint the bombers. A fire engine raced past, its bells clanging frantically, but by then Pam and Richard were lost in each other and totally unaware of anything going on around them.

****

Toulouse, Southern France

Gabriel drove off, heading across the city towards the warehouse where he had met the resistance before.

He would be a little early, but that couldn't be helped. He pulled up in the street where he'd parked the previous time and began the long walk to the warehouse. It was completely dark but the sky was cloudless and there was just enough light from the half moon for him to see by. His shoes echoed off the pavement and, every now and then, he stopped suddenly to make sure he was not being followed. He approached the warehouse and was suddenly aware of a car turning into the street. The vehicle drove slowly towards him and then pulled up.

"Quick! Get in!"

The voice belonged to the woman and, without thinking, Gabriel did as he was told. He scrambled into the back seat. The inside of the car was dark but he could smell her perfume and expensive cigarettes.

"Put the papers on the seat and then we will drop you off. Thank you." He removed the old police magazine containing the papers from his briefcase and placed it on the seat. Before he had time to close his case the car stopped. "Goodnight, we'll be in touch." He got out and looked round to get his bearings.

He was almost back at his own car. He spun around but the vehicle and its occupants were gone. Relieved he no longer had the incriminating documents in his briefcase, he climbed into his car and started her up, smiling at the ease with which the transaction had been accomplished.

****

La Couture, Northern France

Marie stared out into the darkness and waited anxiously for Louis to come back. Their latest two overnight guests had come via Henri and this time Louis had only been keeping watch while Henri spirited them away. But that didn't mean she was any the less worried. She glanced at the clock: he should be back soon. The baby kicked hard and she gave a half smile. Louis' brother or sister was also waiting for him to come home. She tried to ignore the churning nerves in her stomach and then the door opened quietly and he was standing in front of her. She hugged him with relief. "You should be in bed, Mama. You look exhausted."

Marie gave a wry smile. "I wouldn't sleep until you were back safely anyway, so I might as well sit up. I'll make you a hot drink. I take it everything went smoothly?"

Louis sat down at the kitchen table. "Yes, no problems." He yawned. "Sorry, Mama. I think I'll pass on the drink and go to bed instead."

He was about to say something else when there was the sound of a car driving slowly up the lane. Marie stared at Louis in alarm. The geese began hissing and Georges started to growl. Marie and Louis waited, paralysed with indecision. The knock on the door was officious and Marie walked over and slowly opened it, her heart thudding painfully against her chest.

Outside was Major Krug, an apologetic expression on his face. Marie registered this and wondered not only why he was there but what he had to be sorry about.

"Can I come in, madame?" The request was polite, which surprised Louis, who had immediately assumed he had come to arrest them.

Marie stood back, fear causing her to momentarily lose her voice.

Surprised by their attitude, Major Krug glanced from Marie to Louis and back to Marie. They were behaving very suspiciously. He raised an eyebrow and was about to speak when Marie interrupted.

"Major Krug… it is very late. I know you brought us extra supplies and I am very grateful but…" She let the sentence tail off, hoping he would jump to the wrong conclusion which he immediately did.

"No, oh no, Madame. It is nothing like that." He looked embarrassed and Louis was even more puzzled. Perhaps he hadn't come about the escaped British soldiers after all. But the Major's next words took him completely by surprise and his blood ran cold.

"We have been asked to billet ourselves in some of the more rural areas, and I have been assigned to your farm. I realise this is a bit of a shock and I will not be moving in until after Christmas, but I wanted to give you some warning to prepare a room."

Marie stared at him in shock and the room began to sway. Feeling for the chair behind her, she leaned heavily on it and somehow managed to smile at him.

"Well, if it has to be anyone, I suppose you are better than most." She knew she sounded ungracious but she didn't care.

The major's smile seemed a little less certain and then he nodded. "I appreciate this has been a shock for you both, so I will leave you in peace. It is also late and you are looking very tired, madame." He clicked his heels, saluted and left, leaving them staring at each in stunned silence.

****

Toulouse, Southern France

"Yes?" As before he'd been waiting for the phone call.

"Everything's going according to plan. When do you want to spring the trap?"

"Not yet. If we take him now, we'll only get him, then they'll regroup and you won't be able to infiltrate into the wider circle. Much better to let them get more established, then we can grab them all."

The line went dead and he replaced the receiver. He would have loved to have moved against them now, but it would be so much more satisfying to let them recruit hundreds of men, arms and equipment, thinking they were safe and then raid them. He could be patient if he had to and the look on his enemy's face would make the wait more than worthwhile.

****

Libya

The next morning Paul, Antoine and Charles all tried to persuade Marcel he was wrong but the harder they tried, the more he dug his heels in and eventually they relented.

"I think you're a fool, Marcel," Charles said eventually. "But it makes no difference to us; we're still your friends, even if you are an idiot!" The others nodded in resignation and Marcel gave his first real smile since he'd received the letter.

"Thank you. I know how this looks but I can't abandon her, much as I would like to pretend none of this is happening." There was nothing else to say that he hadn't already said. "I'm going to write to her now."

He walked back to his tent, leaving the others watching him. Paul sighed and then said what they were all thinking: "Sounds awful, but Britain's been taking a pounding from the Boche: anything could happen."

Charles shook his head. "If she's killed in the Blitz, he'll probably blame himself. Better he marries her and finds out what she's like. Then he can divorce her eventually with a clear conscience."

Pierre kicked at the sand, his face angry. "This is all my fault. I wish I'd never introduced him to Lilly." There was nothing else to say. Marcel had made up his mind.

"No matter. Maybe the Italians will blow up his letter before it reaches her!" Antoine was grinning.

A glimmer of hope appeared in Pierre's eyes. "Perhaps we could offer to post the reply for him and then we could lose it."

"I don't think he's completely stupid," Paul argued. "Come on, you're grasping at straws. He's made his decision; let's at least respect him for that.'

The others nodded and, after a few moments' silence, began talking about other things.

Back in his tent, Marcel sat on his blanket trying to work out what to say. It was hard enough to choose his words anyway, without having to translate them into English as well.

Dear Lilly…

He looked at the word 'Dear' and crossed it out. She wasn't his 'dear', she had ruined his life. He would marry her for the sake of the child but he didn't have to be more than just distantly polite to her. He started again and, after several attempts, finally found a form of wording that said what he wanted.

> *Lilly,*
> *I have received your letter which was a shock. For the sake of the child I will marry you when I am next on leave in England.*
> *Marcel*

Very short and to the point, but what else was there to say? She had what she wanted. Provided he survived until then, he would keep his word. Writing the letter was the easy part. Now he would have to put away all his dreams and hopes for the future and try to forget they'd ever existed. There was no point in wishing for something that could never happen.

Before he could change his mind, he put the letter in an envelope, copied the address carefully from her letter and then walked over to HQ, a large tent towards the rear of the camp. He handed over his letter and left. To his horror, he could feel tears welling up in his eyes and he half ran back to his tent, praying none of the others would see him.

He flung himself on his blanket, for once oblivious to the searing heat. The only thing he was aware of was his own misery. He had held onto his dream of being with Jeanne and Angel for so long, letting go was almost impossible but he knew he had to, otherwise he would be prolonging the agony, torturing himself when there was no hope of a favourable outcome.

He lay there wishing they could at least go out and raid one of the border posts, anything to take his mind of the unbearably bleak future stretching out like an endless desert of unhappiness and, not for the first time, he wondered what his life was all about. Had he survived the German invasion of France and numerous battles just to spend a future saddled with someone for whom he felt nothing but contempt?

Chapter Thirty-seven

Stalag XXA, Poland

They had been given strict orders not to do anything to offend the Commandant, who would be sitting in the front row with the Senior NCO. Dick, Joe and the others had nodded solemnly and Dick had made sure any digs at the guards would only really be understood by those with an impeccable grasp of English.

The concert started on time, although the arrival of the Commandant and the guards to a chorus of boos and hisses nearly brought the whole thing to a halt. However, after the Senior NCO had poured numerous compliments on the troubled waters of the Commandant's ego and expressed his gratitude for the Commandant's foresight and intelligence in suggesting they use their time in such a productive way, things gradually calmed down and the concert began.

"He only gave in 'cos he knows if he'd tried to stop us, there'd be a riot," Mitchell grumbled under his breath and Joe agreed. The prisoners were crammed in to every available place, many were standing and even more were sitting on the floor.

The concert was a roaring success and, as the laughter began to die down and the various acts took several bows, Dick nodded at Johnstone who was playing the piano. He played the first chord and, before anyone could stop him, Dick began singing the National Anthem. He was joined immediately by the chorus and other acts and, within seconds, as one, the men rose to their feet and sang, *God save the King* at the top of their voices. All the Germans could do was walk out, heads held high, expressions of anger on their faces. To their surprise, the Commandant didn't leave but sat quietly and, when they had finished applauding and cheering, he stood up and indicated silence. Gradually they quietened down, wondering what their punishment would be. However, once he had their attention, he thanked them for their concert and said he hoped they would do many more.

Open mouths and stunned glances greeted the announcement. Most had been expecting him to pull the plug on any future entertainments and then a reluctant, grudging applause echoed round the hut while he left.

"I want a word with you, Coleman."

Dick stepped forward, prepared to defend his decision, but the NCO patted him on the back.

"Well done. You got away with it. If you hadn't, this conversation would be very different."

"Yes, sir." Dick grinned in relief and was then swallowed up by the crowds of men congratulating him on a very professional job.

When they went to bed that night, Joe felt strangely content. He knew the feeling wouldn't last and the next few days would be difficult as they thought about their families so far away celebrating Christmas without them.

There would be no Christmas in the camp; no roast dinner, mince pies, Christmas pudding or crackers. Here, Christmas would be just another day to survive. But who knew what the New Year would bring. Maybe by next Christmas he would be home.

****

Figueres, Spain

Spain felt comparatively warm after the cold grey skies of London and Pam looked round Figueras with appreciation. She'd spent Christmas Day with her parents and flown to Spain on Boxing Day. It seemed such a long time since she'd been in a city that wasn't being bombed, she took a while to adjust to the peace and quiet. Although Figueres was not under aerial bombardment, the city still bore the scars of the civil war, with partially demolished buildings everywhere, and the piles of rubble and bullet holes in buildings were only too reminiscent of London. But there the similarity ended. Despite the poverty all around, the streets were vibrant and full of life, the sun shining down from a cloudless blue sky and bathing the cobbled alleyways and narrow streets in a warm glow, even though it was winter. Within days of her arrival, Pam felt like she had always been there. Although many people spoke French, she was determined to learn Spanish during her stay. Not only would this be another skill she could add to her growing list, but she'd quickly realised understanding and speaking the language would make her task considerably easier, allowing her to blend in and ensure she was not reliant on translators.

Her job was to liaise with the numerous escape lines coming out of France and to provide papers and money to the pilots and other service personnel so they could get back to England. In theory, Spain was supposed to be neutral. In practice, the country was under the control of General Franco whose inclination was to support Germany rather than Britain. This meant Pam had to be careful not to fall foul of the police. She also had to be on her guard against the numerous German and Italian spies, who were themselves looking to catch the very people she was there to help.

Many of the escape lines used the old smuggling routes across the Pyrenees. These had been employed to good effect by those who had fought for the Republicans against Franco and who had to sneak across the border during the Spanish civil war. Now they were bringing British airmen and soldiers out of Vichy France and into Spain. Although some of the escapees had false papers and visas allowing them to enter Spain, this was often as far as they could go. They needed different papers to leave the country, so many had been rounded up once they crossed the border and incarcerated in the notorious Spanish Campo de Concentración at Miranda del Ebro near Burgos.

Her first job on arrival was to meet the other three members of her team. They were already hiding several Englishmen in safe houses in various areas around the country and had just been waiting for the means to get the men back to England.

Pam sat in her hotel, sipped her coffee, pretended to read the local paper and waited for the first contact.

"Would you like some flowers, Señorita?" The girl was petite with long thick black hair, dark almond shaped eyes and sensuous lips. She was wearing colourful clothes and carrying several large bunches of flowers.

"No, thank you," Pam replied, her heart racing. "But perhaps you can direct me to the Café Sol?"

The girl smiled. "Of course, Señorita. If you leave the hotel, turn left, cross over the street and walk to the crossroads and then turn right, the café is a few metres along the road."

Pam thanked her, finished her coffee and set out. The directions were easy to follow and she only stopped once to check no one was following her.

The café was set back from the road, the shutters open, flooding the small building with light. Pam made her way to the back of the café and sat down. Although she had not known the location of the meeting place, she had been briefed on what to do in the café before she left England.

"Violette?" The man was in his early twenties, tall, dark and very handsome. He was clean shaven with flashing black eyes and a smiling mouth. When she nodded, he continued, "I am Adrian." He sat down opposite her. She was about to say something when she heard a rustling of skirts behind him and he was joined by the flower girl.

"Estrella," the girl said blankly and Pam noticed her proprietary hold on Adrian's arm and that her eyes were no longer smiling. She sat close to Adrian and glared at Pam. Not sure what she'd done to cause offence, Pam tried smiling, but to no avail. Fortunately the third member of the team arrived and took the seat next to her.

"Good. You've all met." The new arrival was considerably older than Adrian and Estrella and was only slightly taller than Pam. He was quite stocky with a swarthy complexion and a rather nondescript face. "Patricio," he introduced himself. He waited until Estrella and Adrian had gone to get some drinks before whispering, "Estrella is Adrian's girlfriend. She gets fiercely jealous of anyone who she thinks he finds attractive, so be warned!"

Pam nodded and, when the girl came back, she managed to let slip she was madly in love with an Englishman. After her admission, Estrella relaxed slightly and Pam made a mental note never to appear too friendly towards Adrian, something that was quite difficult because he was very friendly towards her, and obviously found Pam attractive.

It didn't take long before Pam realised that, behind Patricio's seemingly bland exterior, there was a razor sharp mind. He was clearly the brains of the team. She had trouble guessing his age but thought he was probably in his late thirties. This was confirmed when he let slip his role in the fight against the Fascists in the civil war.

"There are some new people coming in tomorrow. Would you like to come with me to collect the new arrivals and take them to one of our safe houses, Violette? "

Pam hesitated. This would probably be a breach of security, because she didn't need to know where the end of the escape line was or the location of the safe houses.

"I'm not sure…" She started to say when she spotted the look of amusement cross Estrella's face.

"Perhaps Violette is afraid?"

Pam smiled back and then turned to Patricio. "I'd love to. What time do we leave?"

****

Honor Oak Park, London

Peggy sighed heavily as the siren went off. After the relative lull in bombing over Christmas and the pleasure of not having to sleep in the shelter every night, she had been hoping the peace would continue. She was curled up snug and warm under a blanket and right in the middle of a really good bit of her book and she certainly didn't feel like putting on her coat and shoes and traipsing down to the communal shelter. It sounded cold and miserable outside, hardly an inviting night for a walk.

Taking care to switch off the light first, she cautiously peeled back the blackout curtain and peered outside. The windows were misted up and droplets of condensation had formed intricate patterns that had frozen onto the windowpanes. The heavy blackout curtains formed an effective barrier to the warmth of the room and she had to scrape away the ice with her fingernail to see through the glass. Outside, the frost glistened on the pavement and she could feel the icy blast of the cold wind coming through the glass. She groaned again. Did she really want to go outside in this? The answer was an unequivocal 'no'. Otherwise, she would have gone with the others when they had left earlier. Blow it, she'd do what thousands of others did every night and hide under the stairs. At least if the raid went on all night, she might get some sleep. And if it was a short one, she wouldn't have gone outside for nothing.

Having made her decision, she closed the curtain and waited for her eyes to adjust to the darkness of the room. Conscious of the precious minutes ticking away, she grabbed her book from the floor where she had put it and, throwing the blanket over her shoulder went into the kitchen. There, she grabbed a couple of candles and some matches, some water, a couple of biscuits and, of course, the chamber pot. After all, she had no idea how long this raid would last and having to come out to go to the toilet would rather defeat the object of sheltering in the first place.

It was quite cramped under the stairs but there was enough room for one. She lit the candle and she shut the door behind her. She was only just in time. The sound of the siren receded and she could hear the muffled boom of the first bombs as they hit their targets somewhere in the distance.

The bombing gradually intensified and then Peggy could hear a different noise; falling masonry and bricks as buildings and houses collapsed. She closed her eyes and hugged her knees in fear, her nostrils filled with the acrid smell of smoke from the many fires raging all around. She began to shake and wondered whether she had made the wrong decision; perhaps she should have gone to the shelter after all. A loud crash sounded much too close for comfort and made her jump and then, before she knew it, the first wave of bombers had passed over and the noise began to recede. Taking a deep breath, Peggy realised she had been in danger of talking herself into a panic. The house was still standing, there was no smoke to be seen and she was still alive. She waited for the all-clear, signalling it was safe to come out, but as the minutes ticked past there was no comforting siren to be heard.

****

Libya

Lost in his own self-pity, Marcel was hardly aware of the passage of time, but looking up into the night sky, he remembered sitting in the barn and watching the stars as they appeared in the sky and how he had promised Jeanne and Angel he would always think of them. It was a promise he could no longer keep. Unable to stop himself, he began to sob. Conscious of the proximity of the other men he buried his head deeper in his bedroll so no one could hear his anguish.

Time passed and his sobs eased, to be replaced by anger at a capricious fate, offering him everything and then casually taking it all away again. The rage consumed him and Marcel began to view life differently. Yes he would be married, but he needn't let it affect his life any more than was necessary. Although he would support his wife and child, he would continue to live his life as if he were a single man. He had nothing to look forward to, everything had been taken away from him, so he no longer cared whether he lived or died and if he was going to die, he intended to enjoy himself first.

****

Honor Oak Park, London

Frowning, Peggy looked at her watch. The bombing had stopped and the anti aircraft guns had fallen silent but she could still hear the fire engines. The minutes passed, the all clear still didn't sound and she wondered whether or not she should come out.

She looked at her watch again; ten minutes had passed and she was sure she could hear more planes approaching. In the distance, the bombing began again and there was a new sound; one she couldn't identify.

Outside the wind became stronger. Starved of oxygen and whipped up by the gale, the fires joined together to create a massive firestorm. The heat was so intense, undamaged buildings were bursting into flames. Fire fighters found themselves encircled by walls of flame, while in the distance, the frantic ringing of the fire engines' bells echoed off the wharves and jetties of the East End as they tried to prevent the whole of London dissolving into a massive fireball. The bombing had fractured many of the water mains so the firemen turned in desperation to the Thames for water. But the river was at low tide and the pumps became clogged with mud. The water pressure in their hoses dropped and the firemen struggled to gain any ground.

Peggy had no idea of the horrors taking place just a few miles from where she was hiding. She tried to take her mind off the horrendous noise by thinking about Joe, but images of Chris kept intruding and eventually she gave up.

She glanced down; the candle was getting low. She was just reaching for another one when there was an almighty crash. The house shook she was showered with dust. The candle went out and she was left in darkness.

****

Glasgow

The German read Olive's letter again. This was the second one they had received that seemed to be full of blatant lies. Perhaps she was trying to tell them something? He thought about that for several minutes and then turned to the man in the trench coat who was waiting patiently for his instructions.

"You're right. Something's going on, although I have no idea what. The security services would not write such obvious rubbish. They would be much more sublte. The letter almost reads as though she's drunk, or mad. You'd better go back down and find out what's going on."

"What do you want me to do?"

"If there is some simple explanation, then try and resolve it. I'd rather not lose her, but if she's been compromised in any way, then you know what to do."

Author's Note

Lives Apart: A World War 2 Chronicle was inspired by the story of my in-laws, Ted and Brenda Taylor (nee Burge). Ted was a young rifleman, conscripted in September 1939 and sent to Calais as part of Calais Force where they fought ferociously against the German 10th Panzer Division for four days, heavily outnumbered and outgunned. Eventually, they were forced to surrender and Ted spent the next five years in POW camps in Poland. He also spent time in a salt mine and Majdanek concentration camp. Brenda, a student nurse in London for the duration of the war, was his fiancée and she waited five years for him to come home, when they were married.

When Ted was captured, he found a discarded signals pad by the side of the road and wrote a note home to his mum to say he was alive and had been captured. Somehow, that message, sealed with the safety pin from his field dressing, found its way back home from occupied France to Ted's Mum, Lou in London. She received his note a couple of months before she was officially notified he had survived.

Although inspired by them, Joe and Peggy, like everyone else in the books, are fictional characters and are not based on any real people. Ted's true story is available from Pen and Sword and all good bookshops/internet retailers and is called Surviving the Nazi Onslaught. From the Defence of Calais to the Death March to Freedom.

http://www.pen-and-sword.co.uk/Surviving-the-Nazi-Onslaught-Hardback/p/7072

Printed in Poland
by Amazon Fulfillment
Poland Sp. z o.o., Wrocław